THE SOCIETY

#ThisIsWar

IVY SMOAK

ISBN: 978-1-942381-47-1

2023 First Edition

To anyone who dares to join the Society.
Let the games begin…

Chapter 1

WINEFLIX AND HANDSY MONKEYS
Friday

As soon as Tanner was pulled overboard by the masked strangers, the monkeys started screeching again. Whatever control Tanner had over them completely disappeared the second he was off the yacht. They resumed running around in their lederhosen, wreaking havoc all over the boat. Ruining the launch party with their perverted little monkey hands.

But none of that mattered.

Because Tanner had been…taken. By DODO.

I lifted up my sword.

"What the hell are you doing with a sword?!" Chastity yelled and tried to grab it out of my death grip.

But I wasn't having it. I pulled back. "Tanner's been taken!" I screamed. "I have to go after him!"

Chastity just stared at me.

Why wasn't she freaking out? I pointed toward the horizon, brandishing my sword and almost hitting a guest.

"Stop it," Chastity said and successfully wrassled the sword out of my hands. "What the hell is happening?"

"DODO took Tanner! They just came and kidnapped him and sped off in a boat…"

The yacht dipped slightly right and I grabbed the rail, narrowly avoiding falling into the Hudson River for the second time tonight. I glared up at the monkey who had taken control of the ship.

"We're all going to die!" some random woman shrieked.

A chandelier crashed and more guests jumped into the freezing cold river to get away from the demon monkeys.

"So DODO took Tanner?" Chastity asked calmly as she looked down at the sword in her hands. "I think the hilt of this is pure gold. And the balance on it is perfect."

She seriously wasn't grasping the gravity of this situation. Screw the gold! "He's been kidnapped!"

"And what happened to your amazing bikini?" Chastity asked.

I looked down at the towel wrapped around me. Had Chastity not seen the last ten minutes of my life? "Where the hell have you been?"

"Below deck," she said with a saucy wink.

I didn't know what that meant. Had she actually been below deck? Or was that some sort of euphemism for kinky butt stuff? "Chastity, I'm freaking out! What are we going to do?!"

A woman ran by us with a monkey's head buried in her cleavage.

"We don't really need to do anything. Because all this…" She waved her hand at the disaster behind us and gave a chef's kiss. "Perfection. Have you looked at TikTok? Or Twitter? Or literally any website worth looking at? The party went viral! Wineflix and Chill is about to make a fortune. And so are we. #WineflixAndHandsyMonkeys is already trending." She pulled out her phone and showed me a TikTok of a monkey motorboating one of the guests. "And don't worry, lots of people are using #WineflixAndChill too. Best party ever! Daddy's going to be so proud of me when I get a raise."

I didn't care about the party. "Why aren't you freaking out about Tanner?"

"Don't you remember how many times we almost got kidnapped back in college? And how many times custom Odegaards got us out of trouble? Surely as the owner of Odegaard Tanner is properly prepared to ward off a kidnapping."

"But he wasn't prepared! They bagged him like a nematode and threw him overboard into a dingy."

"Hmm. Well…maybe he didn't get away because he *wanted* to be taken."

"You know how scared he was of DODO!"

"Exactly. Which means he would have fought them off with his strong biceps and fancy Odegaard gadgets if it was them taking him."

"Or they caught him by surprise and now they're going to torture and rape and murder him!"

"Tanner is not getting tortured or raped tonight. Unless that's what he's into," she added with a wink.

"Chastity! This isn't the time for kinky sex talk!"

"Sure it is. Because clearly the kidnapping was just a Society thing. He was probably just needed for an emergency sex auction or something."

I paled.

"Which he won't participate in, of course. Can you scooch a little to the left? I want to get a few shots of the chaos in case the photographer jumped overboard." She snapped a picture of me looking an absolute mess before I could tell her no.

She snapped another. "Oh! I got a monkey in the background!"

A man with his sleeve on fire jumped off the side of the yacht.

Where had that fire come from? Was there an extinguisher somewhere? The last thing I needed was for someone's dick to catch fire when my mini fire extinguisher wasn't on me. Why had I left it at home? I already had too many incidents to keep track of!

There was a loud clap and all the monkeys froze again. Just like when Tanner had been commanding them.

I turned to see Nigel standing in the center of the deck with his hands pressed together. All the monkeys had turned to him. I had no idea where Tanner had gotten his animal training skills but it appeared that Nigel had been his direct understudy.

"Turn this boat around!" Nigel said in a commanding tone. Although his ridiculous lederhosen costume definitely made it a little less commanding.

The captain lifted the now docile monkey off the ship's wheel and followed Nigel's instructions.

Nigel was as calm as Chastity despite the chaos. And maybe he'd be more helpful. I grabbed Chastity's hand and pulled her over to Nigel.

"We need your help!" I said to him.

Nigel grabbed the sword out of Chastity's hands. "No touching the antiques, whoever you are!"

Chastity ignored him and snapped a selfie of her with one of the monkeys. She made the little guy put his hands on her breasts before snapping another.

"Nigel, Tanner's been taken," I said.

"By…whom?" Nigel asked.

"The Society," Chastity said and finally put her phone away.

"No, it was DODO!" I screamed.

He immediately slapped me across the face. "Stop it, you're being hysterical."

Did Nigel just slap me? I put my hand to my cheek.

"Wait." He blinked at me. "How do you know about DODO?"

"How do *you* know about DODO?" I asked.

"Because I'm Tanner's houseboy!"

"Well I'm Tanner's girlfriend!"

"But there are some secretses you don't share outside your houseboy! There are rules about these things. Good God, what has he done!?"

Chastity slapped Nigel across the face. "Stop it, you're being hysterical!"

Nigel shrieked. "Did you just strike me!?"

"Now we're even."

He raised his hand to slap her back, but she grabbed his wrist.

"I don't think so, Nigel," she said firmly. "You started this when you slapped me in Ash's apartment. Tit for tat."

He pulled his hand out of her grasp, dropped the antique sword on the ground, and then they started swatting their hands against each other's like they were two kittens playing. Two kittens that hated each other very much.

"Would you both cut it out!" I screamed. "Tanner's been taken. Can we please focus for one second? We need to go after him."

Chastity took a step back from Nigel. "I swear he just went to Club Onyx. Let's just stop by and get him."

"You two are not allowed in Club Onyx again without Master Tanner's direct supervision."

"But…" Chastity started.

"No buts, missy. You are both in time-out! Remember?"

Chastity folded her arms across her chest.

"You two will wait here while I check the club."

"No way," said Chastity.

"Yes way," replied Nigel, mimicking her saucy tone.

It looked like they were seconds away from another slap fight. "Stop it!" I yelled. "Nigel, I know that we're not supposed to go back to Club Onyx. But is it really safe for you to leave us here if DODO took Tanner? They might come for me next."

He stared at me for a second. And then he lifted the sword back up, strutted over to one of the lifeboats, and slashed the rope holding it up.

It seemed entirely unnecessary because there was a whole release system for it. But I had to admit, it was pretty badass. "Aren't you two coming?" he asked.

Of course we were! I know that technically we were hosting this party, but I didn't care about that. Not when Tanner had been taken and dirty kidnappers were on the loose!

I grabbed Nigel's hand as he helped me onto the lifeboat. Chastity plopped down ungracefully beside me when Nigel refused to assist her.

"I hate that little man," Chastity said.

Honestly I wasn't a huge fan of Nigel either. But he could help us get into Club Onyx. He could make sure Tanner was safe. And that was the only plan we had.

Chapter 2
A BLESSING AND A CURSE
Friday

A few people stared at us as we walked down the New York City sidewalk.

I was soaking wet wearing nothing but a towel and some sick Odegaard boots.

Chastity was in a bikini and heels.

And Nigel was decked out in lederhosen. And still carrying a sword.

We made an odd threesome. I almost gagged at the thought of a threesome with Chastity and Nigel.

"This way," Nigel said as we tromped through the city.

Surprisingly…no one called the cops on us. Actually, this was the fastest I'd ever been able to walk through the city since everyone on the sidewalk went to great lengths to get out of our way. I made a mental note to dress like a crazy person more often. Because I hated crowded sidewalks. And other humans in general.

"We're here," Nigel said, abruptly stopping in the middle of the sidewalk.

Huh? I stared at the building next to us. "The entrance to Club Onyx is through a Starbucks?"

"Mhm. This way," Nigel said and opened the door to Starbucks.

"I should have known the entrance would be somewhere so basic," Chastity said and walked through the door. "No one would ever even look if they didn't know."

"The entrance to Club Onyx is really through here?" I asked.

Nigel nodded without making eye contact.

That seemed like a yes if I ever saw one. I also didn't like to make direct eye contact with people.

Nigel ignored the line of customers and went straight to the restroom. "In there," he said and opened the door for us.

"Oh, I don't need to go," said Chastity. "And even if I did…I wouldn't use a public restroom. I'd stop by one of the finance buildings and flirt with a guard so I pee in luxury."

"It's the entrance," said Nigel.

"Really?" Chastity frowned. "I don't remember smelling coffee or pastries or pee the first time we went to Club Onyx."

"That's because there was a bag over your head." It kind of looked like Nigel was contemplating bagging her again.

"Come on," I said and grabbed Chastity's hand. "We don't have time to dilly dally." I pulled her into the bathroom.

She stepped over a piece of loose toilet paper and shuddered.

And then the door slammed shut behind us.

We both spun around. Nigel was not standing behind us. And then we heard the click of a lock. Which made no sense because the lock was on this side.

"Nigel!" I yelled and grabbed the doorknob. But the jerk had somehow locked us in. I turned the lock back and forth, but it did no good. "Nigel, what the heck? You're supposed to be showing us how to get into Club Onyx!" And I had a feeling this was definitely not the entrance. Chastity was right. I would have smelled pastries through a bag over my head. I could always smell baked goods. It was a blessing and a curse.

"You're not allowed in Club Onyx. You're in time out!" he shouted through the door.

"Nigel, let us out!" I yelled.

"Never!"

Did he seriously just lock us in a random bathroom to prevent us from finding the real entrance to Club Onyx? And was he serious about *never* letting us out?

"Nigel, let us out right now," Chastity said.

"No!"

"Yes!" Chastity yelled back.

"I don't even know who you are, Chastain!"

"Chastain?" Chastity laughed. "You know that's not my name, Nigel!"

"No I don't. Now silence! I'll be back once I find Tanner. Until then, you two stay put."

"Nigel!" I banged on the door. "Please don't leave us in here! I'm claustrophobic." I'd never been diagnosed or anything, but the walls were definitely closing in on me.

"I'm sorry there's no bath in there to calm you down! But I had to think fast!"

I'd rather die than step into a bath that had been used by others. And I was pretty sure Nigel knew that.

"Au revoir!" he yelled.

"What the hell did you just say to me?!" *That son of a bitch!*

Chastity laughed. "He just said bye in French."

"You know I don't speak French!"

"Take a deep breath. There will surely be a homeless person that needs to pee soon. And the manager will open the door. We'll be in here for a couple of minutes tops."

I never thought I'd need Homeless Rutherford to save me. "I don't have a couple of minutes. I can't breathe!" I tried to take a deep breath, but there was no air. How were we already out of air?

"Ash, snap out of it," Chastity said and shook my shoulders. "Everything is going to be fine."

"How? We're locked in a bathroom and Tanner's been kidnapped!"

"Possibly kidnapped. But probably just taken to an emergency sex auction."

But she hadn't seen what had happened. He'd definitely been taken by DODO. I hip-checked the door. *Ow.* Why did that always work in movies? I grabbed my hip. "I think I broke it."

"The door seems fine to me."

"Not the door! My hip!"

"Here, sit down. No, wait. Don't."

We both stared at the puddle on the ground. I had no idea if it was pee of some sort of beverage. I really hoped it was the latter. Who the hell would pop a squat and piss in the middle of the floor when there was a toilet right there?

I started slamming my fists against the door. "Homeless Rutherford! Save us!"

Chapter 3
SEXY SCAVENGER HUNT
Friday

"Ash, I seriously doubt Homeless Rutherford will be the homeless person that saves us. I mean…what are the chances he'd be using this bathroom out of all the bathrooms in the city? Besides, he'd probably just lick the door and walk away."

I gagged and looked down at my hands that had been banging on the door. "He *licks* doors?!" I ran to the sink and turned on the water. "They're out of soap!" I screamed. "How are they out of soap? I'm going to die in here!"

"Someone will let us out soon."

But the seconds turned to minutes. And the minutes turned to hours. "Chastity!" I screamed. "We've been in here for five hours!"

Chastity checked her phone. "It's literally been one minute."

That didn't sound right. "Are you sure?" The germs were killing me.

A second later there was a knock on the door.

"Occupied!" I yelled out of habit as I dried my hands on way too many paper towels. As if paper towels could help with the germs all over my skin. "No, wait! We're stuck! Help us!" I started banging on the door, keeping the paper towels over my hands for protection.

"Unlock the door," the man said from the other side.

Why is a man trying to get into the woman's restroom?

"It is unlocked on our side," Chastity said. "Unlock it from your side."

"There's no lock on this side," he said.

Chastity and I looked at each other. That didn't make any sense.

"Please just help us, Homeless Rutherford!" I yelled.

"Would you cut it out," Chastity said. "That's not Homeless Rutherford. And you'll scare the person off. Do you want to get out of here or not?"

"Of course I want to get out!"

"Then shush! I'll handle this." Chastity turned back to the door. "We've unlocked it on our side. It must be jammed or something."

"Ma'am, please unlock the door."

"Excuse me?" She turned to me. "Did he just call me ma'am?"

I nodded. Knowing full well that any semblance of calm that Chastity was maintaining was about to be thrown out the window. *Oh God, there are no windows in here!* I gasped for air.

"I'm not a ma'am!" she yelled through the door.

"Oh. Sorry, sir."

"What?!" she screamed. "Let me out of here right this second!"

The knob wiggled but nothing happened.

"Let us out!" She banged on the door with the side of her fist. "Or I'll sue you to oblivion!"

"I need to pee," someone mumbled from the other side of the door.

Honestly we were saving them. They certainly didn't want to pee in this germ-infested hell hole. All I could do was stare at the floor puddle and relive incident #6 over and over again in my head. I'd told Tanner I loved him. And then I flung myself off his yacht. And then I flashed everyone. And then Tanner was taken. It was like the incident that wouldn't stop. Was it actually four incidents in one? "Good God, my life is over!"

Chastity ignored me and kept banging on the door.

It took exactly five hours of yelling back and forth and then another five for the firemen to arrive. "It's been ten hours!"

Chastity laughed. "It's been thirty minutes. Stop it."

"Ten hours!"

Chastity showed me her phone. "Nope."

I was pretty sure her phone was broken.

"How do my tits look?" she asked, sticking out her chest. "These firefighters are gonna be *so* excited when they burst in and see us. Oh! Maybe you should take your towel off."

"I'm not going to do that."

Chastity shrugged. "Suit yourself. But don't say I didn't try to help you. I'm not about to break Single Girl Rule #13: Always wing woman for the girl with the longest active dry spell."

I know she said it had only been thirty minutes. But I was definitely out of air. And severely dehydrated. And starving beyond belief. Being locked up didn't suit me. But I did my best to sob quietly as the firemen hacked away at the hinges of the bathroom door.

The door finally fell away.

"My heroes!" Chastity said and flung herself into the arms of one of the firemen.

I burst through the open doorway. "I need soap! Stat!" I was seconds away from fainting.

The manager quickly grabbed some soap to refill the dispenser. I took it from him and did the last thing I ever expected to do…I ran back into the bathroom.

I washed my hands ten times. And by hands, I mean my hands and arms all the way up to my pits. I finally took a deep breath.

"You used all the soap," the manager said.

What? I looked down. Sure enough, the refill for the soap dispenser was completely empty.

"And the bathroom is for customers only."

I stared at him. We both knew that the public restroom rules at Starbucks weren't regularly enforced. But it didn't seem like he was backing down.

And to be fair…I had just used all his soap. And whatever Nigel had done to the door had pretty much destroyed it.

"I'd like a variety of pastries, please," I said. "And five bottles of water."

He raised his eyebrows. "No shoes, no shirt, no service."

"I'm wearing shoes. And this is a fashionable dress." I gestured to my towel. "Please, I'm starving. And I'm going to pass out from dehydration…"

He held up his hands to stop me. "Fine. But you need to come pay at the register."

I followed him back out of the restroom and past Chastity flirting with the firemen. She'd somehow convinced one of them to take his shirt off. I really didn't know how she could be flirting at a time like this.

I paid for all my food and water with a credit card, because I couldn't fathom touching anything else dirty like loose change.

And then I sat down at a table and ate one pastry after another. Luckily everyone was more focused on the firefighters than on me. Because I definitely had food all over my face. I took another big bite as I looked over at Chastity and all the firemen. One of them was still trying to figure out what had happened to the door. *Stupid Nigel.*

I downed a water bottle and slowly started to feel like myself again. I looked down at the rest of the pastries and bottles of water. Had I ordered too much food? I was pretty sure I'd just panic-eaten three pastries. But I had no idea how to know for sure. I was almost positive I had blacked out. I downed another bottle of water.

The firemen finally left and Chastity walked back over to me.

"Stress eating?" she asked and lifted up a pastry.

"We almost died."

She laughed. "The ceiling had those push-up tiles. We could have been in the vents within minutes."

"Then why didn't we do that?!"

"Because I wanted to see some firemen."

I glared at her.

"We're fine. You're fine. God, how many water bottles did you just pound? You're going to have to go to the bathroom again."

"Never."

She laughed.

But damn it. She was right. I already had to pee. I crossed my legs under the table. "How long do you think Nigel is going to be?"

"I don't know…he probably knew we'd escape fairly quickly. He should be back any minute now."

But the minutes actually did turn to hours. We waited and waited and waited for Nigel. Until I had to use the horrifying restroom again. I refused to close the door and just made Chastity stand guard.

We waited until the hipsters all left. And the manager told us they were closing. And then we waited outside for another hour. Until my fifth water bottle kicked in and we had no choice but to head back to our apartments.

"God, I can't believe my luck," I said as we waited for our Uber. "What are the odds that Tanner would get taken like two seconds after finally confessing his love to me?"

"Whoa whoa whoa. Hold everything! Tanner said he loves you?"

"Yeah."

"And did you say it back?"

"I actually said it first. But I don't think it counts."

She stared at me.

"The punch was spiked and it kind of tumbled out. And then I jumped ship." As I said it, a horrible thought came to me. "Oh my God. Do you think I freaked him out by telling him that I loved him? And then he ran?"

"That depends." She yanked on my towel.

"Chastity!" I screamed and tried to grab it, but it was too late. The Uber had just pulled up. And the driver had definitely seen my boobs.

"What?"

"You can't just pull my towel down on the side-walk!"

"Well I had to check to see if you were topless under there. And good news, you are. Which means Tanner didn't run."

"I don't follow."

"Guys don't run away from naked boobs. It's literally impossible for them to do."

"Are you sure?"

Chastity nodded. "I could have taken my top off and kept the firefighters here all day, but I didn't want the city to burn down in their absence. And the Uber driver is just sitting there staring at us."

"Hmmm...I guess you're right."

"Of course I am! Did Tanner say anything else before he was taken?"

"Uh... He said that he'd known I was special from the moment I started stalking him. And that he liked when I hit him with a door and laughed in his face. And that he loved me. Oh! And that he was done running."

"I really wish you had told me that sooner. I know exactly what's happening."

"You do?"

"Yeah. He's sending you on a sexy scavenger hunt."

"You getting in?" asked the Uber driver.

"Hold on," said Chastity. "We're discussing something very important here."

He looked annoyed, but then she flashed him. After that he seemed more than happy to stick around.

"I really don't follow your logic here," I said.

"He said he loves you stalking him. And then mentioned running. All the hints are there."

"Okay...so where do we start?"

"Well I bet Nigel was in on it. Which means the hunt was supposed to begin in that bathroom."

"Right. That explains how Nigel locked us in. He must have rigged it ahead of time."

"Exactly. Which means..." Chastity's eyes lit up. "Oh my God! The firefighters were part of it! We were probably supposed to suck their cocks to earn our second clue."

"What?! Why would Tanner want us to do that?"

"Uh...because it's a *sexy* scavenger hunt. What else would we do with a bunch of hunky firefighters?"

"I don't know. Thank them kindly for their service to New York City?"

"Oh damn, you think we were supposed to let them gangbang us?"

"What?! No! I said we should have thanked them."

"Right. With a gangbang."

"No. I didn't say anything about a gangbang."

Chastity laughed. "You're not making any sense. It's fine though. It's been a long day. Let's get home and rest a bit, and then we can decide how far we wanna go with the firemen in the morning."

"I'm not gonna sleep with any firefighters."

"So just blowjobs then? Works for me!"

Chapter 4

MATTHEW FREAKING CALDWELL
Saturday

I tossed and turned all night.

I was absolutely dreading whatever Chastity was going to try to make me do at the firehouse in the morning. But I was also kind of hoping she was right about it being the first step of an elaborate scavenger hunt.

Because the alternative was almost unthinkable.

Tanner had either been kidnapped by DODO, or I'd freaked him out and made him run from me.

The latter wouldn't be unprecedented. But this felt different. He'd said that for once in his life he had something real. He'd said I was it for him.

So there was no way he'd run.

I could feel it in my bones. Something terrible had happened to him. And he needed my help.

If he was even alive.

It was equally horrifying and easy to picture him at the bottom of the Hudson River with weights tied to his ankles. Or with a bullet in his head. Or surrounded by sluts at a sex auction.

Gah!

I hated all of it.

I just wished he would call me and explain everything. And as I thought it, my phone buzzed.

Holy shit! Had my wish really just come true?

I jumped out of bed and grabbed my phone. My eyes weren't adjusted to the light so my phone was kind of blinding. I squinted and clicked on the text.

"Ah!" I screamed when the text opened. It was a picture of Chastity giving two thumbs up. She was wearing nothing but a fireman's hat and a face full of cum.

I immediately hit call.

I know, I know. Phone calls are for freaks. But this was important! I needed to know everything.

"Hey girl!" she said. "I wasn't sure if you'd be up yet."

"What about me made you think that I'd be able to sleep a wink?"

"Good point. I couldn't sleep either, so I figured I'd get a head start on the scavenger hunt. I hope you don't mind that I headed to the fire station without you."

"I'm sure I'll get over it," I said. "Find anything helpful?"

"Girl, I found all sorts of helpful things."

"Such as…?"

"Lots of big cocks, mainly."

"I gathered that from the picture you sent. I was more interested in what clues they had for us."

"Oh. Let me ask." Chastity started talking to the firemen, but it was all muffled on my end. "Apparently they've never heard of Tanner or the Society."

"Seriously? Then why'd you send me that selfie with two thumbs up?!"

"Because I had a great time. Didn't you see all that cum on my face?"

"Damn it, Chastity! I can't believe you got me all excited for nothing." She was seriously the worst.

"Well you should still be excited. The firemen said we can come back any time."

"That doesn't make me feel better. Tanner is missing! And we have no clues."

"It'll be fine," said Chastity. "I bet we'll get an envelope from the Society soon telling us what to do."

Hmm… "I can't believe I'm saying this, but that kind of makes sense." Or was I just clinging to false hope?

I had no idea.

The only thing I knew for sure was that I loved Tanner. And he loved me back.

***

No envelope arrived. So we started our hunt again.

We searched for Tanner for days.

Weeks.

Months.

The whole summer went by.

For real. I wasn't just exaggerating because I was locked in a bathroom. I was free and in hell.

Tanner was gone. There wasn't a single trace of him. Or Nigel.

And I had no idea how to find him. I didn't even know where he lived. I'd only ever been to his fake apartment.

I even tried calling the number Nigel had left on my kitchen counter after he'd bagged me, but the number was no longer in service. Neither was Angel's number. Not that I'd had the courage to call him…I'd made Chastity do it. I could never see or speak to Angel or Diablo again. I'd booped their penises like a sex-starved maniac.

We also had the key that Tanner had given me the same night he'd disappeared. But I'd put it into a lot of holes and nothing ever happened. And therefore it was useless. Seriously, who gives someone a key with zero context? It could literally go to anything in the whole city.

The only lead we had was Club Onyx. In Tanner's note that I'd opened early, he'd said if he ever disappeared that I should go to Club Onyx. That it would be where I'd find what I was looking for. And I was looking for him. So…I needed to find Club Onyx. But that wasn't a lead because I didn't know where it was or how to get in without Tanner. The Society app on my phone disappeared the morning after Tanner disappeared. Poof. Gone. Without the app I couldn't even work my way up to getting access to the club. Not that I wanted to go on a date with anyone but Tanner anyway.

And I only had one possible resource to locate Club Onyx – Dr. Lyons. But I couldn't see him because there was no way I wouldn't do something that would result in me going to jail. And he was in three out of my six incidents. You didn't hang out with people who were in half of your incidents.

"You know there's another option," Chastity said as we finished another box of wine.

I'd been finishing a lot of boxes of wine recently.

"Don't you say it." I clenched my jaw. I knew exactly who she was going to say. Tanner's best friend. The one man on this earth I was more embarrassed around than Dr. Lyons. And that was really saying something because I'd tried to rape Dr. Lyons.

Chastity opened her mouth.

"Don't you freaking say it!"

"Matthew Caldwell."

"No! We don't even know for sure that they're friends!"

"I looked into it. He's definitely the Matt from Tanner's phone. We both saw how Nigel reacted to me asking about him."

I shook my head.

"And honestly, maybe this is for the best. You can't date Tanner if he's friends with Matt. You wouldn't be able to handle it."

"Yes I could! I'd do anything for Tanner."

"Anything?"

"Of course."

"Got you. So if you won't see Dr. Lyons, then you can at least contact Matt. End of discussion."

"I can't talk to Matt *or* Dr. Lyons."

"You just said you'd do anything. And we've been searching for months. Matt is our last option. Trust me, I wouldn't mention him if it wasn't dire."

"I can't."

"Ash, Matt's dick is fine. I'm sure he forgives you for setting it on fire."

"No man forgives a girl for something like that." Although it did kind of seem like Matt had forgiven me. The few times I'd run into him after *the incident* he'd been perfectly kind. *Too* kind. He was probably luring me into a false sense of security while he put his case together to sue me for all I'm worth.

"He has reservations in half an hour at that new restaurant with all the rave reviews. Get dressed. We're going."

I looked down at my stained sweatpants. "I am dressed."

"God, you've really gone downhill fast."

Had I? Because I'd dressed like this before I met Tanner. Before my heart had been ripped in two.

I followed Chastity out of the apartment. She kept giving me wary looks. But had she forgotten about the night the people on the sidewalk had literally parted for me because I was wearing only a towel? That was who I was now.

"There," Chastity said and pointed to where a car had just pulled up to the curb.

Matt stepped out as a valet helped his wife to the sidewalk.

"Now's your chance."

I stayed firmly rooted in place.

"Hey, Matt!" Chastity yelled.

He started to turn his head.

And I threw myself into oncoming traffic to avoid his gaze. Literally. I threw myself onto the hood of a car, skidded across it and fell onto the pavement. And then I stayed down for good measure. Although I wasn't entirely sure I could get up. I'm pretty sure my whole body was broken.

But somehow Matt missed the whole thing. It was a miracle.

When Chastity helped me to my feet, I could tell something was wrong. It was all over her face.

"I talked to Matt," she said.

"And what did he say?"

"That Tanner does this sometimes. Goes abroad for long periods of time to close deals."

"He's…abroad? Closing a deal?" He was away on business? That couldn't be right. I'd seen DODO take him. I'd seen it. "I mean, when was the last time Matt talked to Tanner? Are they even really friends anymore? I'm Tanner's girlfriend. I'm…"

"Ash, I'm so sorry." She pulled me into a hug.

I was pretty sure my whole body was broken. And I probably needed a tetanus shot after getting hit by that car. But none of that mattered.

I'd been so sure of one thing. That Tanner loved me. That was all that kept me going. And I was barely going. I was dressed like a homeless person and had almost died tonight.

Now the truth was painfully obvious.

Tanner didn't love me.

The thought echoed around in my head, refusing to settle into place.

He'd run off because I'd stalked him and freaked him out.

Because we both knew I was the stalker in this situation. *Fuck you, Tanner Rhodes.*

Chapter 5

INCIDENT #7?

Friday – Two Months Later

I know you're probably thinking that my entire life was in shambles. But it actually wasn't.

I didn't need Tanner in order to be happy. Technically we had only officially dated for 24 hours. It was the shortest relationship in the history of relationships. It meant nothing to me. Sure, I'd loved him for months before we dated and for months after he disappeared…

No. Stop it. I didn't love him at all. Tanner was a stupid asshattery.

Honestly, I didn't have time for a man in my life anyway. Not when I was working 90-hour weeks. My new therapist said I was exhibiting extremely unhealthy avoidance behaviors, but she didn't know what she was talking about.

So yeah, I was crushing it at work.

All my performance reviews had been amazing. I was on the fast track to upper management. And thanks to my boss getting pregnant, my promotion was going to happen today.

Sucks for her. Soon Bee would be home with a screaming baby, spending all her hard-earned money on diapers. Meanwhile, I'd be making bank, and I sure as hell wouldn't be wasting any money on a dumb baby. Rent, boxed wine, food, boxed wine, healthcare, boxed wine, and Netflix. Those were my only expenses, and I was happier than ever.

Seriously, so happy.

I didn't even think about Tanner at all anymore.

But like…where was he?

Was he in Europe?

Had he found someone new?

Did he still go to the Society?

I did a quick scan of all his closest known associates on every social media platform, but there were still no pictures of him. Which wasn't a surprise since I'd just checked an hour ago.

Okay, fine. I admit it. I still thought about Tanner *occasionally*.

Especially when I had to go into the amazing closet he'd built for me with all the fancy clothes.

I'd been in there earlier this morning picking out the perfect outfit for my promotion. As the soon-to-be VP of Business Development at BIMG, I needed to look the part. And nothing said, "I'm a freaking boss," like a pair of $3000 Odegaards and a matching power suit.

Chastity must have agreed, because she honked my boobs as soon as I walked off the elevator. Which, according to one of Chastity's weird Single Girl Rules, meant that she loved my outfit.

And then she gasped. "Wait a second. That whole outfit is from the Odegaard 2023 Spring collection. Which means…"

"Yup. I went into the closet." It was the first time I'd worn something from his closet since he'd left. Unless you counted the times when Chastity and I had gotten super drunk, dressed up, and tried to find the

Society's secret headquarters. Which had been pretty frequently. At least like four times a week.

"Well that's awfully ballsy of you," said Chastity.

"It's fine. I'm over him."

"Oh, I didn't think it was ballsy of you to go into the closet. But that outfit feels like a premature celebration for you getting the promotion. Aren't you worried about jinxing it?"

Shit! Did I jinx my promotion? "Psssh, jinxes aren't real. And anyway, I'm not celebrating. I'm always super stylish."

"You wore sandals and socks to work last Sunday."

"That was one time! And it was the weekend!" I squinted at her. "And how did you know about that?"

"The security cameras. I know we said we'd only hack them one time to look for Tanner, but that's some good viewing. You should see what Bee and Mason do in the wee hours. Let's just say I'm not at all surprised that she's having a baby. I practically got pregnant watching the things Mason did to her on that desk." Chastity fanned herself.

I cringed and pulled my hand off the desk. "When I get promoted, my first act of business shall be to burn every piece of furniture in this office."

Madison walked over to us. "Oh my God! Did they already announce it?"

"Announce what?" I asked.

"Your promotion," she whispered, as if it was a dirty word.

"No. Why would you think that?"

"You just said it. Which is crazy, because you're totally gonna jinx it."

Damn it! Now I'd double jinxed it? "Now you believe in jinxes too?"

Madison shrugged. "All I'm saying is that you need all the luck you can get. What do you think the odds are that they'd really give this promotion to a woman?"

"High, I hope. Bee wouldn't want this place to become a boys' club while she's away on maternity leave."

Chastity cut in. "You're definitely gonna get it. I mean…I was a shoo-in before I got reported for sexually harassing that hot secretary. There was literally no way for me to know that he was gay. And now that I'm ineligible, you're next in line."

I gave Chastity a sympathetic smile. I felt guilty that I was getting the promotion ahead of her. She'd been here for years more than I had. Hell, she was the one who got me this job. "Well, when I'm in charge, I'm going to hire the hottest, straightest male secretaries. And you can harass them to your heart's content."

"Yes! You're going to be the best boss ever. And I bet you'll even give us unlimited lunch breaks."

"Of course." Just like Tanner had. *No! Don't think about him.* He was dead to me.

"See? The best. And to thank you, I have the ultimate celebration planned for tonight."

Oh God. "Does it involve male strippers?" There was a 98% chance that it did. That was kind of her go-to move for celebrations.

Chastity looked shocked. "How dare you accuse me of such a thing."

"Single Girl Rule #10," I said. "All celebrations of important life events must involve strippers."

She gave me a high five. "Nice job quoting the rules! But no, I actually didn't hire any strippers for this evening. I didn't want to jinx you. And anyway…what I have planned is even better than strippers."

Better than strippers? "I'm not going to an orgy."

Chastity laughed. "It's not an orgy. Or maybe it is. You'll just have to see!"

"I'm not going unless you tell me exactly what I'm getting myself into."

"I don't want to spoil the surprise. But here's a hint…" She rummaged around in her massive handbag and pulled out an envelope. A little black envelope. With lacy trim and a golden wax seal.

I tried to snatch it from her, but she pulled it out of reach. "How'd you get that? Did the Society finally contact you?!"

Was Tanner back?! Had he sent her that envelope? My mind started spinning with possibilities. But just then, Bee arrived in all her pregnant glory.

Chastity gave me a mischievous grin and put the envelope away. "Guess you'll have to wait and see."

"But…" *Damn it!*

With Bee's arrival, the gender reveal party got started. At first everyone was fawning over her and the baby bump. Especially Madison, who could not stop touching her belly and telling her how gorgeous she looked. It was fine at first, but then it got a little aggressive. I was about to step in to save Bee when some random coworker started talking to me.

Ah! Stranger danger! I'd only talked to the lady like once before. Which meant I was terrified to be talking to her now. Making small talk felt like repeatedly getting punched in the boob. Painful and awkward. Only this was worse, because it made me all sweaty too.

The torture didn't stop with Jill from accounting, though. All sorts of people started talking to me. And they were all being way too friendly. It seemed like I was almost more popular than Bee.

What the hell is going on?

I excused myself from the crowd and pulled Chastity aside. "Why are all those people being so nice to me? It's freaking me out."

"They must have heard you're gonna be the boss."

"Ooooh." It all made so much sense now. Part of me was slightly terrified that I was going to have to put up with all that attention, but the other part of me was FREAKING JAZZED. Because it was practically a sure thing now. If all those people were sucking up to me, it was definitely happening. I was really getting promoted!

Mason clinked a glass to get everyone's attention. He was Bee's husband. And the CEO of the company. And Matthew freaking Caldwell's older brother, but we didn't need to get into the OG incident right now because I was already sweaty enough.

This is it!

"Thank you all for coming," he began. "Actually. Why am I thanking you? *You* should be thanking *me* for letting you party during work hours."

Bee slapped his arm. "Don't listen to him. You're all like family to us. Which is why we wanted to share the big reveal with you."

"That's my queue," whispered Chastity. She slipped away and wheeled a giant cake out into the center of the room. And when I say giant, I mean *giant*. Like…big enough for a person to fit inside of.

"But before we do the big reveal," said Mason, "I want everyone to guess what the sex will be. Show of hands for a boy?"

About half the room raised their hands. I didn't.

Mason nodded. "Great. The rest of you are fired."

Everyone laughed and Bee hit Mason again. "He's joking. I'm sure he'll be delighted if we have a little girl. Isn't that right?"

Mason nodded reluctantly.

"Oh come on," said Bee. "Don't you want another little me running around?"

"Well that would be adorable," he conceded. "As long as she never leaves the house."

God, how are they so cute together? It was a total #CoupleGoals moment. For some reason an image of Tanner popped into my head. *No! Go away!* I had no couple goals beyond me and my future cats. *Ew, what?* Why had I subconsciously turned future me into a cat woman? Cats were disgusting little monsters that walked in litter boxes and then walked across the kitchen counter. Imagine if a human casually stepped into a full toilet and then danced on a table? I started gagging just thinking about it. The next time I saw a cat, I'd punt the little demon out a window. And if I ever saw Tanner again…I'd punt his lying ass into a pit of cats. *Take that.*

"Alright," said Bee. "I think we better reveal the gender before Mason hurls any more insults at our unborn baby girl." She rubbed her huge pregnant belly.

Chastity drummed on a desk and counted down. "Three, two, one…surprise!"

A man popped out of the cake. No, not just any man. This was a gorgeous man. Six feet of pure muscle. Dark hair. And the bluest eyes I'd ever seen.

Oh my God. Chastity had really done it. She'd hired a stripper for a baby reveal.

I considered tackling him back into the cake before he could rip his pants off. But he actually kept his clothes on. Instead he yelled, "It's a boy!" and threw blue confetti in the air.

"I thought for sure he was gonna be a stripper," I whispered to Chastity.

"He might be," she said. "Hell, I hope he is. But I didn't hire him."

"Then who is he?"

"Maybe your future husband. It's about time you start talking to men again." She shoved me towards him. Hard. In sneakers I would have kept my balance just fine. But in my sky-high Odegaards, it was a completely different story. I stumbled and reached out to break my fall…by grabbing onto the guy. His butt, to be precise. And my face went into his crotch.

He grabbed me with one of his strong hands and helped me to my feet.

"Nice to meet you," I said, pretending like I hadn't just molested his ass and rubbed my face on his crotch.

"The pleasure is all mine," he said, his beautiful blue eyes dancing with amusement. "Is that always how you greet people?"

"Yup."

He stuck out his hand. "Xander Frost."

"Cool." I slapped his hand as if it was part of some secret handshake and then ran back to Chastity. *Cool? What the hell is wrong with me?!*

"How'd it go?" she asked.

"Terrible!" It probably should have been incident #7, but I promised myself I wouldn't have any more incidents. I'd just have to bury this memory somewhere deep inside of me and never think of it again.

Chastity frowned. "Damn. Small dick?"

"What?"

"I mean, you put your face all over it. I figured you'd at least have some idea of how big it is. Bold move, by the way. To pretend to fall."

"I wasn't pretending!" I whisper-yelled. "You shoved me!"

"You're welcome."

"I wasn't thanking you."

"You should. You must have really made an impression. I think he's staring at you."

"I have to leave. I can never see that man again." I took off for the bathroom.

Chastity grabbed my arm. "You can't leave. They're about to announce the new VP."

Oh, right. I was about to get promoted. "After I burn all the desks, my second order of business shall be to ban that man from this building. Or maybe I'll ban him first..."

"Can't we hire him as a secretary? I'd love to start every morning by slapping his tight ass after he brings me a steaming cup of coffee."

Mason clinked his glass again. "As you all know, Bee is taking some time off to be with Mason Jr. And we need someone to help fill her very large shoes while she's gone."

"They've only grown half a size!" protested Bee. "And we're definitely not naming him that."

"We'll discuss that later. And I meant that you do a lot for this company, not that your feet have grown. Anyway, it's my pleasure to introduce you to our new VP of Business Development…"

I took a deep breath. This was the moment. *Oh no.* Was I going to have to give a big speech? What if I made a fool of myself in front of all my new underlings? I'd already molested the cake stripper. That felt like enough embarrassment for one day.

"Our new VP is one of the most respected marketers in the industry, and I'm sure he'll be a great addition to our team."

He? Did Mason just refer to me as a he? No, I must have heard him wrong. I couldn't hear right with all the blood rushing to my ears.

"So, without further ado, I'd like you all to meet the one, the only, Xander Frost."

I took a step forward. Everyone was cheering. *Wait…Xander Frost?* That wasn't my name!

Xander raised his hand for silence. "Thank you, thank you. I'm so happy to be here."

"What the hell?" whispered Chastity.

"Told you they'd hire a man," said Madison.

I couldn't believe this was happening. That promotion was supposed to be mine. I'd worked my ass off for this company. Yes, I'd only been here a short time. But I'd been putting in so many hours!

What a freaking waste of time.

BIMG could kiss my 90-hour work weeks goodbye. And since I was totally over Tanner, I wouldn't have to work that much anyway. I could finally start living my life again. And the best way to do that was with the little black envelope Chastity had shown me. It was time to rejoin the Society.

Chapter 6

THE ENVELOPE
Friday

"Ready to open this?" asked Chastity. She waved the little black envelope in the air, taunting me with it. Just like she'd been doing all day. It had been pure torture having to wait until after work to open it. But also a great distraction from grabbing my new boss' ding-dong. And for having a new boss to begin with. BIMG was the worst. They all deserved to have their dicks grabbed.

"Yes!" I took my Odegaards off and started cleaning the blue bottoms.

She sat down on my couch and made a show of getting comfy. "Don't you want to know where I got it?"

"Yes."

She just stared at me.

"Are you seriously not going to tell me? You dirty tease."

"Hey! I'm a lot of things, but I am *not* a tease."

That was probably true. Except in this one case. "Then prove it and tell me everything."

"Okay, okay. You can do the honors." She held the envelope out for me.

I grabbed for it, but she pulled it back.

"On one condition," she said.

"Which is?"

"You have to promise to do whatever it says on this card."

That was a dangerous promise to make. It had been months since I'd read the contract, but I still knew what sorts of things the Society expected from their members. Unprotected sex. With strangers. In public. Or as Tanner referred to it - *the pursuit of true love*. Gag. What a little dickwad. He wouldn't know true love if it mollywhopped him right in the face. "I'll do whatever it says. Within reason."

"Nope. You agree, or this card stays a mystery."

"Then no deal. If you're making me agree ahead of time, then there must be something truly awful on that card."

Chastity flipped it around to show me the unbroken seal. "I don't know what it says. But I do know that I can't bear to sit around while you hide from life."

"I'm not hiding from life." *Am I?*

"How many hours did you work this week?"

A lot. "I didn't keep track."

"How many days did you eat dinner at the office this week?"

Four. "None."

Chastity raised an eyebrow. "Liar. I was with you last night. We had Gochujang Palace delivered to the office."

"Gah, fine. But what's wrong with that? I'm working on my career. Investing in my future." *Burying my emotional trauma of only being able to keep a boyfriend for 24 hours.*

"And how's that working out for you? Because last time I checked, you didn't get the promotion."

"Why am I never good enough?"

"What are you talking about? You deserved that promotion. Although I'm not mad about the man candy they hired. Seriously, was his penis really small? That would be devastating."

I shook my head. "It's not just the promotion. It's everything. I wasn't good enough for Tanner, or he wouldn't have skipped town right after I confessed my love to him. And I wasn't even good enough for Joe. Joe! His freaking nickname is Cupcake and he's 5'6 with a tiny little baby penis. I mean…if I'm not good enough for Joe then I should just hurl myself out the window…"

Chastity pulled me into a big hug so I wouldn't go through with it. "Joe's an asshole. And so was Tanner. But there are good guys out there."

"Maybe."

"There are. But you'll never find them if you hide behind a desk. You have to go out and look for them. And yes, I know I haven't found my person yet. But I'm sure as hell having fun trying."

"You really think I'll find my person?" I asked.

"I know you will," said Chastity. She sounded so sure of it. "But you have to start living. You have to start saying yes."

Start saying yes. She made it sound so simple. But saying yes was impossible. My mind wasn't built to say yes to things. It was built to overanalyze and freak out and hide. That's why I had a list of new things to try. Oh my God, what happened to my list? No wonder I was spiraling, I'd lost it. I was listless. Maybe I should just try this saying yes thing instead. It would be easier than keeping track of a piece of paper. Besides, half the things on it had been impossible to cross off anyway.

"Now," said Chastity. "Let's try this again. Will you do whatever the card says?"

No. Damn it! I was supposed to be saying yes. I took a deep breath. "Yes."

Chastity smiled and handed it to me. "Good. I hope you're ready to get gangbanged by a football team."

"WHAT?!"

"Just kidding. I think. Open it!"

I tore through the golden wax seal and pulled out a single sheet of thick parchment.

Raven Black & Chastity Morgan,
Congratulations! You've been promoted to novus (silver) members.
We look forward to seeing you at Club Onyx.

I read it twice to make sure I was reading it right. "I have so many questions."

"Such as?"

"Well for starters, what made them let us back into the Society? And how did we get promoted to novus members?"

"Who could resist this face?" Chastity batted her eyelashes.

"So you found a member and slept with him?"

"No!"

"Of course you did."

"I really didn't!"

"I'm so confused. Usually you're so excited to admit when you use your body to get what you want. Isn't there even a Single Girl Rule about that?"

"Rule #25: Don't be ashamed to use sex to get what you want. If I'd used sex, I'd happily admit it. But I didn't."

"Then how?"

"It's a secret. You've read the Society's rules, right? They take their secrets very seriously."

Gah! "Is that why they didn't bother to give us the address for this mysterious Club Onyx? Because you already know where it is?"

"It's probably on their app."

"My app got deleted."

"You sure about that?"

I was. I grabbed my phone and opened my list of apps. *Tax Codes* was the last app on the list, which was the codename for the Society's app.

"What the hell? I could have sworn that disappeared when Tanner left." *Yup. Chastity definitely slept with someone to make this happen.*

"Well, it's back now."

I clicked the app and navigated to the RSVP page:

Club Onyx Orientation - Open Invitation
Caldwell Hotel
Floor 62
7th and W 52nd St
New York, NY 10019

Below that were two options: accept or decline. But nothing else. No information about what Club Onyx was. Or what we were supposed to wear. Or what filthy things we could expect to happen there.

"I can't believe it!" yelled Chastity.

"Believe what?"

"That it's at the Caldwell Hotel. I freaking *knew* it was there."

She was right - she had guessed it. It was where I'd gone on my first Society date. A bunch of the apartments were filled with hot dudes that I could have dated. And like an idiot, I'd chosen Tanner. Even after Frankie had warned me that his pipes were rusty and his walls were filled with asbestos. I should have listened to her.

And I should have listened to Chastity during our last drunken spy mission to find the Society's HQ.

Chastity shook her head. "I knew that hot liftman was lying to us when he said that the top floors were all apartments. What an asshole!"

"Well what'd you expect him to do? It's probably his job to make sure that non-Society members can't get in."

"You're just defending him because you have a crush on him."

"I do not." *Do I?* "He's not my type. He was too…rugged. I bet he had all sorts of tattoos under that uniform."

"So you've been thinking about him naked?"

"No. I was just saying…"

"And tell me again why sexy tattoos are a bad thing?"

"You're impossible. I want a classy gentleman." But I'd be lying if I said I hadn't had a few dreams about that sexy, tattooed liftman lifting me against the eleva-tor doors and having his way with me. What? You would too if you hadn't been touched by a man since your 24-hour boyfriend disappeared months ago. Un-less you counted groping your new boss. Which I did not. Because that never happened. Why wasn't I better at repressing things?!

"Then what are you waiting for?" Chastity hopped up and opened the bookcase that led to my gigantic closet. "Let's get ready to party!"

"It's just an orientation."

"Then let's get ready to be oriented!"

"Hmmm…yeah, that doesn't have quite the same ring to it. You were right the first time - let's party!" *And hopefully not get AIDS.*

Chapter 7

THE DRESS CHECK
Friday

"Good evening, ladies," said the liftman as we stepped onto the elevator. It was the same one as the other night - the one who probably had tats all over his naked body. Alas, tonight he was fully clothed in a crisp green uniform. His nametag identified him as Cole.

"Club Onyx, please," said Chastity.

"My pleasure." Cole hit a button on his little keypad and the elevator took off.

Well that was easy.

"So…" Cole looked us up and down. "First time at Club Onyx?"

"How'd you know?" I asked. *Oh no. Did I do something weird?* I reached up to make sure my black wig hadn't gotten caught in the elevator doors. And then I looked down to make sure my boobs weren't out. Everything seemed to be in place. *Thank God.* I couldn't have dealt with another awkward naked elevator encounter. Incident #3 still haunted me. I pressed my lips together to make sure I wouldn't strip, curtsey, or say, "Top of the morning, good sir," by accident.

"Most members know to ask for floor 62. It's always good to be discrete when you're running a secret sex club. Especially since we share the building with the Caldwell Hotel."

"Oh." *Oops.*

"And then there's the fact that you guys have tried to sneak in at least five times in the past couple months. Clearly you weren't members yet, or that wouldn't have happened."

He remembers that? I remembered parts of it, but we'd been pretty freaking drunk. I was sure we'd made fools of ourselves.

"But most importantly," he continued, "it would be impossible for me to forget a girl like you."

Was he talking to me? Or Chastity? And what did he mean by that? Was he calling us hot or awkward?

"Oh, one other word of advice. Make sure you always use this elevator. The others can't go above Floor 61."

"Good to know," I said as the doors dinged open.

"Welcome to Club Onyx," said Cole.

A group of handsome men in expensive tuxedos politely waited for us to exit before taking our place on the elevator. I tried not to stare at them.

A doorman dressed just like Cole greeted us. "Good evening, ladies. May I take your dresses?"

"Excuse me?" I said. *Did he just offer to take my dress?*

"They're new," said Cole.

The doorman nodded. "Ah, then it will be my pleasure to give you a tour…"

"Actually," said Cole. "You take over the elevator. I'll take care of our lovely guests here."

"Very good, sir."

Cole swapped positions with the doorman. "Looks like I'll be your tour guide this evening, Miss…?"

"Morgan," said Chastity. "Chastity Morgan. And this is Raven."

Ah, how I loved hanging out with Chastity. I hated introducing myself.

"Pleasure to meet you both. Now, where were we? Ah, right. I'll need your dresses."

"I'm sorry," I said. "But are you asking me to…you know…"

"Take off your dress, yes," said Cole as if it was the most normal thing in the world.

"And why in the world would I do that?"

"Because it's a Friday night. Which means the dress code is black tie lingerie."

"Great," I said. "I think this cocktail dress qualifies as black tie."

"The black tie is for the men."

"Well that's very unclear. How was I to know that the lingerie part applied to women?"

"What did you expect? For all the guys here to be wearing lacy thongs?"

"Hey man, I don't know what you're into. Don't ask, don't tell. That's a thing, right?"

Cole looked at me like I was crazy. "I'm pretty sure that applies to gay guys in the army."

I shrugged. "Gay guys in the army, lingerie-clad men at sex clubs. Potato, potahto."

"She has a point," added Chastity. "Those two things seem closely related."

Cole sighed. "Look around. Everyone else understands the dress code." He gestured to a group of women walking down the grand staircase wearing nothing but lingerie and heels. And the men with them were dressed to the nines. "If you're not wearing appropriate undergarments, I can have someone escort you to the boutique in the Ladies' Lounge. They'll fix you up with some great lingerie."

I shook my head. "I'm not taking my dress off."

Cole frowned. "I assure you, our dress check is first rate. Your clothes will be safe with us."

"I was more concerned with the whole being naked thing."

He gave me the up-down. "Are you not wearing any underwear?"

"What? Of course I am!"

"I don't know…it sure seems like you're not. Like I said, the boutique has plenty…"

"You're ridiculous." I was about to turn around and get back on the elevator. But then I remembered my new mantra. *Say yes.* It was time for me to start living.

Would it really be so bad to walk around Club Onyx in my underwear?

All the other girls were doing it.

And at Chastity's insistence, I'd worn a super sexy set of strappy lingerie, complete with a garter belt and stockings. I'd told her that I wasn't going to sleep with anyone tonight, but she said it was always good to be prepared just in case. She was indeed correct.

And if that wasn't enough, I'd also just gotten a fresh wax at the spa yesterday. That was the one link to the Society that hadn't disappeared along with Tanner. But everyone at the Shifting Sands Spa had gotten mysteriously worse at English this summer.

Anyway, I really couldn't have been any better prepared to strip down.

But I didn't do stuff like this. I was sweet, innocent Ashley Cooper. I was the girl who had saved myself for marriage and never drank at parties until I was 21. Except I wasn't her. Because an hour ago, I'd put on my black wig and transformed into Raven Black. And Raven Black was fearless.

"Of course I'm wearing underwear," I said as I pulled my dress over my head and tossed it at Cole's face. "See?" I put my hand on my hip for some added sass. *Take that.*

Chastity looked like she was about to faint. She had definitely not been expecting me to strip down.

That's right, bitch! I said yes! Raven Black was the kind of woman who got down on her knees and blew fancy paintings in museums. She could definitely strip down to her lingerie at a sex club. #SexClubReady. I'd also gotten surprisingly good at hashtags in my free time this summer. Tanner was missing out on so much. Loser.

Cole's eyes feasted on my half-naked body. "I stand corrected."

Chastity handed me her gigantic purse and then slid out of her dress. Her striptease was way more graceful than mine, but it didn't matter. Cole's eyes stayed glued on me.

"Give me one moment please," said Cole. He ran our dresses over to the dress check. Since apparently that was a thing at Club Onyx.

"Cole is so hot!" whispered Chastity. "And he's totally into you. I think he's the one."

"The one?" I asked.

"Yeah. The one you're gonna sleep with to get over Tanner."

"I'm not gonna do that." *Right?* I gulped. This *was* a sex club. And I was supposed to be saying yes to everything…

"I dunno, he got you out of the dress pretty easily. I wonder how long it'll take him to get you naked."

"I'm not…" I stopped mid-sentence, all my confidence vanishing when I remembered that I was wearing a thong. A thong! I turned to prevent a nearby group of men from being able to see my bare ass. *Oh my God. Why did I take off my dress?!* I'd been working out a lot, but still. My ass wasn't ready for public viewing, and it never would be. "We should go. This was a mistake."

"You really want to walk home in your underwear?" asked Chastity.

I glared at her. Of course I didn't want to walk home in my underwear!

"Your tickets, ladies," said Cole. He'd snuck up behind us. Which meant he'd just seen my ass. *Fuck my life.*

I reached for my ticket, but Chastity snagged both hers and mine and put them in her purse. I was officially stuck here at her mercy.

"Now that you're properly attired, we can begin orientation. Please follow me." Cole stuck out an arm for each of us. I reluctantly looped my arm through his as we walked up the grand staircase. I was already half naked - I didn't want to further embarrass myself with a tumble down the stairs. It had nothing to do with wanting to feel his arms. *I think.* But God was he strong. I held on to him a little tighter.

The velvety red carpet on the grand staircase muffled the noise of my heels, but I was more focused on the group of models passing us. They were all ridiculously tall and skinny and tan. Them strutting around in lingerie just made sense. I expected Cole to stare at them, but when I looked up at him, he was staring at me. My boobs, to be precise. Which did kind of look amazing in my push-up bra.

The door at the top of the stairs opened right into the heart of the club. Just like the foyer, everything was gold and leather and wood. The whole place oozed class. And the men...*damn*. I had never seen so many fine men in one place. Maybe it was a trick of the dim lights, but every guy was well-groomed, well-built, and handsome AF. I thought for sure they'd all be acting like assholes and staring at every girl who passed, but they were actually quite respectful.

"Care for a drink?" asked Cole.

"Yes please." *God yes.* I desperately needed a drink. Or ten.

"What can I get for you?"

"Tequila shots," said Chastity.

Cole nodded approvingly. "Tequila shots it is. While I get those, please turn your attention to our wall of fame." He gestured to a wall of paintings. Each one was a hand-painted portrait of a couple. "Those are all of the happy couples that the Society has brought together."

I crinkled my nose. "Ew. They paint you every time you bang someone?"

Cole laughed. "No. These are couples that have gotten married. The Society is quite good at creating lasting relationships."

"Aw," said Chastity. "That's so cute! Maybe my picture will be up there soon."

Give me a break. Was Chastity actually buying this nonsense? At one point Tanner had almost convinced me that the Society was about love. But then I'd told him I loved him, and he'd responded by faking an elaborate kidnapping just to get away from me. There was no way this place was about true love. If it was, they wouldn't have had us parading around in lingerie.

"You really believe that?" I asked.

"Of course," said Cole. "The proof is in the paintings."

And then a horrible thought occurred to me. What if one of the paintings was of Tanner and whatever girl he undoubtedly met after leaving me? I looked for his picture while Cole went off to get our drinks from the ridiculously well-stocked bar.

"I wonder what's up there," said Chastity, pointing to a second story section. "That's probably where people go to bang."

I turned my attention away from the pictures. Much to my relief, none of them had been of Tanner. "Oh, maybe."

"Wanna check it out?" she asked.

I laughed, but I wasn't sure she'd been joking. I was busy trying to get a better look at the second story when I saw someone out of the corner of my eye in a bright blue suit and a man bun. My heart started racing.

"Is that Tanner?" I muttered. If that asshole was here...

"Where?" asked Chastity.

"Three o'clock." But when I looked back to where I'd seen him, he was gone. "Just kidding. False alarm." *Thank God.* If one thing could ruin this night, it was running into Tanner.

"Three tequila shots," said Cole, handing us each a shot glass.

Usually I avoided tequila at all costs, but tonight called for drastic measures. Especially if I was going to have to face Tanner.

I downed the shot and tried not to cough as the liquid seared my throat. Then I grabbed another and downed it too, just for good measure. All the alcohol in the world wouldn't be enough to make me feel comfortable running around in my underwear. But two tequila shots was a good start.

"So where were we?" asked Cole.

"You showed us the wall of fame. And that was about it."

"Ah, right. This is the main bar. It's open every night from 5 to 2. And the restaurant has the same hours." Cole gestured to a set of double doors with a hostess standing out front.

"Restaurant?" asked Chastity. "Is that Society slang for the sex dungeon?"

Cole laughed. "Nope. Not a sex dungeon. Just a normal restaurant. In fact, having sex there would be a great way to get thrown out of the club."

"Say what?" Chastity looked personally offended. "What kind of sex club doesn't let you have sex?"

"Oh, you can have plenty of sex at Club Onyx. Just not by the bar or in the restaurant…at least not tonight."

"Up on the sex balcony then?" asked Chastity.

Cole shook his head. "That's part of the bar. And so is the roof deck. See those blue lights? That means this is a sex-free zone."

"Then where *can* you have sex?"

Cole gave us a mischievous grin. "Follow me."

Chapter 8

CLOWN PENIS
Friday

Cole led us to a hallway at the back of the club. But before we could enter, he put his arm out to block us.

"This, ladies, is where the real Club Onyx begins. Once you cross this line and enter this hallway…" He gestured to a red line on the floor. "…The rules change."

So it's just a big sex hallway? I squinted to try to see into the dark hallway, but I couldn't make out much. Just lots of wood detailing on the walls and chandeliers hanging from the ceiling. It looked like it was leading to a vampire lair. I remembered when I used to think Tanner was a vampire. When really he was just a lying trollop. The hallways probably just led to a normal lair. *Or if Chastity was right…a sex dungeon.*

"Through this door, you'll be able to live out your wildest fantasies - and some fantasies you never knew you had." He smiled at me when he said it, as if he thought *he* was my wildest fantasy.

I gulped.

"But I have to warn you. It's not for the faint of heart."

"Raven can handle it," said Chastity. "Which of her fantasies are you gonna fulfill first? She's always had a thing for hot teachers."

My face turned bright red. *I had the teacher fantasy one time!* And I had told her about it in confidence. How dare she betray me!

Cole's eyes danced with amusement. "Nothing to be ashamed of. That's actually quite a common fantasy, and definitely one that the Society can fulfill for you. If you're lucky, maybe it'll even happen tonight."

I gulped. It was hard to picture Cole as a teacher, with his tattoos and his chiseled jaw. He belonged in a leather jacket, not a sweater vest. Although now that I was picturing it, I was kinda into it. Who said bad boys can't be teachers?

"So before I leave you to your own devices, I have…"

"Wait," I said. *No! Don't leave us!* "That's the whole tour? You showed us like…two things. And I have so many questions."

"Such as?" asked Cole.

"How do these fantasies work? Do we make wishes through the app? Or do people just pop out and molest us? Or…?"

Cole gave me his devilish grin. "You'll just have to wait and see."

I glared at him. This was the most useless orientation ever. Hadn't he ever been to a summer camp? Now *they* knew how to do orientations right. "Oh, okay. Thanks for being so helpful."

"My pleasure."

What? No! I was being sarcastic, you dumb, handsome meat tower.

"Before I go, I have a gift for each of you." Cole pulled out three golden keys that were straight out of the 1500s. "Choose wisely."

They all looked the same to me, so I randomly chose the one in the middle.

"What'd you get?" asked Cole.

"Uh…" *How should I know?*

"Flip it over."

I did. The back was etched with an outline of some dice.

"Oh!" squealed Chastity. "I got handcuffs."

"Interesting choices," said Cole.

"Why?" I asked. "What do these symbols mean?"

"Oh, you'll find out soon enough."

"Can't you tell us?" I asked.

"That would spoil all the fun. Not to mention it's strictly forbidden by the Society. What happens in this hallway stays in this hallway."

"I thought that was Vegas?"

"Vegas has nothing on Club Onyx. Good luck." Cole gave me a wink and then left us alone at the entrance to the weird sex hallway.

"Oh my God," said Chastity. "He was so into you."

"You think?"

"Uh, yes. He couldn't take his eyes off you."

"Probably because I'm half naked."

"I am too, and he wasn't looking at me like that."

Fair point. "If he was into me, then why did he leave us alone? He could have kept the tour going as long as he wanted."

"Isn't it obvious?" asked Chastity.

"No."

"He's going to go dress up as a teacher so that he can fulfill your fantasy." She sounded so sure. "Come on." She grabbed my arm and pulled me towards the hallway.

I yanked her back just before she crossed the threshold. "You can't just run into a sex hallway guns a-blazing. You have to be careful." I slowly edged my toe over the red line. I half expected a giant dildo to swing down across the doorway, like one of those swinging axes that you'd see in a horror film. But nothing happened. I peered into the hallway.

"Come on," said Chastity. "We've been in this hallway before and nothing bad happened to us."

"I mean…I ended up on stage and nearly got fucked in front of like a thousand people."

"Exactly! This hallway is amazing."

"You say that now, but you'll be singing a different tune when you see all the clown penises."

"Clown penises? I've never heard you talk about that fantasy before."

Oh God. "That's not… You know what, forget it." If I explained that I was scared of clowns and hence their penises, she'd probably blab it to Cole. Getting attacked by a clown penis needed to be added to my list of greatest fears. Somewhere under centipedes.

Chastity walked into the hallway. No clown penises attacked her. "Are you coming?" she asked. "Or do you want me to leave you all alone in this sex club?"

Damn her. I had no choice but to follow. "Fine, I'm coming." I joined her, and together we walked farther into the hallway.

Rap music began to shake the entire hallway as we approached the first door. Through the archway, dozens of scantily clad women were grinding up against tuxedoed men on the dance floor. If it had been a high school dance, the chaperones would not have not been pleased. They were definitely not leaving room for Jesus.

"Wanna dance?" asked Chastity.

"Um…" *Not really.* Grinding on some sweaty stranger wasn't at the top of my to-do list. There were probably so many germs on that dancefloor.

"Come on! You promised you'd play along!"

"I will. I just uh…" I looked down at the key in my hand. "Don't you want to find out what this dice symbol means?"

"Uh, hell yes I do. Good call." She dragged me deeper into the hallway.

I hoped I hadn't just made a terrible mistake. Dancing was a known entity. But this key? There was no telling what kind of sexy horrors it would lead to.

"What do you think will be behind the handcuff door?" asked Chastity, looking at the handcuff symbol on hers.

"A sex dungeon?"

Chastity twirled a strand of hair around her finger. "My first thought was bondage too, but I also wouldn't mind being manhandled by a hot cop."

"Sounds romantic."

"Right? Oh! Or maybe I'll get thrown into a co-ed prison cell and get gangbanged by a bunch of prisoners." She let out a squeal. "This is so exciting! What do you think your dice will be?"

"That depends. What kind of sexy things can you do with dice?"

"One time I saw this girl put one in her…"

"Hold on," I said, stopping in front of a heavy wooden door. It was at least ten feet tall and looked like it had been carved out of a solid block of wood. I pointed to the tablet on the wall next to it. The screen was all black except for the red outline of handcuffs - the same symbol as Chastity's key. "Looks like we found your sex dungeon."

Her eyes lit up. "Wish me luck," she said as she stepped towards the door with her key in hand.

"Whoa whoa whoa. You're just gonna leave me out here all alone?" *Not cool.*

A door creaking made me jump. I turned around to see a man smoothing his trousers as he exited a room across the hall. I caught a brief glimpse inside where women covered in gold body paint were feeding grapes to a man in a toga. *Weird.*

"Boo," said Chastity.

"What?" I turned back around. Chastity had her key in the handcuff door. But the door wasn't opening. A message scrolled across the tablet:

Session in progress.

"Lame," said Chastity. She tried again and got the same result. "Guess we have to go find your dice room."

I breathed a sigh of relief. There was no way I was going anywhere without her. We continued on down the hallway, checking the symbols on the doors as we went. There was a masquerade mask, an eyeball, an apple, a trident…or was it a pitchfork? Then there was the letter V. But no dice.

Chastity kept pulling me around corner after corner. Before I knew it, I was all turned around. *Great. This is where I'm going to die.*

I picked up my pace and tore around a corner.

"Oh my God!" I screamed as I ran into a chiseled body. The man steadied me in his strong arms.

"Sorry," he said. "You okay?"

I took a deep breath and tried to gather my nerves.

"She's fine," said Chastity. "And so are you."

The guy smiled. "You flatter me."

"I'd like to do more than that to you." Chastity bit her lip seductively.

"Oh you would, would you?"

She nodded.

"In that case, come to the sky box at 7 pm tomorrow night." He handed her a key from his pocket engraved with a cloud symbol.

"It's a date," said Chastity. "Hey, do you know where the dice door is?"

"Try the casino room." He gave us directions and then walked away.

"See ya tomorrow," called Chastity.

Damn. I'd seen Chastity flirt before, but I still couldn't believe how easy it was for her.

"Well he seemed nice," she said.

"What the hell is a sky box?"

"No idea. But I'll let you know when I find out tomorrow night."

We brainstormed what the sky box might be as we followed her new boyfriend's directions to the casino room. We did have a few clues. I remembered them talking about the sky box during the Onyxies award ceremony we'd been bought for the last time we were here. The sky box had won best new room. And Tanner had also looked really concerned when he'd asked me if I'd gone to the sky box. Now I kind of wish that I had, just so I could have rubbed it in his face back then.

My guess was that the sky box was just another name for a penthouse. But Chastity thought it would be a skydiving simulation room. I was still working out the logistics of how sex in one of those things would work when we entered the casino.

It felt like we'd been transported to Vegas.

A cocktail waitress wearing an elephant mask made of mirrors offered us champagne. I took two flutes and downed them both.

"So where do you think your dice door is?" asked Chastity, looking around the room.

"Hmmm…" My first thought was craps. I was pretty sure that used dice. But the symbol wasn't there. The roulette table was similarly disappointing.

Wait, why is that disappointing? I didn't want to go into some weird sex room. *Right?*

I started to say something to Chastity, but she'd disappeared to go get some chips from the cashier. I went over to join her. And then I saw it. Next to the cashier were a bunch of safes. One of which was marked with the dice symbol.

Just a safe? That couldn't be so bad. Unless there was a naked leprechaun stuffed in there or something.

No, then it would be marked with a four-leaf clover. But if not a leprechaun, then what?

I knew it was a bad idea to open it. Everything about the Society was a bad idea. Meeting Tanner had been bad. Making wishes had been bad. It was all bad.

But as bad as it was, it was also extremely distracting. I'd only thought about not getting the promotion like five times since we'd gotten to Club Onyx, which was a major improvement compared to earlier in the day. And I'd only thought about Tanner when I thought I'd seen him...

Maybe that was the whole point. Club Onyx was an escape. It was a place to break the rules and act a little crazy. And that was exactly what I was going to do. Hell, I'd already been running around in nothing but lingerie for thirty minutes, and it hadn't killed me. Neither would opening this safe.

Please don't be a naked midget.

The lock clicked as I turned the key.

Chapter 9

THE DICE DOOR
Friday

I opened the safe slowly, not sure what would pop out. Was I about to get hit with a giant dildo, like some sort of weird jack-in-the-box? Nope. I didn't get hit with anything. The only thing inside was a huge pile of casino chips.

Chastity grabbed a chip out of the safe and rolled it over her fingers like one of those dudes on the World Series of Poker. *$1000* was written on both sides of it.

Holy shit! "Guess I chose the right key," I said. "Maybe the dice meant this is my lucky day." I pulled the chips out and counted them one by one. Near the bottom, I uncovered a little black envelope. *A wish?* What did I need a wish for? I'd just won 100 grand. That felt like enough of a wish come true already.

I broke the gold seal and pulled out the card. It had the dice symbol at the top, and then a few lines of text:

Welcome to the Club Onyx Casino!
Your challenge is simple:
Double these chips. If you do, they're all yours.

Challenge? Damn it! So much for getting lucky. "How do you think I double them?" I asked. "By selling my body to some handsome investment banker?"

"I mean…that's one option. I'm loving your energy right now. But I think you're probably just supposed to gamble. Since we're in a casino and all."

"Ha, right," I said as casually as possible. "I was just messing with you." *What is wrong with me?!* Running around a sex club in lingerie was messing with my head. And it was possible that double-fisting that champagne had been a little aggressive. *Speaking of which…* I flagged down the nearest waitress and plucked another drink off her tray.

"So what's your game?" asked Chastity. "Blackjack? Craps? Poker?"

"Hmmm…" There was a huge crowd around both craps tables. Pushing through crowds wasn't for me, so that was out. Same for the roulette wheels. Not that it really mattered. I'd never been to a casino before. I had pretty much no idea how any of these games worked. "Let's start with the slot machines."

We shoveled my chips into Chastity's oversized purse and headed to the slots. The sign above the machines promised a million-dollar jackpot. All we had to do was get four of a kind. That was pretty likely, right?

I put a chip in and pulled the lever. The symbols spun and spun and then settled one by one. Lollipop, lollipop, heart, and… *Is that a pair of jelly donuts?* I studied the final symbol. *Nope. It's boobs.*

"Oh yeah!" yelled Chastity as chips poured out of her machine. "Give me those big black dicks!"

She'd gotten three big black dicks and one foot. According to the payout chart, three-of-a-kind was worth $5000. *Not a bad start.*

It was all downhill from there. Chastity and I lost on our next 20 spins. Seriously, every single spin was a big fat nothing. We didn't even get a two-of-a-kind! And just like that, we'd lost $15K. Granted, it wasn't our money to begin with. But still. If we could get it up to $200K, we'd get to keep it all. And then I could walk into BIMG and flip a desk and tell those fuckers that I quit. Or, you know…not do any of that and just keep working there like the good little employee that I was.

I was about to pull the lever again when a douchy guy in a white tux leaned on my machine. He looked like the kind of person who loved to steal promotions from more qualified women. I wished there was a candle nearby. Unlike Matthew Caldwell, this arrogant guy was the type of person who should 100% be set on fire. I wanted him to light up like a Christmas tree. I pressed my lips together. Apparently losing lots of money made me a little bit of a pyromaniac. And I was scared of pyromaniacs. Why did I keep leaving my mini fire extinguisher at home?!

"Hey ladies," he said, shamelessly staring at my breasts. "Looks like you've hit a bit of a dry spell."

"Excuse me," I said, pushing his arm off my machine. "I'm trying to win a jackpot here."

"I'm not stopping you."

I pulled the lever. No matching symbols. Not even one big black dick. *Damn it!* How was I so bad at this?

The guy shook his head and put one of his own coins in the slot. "Maybe this will change your luck."

"Dude, take a hint," said Chastity. "She's not into you. Paying for one spin isn't going to get you laid."

I started to blush. "Actually, we were just about to uh…go play poker. The machine is all yours." I yanked on Chastity's arm to get her to stand up with me.

We made it about three steps before a siren started blaring right behind us. I turned around. My machine was lit up with a bajillion strobe lights. Four breast symbols were showing and the JACKPOT sign above it was flashing.

"Are you freaking kidding me?!" I yelled.

Four topless cocktail waitresses in the weird elephant masks came out of nowhere carrying a treasure chest overflowing with chips.

"Your winnings, sir," said one of the girls.

"A million dollars and four lovely pairs of breasts," added another. They all waved their hands over their boobs as if they were showing off a prize on a game show.

"So the symbols correspond to what you win?" asked Chastity. "Man, I was so close to getting four big black dicks!"

"It's a shame he got the boobs instead of the dicks," I said. Seeing his treasure carried by four naked men would have made me slightly less depressed about missing out on the jackpot. But then I would have been sad that I wasn't getting railed by the four hot guys. *Seriously, what the hell am I saying?* I needed to stop it with the champagne. Although…I blamed Tanner for my current wanting four men mood. He'd left me and I'd become a horny spinster and I hated his perfect disappearing face.

Chastity laughed. "So poker next, huh?"

Thinking about Tanner made my stomach churn. And whenever that happened, I thought about when I incident #4'd all over Dr. Lyons. I was spiraling. "Or maybe we should just dump all our chips on the floor and leave."

"Why would we do that?"

"Because we're gonna lose them all anyway. Clearly today is just not my day. First I lost the promotion to Xander Frost, and now I just lost a million dollars to that jerk. And then there's the little issue of me not knowing the first thing about poker. All I know is that you try to get 21. Or is it five of a kind?"

Chastity gave me a funny look. "Wow, okay. Blackjack is where you try to get 21. And it's impossible to get five of a kind in poker. There's only four of each card."

"I rest my case. Do they have a table for Uno? I'll freaking own everyone in that."

"Since this is a casino instead of a five-year-old's birthday party, I think it's safe to assume that they don't have Uno. But poker is even better. Come on…I'm a beast at it. I'll double our money in no time." She pulled me over to a table and forced me to sit. The dealer dealt us in on the next hand.

We had two aces. *Is that good?* It seemed good. Chastity whispered in my ear that I should play it. So I pushed a bunch of my chips into the center. Everyone else at the table immediately folded.

"What the hell?" hissed Chastity.

"What?" I said. "I won the hand. Isn't that the goal?"

Chastity shook her head. "You had the best possible starting hand. And by bidding so high, you telegraphed that to everyone at the table."

"Since when are you a poker expert?"

"Since always. Daddy and his friends love to play poker. At least…they did. Until freshman year of high school when I took all their money. Now follow my instructions and we can do the same to all these losers."

Everyone at the table was staring at us.

"I'm not falling for this trick," said a serious-looking dude hiding behind a pair of aviators. "I know a sandbagger when I see one."

"Sandbagger?" I asked. "Is he implying our boobs feel like sandbags?" I grabbed one of my boobs but it still felt normal and un-sandbaggy. Everyone was staring at me groping myself. I immediately dropped my hand.

Chastity laughed. "No. But props for the *Forty-Year-Old Virgin* reference." She high-fived me. "What he meant was that he thought we're pretending like we don't know how to play."

"I don't…"

"Yeah, right," he scoffed. He gathered his chips and left the table.

Screw you too.

We went back to playing. Things started off shaky, but after a while we came up with a system of signals. And then we got on a roll. In a flash, we cleaned out all three of the guys at the table. Our bankroll was up to $180K. *We're so close!*

But then Cole sat down. I almost didn't recognize him out of his liftman uniform.

I grabbed another drink from a passing waitress.

"I see you found the dice door," said Cole. "And by the looks of it, you're doing quite well."

"Yup," said Chastity. "We only need 20K more. And it's going to be a pleasure taking it from you."

Cole raised an eyebrow. "We'll see about that." He slid on some sunglasses and rolled up his sleeves. Just as I suspected, tribal tattoos snaked up his forearms. I wanted to trace them with my tongue and see where they stopped. *Oh God, I'm so drunk.*

I shook my head and focused back on the task at hand. I couldn't let him distract me.

The next dozen hands passed without much action. I won a few chips, then he took them back. Then I got them back. And so on.

Then we got dealt a king of hearts and a jack of spades. Chastity kicked my chair - our secret signal that I had a good hand.

I slow played it just like she'd taught me. The flop (Chastity's fancy name for when the dealer flipped the first three of five cards) gave us a straight. *A straight!* Unless something went horribly wrong, we were definitely going to win. The best part? I'd played my bets perfectly, slowly tricking Cole into risking $50K on this hand. So if we won, we'd be well over the threshold to cash out our chips. I was already dreaming of buying a new TV with the winnings. I was determined to binge-watch season 3 of *Riverdale* on nothing less than an 80-inch screen.

"All in," said Cole, leaning forward and pushing all his chips into the center of the table. He lowered his glasses and stared into my soul. I could either call him and risk all my chips too, or fold and let him take my 50 grand.

"He's bluffing," I said to Chastity.

"You sure?" she asked.

"Yes?" I did not sound sure.

She shook her head. "I think we should fold. Live to fight another day."

"What?!" I couldn't believe she was being such a chicken. "Are you blind?" I showed her our cards again.

"He could have..."

I didn't let her finish. There was no way I was going to let Cole bluff us. "Call." I pushed all my chips into the center.

Cole flashed me his devilish grin. "Bold move."

I smiled back as I flipped my cards over. "Read them and weep, buster." *Buster?*

"Oh," said Cole. "King high straight. Very impressive. Not sure that's worth risking your body, though."

"Excuse me?"

He dug through my chips until he found one engraved with the dice symbol.

"So you found a chip with some dice on it," I said. "So what?"

His devilish grin got even more devilish. "You didn't read the whole card, did you?"

"Of course I did." I fished the envelope out of Chastity's purse and read it again. "Welcome to the

Club Onyx Casino! Your challenge is simple: Double these chips. If you do, they're all yours."

Cole reached over and flipped the card. There was more writing on the back:

Be careful, though.
If someone wins your dice chip, they own your body
until sunrise.
Do you dare risk it all?

I read it again. And again. *Shit. Shit, shit, shit!* What the hell had I gotten myself into?

Chapter 10
THE GAMBLE
Friday

Cole stood on his chair and cleared his throat. "Ladies and gentlemen!" he yelled.

What is he doing? No! Don't call everyone's attention to us!

"We have a dice chip in play!"

Cheers went up around the casino as a crowd swarmed our table. Everyone was pushing and shoving to see the action. A few guys even stood on nearby tables and slot machines.

Oh my God. This was my worst nightmare. There were so many people watching me. And I was still half naked. I crossed my arms to try to cover my boobs, but all it did was push them up more. *Damn it!*

"It's okay," whispered Chastity. "You got this." She squeezed my shoulder.

To make a better show for our spectators, Cole flipped his cards. A two and a seven.

"Oh yeah!" I yelled in celebration. "I knew you were bluffing. Our straight beats your trash hand. Boom." I pretended like my fist was exploding in his face.

Cole responded with a confident smirk.

What am I missing?

"Don't celebrate yet," said Chastity. "He has a shot at a flush."

I looked at his cards again. They were both diamonds. And two other diamonds were showing. If one of the final two cards was also a diamond, he'd win. *My chips and my body.*

I held my breath as the dealer flipped the next card. An ace of hearts. *Yes!* I was still safe.

"One card to go," said Cole.

"Yup," I agreed. "Get ready to lose."

"How confident are you?" asked Cole. "I'll tell you what. I'm a gentleman, so I'll still let you fold."

"Now why would I do that?"

"Because if you do, then I'll settle for a blowjob."

"And if I don't fold and you win fair and square?"

He stared right at me. "Then I'm going to bend you over this table and fuck you senseless in front of the entire casino."

I gulped. Was he serious? The way he was devouring me with his eyes said he was *very* serious. I crossed my legs under the table, hating my body for kind of wanting him to be serious. *No.* No, I definitely didn't want that. Not in front of all these people. Why couldn't he fuck me senseless back at his place like a proper gentleman?

"So what'll it be?" he asked. "Fold or play?"

I looked to Chastity for help.

"Well..." she said. "It's your choice. But the odds *are* in your favor."

My heart was beating out of my chest. I'd literally die if I had to bang Cole in front of all these people. Would it be better to fold and blow him instead? At least then I'd get to keep my lingerie on...

"I..." My mouth was too dry to speak. Which would be really bad for a blowjob. And I'd much rather feel him deep inside of me...

"Play!" yelled one of the spectators. Then another guy joined in. And another. Soon the whole casino was chanting for me to play.

I looked around for some sort of sign. And there he was again. *Tanner.* Standing by the slot machines staring daggers at Cole. I tried to catch his gaze, but someone walked in front of him. And then he was gone.

Was I hallucinating? The stress of all this was messing with my head. It wouldn't be the first time I'd seen a ghost. Three years ago when my sister had disappeared, I'd kept catching glimpses of her face in crowded places. At restaurants, on buses, on the sidewalk. My therapist had said it was just wishful thinking. I had desperately wanted to see her, so I had.

Chastity tapped my shoulder. "You have to decide."

I stared at Cole. He raised his eyebrow at me and then his eyes scanned down my body like it already belonged to him. What a cocky asshole. There was no way I was gonna give him the satisfaction of scaring me into folding. Raven Black didn't fold.

"Play," I said.

Everyone cheered.

Oh God, oh God, oh God. I could feel my heart in my throat. Sweat poured down my sides.

"Let the lady do the honors," said Cole.

The dealer slid the top card off the deck and put it in the center of the table face down. He motioned for me to flip it over.

I took a big gulp of my drink to stall for time. I could still fold. I could still get away with just a blow-job. But Chastity had said the odds were in my favor…

I put my hand on the card. *Anything but a diamond. Please be anything but a diamond.* I pulled one corner up ever so slightly so that I was the only one in the room who could see.

First I saw that it was a queen. But what mattered was the suit. If it was a heart, spade, or club, I won. But if it was a diamond…well, I didn't want to think about that.

Anything but a diamond, I repeated in my head as I peeled the card up a bit more to see the suit. And it was the queen of…diamonds.

Fuck.

Fuckity fuck fuck shit!

I went into total panic mode. Rather than flip the card, I slammed my hand on top of it and pinned it to the table. If no one saw it, then my body was still safe.

But it was only a matter of time until Cole would force me to flip it.

And then what? Would Cole tear my lingerie off? Or would he make me get on the table and strip? The thought was horrifying, and I hadn't even gotten to the really crazy part. I pictured myself lying on the table, the chips digging into my flesh as Cole thrust into me. Would the crowd cheer when he claimed me? Would Chastity watch? And how big was he? Because he looked like he was packing.

I shifted in my chair and tried to look for an escape. But there was none. The crowd around us was too thick. I'd never be able to push my way through them. I was trapped.

"What's wrong?" asked Cole. "Didn't like what you saw on that card?"

"Can I still fold?" I asked. My voice squeaked as I said it.

Cole laughed. "I'm afraid it's too late for that. Flip the card."

Chastity gave my shoulder another sympathetic squeeze.

"Flip the card!" chanted the crowd. The crowd that was about to watch Cole ravish me.

Could I just refuse? Rape was strictly forbidden in the Society. So if I said no, he'd have to honor that. Or did the dice challenge trump that? It had been very clear that my body would belong to him if I lost.

And I'd lost.

"Flip the card!" continued the chant.

I was out of options. And honestly? As mortifying as this would be…I couldn't stop staring at Cole. He was so handsome. Would it really be the worst thing in the world if I climbed on this table and spread my legs for him? I took a deep breath. Raven Black was filthy. Or maybe I was just turned on because I'd just seen Tanner's ghost. *Fuck you, Tanner.* I removed my hand and flipped the card. And Cole's face…sunk?

Huh? Why was he upset? He had won. I looked at the card. It was a two of clubs. I blinked to make sure I was seeing it right. *How is that possible?* A second ago it had been a queen of diamonds. I was sure of it.

But now it was definitely a two of clubs. I looked back over my shoulder to where I thought I'd seen

Tanner. But he wasn't there. Because of course he wasn't.

I looked back down at my cards. It took a second for it to sink in that I'd just won. I'd freaking won!

"Ha!" I yelled right in Cole's face. "You suck!"

"Should have let her fold, sucker," said Chastity as she scooped up all the chips. $360K worth.

Cole shrugged. "It's your loss, really. You could have had the night of your life." He gave me another stupid cocky smile and left the table.

***

I was exhausted by the time I got home. I'd had way too many drinks without nearly enough food. And it was about six hours past my bedtime. I stumbled through my tiny family room and into my giant closet. The two rooms could not have been more different. My apartment was one step above homelessness, while the closet was fit for a queen.

Queen. The image of the queen of diamonds popped into my head. That had magically become a two of clubs. How was that possible?

It didn't matter. Because despite being exhausted, I felt alive for the first time in months. Every ounce of sense I had told me to forget about Cole. He was clearly a total manwhore. And he would have been more than happy to strip me down in front of an entire room of people and have his way with me.

And yet…I couldn't stop thinking about him. More than once since he'd walked away from that table, I'd found myself wishing that I'd lost. Especially after I went to the cashier and found out that my $360K in winnings was actually just Monopoly money.

When could I see Cole again? I could probably convince Chastity to go back to Club Onyx tomorrow night. But first I needed to get out of these clothes and get some sleep.

I pulled my dress over my head and hung it up on a rack before slipping out of my bra. God, it felt so good to get out of that push-up bra.

"You should be more careful," said a deep voice.

I screamed and nearly fell over. *What the hell!? Who's in my closet?!* I covered my boobs and spun around.

"AH! Die, pervert!" I chucked my bra at him, dove behind a table, and started throwing shoes.

He dodged them all easily.

"Are you stalking me, baby?"

Oh God, the last thing I needed was another stalker... *Wait.* That's not what he'd said. He'd asked if I was stalking him. And I only knew one person that would say that to me. I poked my head above the table.

What the hell? My heart started beating even faster. And tears welled in the corners of my eyes. It couldn't be. "Tanner?" My voice cracked.

"That's my name."

"Tanner!" The tears spilled down my cheeks. I ran over and gave him a big hug. It was really him. He was here.

"Ash." His arms wrapped protectively around me, holding me firmly against him.

The smell of blueberries washed over me. God, I loved his smell...

No! I hated him. And his stupid smell.

I pushed him off and covered my boobs again. My heart was still pounding. But I wasn't scared now. I was fucking furious. "What are you doing in my closet? You can't just sneak in and watch a girl undress."

"Technically this is my closet. I never transferred the deed to your name. And you're not just any girl. You're my girlfriend."

"Girlfriend?" I scoffed. "I think you might be forgetting something important. Like, oh, I don't know…the fact that you faked your own kidnapping just so you could get away from me."

Tanner laughed.

I slapped him. *Where did that come from?! Go me!*

He rubbed the side of his jaw. "Wait, you're serious?"

"Yes!"

"I really did get kidnapped."

"I want to believe you. I really do. But if you got kidnapped, then how are you standing here right now?" He was such a dirty liar.

"DODO let me go."

"How convenient."

"It was convenient."

Did he think I was an idiot? DODO probably didn't even exist. He clearly got off on toying with my emotions. I narrowed my eyes at him. And then I realized my boobs were everywhere, so I grabbed them again. "Would you stop staring at me so I can change?"

"Since when are you so concerned about people seeing your body?"

"Excuse me?"

"You certainly didn't have any problem stripping down at Club Onyx tonight."

"I knew I saw you there!"

"You're welcome, by the way. Since you know…I saved you from getting banged in front of all those people."

I just stared at him. He hadn't saved me. I'd just pulled the right card. *Kind of.* I'd thought I pulled the wrong card, but…that didn't mean he'd fixed it. Tanner Rhodes wasn't saving me. He was fucking ruining my life. "Oh, you saved me, did you?"

"Yes."

"You're my hero. Except…no, you aren't. Because you freaking broke up with me by leaving me half-naked on a yacht and then ghosting me for three months. Three fucking months, Tanner! And for your information, I knew exactly what I was doing tonight. I love gambling my body."

His eyes lit up for just a moment, as if he was excited by the thought. "Is that so?"

"What I do with my body is none of your business." *You freaking asshole.* "So if you would be so kind, please leave. And stay out of my life." Saying the words felt like a knife in my chest. I'd been dying to see him again. Praying that he was okay. Somehow hoping that he hadn't ghosted me, but also hoping he had. Because otherwise the unthinkable had happened. I'd thought he was dead. I'd been so worried about him. A confusing mix of worry and hate and fear. And clearly he hadn't been worried about me at all. Not even a little bit.

"You don't mean that," he said.

"I do." I didn't. And I hated that I didn't. I swallowed hard. "Now get out." I put my hand on my hip and pointed to the door.

He smiled at me and his eyes went to my chest. And I realized that I had left my breasts completely uncovered again. I quickly threw both arms over myself.

"I'm serious," I said. "Get out." My bottom lip started trembling. I clenched my jaw to stop it.

"It's been a long day. Let's talk about this tomorrow."

I shook my head. Tanner was toxic. I was only just recovering from our first break-up, if you could even call it that. A 24-hour relationship was hardly a relationship at all. "I'm sorry," I said, "but I can't have you in my life. Now I'll ask you nicely one more time. Please leave."

He opened his mouth to speak, but no words came out. He shook his head. "That's not what you really want..."

"It is." And how dare he tell me differently? How dare he? I clenched my jaw harder. He had to go. I was seconds away from falling apart.

But he didn't turn to go. He just stared at me. So intensely that it felt like he could see right through me.

And maybe that was the whole problem. That he could so easily see through me. I just wanted him to see me. My thoughts were at war with each other. I wanted to jump him and remember what it felt like to be devoured by one of his kisses. I wanted to punch his perfect face and throw all these stupid shoes at him.

I just wanted to cry myself to sleep. Because I couldn't stand here another second and look at him. He'd broken me. I'd barely been holding on from my divorce when Tanner had stumbled into my life. He'd kicked me when I was down. Twice. Because he knew Rosalie had disappeared. He knew and he did it to me too. And I didn't know how to pick myself up again.

"Just be careful, okay? The Society is a dangerous place for a sweet girl like you."

Fuck him. He didn't know anything about me. I wasn't sweet. I'd show him. "Goodbye, Tanner." And this time, I really meant it.

"Bye, Ash." He lifted the hat that was in his hand and put it back on his head, low enough so I could no longer see his piercing gaze. And then he walked out of the closet without looking back at me. Just like he'd walked out of my life the first time. Without a care in the world about the destruction he was leaving in his wake.

I heard the apartment door close. And I fell to my knees sobbing.

I hated him.

I missed him.

I hated how much I still missed him.

I pulled my knees into my chest as I sobbed.

Tanner Rhodes was alive.

And I was an idiot.

Because I still loved him. Almost as much as I hated him.

Chapter 11

THIRTY SECONDS OF PURE HELL
Saturday

I rolled over and pressed my pillow against my pounding head. It felt like I'd been run over by a dump truck. And then it had dumped its entire load right onto my temples.

"I'm never drinking again," I groaned. Not that the ridiculous amount of alcohol I'd consumed was my fault. It was Tanner's. Seeing him had made one of my wine bottles magically disappear down my gullet on top of everything I'd already had to drink last night.

How *dare* he show up and mess with my life after ignoring me for months? He was the absolute worst. Or was I overreacting? *Stop it.* There was no point in analyzing this. Especially because Chastity would know what to do.

I grabbed my phone to text her. The screen was about a million times too bright, but turning it down to the lowest setting and squinting made it somewhat bearable.

I had three texts from Chastity. But none from Tanner. Which was good. Because I was done with him. *So why am I even thinking about him?*

Chastity: Hey girl, how you feeling?
Chastity: Wanna grab lunch and game plan for tonight?
Chastity: I'll be over in 10 with some salads.

I checked the time stamp on the last one. It was from ten minutes ago. Right on cue, I heard a knock on the door.

"Why are you knocking so loud?!" I yelled as I rolled out of bed. If she knocked one more time I was pretty sure my brain would literally explode.

Chastity cringed at the sight of me when I opened the door. "You look like hell," she said way too loudly.

"How much did I drink?" I whispered, hoping she'd get the hint that my head was throbbing.

"A lot," she whispered back. "Did you black out?"

I rubbed my head. "I wish. Because then I wouldn't remember Tanner coming to visit."

"Tanner came back?!"

"Sssshhh!" I hissed.

"Sorry," she whispered. "Tanner came back?"

I nodded.

"Well I need to hear this entire story immediately." She tossed me the takeout bag from Salad Central and made herself comfy on my couch.

I got about three sentences in before Chastity interrupted.

"That. Freaking. Asshole." She looked like she was ready to flip my coffee table. If not for our salads and drinks, she might have.

"Tell me about it," I agreed.

"How dare he come back after three months and mess with your love life."

"That's what I said to him. Among other things."

"Please tell me you told him off."

I thought back to the conversation. It was all kind of foggy, but I was pretty sure I hadn't been very nice to him. "I think I told him to stay out of my life. And that I love gambling my body."

Chastity gave me a high five. "So what are you gonna do now?"

"I'm gonna go back to Club Onyx. And I'm going to do whatever I damn well please." There was a high probability that I was still drunk. "I'm done thinking about Tanner. I'm officially single and ready to mingle." *As soon as I get rid of this wicked hangover.*

***

"Remind me not to drink as much tonight," I said as we waited for the elevator in the lobby of the Caldwell Hotel. It had taken three cups of coffee and two naps to get my hangover to subside. I wasn't about to go and give myself another one.

"Will do," said Chastity. "But it probably won't be necessary. I mean…it'll be hard for you to drink too much when you have Cole's cock jammed down your throat."

I laughed and then nervously looked around to make sure no one else had heard her. Was that where tonight was headed? I decided to change the subject, especially since the elevator doors could open at any second. And I was pretty sure Cole would be inside. "What about you?" I asked. "Will you be going to the sky box with your mysterious gentleman suitor?"

She shook her head. "Not tonight. He canceled during your last nap."

"Darn. I'm so curious about what the sky box is."

"Me too. But it's okay. Because this means that I can devote my entire night to being the best wing woman you've ever had."

Ding.

The elevator doors slid open and Cole greeted us with his signature cocky smirk. "Good evening, ladies," he said, holding the door open for us.

We walked in. I'd come up with a million sexy things to say to him. But the sight of him in his fitted liftman uniform made me forget half of my pickup lines. And the half that I did remember suddenly seemed horribly corny. Luckily Cole did the talking.

"What floor?" he asked.

"Club Onyx, please," I said.

He shook his head. "I'm sorry, I don't know what you're talking about."

"Floor 62," said Chastity.

"Ah, why of course." Cole hit a button and off we went.

Oh, right. We were supposed to talk in code. But he didn't have to be an ass about it.

"Does your presence here mean that you enjoyed yourselves last night?" he asked.

"We did," I said.

"It was quite the evening," agreed Chastity. "One of the high rollers was so impressed with Raven's poker skills that he invited her to the sky box tonight." She flashed him the key that she'd been given.

Cole's eyes darkened. "Oh really?"

"Yup," she said, nudging me in the ribs.

"Yes indeed," I agreed. Making guys jealous wasn't my usual MO, but I kind of loved that possessive look in his eyes. And it had worked with Tanner… Gah, why did I always start thinking about Tanner at the worst times?!

"Sounds fun," said Cole dismissively. His possessiveness had vanished in the blink of an eye.

No! Be jealous! I didn't want some made-up high roller. I wanted Cole. "It will be. And I definitely won't be needing this," I said, stripping off my dress. I shoved the thin fabric into his arms. *Jealous now?*

A smile played on his lips as he took the dress from me. The doors dinged open. "Welcome to Club Onyx." He held the door to allow us to exit.

"That was awesome," whispered Chastity as we strutted off the elevator. "There's no way he won't come find…" She stopped mid-sentence.

"What?" I asked. But before she could answer, I followed her gaze to the center of the foyer.

A bunch of teens in blazers and khakis were staring at me. In my super sexy lingerie. Push-up bra, garter belt, thong, stockings, heels. The whole nine yards. The set even came with some weird harness that went over my bra to push my boobs up even more.

I froze. They froze.

What the hell are a bunch of high school kids doing here?!

The woman with the students - a librarian-looking type with a severe bun, horn-rimmed glasses, and a pencil skirt - glared at me and tried to block the view of her students.

"Sorry, wrong floor," I said. I slowly backed up towards the elevator. I was devastated when my bare ass hit the cold marble of the closed elevator door.

"Hit the button!" I hissed at Chastity.

The next thirty seconds were pure hell. The librarian told her students to ignore the "perverted lady," but telling a bunch of horny teenage boys to not look at a woman in lingerie was never going to work. I considered covering myself, but that seemed like it would make it more obscene. So instead I just stood there.

Every second felt like an eternity until the elevator doors dinged open. I backed on and, for a reason that I will never be able to explain, waved goodbye to the kids.

Cole smirked at me as the doors slid shut. "So I take it you didn't realize that tonight was take your kids to Club Onyx night?"

"Who the hell thought it was a good idea to invite kids to a sex club?! And give me that!" I snatched my dress out of his hands and pulled it over my head.

"It's actually a great idea," said Cole. "A lot of our members have kids. And those kids wonder where their parents go all the time. So once a year, we make the place kid friendly and frankly quite boring. Then they come, see it, and never ask to come back. Or at least…that was how it was supposed to go until you decided to give them an eyeful. You, Miss Raven Black, are going to be the talk of Empire High on Monday. It's not every day those kids get to see a California 10 half-naked."

I *really* wanted to slap him. "You didn't think it was worth warning me that I was about to flash a group of horny teens? God, I'm a child predator!"

"So you're saying you liked it?" asked Cole.

"What? No! I hated it."

"Then I think technically that would make you more of a flasher than a predator. Although the sex offender registry probably won't specify that when they add your name..."

"What?!"

Chastity laughed. "Relax. He's joking."

Is he? I turned to see the smile on his face. "Ha ha. Very funny, pal." I punched him in the arm playfully, but all I did was hurt my own hand thanks to his rock-hard bicep.

The elevator came to a halt. I yanked Chastity off the elevator the second the doors were open.

"Have a great evening," called Cole. "Always a pleasure."

"That was amazing!" said Chastity when we were safely out of the Caldwell Hotel.

"What are you talking about? That was literally the most mortifying moment of my entire life."

"Who cares? Cole thinks you're a #California10."

"What parallel universe are you in? He doesn't think I'm a 10. He thinks I'm a child molester."

A guy passing us on the sidewalk gave me a weird look.

"He was joking about that. But he wasn't joking when he said, 'It's not every day those kids get to see a California 10 half-naked.'"

"He didn't say…" *Wait a second.* I replayed the scene in my mind. Usually my memory wasn't so vivid. But the past five minutes had been so horrifying that I would forever remember them in perfect detail. *Fuck.* I'd remember it forever? Noooo. That meant it was incident #7, right after my last incident of face-planting Xander Frost's penis.

Shit! I thought I'd repressed that! But apparently it wasn't going anywhere. Which meant the penis grab was officially incident #7. And this was #8. I was almost into double digits. I stood there reliving the horrors of the high schoolers staring at me. And Cole's cocky smile. As the scene unfolded in my mind, I realized that he had in fact called me a California 10. "He was just messing with me." *Right?*

"No way. He's so into you."

"Complimenting people is probably just part of his job. It's like how doormen always act excited to see you and hand you packages. You know they're just faking it."

"Oh, I bet Cole would be more than happy to hand you his package," said Chastity.

"Well I can never show my face in that building again, so he'll never get the chance. And anyway, I'm officially done with men. They're all assholes."

"We've been over this," said Chastity. "They aren't *all* assholes. And as your wing woman, I think you should give Cole another chance. You two are totes adorbs together. You totally owned him in poker, and tonight he got you back by having you flash a few schoolboys."

"Ew, don't call them that."

"So now that you've calmed down, should we go back in?"

"I told you. I'm never going back."

"Not even to mess with Cole?"

"Nope. But if I happened to change my mind, how would you suggest we do it?"

Chastity scrunched her mouth to the side in the way she always did when she was thinking hard. "I don't know."

"Well…when you think of something, I'll be happy to come back."

"Promise?"

I nodded. But the sinister look on Chastity's face made me immediately regret it. She would stop at nothing to try to get me a new boyfriend. Or boy toy. Or whatever weird relationship Chastity was trying to get me into.

Chapter 12

MR. FROST
Monday

"It's going to be fine," said Chastity as we stood outside the BIMG office building. "Xander Frost probably doesn't even remember you."

I stared at her.

"I mean…it was a busy day. He met tons of people."

"And how many of those people do you think grabbed his ass while sticking their face in his crotch?" I cringed at the memory of inadvertently molesting my new boss.

"Probably just you…"

I nodded. "I rest my case."

"Okay, fine. He'll definitely remember you. But what does that matter? I bet he liked it."

This is going to be a disaster.

But somehow, it wasn't. At least…not right away.

For some reason I had been expecting Xander to greet us the second we stepped off the elevator. Or maybe have security waiting by my desk to escort me out. But neither of those things happened. Because that wasn't how new bosses worked. His job was to go out and land big clients, not micromanage all of his employees.

In the short time that I'd worked for Bee, I'd only had a handful of face-to-face conversations with her. The same would probably be true with Xander.

I relaxed and got to work prepping for my noon meeting with a prospective client.

The first hour flew by. But then Chastity poked me.

"What?" I hissed. I had been in the zone.

"What do you think is going on?" she asked, pointing to Xander's office. He was having a meeting with a guy that I vaguely recognized as being from one of the other marketing teams.

"It looks like a meeting to me." I turned back to my notes, but Chastity kept talking.

"That's the eighth meeting he's had this morning. Each one lasts a few minutes and then they send the next person in."

I watched for a second. Just as Chastity had said, the meeting ended after a minute. The guy walked out, tapped another person on the shoulder, and pointed to Xander's office.

So much for not having any face-to-face conversations with the new boss.

I tried to get back to work, but I couldn't focus. I kept looking up every five minutes to see how close I was to being summoned to his office. But there didn't seem to be any rhyme or reason to the order in which he was calling people.

"Should I apologize for molesting him?" I asked. That had been the question plaguing my mind ever since I'd face-planted his crotch.

"Definitely not. Just don't bring it up."

"But what if he brings it up?"

"He won't." She sounded so confident.

"Are you sure?"

"Yes. But if he does, just say you fell. And then give him a saucy wink."

"A saucy wink?" *What the hell is that?*

"Yeah. You know. Like this." Chastity bit her lip slightly and gave me a wink. It was a good thing that Madison was working on-site with a client today, because if she had been here to see that wink, she would have gotten a total lady boner.

"So like…this?" I bit my lip way too hard and scowled in pain.

"Uh, no."

"Let me try again." I did it again with a more appropriate amount of lip-biting.

"Better. But try to smile a little bit."

I tried again. And again. And again. I was *so close* to getting it right. I could feel it. This next one was going to be perfect.

Just as I executed the perfect saucy wink, Chastity bent down to grab something off the floor. Which left a clear line of sight between me and Xander's office. He locked eyes with me as I winked.

"Fuck!" I whisper-yelled. "Why did you duck?!"

"What?" asked Chastity, brushing off the pen she'd dropped.

"I just gave Xander the sauciest of winks."

Chastity raised her eyebrows. "Ohhh…you naughty minx. I didn't know you were so into him."

"I'm not! It was an accident. I was just practicing and then you ducked and he and I locked eyes, but by then it was already too late! I couldn't just stop mid-wink. It would have looked like I was having a stroke."

"Suuuure."

"I'm serious!"

The guy meeting with Xander got up and walked out of the office.

Please don't talk to me next. Please don't talk to me next. I repeated it over and over in my head, but it didn't stop the inevitable. The guy came directly for me.

"Ashley?" he asked.

"Yes?"

"Mr. Frost would like to speak with you in his office."

No!

"Good luck," said Chastity. "And remember…everyone can see right into his office. So don't do anything too crazy."

"I'll try to control myself." I got up and took a deep breath. *Here we go.* When I was halfway to his office, I strongly considered just making a sharp left turn, getting on the elevator, and never coming back. But then I'd be unemployed again. And while I'd been able to save up some money over the past few months, it wasn't nearly enough to go for any length of time in NYC with no job. *If only Monopoly money was real currency.*

So I walked into Xander's office.

"You wanted to see me?" I asked.

Xander looked up from his laptop. "Please take a seat."

I sat down. On my hands for some reason. *Is this how normal people sit?* Why could I no longer remember how seats worked? Should I get up and pop a squat on the armrest instead? That seemed better… But he started talking so I just sat there on my hands staring at him.

"It's a pleasure to meet you again, Miss Cooper."

Does that mean he remembers me? Damn it! "Same to you, Xander."

"Call me Mr. Frost."

"Uh, okay." *Weird.* "So what did you want to talk to me about?" *Please don't mention the molestation. Or the saucy wink.*

He leaned back in his big leather chair. "I was hoping you could bring me up to speed on the accounts you handle."

Thank God. "Well, I'm the account manager for Mills Winery, and..."

"That's the Wineflix and Chill brand, right?"

"Yup. I was actually the one that came up with that idea for rebranding."

Mr. Frost nodded. "Is that why everyone thought that you should have gotten this job instead of me?"

"Yeah," I said without thinking. *Shit! Why did I say that?*

"And what do *you* think?" His icy blue eyes bore into my soul.

"No, I... I just..." I couldn't find the right words.

"You just what? Think you're better than me?"

I had no idea how to respond to that. I was sure I was moments away from getting fired. And now my hands were starting to sweat. I pulled them out from underneath of me and the chair made a weird noise. Almost like a tiny fart. Did he hear that? I felt my face turning red. Now he probably thought I was farting *and* that I thought I was better than him.

But then his piercing stare turned into a surprisingly warm smile. "I'm just messing with you. You only have what…like six months experience? Of course they weren't going to promote you to VP." He laughed like it was the most ridiculous thing he'd ever heard.

I forced myself to laugh too.

"Now that we've gotten that out of the way, let's get down to business. I took a look at your accounts and came up with a few new ideas. Nothing major. Just a few tweaks here and there of things that I thought we could improve." He handed me a thick binder.

Who uses binders anymore?

"That'll be all for now. Can you send in…let's see…" He glanced at his screen. "Winston Powell."

"Sure." I got up to leave. When I was halfway out the door, he stopped me.

"I'm looking forward to your presentation today for Masquerade Records. Make sure you check out my notes on that." He gestured to the binder.

I nodded and went back to my desk, stopping along the way to give Winston his summons.

"How'd it go?" asked Chastity.

"He hates me."

"What makes you say that?"

"He knows I wanted that promotion. So he thinks I'm gunning for his job. But hey, I didn't get fired. So there's that."

Chastity shrugged. "Nothing to worry about. After you sleep with him, he won't be able to fire you. And if he does, you can sue him for sexual harassment. Oldest trick in the book."

"I'm not going to do that."

"Never say never."

"I didn't…"

Chastity's eyes lit up. "So you might sleep with him?"

"You're impossible."

I was about to start looking through the weird binder that he'd given me when Chastity spun her laptop around to show me some sort of spreadsheet.

"Check this out," she said.

I scooted my chair over to get a closer look. "What am I looking at here?"

"As your wing woman, it's my duty to keep track of all your lovers."

"I don't have any lovers. I've been celibate since the divorce." Despite the fact that I was in a sex club. And despite the fact that I'd had a boyfriend for a bit there. Fine, a day. I'd had a boyfriend for a day. If I ever saw Tanner again I was going to punch him.

"And if I do my job right, then you won't be for much longer. The only question is...who will be the lucky man to break your dry spell? Will it be Tanner?" She pointed to a blurry picture in column A. Under it was a list of pros and cons.

PROS
- Billionaire
- Super Hot
CONS
- Total Asshole

That about sums it up. "You should also add that he has a flaming genie penis that melts anything it touches. So I'm guessing he won't be the one to break my dry spell."

Chastity laughed but didn't add it to the list of cons. You know…because it was made up. Because everything Tanner said was a lie.

"Okay," said Chastity. "Moving on to suitor #2: Cole the handsome liftman."

"I've known him for three days and he's already tried to fuck me in front of an entire casino and tricked me into flashing a bunch of teens. He's a real keeper." *So why does thinking about him make me feel all giddy?*

"Exactly. He's the perfect candidate for some great rebound sex. It's at least worth considering his pros and cons."

PROS
- Tattoos
- Definitely into you
- Super Hot
- Bad Boy Vibes
CONS
- Total Asshole

"I'm seeing a theme here," I said. Is there something I'm doing to attract super hot assholes?"

"In my experience, those two things generally go together. Except for with your third suitor…"

Column C had a picture of Dr. Lyons at the top.

PROS
- Nine Inch Penis
- Doctor
- Veteran
- Super Hot

- Nice
Well that order says a lot about Chastity's priorities...
CONS
- None

"No cons? Really? You do remember that I tried to rape him. And that we both cheated on each other with each other and then I ghosted him, right? Oh, and then there was the time that I threw up all over him!" I needed to give her a printout of all my incidents.

"Yes, but I have a feeling he might still be interested."

"And why would you think that?"

"Oh, I don't know. Maybe because he was willing to pull some strings to get us invited to Club Onyx on the one condition that I do everything in my power to set you two up on another date."

"Say what now?"

She waved my question aside. "I'll work out the details later. But first we need to discuss your 4th and final suitor..." She scrolled over to reveal a picture of Mr. Frost.

I shook my head emphatically. "Why is he on the list?"

"Just keeping your options open..."

Before I could see what she listed as the pros and cons for him, I saw Mr. Frost approaching out of the corner of my eye.

I slammed her laptop shut just as he walked up. *Did he see her list?*

"I'm surprised you're still here," he said.
"Why?"

He picked up the binder and opened it to the first page. It was an hourly breakdown of everything I was supposed to do today, including a line item for 10:30 to leave and go pick up lunch from some place called The Sausage King. And it was almost 11.

"Better hurry if you don't want to be late for your meeting with Masquerade Records," said Mr. Frost.

"Why? Our meeting isn't until noon. And can't we just get it delivered?" I wasn't his assistant. Didn't he have someone else who could go fetch him food?

"They don't deliver."

"Let's just order from somewhere else then. Gochujang Palace is pretty great." I immediately regretted what I'd said. Mr. Frost's gaze made me want to crawl under the desk. "Actually, I'll just go pick up lunch from The Sausage King."

"Good," growled Mr. Frost. "I already placed the order under your name." He spun on his heel and left.

I pulled out my phone to see where this Sausage King place was. Wherever it was, I definitely didn't need to leave at 10:30 to pick up food for a noon meeting. That was the craziest... *SHIT!* Google maps said that The Sausage King was 24 minutes away based on current traffic. It was almost 11. I'd only have a few minutes to spare if traffic stayed the same, but it was almost lunchtime and there would surely be an accident. Why had Mr. Frost just let me sit here when he could see me through his office window?

I officially had the worst boss ever.

Chapter 13

THE SAUSAGE KING
Monday

I told my Uber driver to hurry, but we pretty much hit every red light possible. And it didn't help that construction took traffic down to one lane for a few blocks. As usual, no actual construction was being done. *Thanks for making me late for the most important meeting of my career. Assholes.*

Actually, that wasn't entirely fair. While the construction workers were definitely assholes for putting up those cones when they clearly weren't working, the real asshole was Mr. Frost. There were literally thousands of restaurants in NYC. But I was pretty sure Mr. Frost had intentionally picked the one that was farthest away just to mess with me.

Despite all that, my Uber driver did his best to earn his 5-star rating. At 11:25, we turned onto a street that looked like it was straight out of Germany. Most of the buildings were half-timbered, while the rest were super modern with lots of concrete and sharp angles. The street was lined exclusively with Audis, BMWs, and Volkswagens. So. Many. Volkswagens. And all the store names had weird umlauts in them. There was Schläfriger Bär, Schön, The Sausage King... *Ah! The Sausage King! We're here!*

I was out of the Uber before the driver could even put the car in park.

"Wait here!" I called back to him as I ran up to the front door of The Sausage King. As long as they had the food ready, I would be able to make it back in time for my meeting. Hell, I might even have a few minutes to spare.

I let out a deep breath and pulled the door open. But it didn't budge. I pulled again. Then I tried pushing just for good measure. Still no luck.

Shit!

Was this the wrong door? Some restaurants were weird and had different doors for takeout. There was writing on the door, but most of it was in German. The only thing I recognized were the store hours: Monday - Friday: Noon to 2 a.m.

Noon? Noon!?!? You've got to be kidding me.

I put my face to the glass and peered in. There was a nasty glare so it was hard to tell exactly what I was looking at, but I definitely didn't see any movement. The place was deserted. Part of me wondered if it was even still in business.

Mr. Frost was probably sitting at his desk laughing his ass off. His plan was suddenly so clear. He wanted me to miss the meeting so that he could take credit for landing Masquerade Records. What better way to show that he was the right choice for the job than to make his competition look completely inept?

Shame on me for falling for it.

I got out my phone to call Mr. Frost. It was time to give him a piece of my mind. Except…I didn't have his number. So I called Chastity instead.

"Do you have the food?" she asked.

"Put him on the phone right now." I was practically yelling.

"Who?"

"Mr. Frost."

"Um…okay. Why?"

"That asshole sent me on a wild goose chase. This freaking place isn't even open yet. I bet he didn't even place an order. He just sent me here so he could poach Masquerade Records."

"Let me ask him. One sec." There was silence on the line for a minute. "He just showed me the order confirmation. It clearly says pickup for 11:15."

"Then why the hell is this place empty? What happened to Germans being punctual? And who the hell orders German food? German cuisine isn't a thing that people like. No one wants beer and pretzels and sausage. Actually, no one wants anything from Germany. What have they ever done for the world? They just run around yodeling in their stupid lederhosen and Hitlerstaches. As far as I'm concerned, the Sausage King can take his sausage and stick it up Mr. Frost's ass." As I finished my tirade, I couldn't help but notice the delicious aroma of gingerbread wafting into my nose.

"Miss Cooper?" asked a deep voice behind me.

I spun around and came face to face with the source of the aroma - the Sausage King himself. He looked like he was straight out of some weird crossover between Top Chef and an NFL broadcast. *Chiseled beef tower* was, for some inexplicable reason, the first phrase that popped into my head. The second phrase was *shit,* because he had definitely just heard my entire speech about how much German people sucked. And based on his blue eyes, blonde stubble, and the swastika on his sleeve… Just kidding. There was no swastika. The Nazis probably hadn't even made arm bands big enough to fit his massive biceps.

What were the odds that he identified enough with German culture to be offended by what I had said? I mean…sure, he had apparently devoted his life to bringing German cuisine to the streets of New York, but that didn't mean anything. I'd seen plenty of white dudes slinging Thai food. It didn't mean they were from Thailand.

"Miss Cooper?" he said again. "I believe this is your order, ya?" He held up a big bag of takeout, but I was more focused on his very-German accent.

So much for him not really being German. "Uh, yup. That's me."

"I am so sorry to make you wait. May I offer you some complimentary wienerschnitzel?"

Weiner what? "No!"

He looked at me like I was crazy. "You do not like the wienerschnitzel? Perhaps you prefer lebkuchen? Or stollen?"

"Stalin? What does he have to do with this?"

The Sausage King laughed. "Not the Russian dictator. *Stollen* is a traditional German fruit bread."

"Well I don't have time for any of that. I have to be back at my office in Midtown by noon."

"Midtown? By noon?" He checked his expensive-looking watch. "How will you make it in time?"

"My Uber driver is…" I turned around to gesture to his car, but it was gone. *Shit!* "Where'd he go? I told him to wait."

"That is not how the Uber works."

"Yeah, I know."

"So what will you do?"

"I guess I'll be late." I got all sweaty as the harsh reality sunk in. One of my greatest fears was officially happening. I was going to be late. And then I was going to get fired. And then I was going to be homeless and die. My life was over.

"That is not acceptable."

"Yeah, tell me about it. This is the most important meeting of my career, and I'm going to miss it."

"No. You can still make it."

"How? This is NYC, man. You can't just hop on the autobahn and drive a million miles per hour."

"Follow me." He grabbed my hand and pulled me into his restaurant.

"Cooking me some complimentary wienerschnitzel isn't going to help much when I get fired."

He didn't respond. He just laughed and kept pulling me through the back halls of his restaurant. And then he pulled me onto an elevator.

Great. I had survived getting roofied at the Shifting Sands Spa only to get raped and murdered by some weird German chef. If I could just wiggle out of his grasp I might be able to grab the knife in his pocket...

I had my plan of attack all ready when the elevator doors opened. Wind whipped at my hair. *Wind? What the hell?* I took my eyes off the knife and stared out the doors in disbelief. We were on the roof of his building. And there was a helicopter in the center of it.

"Does your building have a helipad?" he asked.

"Uh..."

"We will make it work. Come." He pulled me over to the helicopter and strapped me into the back seat. Then he hopped into the cockpit and started playing with controls. Despite the earmuffs he had given me, I could still hear the engine roar to life.

"Do you know how to fly this thing?" I shouted, but it was too late. He had already taken off. There was no going back now.

Once we were comfortably above the skyscrapers, he turned and looked at me with his blue eyes. Unlike Mr. Frost's, they weren't icy at all. They were filled with life and warmth. Looking into his eyes was like looking into the crisp, clear water of the Caribbean.

"The city is beautiful from up here, ya?" he asked.

I leaned over to get a better look. It really was breathtaking. But I had so many other questions. "Why are you doing this for me?"

"In Germany we have a phrase. *Wer zu spät kommt, den bestraft das leben.* Life punishes those who come too late."

Did that saying extend to sex as well? Were all Germans premature ejaculators? *Gross.* But I was more into the actual meaning of what he'd just said. "Germans hate lateness so much that you would fly me back to work? That's the coolest thing anyone has ever done for me." In that moment, I was pretty sure I had found my soulmate. No one had ever shared my passion for punctuality the way he clearly did.

"Yes. See? We are not all lederhosen and Hitler-staches."

"Oh God. How much of that did you hear?"

"Enough to know that you have never eaten at The Sausage King before. Because if you had, you would know that German food is the best. You have not lived until you have tasted my sausage."

I stifled a laugh. Was he aware of the innuendo there? Based on how serious he sounded, I assumed he wasn't.

I couldn't decide what to ask him next. I had a million questions. What was his name? Did he grow up in Germany? When did he open his restaurant? Most importantly…how did he get his own freaking helicopter?!

But I didn't get to ask any of my questions.

"Which building is yours?" he asked.

I gave him the address. A minute later, we touched down on the roof of BIMG. By some miracle, the building actually did have a helipad.

"Thank you so much," I said as I unstrapped myself.

"There is no time for thanks. You will be late."

"But I didn't even get your name."

"Otto von Wurst. Now go!"

Chapter 14

OVERSIZED SAUSAGE
Monday

"You made it back!" said Chastity when I appeared at our desk. "You better hurry though…I think Mr. Frost was just about to start the meeting."

"What a jerk. Can you get this on a serving tray?" I tossed her the takeout bag and ran to the meeting room.

As I approached, I heard Mr. Frost say, "Well, let's give her one more minute. If she's not here then I guess we'll just have to go on without her."

I waited for him to finish his sentence before making my triumphant entrance. "That won't be necessary."

The shocked look on Mr. Frost's face was priceless. But it was only visible for a second. He quickly concealed it with a look of relief. "Where were you?" he asked. "Is everything okay?"

"Everything is fine. Now, please take a seat and let's begin." I strode to the head of the table and clicked on the first slide.

I was so freaking nervous, but my months of practice paid off. The presentation went flawlessly until I accidentally looked into Mr. Frost's icy blue eyes. It wouldn't have been a problem, but I was using the tried-and-true method of picturing my audience naked. So Mr. Frost's innocent gaze seemed a lot like he was eye-fucking the hell out of me while I talked about how important TikTok is for up-and-coming musicians. Or maybe it wasn't an innocent gaze after all. *Gah! Focus!* Chastity's pro and con list was just stuck in my head.

As I tried to get back into my flow, Chastity brought in a serving tray piled high with sausage. All sorts of sausage. Dark sausage, white sausage, long sausage, fat sausage. Every type of sausage imaginable. It looked absolutely repulsive. But Mr. Frost and the owners of Masquerade Records were more than happy to dig in.

I kept going with my presentation while everyone stuffed their faces full of sausage. I tried to stay focused, but something about the whole thing was deeply homoerotic. When there were only two sausages left, the owner of Masquerade Records snatched them both up and double-fisted them.

"So, any questions?" I asked when I finished my totally awesome presentation. I was sure I had nailed it. They'd probably have a million questions, but I was super prepared. *Wanna know your expected CPC on ads? Thirty-five cents. Wanna know the CTR on a banner placement? One to two percent. Yeah, I know those are good numbers. But I'm good at what I do.*

Only they didn't ask those questions. In fact, they didn't ask anything at all. They just shook hands with us, thanked us for lunch, and walked out.

What the hell? People *always* asked questions. In my experience, more questions equated to a higher probability that the client would sign. So what did no questions mean? Did they hate my presentation that much? No way. I did awesome. They must have been insulted that I served them stupid German food. Because even though the Sausage King was a badass helicopter pilot, it didn't change the fact that no one liked German cuisine.

Mr. Frost had tricked me again. That sly bastard.

"Great job," he said with a smug smile. "But next time don't cut it so close. I put a lot of thought into that binder. Maybe you should try reading it."

Screw you. I nodded and walked out.

"How'd it go?" asked Chastity when I got back to my desk.

"I honestly have no idea. They didn't ask a single question."

"Oh. Well…that's probably a good thing. Right?"

"I guess."

"Great! Then let's have some celebratory bratwurst!" She slid a plate across my desk. I nearly gagged at the sight of the tubular meat.

"No thanks."

"Well at least tell me all about the Sausage Duke. Was he dreamy?" She absentmindedly smacked a bratwurst against her lips.

"The Sausage *King*. You have your royal titles mixed up."

"Right. His restaurant is The Sausage King. But he's the Duke of Sausage. Or I guess technically the Duke of Wurst."

"Say what now?"

"I looked him up while you were gone. Germany abolished their monarchy in 1918, but you can still trace the royal bloodlines. His family has ruled the village of Wurst for centuries."

"You're joking."

"I'm not." She spun her laptop around and showed me the Wikipedia page for Wilhelm von Wurst, father of Otto von Wurst. "And check out this castle they own." She scrolled down to a picture of a ridiculously awesome castle nestled in the mountains above the cutest little ski resort village.

"Well that explains the helicopter," I said.

"The what?!"

I told her the whole story while she kept nibbling at the oversized sausage.

"Please tell me you gave him sky head."

Really? That's her takeaway from this whole story? "Sky head? Is that like road head in a helicopter?"

"So that's a yes then? Oh my God." She slapped my hand with her half-eaten bratwurst. "You naughty girl."

"What? No! I didn't do that."

"Suuure. So how big was he?"

"I don't know."

"You're really not going to tell me?" She looked so mad. "That violates Single Girl Rule #9: If you hear about a well-hung man, share the news."

"No. Because I didn't blow him."

"What if he's one of the famous descendants of Hansel and Gretel and the wizard?"

"Wasn't it a witch?" It was definitely a witch.

"Yeah, in the dumb kids' version. Have you not heard the *real* version?"

"No?"

"Well…once upon a time, there was a husband and a wife: Hansel and Gretel."

"Pretty sure they were brother and sister."

"Shhh. They were a couple. And Gretel was a total babe. Anyway, they tried and they tried, but they couldn't conceive."

"I thought they were starving?"

Chastity shook her head. "Maybe. The story doesn't say. But they definitely couldn't make a baby. So they set off in the woods in search of a cure for Hansel's erectile dysfunction. Gretel suggested they leave pebbles so that they could find their way back, but Hansel was all like, 'Na, real men don't need directions.' So of course they got lost in the woods."

I thought about correcting her, but I didn't want to interrupt. I genuinely couldn't wait to hear how she was going to make this story make any sense.

"They walked and walked until they were practically starving…"

"See!" I said. "I knew they were starving."

"Well yeah, now they are. But as luck would have it, they stumbled upon a house. All around the house, sausages were hung up to dry. Hansel and Gretel immediately started downing sausage after sausage until the wizard who owned the house came out and invited them inside. He pretended to be a nice young man, offering to feed them and give them shelter."

Definitely a witch.

"One night, the wizard heard noises coming from Hansel and Gretel's room. He thought someone was hurting Gretel, so he didn't even bother to put on his nightclothes before going to check on them. As it turned out, they were making love. But Gretel took one look at the wizard's footlong cock and immediately realized that she needed a real man to get her pregnant.

So she locked Hansel in a cage and made him watch her get absolutely plowed by the well-endowed wizard."

I blinked a few times as I tried to process what I'd just heard. "Well that took a weird turn. And isn't there supposed to be something about an oven?"

"I'm getting there!"

"Please continue."

"That continued every night for weeks, until Gretel's belly swelled with the wizard's bun in her oven. She had the baby, and they all lived happily ever after. Even Hansel, who begrudgingly accepted his role as their bitch and went into town every day to sell the wizard's sausages."

"Wow." I honestly didn't have any other words to respond to that story.

"Right! There aren't any official records, but people have speculated that Gretel and the wizard's baby grew up to be the duke of a small village. Because what else would he have done? He was clearly a total alpha if his dad was a freaking hung wizard."

"That checks out."

"It follows that the village would be renowned for sausages - both culinary and anatomical. Ever since this version of the story surfaced, girls have been backpacking around Germany trying to find these mythical sausages. But I think we just found the duke himself! I mean...he's the Duke of Wurst. That translates to the duke of sausage. He's Gretel and the wizard's great great great grandson! It has to be him! And he's #HungLikeAGermanSausage."

Well that was officially the weirdest story that I had ever heard. "I'm curious," I said. "What was the moral of that story?"

"Who says there has to be a moral?"

"That's literally what a fable is. A short story designed to teach a moral."

"It's not a fable either. It's a true story."

"Oh right, because wizards totally exist."

"They do. I still have my suspicions that Tanner might be one…"

Is that how he switched that card to make me win in poker? No. Of course it wasn't. Because magic wasn't real. And Tanner was dead to me. Unless I ever saw him again and kissed him. I shook my head. I meant throat-punch him.

"You really never heard that story when you were a kid?" asked Chastity.

"Not in that form."

"Weird. I need to have a chat with your mom about that."

"Please don't."

"Suit yourself. Aren't you hungry?" She gestured to the sausage on my desk.

"I'm not really a fan of sausage…"

"The great great great grandson of Gretel and the wizard just gave you a free helicopter ride across the city so that you wouldn't be late for your meeting, and you won't even *taste* his sausage? That's messed up."

I looked at the gross link of mystery meat and scrunched up my face. I really did not want to eat it, but she did have a point. "Fine. Do you have a fork?"

"No. Just barehand it."

I gave her a look. "You know perfectly well that I would never do that. I'm not a barbarian."

"You're impossible." Chastity grabbed the sausage off my plate and held it up to my mouth. I tentatively licked the tip of it. I expected it to be the grossest thing ever, but it wasn't. In fact, it was pretty delicious. I licked a little more. And then I went to take a bite.

Just then, Mr. Frost walked up behind Chastity. "Hey, just checking in…"

Chastity must not have seen him coming, because she jumped. And in doing so, she jammed the entire sausage down my throat. My eyes got big and I gagged.

"Am I interrupting something?" asked Mr. Frost.

I pulled back from the sausage and wiped the spit off the side of my mouth. I was fully aware of the fact that I had just deepthroated a bratwurst in front of my new boss. The same boss that I had already molested and then given a saucy wink.

"You're not interrupting anything at all. I was just taking a quick lunch break." To drive the point home, I grabbed Chastity's hand and brought the sausage up to my mouth so I could take a big bite. I started chewing and… *Oh my God.* I had always thought sausage was gross, but this thing melted in my mouth. It was an explosion of delicious savory yumminess. I actually moaned it tasted so good.

"You were supposed to take a ten-minute lunch break after the meeting. And then you were supposed to do Facebook ads for Wineflix and Chill from 2 to 3, and then…well, I don't have to tell you. It's all in the binder." He tapped the binder and walked away.

"I guess we better look in the binder, huh?" I asked.

Chastity nodded.

I opened it up, and it was even worse than I thought. Not only had he broken down my day by the minute, but he also had painfully detailed instructions on how to do each and every task. *Scale ads to 2000 x 2000 pixels. Duplicate ad sets, not ads. Have six ads per ad set. Yadda yadda.*

We both got to work. And worked. And worked some more. By 5 o'clock - the time when work was supposed to be over - I still had hours and hours of work to do. But you know who didn't? Apparently Mr. Frost. Because he was all packed up and out the door at 5 pm sharp. Chastity and I didn't leave until the sun had long since set.

I hoped that he just had somewhere really important to be, but the same thing happened Tuesday. And Wednesday, and Thursday.

I was a fast worker, but thanks to Mr. Frost's stupid binder, everything took twice as long as it used to. By some miracle, I was able to catch up on all my work by 4 pm on Friday. One more task and then I would finally be free from his tyranny. Or at least…free from it for one weekend.

I opened up the binder and scanned my final assignment.

Friday - 4 pm - Draft 6 new creatives for Wineflix and Chill's October campaign.

There were a ton of criteria under that, but one in particular stood out: *ONLY buy images from PicStock.*

"You ever heard of PicStock?" I asked.

"Nope," said Chastity. "What is it?"

"I'm guessing some stock photo site. Apparently that's what we have to use for images now." I brought it up on my computer and started searching for images we could use in the new Wineflix ads. The first thing that caught my eye was that you could only buy exclusive rights to images. You couldn't just buy a normal license like you do on most sites. The prices reflected that. Instead of $10 per image, this site charged $1000. "They better have some good stuff on here…"

I did a few of my usual searches. Wine glass. Beautiful model drinking wine. Fashion model party. I had to admit, the images were good. And for a nice change in the stock image space, there were actually photos I hadn't seen before.

Chastity watched over my shoulder and helped me save images that might work.

"Whoa, go back," said Chastity suddenly. She sounded concerned.

I clicked back. "What? Did we miss one?"

She took the mouse from me and clicked on an image of a girl sitting on a cliffside looking off into the distance. I nearly fell out of my chair when I saw the larger version of the photo. It wasn't just some random model in the picture. It was Rosalie. My sister. Who went missing three years ago. I felt my throat constricting.

"That's Rosalie, right?" asked Chastity.

I nodded.

"Did you know she did any modeling?"

"Never." My brain was working overdrive. Was it at all possible that this was a new photo? If it was, it meant that Rosalie was still alive. And even if it wasn't, it was still new information. A new lead to someone who might know what happened to her.

I stared at the image and tried to blink away my tears. I needed to tell Marty, Tanner's PI, about this immediately.

My heart sunk. I couldn't tell Marty. I wasn't dating Tanner anymore. There was no way he was still looking into Rosalie's disappearance now. And he'd totally ignored me the entire time Tanner had been missing.

I shook the thought away. I didn't need a fancy PI anyway. And I definitely didn't need Tanner. I was a freaking amazing stalker.

Chapter 15
APOLOGY NUDIES
Friday

I searched high and low on PicStock for information about the picture of Rosalie - who took it, when it was taken, where it was taken - but I couldn't find a thing.

Come on! Shutterstock at least gave the username of the photographer that posted the photos on their site. But of course this stupid site that Mr. Frost demanded we use wasn't nearly as helpful.

"Maybe try their customer service chat?" suggested Chastity.

I went to the *contact us* tab. But they didn't have a chat option either. *Stupid trash site!* "Gah, they only have a phone number."

"I'll call," said Chastity.

And that was why she was the best. She totally understood that I hated calling people.

She put her phone on speaker and placed it on the desk between us.

"Thank you for calling PicStock. We're currently experiencing a higher-than-usual call volume, but a representative will be with you shortly."

Twenty minutes later, someone finally answered.

"Hello, this is Olivia with PicStock," said a man with a very thick Indian accent. "For quality assurance purposes, we are recording this call. How may I help you?"

For starters you could stop lying about your name, Olivia the Indian man.

"Hey, Olivia," said Chastity. "I was just looking on your site and I found an image I really like. I'd love to hire the photographer to do more photos for me, but I can't find their name on the site. Can you possibly give me their name?"

"What photo is this in reference to?" asked Olivia.

"Uh…" Chastity looked at the screen. "ID# 751495."

"Thank you. One moment please." Olivia treated us to five minutes of elevator music before returning. "Hello?"

"I'm here," said Chastity.

"Wonderful. I regret to inform you that I am not able to share the name of the photographer with you."

"Why not?"

"We sign nondisclosure agreements with all of our photographers."

Chastity glared at Olivia through the phone. "But I'm trying to hire this photographer," she lied. "Why would he not want that?"

"I'm sorry, but it is company policy to keep all photographer and model names confidential."

Chastity kept trying different angles to get the information, but Olivia was a stone wall. Even when she flirted with him. I was pretty sure it was the first time I'd ever seen Chastity's flirting fail. Eventually she told him that Olivia was a girl's name and then hung up.

"I'm sorry, Ash. I tried," she said.

"That was amazing. It's not your fault Olivia is a total ass."

Chastity said she'd try to call again in hopes of talking to someone other than Olivia. Meanwhile I tried searching for more information about PicStock. They were privately held. The CEO was a guy named Vance Williams. They were founded in 2014 as a division of Odegaard, LLC. *Wait, what?*

I read that last sentence again. I must not have been reading it right. Odegaard was Tanner's fashion label. What were they doing selling stock photos? Honestly, it didn't really matter. What mattered was that Tanner probably had access to the photographer's name.

There was just one problem: he was a total idiot and I never wanted to talk to his stupid face again.

I tapped Chastity on the shoulder. "Check this out."

"Tanner owns PicStock?"

"Apparently so."

"Well that's amazing! Call him and get all the info. And while you're at it, tell him to fire Olivia."

"Can you call him for me?" I asked.

"Why? He's your boy toy." She looked confused for a second before nodding. "Oh right, you told him to stay out of your life forever."

"Yeah."

"Well, he's more likely to answer you," said Chastity. "Just text him a nudie and apologize."

"I'm not going to do that."

"Not even to find Rosalie?"

Damn it! She was right. A few awkward minutes were totally worth it if it led me to finding out what happened to Rosalie. "Fine."

"Thatta girl." She grabbed my phone and pointed it at my chest. "Pull a boob out and let's do this."

"What? No!" I wasn't going to pull out my boob in the middle of the office! "I meant I'd call him."

"With no apology nudie?" She shook her head. "As your wing woman, I strongly advise against that."

"Noted." I took my phone and dialed Tanner's number. The faster I got it over with, the sooner I'd stop sweating.

"Hello?" said Tanner.

"Tanner. Hey. It's Ash."

"What's up?" His voice was unreadable. Was he excited to be talking to me? Or did he hate my guts?

"Listen, I'm really sorry about the other night. I'd had a lot to drink and…it had been a long day."

There was a long pause. "I'm sorry too. I had no business telling you what to do. You're a grown woman."

"Don't worry about it." How could I segue into asking about Rosalie? I decided to just go for it. "You own PicStock, right?"

"Yes." He sounded very confused by the sudden change of topic. "Why?"

"So you know how I told you that my sister went missing a few years ago? Well…I just came across a picture of her on PicStock. I was hoping you could give me some info about the photo. Like when it was taken. And who the photographer was."

"Are you serious? That's amazing! Of course I can get that info. What's the photo ID?"

"751495."

"Great. I'll see what I can find." The line went dead.

I smiled at the phone. I tried not to get my hopes up too much. But with this new lead and Tanner helping…it felt like I might actually have a shot at finding out what had happened to Rosalie. Afterall…Tanner was a better stalker than I was. Since technically he was the one who'd been stalking me, not the other way around.

"Well that sounded like it went surprisingly well," said Chastity. "Imagine how well it would have gone if you had sent a nudie first, though."

I tapped my fingers on the desk while I waited for him to call back. It was probably only about 5 minutes, but it felt like an eternity.

When he finally called, I picked up on the first ring.

"Are you at work?" he asked.

Weird greeting. "Yeah. Why?"

"Good. Go wait out front. I'll pick you up in ten." And then he hung up.

I looked at the phone as if the screen would magically give me more information about whatever the hell had just happened.

"What'd he find?" asked Chastity.

"He didn't say. He just told me to wait outside. And that he's going to pick me up in ten minutes."

"Ooh la la. I bet he's going to take you to Club Onyx to punish you for talking back to him the other night."

"What does that have to do with the picture of Rosalie?"

"No idea. But I bet you're gonna have a wild night."

"Wild night?" asked Madison.

I jumped at the sound of her voice. How long had she been creeping on us?

"Yeah," said Chastity. "Tanner is picking Ash up in ten minutes."

"For what?"

Chastity's eyes lit up. "We aren't sure. All we know is that it involves handcuffs, a bed, and a whip. Oh, and lots of spectators." She said it loud enough for all of our coworkers to hear.

Kill me now. "We definitely do *not* know that. He just said he was coming to pick me up in ten."

"Right. But the subtext…"

"There was no subtext!"

"Sounds to me like he's gonna murder you," Madison said. "You should probably just stay in. We can watch baseball. It'll be amazing."

"No thanks."

"But it's Friday night," said Madison. "Doesn't Chastity have some weird rule about that? Single Girl Rule #14: Fridays in September are reserved for baseball with your bitches."

Chastity looked horrified. "Wow. No. Rule #14 is: If a girl forgets her purse, she must attempt to pay with her body."

Madison made a gagging noise. "Your rules are disgusting."

"They're not *my* rules. They're the Single Girl Rules. They belong to all single girls."

"Whatever." Madison turned to me. "Are you seriously gonna get into Tanner's car?"

"Of course," I said. "Why wouldn't I?"

"Um…aren't you even a little worried that he's the one who murdered Rosalie? And now he knows you're onto him. What if he's going to drive you to a remote location and cut you up into little bits and eat you?"

"Well I wasn't worried about that before. But now I kind of am." *Tanner's not a killer, right?* "I have to go, though. I'll keep my phone on and text you guys every 20 minutes. If you don't hear from me, use Find My Phone." I gave Chastity my password and headed to the elevator.

It was exactly 5 o'clock, so I had the displeasure of sharing the elevator with Mr. Frost.

"Leaving so early?" he asked.

Really? How dare he have the nerve to ask me about leaving at 5 when he did it every single day. "Thanks to your very thoughtful and detailed instructions, I was able to budget my time effectively and finish my work right on schedule." I tried to say it nicely, but it came out super sarcastic.

"So you hate the binder that much, huh? Good to know. I'll come up with something better for next week."

Is that a threat? It really sounded like a threat. *Oh God.* What had I gotten myself into? I was pretty sure Mr. Frost was going to do everything in his power to make next week a living hell. But honestly, I didn't care. All I could think about was that I was about to find Rosalie.

Chapter 16

YOU HAD SEX IN FIFTH GRADE?!
Friday

Tanner was waiting for me on the front steps of the BIMG building. He gave me a smile like everything was totally normal. "Are you stalking me, baby?"

"Hey." My voice squeaked and I had no idea why. It wasn't because I loved when he said that. Or because his face was perfect. Or because he was staring at me like he missed me too. Or because I'd been dying to see him ever since he broke into my closet. I cleared my throat. I could keep this professional. "What'd you find?"

"I'll tell you on the ride over. Shall we?" He gestured to the street. I didn't see his usual black Phantom limo, but there was a bright red Ferrari.

Where was he planning on taking me? "Trying to impress me with your fancy cars, huh?" I said and crossed my arms. But what I really wanted to do was hug him. I hugged myself tighter to stop myself from hugging him.

"Only a douche would take a Ferrari where we're headed. We're over here." He clicked his key fob and the lights blinked on a futuristic-looking silver SUV.

"What even is that thing?" It looked like what an alien would design if they wanted to blend in on Earth but couldn't *quite* get it right.

"You like it? Elon sent it over a few weeks ago for me to test drive."

"Elon? As in…Elon Musk? As in…the richest man in the world?"

"Second richest," corrected Tanner.

"Oh. Did Bezos get ahead of him again?"

"No idea. But I know someone richer than both of them."

"Who?"

He just gave me a knowing smile. Which made me think…

"*You?*"

"Of course. That's the beauty of compound interest."

"Right… But that takes time. And you're like half their age."

"I started investing early."

"How early?" An image of little baby Tanner popped into my head. He was sitting in front of three huge monitors trading stocks while wearing nothing but his man bun and some diapers. It was adorable. "Wait, were you the inspiration for the E-Trade baby commercials?"

He laughed and opened the passenger door for me.

"Where are we going?"

"Just get in."

I shook my head. Madison had really gotten into my head about him being a murderer. And him being *so* rich was super sus. He claimed it was compound interest. But I was starting to think it was more likely to be human trafficking…

More importantly, though, I couldn't trust myself to be near him. I was finally piecing my heart back together. I couldn't risk letting him shatter it again.

"Don't you trust me?" asked Tanner.

Was he serious right now?

He looked at the car and then back at me. "I promise, I'm just trying to help."

I slowly exhaled. I needed answers. And if getting in a confined space with Tanner meant I was closer to finding Rosalie…then I guess I could bear it. A minute later we were speeding off through New York City traffic. And his stupid blueberry cologne was invading my senses. I leaned away from him and toward the window, trying my best to avoid his alluring scent.

"So do you want the good news or the bad news?" asked Tanner.

My heart immediately started racing. That meant he had found something…but that I might not like what he had found. "Um, bad news."

"I couldn't find the name of the photographer."

"Really?" Then why had I gotten in the car?

"But I did find some other information. The photo was uploaded to our system three years ago."

"What month? Rosalie went missing in May."

"September."

"Really?! That means she's alive!" I couldn't believe it. I wanted to scream and dance and sing.

"Not necessarily. It could have been taken a while before that. Photos can sometimes sit on hard drives for years before they end up on stock photo sites."

"Oh." *Damn.* "So what's the good news then?"

"Well…when I looked at the photo, I thought that the scenery looked familiar. I couldn't quite place it, though. But then when I pulled up the metadata, I noticed that the model's name was listed as Oaklyn Hope."

"So it's not her? That's not possible…it looks just like her. She's even wearing the bracelets she always wore. Maybe that's what she changed her name to after she disappeared."

"I had the same thought. But then I ran the name through the Society database. And bingo…"

Why did he have access to the Society database? But my question fell away as he handed me his phone. The screen was open to a profile on his Society app for Oaklyn Hope. There was a picture of Rosalie that I'd never seen before, a few stats about her height, weight, and birthday, and the date of her last spa visit: May 18, 2020. Exactly one week before she disappeared.

I had so many questions. How long had she been part of the Society? Why had she never told me? Who had she been dating? But most importantly… "Did you know her?"

Tanner shook his head. "Nope."

I breathed a sigh of relief. I tried to scroll down to get more info, but the profile ended with the spa visit date. "Can you see her ratings? And who she dated?"

"For security reasons they purge most member data every six months."

"Damn." I leaned back and looked out the window, trying to process everything I had just learned. The sight of the trees whipping by was soothing. *Wait…trees?* I blinked and looked around. We were cruising down the highway, surrounded by thick forest. *Oh no!* Had Madison been right about Tanner? Was he really going to drive me into the woods and chop me up into little bits? I stared at the slight smile playing at the corners of his mouth. He wasn't going to chop me into little bits. Or sell me on the black market. He was more likely going to suck my freaking blood. Because he was a vampire. It was the only thing that made sense. *Yup, he's definitely going to murder me.* "Where the heck are we?"

Tanner laughed. "That's the other part of the good news. After I figured out that Rosalie was part of the Society, I was able to place the scenery in that photo. The reason I recognized it was because the photo was taken at the Emerald Oasis - a resort in the Catskills."

"Resort? With pools and piña coladas and heart-shaped hot tubs?"

"Eh…more like bonfires and zip lining and a big lake."

"That sounds like my 5th-grade summer camp."

Tanner looked shocked. "You had sex in 5th grade?!"

"What? No! Of course I didn't have sex in 5th grade." I hadn't even been kissed until college. But Tanner didn't need to know that. "Who said anything about having sex?"

"You said that this resort reminded you of summer camp in 5th grade."

"Right. The bonfire and zip lining and big lake parts."

"Oh, I get it. I should have mentioned that the Society owns this particular resort. So naturally there's quite a bit of sex."

"Why does the Society own a resort in the Catskills?" I thought that only New York Jews in the 50s hung out in the Catskills. Or maybe I had just been binge-watching too much of *The Marvelous Mrs. Maisel*…

"A while ago I saw one was available for purchase. So I put in an offer. Now the Society hosts weekend getaways there."

"I'm sorry, *you* purchased it? For the Society? Why didn't they purchase it themselves?" I knew he was some kind of prestigious member of the Society because he had that weird badge with the Society logo on it. He'd used it to stop me from getting double-teamed by Angel and Diablo.

"Oh." He laughed. "I meant I found it for them. Of course they bought it since I'm just a normal member of the Society. Just a normal boy on the town."

What the hell was he talking about? "And why do you have access to their database? And know how often they purge their member data?"

"I know people who know people. And I've been a member of the Society for quite some time."

I bet he had. *Whore.* I stared at his perfect jawline. Really, how many women had he dated in the Society? And where had he been for three months? And why was he here now, torturing me with his flawless bone structure?

"Do I have something on my face?" he asked.

"What? No. You're perfect." I cleared my throat. "I mean, it's nothing. So…that's where we're headed? The resort?"

"Indeed it is."

"What good will that do us?"

"Well…the Society servers might not have any info about Rosalie, but that doesn't mean people don't remember her. A lot of the staff at the Emerald Oasis are townies who have worked there for years. I bet at least one of them remembers her. And if we're really lucky, maybe they'll remember who she used to hang out with."

I couldn't believe it. After all these years, I finally had hope of finding Rosalie. I pinched myself to make sure this was actually happening. *Ow.* "You're the best." I could never repay him for this.

"I know." He flashed me his cocky smile.

I immediately wanted to take my comment back. He was the worst.

And yet…that smile was the one that I'd fallen for when I first met him. I wanted to lean over the center console and kiss him with joy. But I knew better. My heart had only just healed from when he'd shattered it. It would be careless to let that happen again. I turned away from him and checked my phone. There were a bunch of texts from Madison and a few missed calls.

Madison: What'd he say?
Madison: Where is he taking you?
Madison: Why are you leaving the city?
Madison: Ash?
Madison: Ash?!
Madison: Is he taking you into the woods to chop you into little bits?
Madison: ASH! Write back to me this instant or I'm calling the police!

I laughed. "Oops."

"What?" asked Tanner.

"Hold on." I dialed Chastity. I figured she'd be calmer than Madison.

"Hey girl!" said Chastity.

But then Madison screamed, "Ash?! Is that you?!"

"Yes, it's me."

"Are you okay?" asked Madison. She must have taken the phone from Chastity. "Shit…he's probably listening. We need some sort of code. Pretend like everything is okay if you're in trouble."

"I'm fine."

"So you're not fine?"

"No."

"No as in you're fine? Or no as in…no, you're not fine." Madison sounded frantic.

"This is too confusing. I'm really okay. He's not going to murder me."

"What now?" asked Tanner.

"Madison thought that we had outed you as Rosalie's murderer. And that you were coming to pick me up so that you could drive me out into the woods and chop me into little bits."

"Aw man, how'd she figure it out so easily?" said Tanner. "I thought it was going to be the perfect murder."

"Did he just confess?!" yelled Madison. "It sounded like he confessed!"

I put Madison and Chastity on speaker phone and Tanner told them everything he had just told me. That seemed to calm Madison down enough to let Chastity have her phone back. I thought for sure Chastity was gonna say she wanted to come. But apparently her sky box date with her gentleman suitor had been rescheduled for tonight, so she hung up pretty quickly.

I was still curious about what the sky box was. Waiting until tomorrow to hear all about it was going to be torture. But maybe I wouldn't have to wait. I mean…Tanner probably knew all about it. "Do you know what the sky box is?"

He raised his eyebrows. "I do. And all I can say is that I hope Chastity isn't afraid of heights."

"So she's gonna have sex in a…helicopter?" My mind flashed back to my ride with the Sausage King. I couldn't help but smile at the thought of him.

"Why do you look so happy about that? Have you ever been in a helicopter?"

"Maybe. Does that mean I'm right?"

"That's classified information."

"You're seriously not going to tell me?" I asked.

"Nope. The only way to find out what happens in the sky box is to go in the sky box. And I'm pretty sure the only challenge you've completed is the casino. Speaking of which…I got you a present." He gestured to the back seat. "Go ahead and open the top compartment of your suitcase."

"*My* suitcase?" I looked back. There were two suitcases in the back. One was super cute with red flowers. The other was covered in all sorts of bright green zigzags.

"Yeah. I figured you wouldn't want to be running around in your business clothes all weekend."

"Whoa whoa whoa. *All* weekend?"

He gave me a funny look. "Of course we're staying all weekend. What kind of crazy person would only go to a resort for one night?"

I stared at him. Part of me wondered if that photo of Rosalie had really been taken at this resort. It was entirely possible that Tanner had just made it up to get me to agree to go on a romantic weekend getaway with him. But if he thought he was going to win me back, he was dead wrong. Just because he was super handsome and muscular and fun to be around, it didn't mean I would come crawling back to him. That would be insane. Or would it be insane not to?

"Aren't you going to open your present?" asked Tanner.

Oh, right. I turned back to the suitcases. "Which one is mine?"

"Which one do you think is yours?"

"The green zig zags?" I joked.

"Oh yes. You know how I love my super feminine floral luggage."

"It's okay. Your secret is safe with me." I opened the top pocket on the floral luggage and pulled out a little wrapped package about the size of one of those boxes of fancy assorted chocolates.

"You look grossed out," said Tanner.

"Sorry. I was just thinking about how this box was the same size as those stupid chocolate variety packs."

"You mean the ones where you have to eat all sorts of awful milk chocolate trash in order to get the one good dark chocolate turtle?"

"Yes!" He totally got me. "Those things make me so mad!" I pressed my lips together. No, Tanner did not get me. He didn't know me at all. And he'd disappeared for three months like an ass hat.

"Oh. Then I guess you probably shouldn't open that." He sounded so disappointed.

My eyes got big. Had I seriously just insulted his gift? What had I been thinking?! My mom had always told me that I was so good at receiving gifts. No matter what she had gotten me, I'd always just plastered a smile on my face and pretended to be so excited. Could I still backtrack and make him think I appreciated his gift? "The thing I love about chocolate samplers is that the one dark chocolate turtle is so good that it makes up for all the trash chocolate. Not that your gift is trash..." I cringed at my own words.

Then Tanner started laughing. "This isn't the first time someone's told me I gave them a trash gift. But do you really think I got you a chocolate sampler? Why would I do that?"

I glared at him. Of course he had been messing with me. "I forgot how annoying you are."

"Annoying, huh? In that case, I guess I should just take this back..." He reached over and tried to snatch the present out of my hand. I swatted his hand away.

"No takesie-backsies, mister. Didn't anyone ever teach you any manners?"

"Nope. Now hurry up and open your present."

I tore into the paper. I was relieved to see that the gift was *not* chocolates. Instead, it was a black box emblazoned in gold lettering on the lid. *Jewelry?* I opened the lid and nearly got blinded by the sun reflecting off the gold necklace inside.

"Try it on," said Tanner.

I pulled it out and clipped it behind my neck. Then I pulled down the mirror to check it out. There were three gold chains all connected in the back. One was kind of a choker, the next hung a little lower, and the third hung down between my breasts. There was a charm on the end that looked like an old-fashioned coin. I expected it to be etched with some Greek letters or something, but instead it featured the same dice symbol that had been on the key Cole had given me. "Why's this on there?"

"To show which challenges you've completed. Once you get seven coins, you'll be elevated to a gold member. If you don't like it there are a bunch of other styles to choose from. I just thought this one would look best on you." His eyes followed the necklace down between my cleavage.

"Eyes on the road, buddy."

Tanner quickly averted his gaze.

I looked back down at the necklace. "I love it." I really did. It was classy and sexy and super shiny. And the fact that Tanner had picked it out made it even more special. "Thank you."

"My pleasure."

"I'm sorry again about what I said to you last weekend. I didn't mean that I never wanted to see you again. I was just still mad at you for leaving."

"You really don't believe that I got kidnapped?"

"Not even a little bit."

"But you saw me get bagged."

"Mhm. I saw it. And I fell for it. I searched for you all freaking summer, Tanner. Luckily I talked to your friend Matt and he told me that you were just out of town on business."

"Huh?"

"That's right. Your best friend blew your cover."

"Wow. Okay." He pushed a few buttons on the built-in display and his car started calling Matt. As in Matthew freaking Caldwell. Who I set on fire. *The incident* flashed through my mind and I immediately started sweating profusely.

"Hey man," said Matt. "What's up?"

Hearing his voice made me want to scream. But also I suddenly wanted to jump out of the car and die. It was hard to choose which reaction was best. Instead I just stared in horror at the dashboard and pretended this wasn't happening.

"Quick question. What did you say to Ash about me being gone the past few months?"

"Ash? As in the crazy girl who lit my dick on fire?"

Fuck my life. I needed to jump out into oncoming traffic immediately.

"That's the one," said Tanner.

I freaking knew that he knew about that! I hadn't been sure before…but now I was certain the flaming genie penis thing was him just messing with me. Because he knew I set dicks on fire in my free time. Why did he not tell me that he knew what I'd done to his best friend? And why wasn't he scared of me? I pulled my purse a little closer, happy that I'd remembered my mini fire extinguisher.

"I haven't talked to her in months," Matt said. "But her friend Chastity accosted me on the street and asked if I'd heard from you. She was very forward."

Gah Chastity. Why had she hit on him right in front of his wife?!

"And what'd you tell her?" asked Tanner.

"Uhh…" Matt took a second to think about it. "I told her that sometimes you go abroad for long periods of time to close deals. Which is really getting annoying, by the way. You could at least give me some warning next time."

"Sure thing. Maybe you could send me a voice message telling me that as your very best friend in the whole world it's my duty to not leave town without telling you?"

Well that was oddly specific.

Matt laughed. "Hmm…that's a good point. Rob has *never* left town without telling me first."

"What does Rob have to do with this?" asked Tanner. "This is a conversation about best friend behavior."

Matt laughed again. "I'm not gonna send you that voicemail to help you antagonize Rob. And I have to go. Let's get together next week though. Later." He hung up.

I stared at Tanner. "What was that supposed to prove? Other than that someone named Rob is definitely best friends with Matt."

"No! You take that back. I'm Matt's best friend."

"I don't believe you. Because you're a liar. Matt even just confirmed it. He said you were away on business, just like he'd told Chastity."

"Matt doesn't know anything about DODO. So whenever I have to skip town to avoid DODO agents,

I always tell Matt I'm away on business. He must have just assumed it this time."

"So you admit that you skipped town?" I asked.

"Nope. I should have. I had a feeling that DODO was after me. But I went against my better judgment because I couldn't imagine being away from you." He tried to grab my hand, but I pulled away.

Was he serious right now? "You're lying."

"I'm not."

"Yes you are. You told me that DODO was an ancient all-powerful organization that was worse than a cartel. You really expect me to believe that they caught you and then just…let you go?"

"Yes. I still owe them a great debt, and I couldn't exactly repay that debt while sitting in a prison cell in Morocco."

"Morocco?"

He cleared his throat. "What? I didn't say anything about Morocco. Anyway, where was I? Ah yes, DO-DO. They sent me back here so that I could repay my debt. And they specifically warned me *not* to get distracted."

"Which means what?" But I had a feeling that I already knew.

"It means dating is off the table for me."

Then why are you buying me jewelry and whisking me off on a romantic getaway and trying to hold my hand? I almost asked that, but then I realized I didn't want to hear the answer. He was a crazy person. And I wasn't here to flirt with him. I was here for Rosalie.

"Yeah," I said. "I'm not really interested in guys either." *Shit!* That made me sound like a lesbian. "I mean

I'm not interested in a serious relationship. I'm all about that casual sex now. But not with people I know. Strangers only." *Oh God what I am saying?!* "Anyway, let's focus up. What's the plan for finding info about Rosalie?"

"Well, for starters, you need to change into something more camp-appropriate."

"I assume that's what's in the suitcase?" I asked.

"It is."

I reached back for my suitcase and someone handed me a bikini.

Wait, what?

I screamed at the top of my lungs. And then the person in the back screamed too.

Chapter 17

NIGEL!
Friday

"Nigel!" yelled Tanner. "Stop screaming. You're acting hysterical."

Nigel?

I looked back. Sure enough, Tanner's weird little houseboy had taken the place of Tanner's suitcase. He was dressed in his full butler's uniform, which somehow was the most normal thing I'd seen him wear. But what wasn't normal was that he was sitting there at all. Because I swear he hadn't been a minute ago. "Where the heck did you come from?"

"Hello, Mistress Ash," he said. "Forgive me for startling you. I would have stayed in the trunk, but it was getting cramped."

I glared at him. The trunk was exactly where his weird little ass belonged. "Forgive you? I absolutely do not forgive you. You locked me in a Starbucks bathroom and left me for dead."

"It was for your own safety."

"There was nothing safe about that bathroom," I said. "You should have seen the puddle on the floor. It still haunts me…"

"Nigel, is that true?" asked Tanner.

Nigel shrugged. "How should I know if the puddle haunts her?"

"I didn't mean the puddle. I was asking if you really locked her in a bathroom?"

"I did. So that she'd be safe from DODO."

"Good job."

"What?!" I screamed. "No! Don't encourage that behavior." I hit him with the bikini Nigel had handed me, but there was so little fabric that I didn't even think he felt it. "Wait, do you really expect me to wear this tiny bikini?"

"Pretty sexy, right?" asked Tanner.

"I'm not running around this camp in a thong."

"Well I figured you'd wear some jean shorts with it. Nigel, your assistance, please."

Nigel tossed a pair of jean shorts onto my lap.

Thank God. But wait... I was supposed to be living. And acting wild. And saying yes to everything, even thongs. "Actually, I don't need these shorts. Single Girl Rule #43: Bikinis are the only acceptable girls' trip outfit. Er...summer camp outfit."

Tanner gripped the wheel a little tighter.

Ha! Take that! For the first time ever, Chastity's ridiculous made-up rules had come in handy. Fine, not the first time. They'd helped me make Tanner jealous before. Which ultimately won him over for a day. I wondered if making him jealous again would get me a 48-hour boyfriend this time.

"Aren't you gonna change?" asked Tanner.

"Yeah. I'll change when we get there."

"Wow. Bold move."

"What? Why?"

"You'll see." He started humming like the conversation was over. But it definitely wasn't.

"No. Tell me! Why is it a bold move to wait until we get there to change?" I had started to sweat so much thinking of all the crazy things that might happen to me at this sex camp.

"It's not a big deal, really. Don't worry about it. I'm sure you'll enjoy it."

"Enjoy what?! Tell me right this instant!"

"It's tradition to strip anyone who arrives in business clothes and then throw them in the lake."

"What?!" I was totally freaking out. I didn't want to be stripped naked. Or thrown in a lake. I actually wasn't sure which was more horrifying. I'd read about these brain-eating amoebas that liked to live in lakes…

"Don't worry," said Tanner. "It's all in good fun." He seemed so relaxed. He wasn't even gripping the wheel tightly anymore.

Which was suspicious. And it was even more suspicious that Tanner was wearing a suit. And Nigel… I turned to look back at him. "If that's a tradition, then why is Nigel in his butler's uniform?"

Nigel gave me a *huge* grin. Which made me think that he was very much looking forward to being stripped and thrown into the lake.

"Ugh, never mind. I don't want to know."

"I'm good at changing quickly," said Tanner. "Hopefully you are too."

I wasn't. If I tried to change quickly, I'd end up putting both feet through the same leg hole and falling on my face. Or putting the thong on backwards and ending up with the world's worst front wedgie. Either would be mortifying. But not that bad, really, because it would be Raven Black doing it. *Oh God…* I didn't have my wig! Which meant that I was about to have to parade around in a thong bikini as myself.

I turned back to Nigel. "Is my wig in there?"

"Let me check…" Nigel started digging in my suitcase. And then he handed me what looked like a powdered wig from the 1700s.

"What the hell is that?" I asked.

"Your wig, Mistress."

"Unless we're going to some weird colonial history camp, then that is not my wig."

"Hmm…" said Nigel. "Are you certain?"

"My wig is black. And not curled. Or powdered."

"Try this," said Tanner. He pulled a silver bracelet out of his pocket and handed it to me.

"Okay, but I don't know how that's going to help."

"Just try it on. You need it anyway now that you're a novus member. Initiates just wear black, novus members wear silver. And veritas members wear gold."

I looked at his wrist. He was just wearing a black watch. "And what are you?"

"What do you think I am?"

"I assume you're veritas. Or is there something higher? I know you have some fancy badge that lets you order other members around, right?" He'd used it months ago at Club Onyx to make Angel and Diablo stop flirting with me.

"You should really put that bracelet on and change. We're getting pretty close."

Gah! I hated when he ignored my questions. But if we were close, then he was right. I needed to change. And fix my makeup. I slid the bracelet on and then opened up the mirror and…

"How…?" I gasped. Somehow, my hair was jet black.

"Pretty cool, huh?" asked Tanner. "It's some new tech I've been working on for the CIA."

"The CIA?" I slid the bracelet off and my hair changed back to red. And then I slid it back on and my hair turned black again. "Whoa."

Tanner smiled. "Now you don't have to worry about your wig flying off."

"Thank God. That was one of my biggest fears. You don't happen to have one that magically changes my clothes?"

"Magic?" asked Tanner. "Who said anything about magic? That bracelet is 100% technology. It's filled with microchips and things."

"It was just a figure of speech. But now I'm kind of suspicious about it actually being magic." Seriously, why was he acting so weird about it?

Tanner laughed. "Fine, you caught me. It's a magic hair-changing bracelet."

I hit his arm. "Oh, right. Just like your flaming genie penis?"

Nigel gasped. "You told her!?"

I shook my head. "You two are ridiculous. I know you just said you had a flaming penis because I accidentally set Matt's penis on fire."

Tanner laughed.

"It's not funny! It was one of the worst moments of my life."

"Worse than it was for Matt?"

I didn't want to think about that. "But he said he was okay. He is, right? I mean, he must be. He has a baby."

"Don't tell me you're stalking him too?"

"I'm not stalking Matt or you or anyone else. It's just important to follow through with these things. You wouldn't understand because your dick has never been set on fire so you don't need to be checked up on." *What am I even saying right now?* A blue sign in the distance caught my eye. "Hey, there's a gas station coming up! Let's pull over so we can all change and avoid being tossed into the brain-eating-amoeba-filled lake."

"Great idea," said Tanner. "I just hope the floor in the bathroom there isn't too slippery."

"Slippery? Oh God. Why would the floor be slippery?" I flashed back to my time in the Starbucks bathroom. And *the puddle.*

"I can think of a lot of reasons. Someone might have missed the toilet, or maybe changed some diapers on the floor…"

I dry heaved. "Fine. Fine! I'll change in here. Just don't look."

"I would never."

"Just like on our first date when I caught you looking?"

"If I recall correctly, I caught *you* looking."

"You're impossible. Now, don't look." I pushed my hair aside and started to unbutton my blouse. But my fingers paused when I felt eyes on me. Tanner was focusing on the road. Which meant… I turned around to see Nigel staring right at me. "Hey, you don't look either."

"Would you rather I help?" He reached toward my buttons. And therefore my boobs.

I swatted his perverted little hand away. "No! I don't need your help. Now turn around."

Nigel looked out the window. For literally one second. And then he turned back and stared at me. He seemed surprised that I hadn't already changed. "Are you sure you don't need my assistance, Mistress Ash? It seems like you're having a bit of trouble."

No. I turned back to Tanner. "Seriously – do you have a bracelet that can change my clothes?"

"I do," said Tanner. "Well, kind of. It's a ring." He pulled a ring out of his pocket and slid it onto his finger. And right before my eyes, his clothes changed from a suit to a fitted T-shirt and some swim trunks that cut off just above his knees.

I blinked. *How the hell did that just happen?!* His tech was seriously impressive. I couldn't even imagine what must have gone into designing something like that.

"Wow," I said. "That's amazing. Do you have one for me?"

"I do." He tossed me a ring.

I was about to put it on, but he reached out to stop me.

"Before you use it, I should probably warn you that it's still just a prototype. Sometimes it…glitches."

"Glitches? What does that mean?"

"Well…it is pretty good at making your current clothes disappear. But the part that replaces them doesn't always work."

"Really?" *Damn it! Why hadn't it glitched when he used it on himself?* It would have been so great if he had accidentally lost all his clothes. Not because I wanted to see him naked or anything. *Nope. Definitely not.* Because I wasn't interested in him. I just thought it would be funny if he messed up.

"Yeah. But it only glitches like 70% of the time. So the odds are…well, I guess they're not really in your favor. You willing to risk it?" His eyes went to my breasts. And I started to think that it wasn't really a glitch at all. That little pervert had just given me a ring that would leave me ass naked!

And I wasn't going to give him the satisfaction.

"I think I'll just change the old-fashioned way."

He turned off onto a gravel road. "Okay, but you better hurry. You only have about 90 seconds before we arrive at the Emerald Oasis. And unfortunately for you, Elon didn't bother to send me the model with tinted windows."

Chapter 18

HUGGING A NAKED WOMAN
Friday

We pulled up to the Emerald Oasis just as I buttoned my jean shorts. *Phew.* That had been close.

"All done?" asked Tanner, as if he hadn't been stealing glances at me the entire time I was changing.

"Yup." I would have called him out for peeking, but I was too distracted by the massive castle that we'd just pulled up to. Or maybe *palace* was a better word to describe it? Either way, it was *not* what I had pictured. I'd assumed the clubhouse would be a rustic little cabin type deal, which was kind of dumb given how much money the Society clearly had to throw around.

Tanner hopped out of the car and started to walk over to open my door, but someone else beat him to it.

"Welcome to the Emerald Oasis," said a familiar voice. I looked up and saw Cole the liftman holding the door open for me. Instead of his usual uniform, he was now wearing swim trunks and a bright blue T-shirt with *Emerald Oasis* written across the chest.

"What are you doing here?" I asked. He wasn't supposed to be here! Chastity hadn't had time to devise a proper prank to get him back for embarrassing me at Club Onyx.

He laughed. "Now what kind of way is that to greet your favorite Society member? We missed you this week at Club Onyx. I was especially surprised not to see you when we hosted an elementary school science fair Wednesday night. I thought for sure you'd show up nude."

I tried to turn away so he couldn't see me blush, but it was too late. My damned cheeks always betrayed me! And that made me even more embarrassed.

"Everything okay?" asked Tanner. "Is this camp counselor bothering you?"

"He was just offering to carry my bags," I said.

Cole raised an eyebrow at me but didn't fight back. I had a feeling he'd get me back for that comment later. Once our bags were out of the back seat, Cole pulled out a clipboard. "So will you two be staying as a couple?"

Uhh... "Nope," I said. Tanner had made it very clear that we weren't dating.

And yet...Tanner looked disappointed by my answer.

"Great," said Cole. He turned to Tanner. "Someone will be with you shortly. Raven, please come with me." Cole grabbed my suitcase and tossed it onto a golf cart. Then he patted the passenger seat to get me to join him.

I hopped in and we sped off down the gravel road. It took every ounce of restraint I had not to look back to see Tanner's reaction. Not that I cared what he thought. I pulled out my phone and texted Chastity to distract myself.

Ash: We made it to the camp. Tanner didn't cut me into little bits. But...Cole is here!

Chastity: Cole?! What is he doing there?

Ash: He's one of the camp counselors or some-thing.

Chastity: We still need to prank him.

Ash: I know! Did you ever pull any good pranks at summer camp?

Chastity: Uh…one time I showered with a bunch of guys. Does that count?

Ash: No.

Chastity: Hmm…okay. Well, I'll try to think of something. Just don't let him trick you into getting naked and everything should be fine. Or do. ;)

I glanced at Cole out of the corner of my eye. Chastity didn't need to warn me that he might try to get me naked. My radar had been on high alert since the second I saw Cole's stupid handsome face. There was no way he was going to trick me again.

"Here we are," said Cole as we pulled to a stop in front of a super cool looking cabin with a giant window overlooking the lake.

Damn this is nice. So much for this being like my 5th-grade summer camp. Those cabins had looked like they were straight out of the 1700s. Meanwhile, this cabin could have been on the cover of *Architectural Digest*.

Cole grabbed my suitcase out of the golf cart and took it into the cabin. As I walked in, I nearly tripped over a suitcase overflowing with bikinis and makeup and beauty products. And another suitcase. And anoth-er. It reminded me of when I'd visited my extremely messy older sister in college one time. She'd had so much stuff everywhere that we literally could not open the door to her dorm.

I hadn't realized I'd be rooming with other people when I turned down the couples cabin. *Speaking of which...how did the couples cabins work?* Were the couples all together in one big room...orgy style? I swallowed down the lump in my throat. I'd made the right call saying Tanner and I weren't together.

Especially because we clearly weren't together. And we never would be. Because DODO said he couldn't be distracted and apparently dating me was a distraction. Stupid DODO. Or stupid Tanner, because I was really starting to think DODO didn't exist at all.

"You'll be rooming with..." Cole looked down at his clipboard. "Vanessa, Soraya, Alessandra, Isadora, and Giovanna."

"Are you sure that's all?" I asked. "Because I count at least 18 suitcases."

Cole laughed. "Based on what I've seen in some of the other cabins, you actually got lucky. Well...maybe. I guess that depends on if you remembered to bring earplugs. Rumor has it that Soraya had a few ribs removed and now she snores like a 90-year-old man."

Was rib removal still a thing people did? "Are those two things even related?"

Cole shrugged. "I guess you'll find out."

"Aren't any other rooms available?"

"Don't think so. In fact, you're lucky this one was. The Emerald Oasis fills up fast on Friday afternoons. But let me make a call."

He dropped my suitcase and stepped out of the cabin. I took a minute to look around. All of the top bunks had been taken, which left one lower bunk for me. *Probably under Soraya.* And then I realized that I really needed to pee after the long car ride. I hopped over a few suitcases to the bathroom. There were a bunch of sinks, a few toilet stalls, and one giant group shower occupied by two beautiful models soaping each other up. *Oh no, it's an orgy here too.*

"Hey," said the one getting soaped. "You our sixth?"

"Uh…yeah. I'm Raven."

"Isadora," she replied.

"And I'm Giovanna," said the other. I was pretty sure she'd been one of the other girls at the sex auction a few months ago.

I stuck my hand out for them to shake. Which was awkward because she was naked and soapy. What the hell was I doing?

"I'm a hugger," said Isadora. Before I could process that information, she bounced over and threw her arms around me. I died a little inside as her soaking-wet body pressed against me.

Well…at least I can cross "Hugging a naked woman" off my bucket list. Not that it was on there in the first place. But if it had been, I'd done it. I patted her awkwardly on the back and prayed she'd let go of me.

"Wanna join us?" asked Giovanna. "We were just getting ready to head over to the mess hall for dinner."

"Uh…I'm pretty clean already. I'll just wait for you guys out there."

They nodded and went back to awkwardly soaping each other. I turned and got the heck out of there, completely forgetting about my need to use the restroom.

Cole was waiting for me by the bunks.

"Please tell me you found me a better room," I said.

"Why are you so soapy?" he asked. "Did you just take a shower with your clothes on?"

"I don't want to talk about it."

"Well, I do have some good news. There was a last-minute cancellation for one of the princess suites. You interested?"

"Is this a trick?"

"You don't trust me?" He acted like he was hurt, but his acting was way over the top.

"I do not. The last time I trusted you I ended up naked in front of a bunch of high school kids."

"That wasn't my fault. You took your dress off all on your own."

"And you didn't stop me!"

He shrugged like it was no big deal. "Do you want the princess suite or not?"

"I need more information."

"The princess suite is just what it sounds like...a suite fit for a princess."

"But I have to share it with twelve other girls who like giving naked soapy hugs?"

Cole's eyes lit up. "Is that what's going on in there?" He craned his neck to try to look into the bathroom.

I blocked his view. "Hey, focus, buddy. You were telling me about the princess suite."

"Right. No, you don't have to share it with anyone. You get it all to yourself."

I squinted at him, trying to see through his lies. "What's the catch?"

"No catch."

"Then why is it available?"

"I think a lot of the girls like sharing cabins. It's part of the experience."

I thought back to what I'd just witnessed in the shower. *Okay, that checks out.* These girls were crazy, though. Having a room all to myself was a dream come true. Although…staying in a cabin with lots of girls might be better for detective work. One of these girls might have known Rosalie.

Nope. I couldn't deal with the group showers and all these suitcases. And the snoring. Nope, nope, nope. But I still wasn't *quite* ready to say yes to Cole. I still had more questions. "So I'm not going to wake up handcuffed to the bed surrounded by naked men?"

"I mean…I could probably arrange for that to happen. Is that what you want?"

"No!"

"Then I guess it won't happen."

"Is it like a three-hour hike from the princess suite to the rest of the camp? Is there a pet crocodile that the occupant of the princess suite must care for? Is the suite filled with nanny cams…like a Big Brother situation?"

"No, no, and no. It's just a normal room."

"Alright. But if you're lying, I *promise* you'll regret it."

Chapter 19

THE PRINCESS SUITE
Friday

"Here it is," said Cole.

"This is the princess suite?" I looked up at the four-story-tall stone tower in front of us. "So the catch is that I have to man the ballista when the goblins come attack?"

Cole laughed. "Princesses can live in towers. Haven't you ever heard of Rapunzel?"

"Oh, great. So I'm going to be stuck up there for the rest of my life? Well if you think I'm going to let you climb my hair, you're crazy." *Especially since I'm wearing a wig. Kind of...* I wasn't sure how exactly Tanner's bracelet worked, but I doubted my black hair would be strong enough for Cole to climb. And anyway, it wasn't nearly long enough.

Cole ignored me and pressed a few buttons on a keypad next to a heavy wooden door. Instead of swinging open, the door slid back into the wall to reveal a fancy elevator.

"I don't remember Rapunzel having an elevator," I said.

"You'd rather take the stairs?"

Up four stories? No way. I got on the elevator and up we went.

My jaw dropped when the doors opened to the princess suite. It was like a cross between a casino penthouse and something out of a fairytale. A Disney fairytale. Not the real ones where babies get eaten by evil monsters. Or whatever the Rapunzel equivalent was of Chastity's version of Hansel and Gretel. If I was living in that deranged fairy tale world, then I was in serious trouble.

"What do you think?" asked Cole.

"This is freaking amazing!" I ran over and collapsed back on the gigantic round bed. It felt like I was lying on a cloud. For some reason, my mind went immediately to the Sausage King. Did his family have a castle like this back in Germany? I'd have to go back to his restaurant soon...

"See? And to think that you didn't trust me..." Cole made a *tsk tsk* noise and shook his head back and forth.

"I still don't trust you." I stared at him. He still had that stupid cocky smile, but I was starting to find it kind of endearing. Fine...*a lot* endearing. But it wasn't my fault. Tattoos did something to me. I shook the thought away. I was in love with Tanner. *What?! No.* I shook that thought away too. "But maybe you're not as awful as I originally thought."

"I'll take that. Well, enjoy the princess suite. I'm gonna go grab some food before the dining hall closes." He started to walk out.

"Wait up," I said. "I'm starving."

I pulled out my phone and texted Chastity during the golf cart ride to the dining hall.

Ash: So I think I might be going to dinner with Cole.

Chastity: I love that for you. But we still need to prank him.

Ash: He might not be as bad as we thought.

Chastity: Does that mean you saw his dick? Was it magnificent? Tell me everything!

Ash: He saved me from living with a bunch of naked soapy shower lesbians. And you should see the room he got me…

Chastity: Naked soapy shower lesbians? Wow, you've got some competition. You're definitely gonna have to suck his cock if you want his help finding Rosalie.

Right. I'm here to find Rosalie. How had Cole distracted me so easily? I glanced over at him and my eyes gravitated to his muscly tattooed arms. *Oh yeah, that's how.* But no more! From here on out I was going to be in full detective mode.

I slid my phone back into my purse. "So how long have you been a part of the Society?"

"A few years."

"A few as in…three?"

"Something like that. You?"

"A few months." *But that's not important!* I needed to know if he was in the Society with Rosalie before she disappeared.

"I'm surprised you haven't been to the Emerald Oasis yet then," he said. "Where were you all summer?"

"Working." It didn't seem necessary to tell him that the app had disappeared from my phone all summer.

Cole turned onto another gravel path. "Well, as your camp counselor, it's my official responsibility to ensure you have the best experience possible."

And help me find Rosalie. I glanced down at his crotch. Was I really gonna have to blow him in order to get his help? Or could I just ask the right questions?

"What's that over there?" I asked, pointing at a group of cabins.

"Those are the couples cabins."

I bit the inside of my lip. I could have been there with Tanner. But Tanner was the worst, so I'd definitely made the right choice. But like…where was he now? Was he in a cabin like they'd tried to put me in, only his was full of soapy gay men? Or did he have a prince suite? Probably a prince suite. God, did he have another woman there with him?

I felt Cole staring at me. I needed to stop focusing on these stupid distracting men. I pointed to a clearing across the path. A bunch of guys in Emerald Oasis t-shirts were rearranging picnic tables and piling firewood next to a giant unlit fire pit. "And that?" *Of course I just pointed to more distracting men.*

"That's where we'll have the post-games spit roast tomorrow night."

That thing where they roast a pig over an open fire? "Oh my gosh! I've always wanted to have a spit roast."

Cole looked over at me with a raised eyebrow. "You have?"

"Yeah! I never knew it was a thing until one of my ex-husband's friends suggested we have one for our 1st wedding anniversary. But of course my stupid ex wouldn't let us do it. Said it was too dangerous."

"Well that was extremely lame of him."

"I know! He was the freaking worst."

"It sounds like it." Cole pulled to a stop outside the clubhouse and opened the heavy wooden doors for me.

Since when was he such a gentleman? I had really underestimated him.

The dining hall was mostly empty, but there were still a few stragglers. More importantly, the buffet was still well stocked with all sorts of good stuff. Burgers, pasta, even some waffles. Breakfast for dinner? Yas queen! Sign me up for summer camp.

We each made a plate and then sat down at an empty table.

As much as I wanted to go back to the topic of how much Joe sucked, it was more important for me to collect more intel. And devour an inappropriate amount of waffles.

"So you were saying you've been a part of the Society for a while," I said as I smothered my waffles in syrup. "How'd you get started?"

"A few years ago I was invited to come be a counselor here. The members must have liked me, because after that first weekend they asked if I wanted to work at Club Onyx too."

"So you're not a member?"

"I wasn't at first. But for two years of loyal service, they rewarded me with membership into the Society. How'd you get in?"

"Ryder invited me after my divorce," I said. I was so proud of myself for remembering to use Tanner's Society name.

Cole nodded and took a bite of his burger. "Ah, classic Ryder."

"What do you mean?"

"He's by far the Society's most active recruiter. It seems like he has a different girl on his arm every night at Club Onyx."

"What?" I asked. From the Onyxies I knew that Tanner recruited tons of members. But had he been recruiting members all summer? *That little asshole!* He was hiding out in the city instead of in jail in…Morocco? Is that what he'd said? I was going to kill him.

"You didn't know?"

I was going to get so much more information, but then Tanner sat down next to me with a tray of food. "Didn't know what?" he asked.

"Nothing," I said. I couldn't believe that he'd really just disappeared from me this summer so he could go bang a bunch of new members.

"How's your room?" asked Tanner as if everything was totally normal.

"Amazing. I'm so glad I passed on the couples cabin." The princess suite really was everything. I couldn't wait to get back and send Chastity some pictures of it. She was gonna be so jealous.

"She wasn't happy with the first cabin we had for her," said Cole. "But I pulled a few strings to get her an upgrade."

"Thanks for looking out for her," said Tanner.

Looking out for me? What did Tanner care about someone looking out for me? Didn't he have some newbie to go bang or something?

"It's my pleasure. I told her I'd do anything I could to make her weekend as enjoyable as possible."

Tanner narrowed his eyes at Cole and slid a little closer to me. "It sounds like you've already gone above and beyond."

Cole popped a French fry into his mouth and stared back at Tanner. "Just doing my job. Speaking of which…is everything good with your cabin?"

"It is," said Tanner.

"You're on the red team, right?" asked Cole.

Tanner nodded.

"I guess that makes us enemies."

"Red team? Enemies?" I asked. I was so confused. Both about the teams and about why Tanner was acting all protective. He'd made it abundantly clear he didn't want to be with me. If the three months of ghosting wasn't proof enough, him literally telling me he couldn't date me because of DODO was.

"For the games tomorrow," said Cole. "Everyone splits into two teams - red and blue - and then we battle it out over 23 events. At the end of the day, we crown a winner."

"Which team am I on?"

"You're on red with Ryder. Unfortunately, I'm blue…which means you guys are going to be on the losing team."

"Oh yeah?" I asked.

"Yup. Not to brag, but my team has won 9 weeks in a row. And there's no way I'm going to miss out on breaking the record with a 10th."

Cocky bastard. "Sorry to burst your bubble, but Ryder and I are going to crush you."

"Wanna bet?" asked Cole.

"Sure," I said through a mouthful of waffles. "What are we betting?"

He didn't even have to think about it. "When blue wins, you go out with me tomorrow night."

Fat chance. I swallowed down the lump of sugary goodness. "And if Ryder and I win?"

Cole gave me his cockiest grin. "Then I'll let you go out with me tomorrow night."

I laughed. "Nice try. How about this. If Ryder and I win, then you have to get naked at a future time of my choosing. No questions asked." It wasn't the perfect prank, but it would be good enough payback for all the times he'd tricked me. And Tanner choking on a French fry as I said it was a nice little bonus.

"What?" asked Tanner.

I had no idea what his angle was. Despite what he'd said in the car about dating being off the table, he sure was acting like a jealous boyfriend whenever Cole was around.

Because he was a crazy person.

That was the only logical explanation, right? I would have just said he was weird. But I was weird. And I didn't want Tanner to make being weird a bad thing. I used to love that he was weird like me... He was definitely just insane.

Either way, I couldn't worry about his feelings. I was here for one reason, and one reason only: to find Rosalie. And maybe to flirt with Cole and make Tanner jealous...

"Deal," said Cole. He stuck out his hand and we shook on it.

"Hope you're ready to get naked," I said.

Cole wasn't fazed by my threat. "You don't even know what the events are."

"It doesn't matter. With Ryder on my team, there's no way I'm going to lose." I squeezed his massive bicep to drive the point home. If Tanner was going to send me mixed signals, then I could do the same. Besides, I really liked touching him.

"She's right," said Tanner. "I hope you enjoyed your winning streak while it lasted, because it ends tomorrow."

"We shall see." Cole popped one more fry into his mouth. "May the best team win. See you tomorrow, Raven," he said with a wink. And then he got up and walked out of the dining hall.

I turned to Tanner. "This is going to be so great. I can't wait for his stupid cocky grin to disappear when you whoop his ass tomorrow."

"Me either," said Tanner. "That guy is so annoying. Did he at least have some information about Rosalie?"

"He said he's been a counselor here for *about* three years," I said. "It's possible he was here when that picture was taken, which means he might have known her."

"I doubt it."

"Why?"

"It just seems unlikely. Let's talk to some other people instead."

"Wait, are you jealous of Cole?" I asked.

"No. Why would I be jealous?"

"Because he was hitting on me."

Tanner shrugged like it was no big deal. "He can hit on you all he wants. Clearly you were just flirting with him to try to get info about Rosalie. I know you'd never actually fall for a peasant like Cole."

A peasant? I laughed. But I wasn't so sure Tanner was right about my intentions. I mean…I was kind of already falling for Cole. Or at the very least I was flirting back for real. As far as I was concerned, the bet we'd made was a win/win. Either he'd take me out on a date, or I'd get to see him naked.

"So how were you planning to figure out if he knew Rosalie?" Tanner asked.

"I guess I'll just show him a picture of her."

"But what if he was involved in her disappearance?"

"Hmm…I hadn't thought of that." The thought that Rosalie's killer could be anyone at this camp sent chills down my spine. "How can we find any clues if we can't ask people about her?"

Tanner gestured to the wall of the mess hall. It was covered in more art than the wall of a TGIF. But instead of random album covers and canoes, these were pictures from the camp. *Jackpot!*

I jammed the rest of my waffles in my mouth and ran over to the wall. With so many photos, she had to be in at least one of them.

But…she wasn't.

We spent hours looking, but I didn't see a single girl that could possibly be her.

"Are you sure you looked at all of those?" I asked, gesturing to the half of the wall that Tanner had been responsible for searching.

Tanner nodded.

"Even the people in the background?"

"Yup. I checked them all twice. She's not in any of them." He pulled a photo off the wall and checked the back. It was from two months ago. We checked a few more, and they had all been taken within the last year.

"Well that explains it," I said. "Think they have an archive of old photos?"

"Maybe."

"Don't you like…have access to their databases and stuff? Shouldn't you know?" I was pretty sure he'd said that on the way here, but his face had been very distracting…

"No. And even if I did, what kind of horrible micromanager do you think I am?"

Oh God. The word micromanager reminded me of Mr. Frost and his promise to come up with something better than the binder. Just thinking about it reminded me how thoroughly exhausted I was. If I was going to get any solid detective work done, it would only happen after I got some rest.

"Let's call it a night," I said. "I'm sure something will turn up tomorrow. And I want to make sure we're well rested so we can kick Cole's ass."

Chapter 20
SOCIETY WARS
Saturday

"Rise and shine!" said a sing-songy voice.

I opened my eyes just in time to see a girl yank open the curtains. The morning sun hit me right in the eyes.

I put my hands up to block it. "What the hell? Who are you?!"

She turned around. "It's me. Frankie."

I squinted to make sure it was really Frankie and not some serial killer. "What are you doing here?"

"I'm your handmaid for the day, milady." She gave an exaggerated curtsey.

"Handmaid?" Everyone in the Society had such weird jobs. First Cole was a liftman, then a card shark, and now he was a camp counselor. And Frankie had gone from a real estate agent to Ocelot's assistant to now being my handmaid. Whatever the hell that meant.

"Yeah. You're the princess of the red team. Of course you have a handmaid." She said it as if it made all the sense in the world.

"Right…"

Frankie plopped a breakfast platter in front of me. "Eat up."

Maybe having a handmaid isn't so bad after all. I scarfed down the eggs and bacon while Frankie heated up a straightening iron and organized her makeup bag.

"So what are my duties as princess?" I asked. I had a feeling that I was about to find out why Cole had been able to get me into the princess suite on such late notice.

"Just look hot and do whatever you can to motive your team."

Oh no. "By like…having sex with them?"

Frankie shrugged. "You can certainly do that if you want. But I'd probably advise against it. One girl tried that last month and her team lost horribly. All the guys were exhausted after their pre-game gangbang."

I gulped. "But I don't *have to* do that, do I?"

"Nope."

"And I don't have to do anything else weird either?"

Frankie shook her head.

Thank God. I'd eaten too many eggs to participate in an orgy. Just the thought made my stomach churn. Which reminded me of incident #4. And Dr. Lyons face when I'd regurgitated my dinner all over him. *Never again.* Why had I just eaten so much?

"Here, put this on and we can start your makeup." She tossed me a lacy red robe and pulled out a chair by the vanity.

While she did my hair and makeup, I couldn't help but be taken back to the good old days when Rosalie and I would stay up late doing each other's hair. Or really…Rosalie would stay up late doing my hair. She could always do the coolest braids.

And if I was a good enough detective this weekend, maybe I could experience that again. What better place to start than by interrogating Frankie? Afterall…her real estate roleplay seemed to be a part of the initiation process for female members. With any luck, she would have gone through that same song and dance with Rosalie.

"How long have you been doing this?" I asked.

"Oh geez…pretty much as long as I can remember."

"Huh? You've been in the Society as long as you can remember?"

She laughed. "Oh, I thought you meant makeup. I've only been in the Society for two years. Or I guess two and a half now. It's crazy how time flies."

Damn. So she didn't know Rosalie. But it did at least give me some information. It meant that Frankie wasn't the killer. Or kidnapper. Or whatever the crime had been. So maybe she could help.

"It seems like no one has been a member for much longer than a year or two," I said.

Frankie nodded. "Yeah, there are a few long-time members like Ryder, but most find love and settle down."

For real? Tanner always told me that the Society was about finding love, but I never really believed him. That wasn't what was important here, though. "Do you know any other long-timers?"

"Hmm…do you know Sebastian?"

I shook my head.

"What about Callum?"

"Nope."

That continued for a while. She'd say a name, and then I'd shake my head and try desperately to commit the name to memory. Eventually it seemed like she had exhausted her list, but then she snapped her fingers.

"I can't believe I forgot! Angel and Diablo are long-timers. Surely you haven't forgotten them," she said with a saucy wiggle of her eyebrows.

"I certainly have not." I would never forget the image of the two brothers standing there completely naked in that bathroom. Or the way they'd flirted with me in the green room. Or how I'd touched both their cocks while trying to make Tanner jealous. And I'd dreamed of so much more. Usually I'd picture what would have happened if I'd let them double-team me in the shower when we first met. I pressed my legs together. "Do you know how long they've been members?"

Frankie pushed her mouth to one side. "Five years? Six Years?"

Six years! That meant they might have known Rosalie. *Finally, a clue!*

Frankie got back to work on my hair and makeup. Thirty minutes later, I looked hot as hell.

Frankie had given me eye makeup straight out of an episode of Euphoria. And she'd pulled my black hair into a high ponytail. The best part was the outfit, though. My red t-shirt had the same Emerald Oasis logo that had been on Cole's shirt, but it was super tight and tied on the side to leave my midriff exposed. And my high-waisted booty shorts made my waist look impossibly small and my butt impossibly big. Usually I would have been horrified to have a little butt cheek hanging out the bottom, but in this case, it worked. Besides, what happened at summer camp stayed at summer camp. And it was certainly better than the minuscule bikini Tanner had packed for me. *I wonder what he's up to this morning…*

I threw on a pair of sneakers and we were ready to roll.

I'd been worried that I would be cold in this outfit, but those fears dissipated the second I stepped off the elevator. It was unseasonably warm for late September - the perfect day for a good old-fashioned summer camp competition.

Both teams were waiting by the lake. Cole was making a show of stretching his very muscular quads while the red team - my team - was doing a group stretch. *Damn, they take this seriously.* But I didn't see Tanner anywhere.

What really got my attention, though, was the guy standing on a raised platform between the two teams. I'd never seen a referee with such voluminous hair. Or with such a well-tailored uniform.

I immediately started sweating when I saw who it was.

Ocelot.

He was in charge of Club Onyx or something. I think they called him the imperator, whatever that meant.

More importantly, he was a deranged pervert.

The last time I'd seen him, he'd tried to get me to choose a guy to fuck on stage in front of like a thousand people. And now he was standing on another stage…

Oh God, oh God, oh God.

"Please tell me Ocelot isn't about to make me fuck someone on that stage," I said to Frankie.

"Nope. Or at least, I don't think that's one of today's events."

"What?!"

"I'm like 99% sure Ocelot won't start with something crazy. He's all about the drama, so he'll want the competition to build to a crescendo. Anyway, it's time for you to join him on stage for the opening ceremonies." She pushed me towards the stage.

That wasn't super reassuring.

But I was in sneakers and Ocelot was in black and white striped loafers, so if things went south, I could always make a run for it.

I went up on stage and…

"Chastity?!"

She smiled at me from across the stage. I suddenly felt less confident about my hotness, because she was absolutely *slaying* the same outfit as me. But she was dressed all in blue. And she'd torn her top up so that one shoulder was out. And the bottom of her breasts. I didn't know how she did it, but she made underboob look classy as hell.

She ran over and honked my boobs. "You look so freaking hot. #LegsForDays. Tanner and Cole must be losing their minds."

Oh God. I tried to pretend like the entire camp hadn't just seen her honk my boobs. That Single Girl Rule really needed to be amended to make complimentary boob honks a private activity.

"What are you doing here?" I asked. "I thought you had your sky box thing."

"Psssh, a sky box sounds great. But literally getting to be a princess for a weekend? I was made for this."

"Campers!" yelled Ocelot into his megaphone. "Welcome to this summer's final edition of Society Wars. Today we have the red team, led by Princess Raven…"

The red team all cheered wildly for me. I had been so distracted by Chastity appearing that I hadn't really processed the fact that I was standing in front of at least a hundred people. My extreme stage fright immediately kicked in.

Why are there so many people on each team?!

"And the blue team, led by Princess Chastity!"

Instead of standing there like a deer in the headlights, Chastity waved and jumped up and down like a high school cheerleader. Her enthusiasm whipped the blue team into a frenzy. Or maybe they were just cheering because her boobs were bouncing so much. Either way, the guys on her team loved it. Including Cole.

Stupid boy.

"The rules are simple," continued Ocelot. "Throughout the day, both teams will compete in 23 events. The winning team for each event will earn one point, except for the finale, which is worth five. Whichever team has the most points at the end will be declared champions of Society Wars. Any questions, Princesses?"

Chastity shook her head. I had a million questions, but my stage fright forced me to keep my mouth shut.

"Okay. Shake hands, and then we'll begin."

"Good luck!" said Chastity. She pulled me into a hug and lowered her voice. "You're gonna need it after you ditched me last night. Single Girl Rule #2: Girls' night is every Friday. No exceptions."

"I had to," I whispered back. "To find Rosalie."

"No exceptions!"

"But…"

She laughed. "I'm just messing with you. You said that Cole is gonna take you on a date if you lose, right?"

"Yes."

"Then you're in luck. Because I think it might be impossible for me to lose at anything. #Blessed."

Oh no. Usually I loved that Chastity was amazing at everything because I was almost always on her team. But today, she was the enemy.

Luckily for me, the only thing she loved more than winning was the idea of a single girl getting to see, play with, or otherwise interact with a huge cock.

"It's a shame you're gonna beat me. Because if I win, Cole promised that he'd get naked at a time and place of my choosing."

"Hmm…" Chastity scrunched her mouth to the side. She was definitely contemplating throwing the competition for me. "I do love the idea of that. But I like the idea more of him taking you on a date and ravishing your body." She winked at me and looked over at Ocelot.

He put the megaphone to his mouth. "Let the games begin!"

The crowd cheered as we both hopped off the platform. I ran over to where Tanner had suddenly appeared. I was so happy to see him. I mean…mildly happy. Like just a normal amount of happiness you'd have when you see an acquaintance. And the amused look on his face made me uncomfortable.

"Why do you look so happy? Did I do something weird?"

"I'm just surprised you volunteered to be a princess. Bold move."

"Well Cole offered to upgrade me to the princess suite so I wouldn't have to room with the naked soapy shower lesbians."

"I bet he did."

"What does that mean? And why is being a princess a bold move? And why didn't you say any of this last night when I told you that Cole put me in the princess suite?"

"I just thought he put you in a different dorm. Not the princess suite."

"And is it bad that I'm in the princess suite? Oh God…what's going to happen to me?"

"Nothing. Because we're gonna win."

"But what if we lose?"

"Then that's a different story. Have you ever…" He didn't get to finish the thought because a bunch of our teammates had just run over. Among them were the shower lesbians themselves, Isadora and Giovanna. Thankfully they were clothed, but just barely. Apparently they thought red push-up bikinis were the proper attire for this competition. Although…maybe it was. Because they were definitely going to distract the boys on the other team.

"Hey!" they said in unison.

"Hi again," I said and honked one of each of their boobs. *Oh God why?* Being up on stage and then seeing

Chastity and having her honk my boobs had put me in a weird headspace.

"Ready to kick the blue team's ass?" asked one of them.

"Yup," I said.

"Me too," said Diablo.

"Ah!" I said. I'd screamed from terror. But I tried to play it off like I was excited. Maybe he wouldn't even remember me...

"Hey, Raven," he said.

So much for that. "Diablo!" I said way too enthusiastically. I punched his arm. *Stop touching him.* "You're just the person I was hoping to see." *Not really.* But also kind of...because I couldn't wait to ask him about Rosalie.

"I get that a lot." He reached out and honked my tits.

I slapped his hand away. "What are you doing?!"

"He didn't mean to offend," said Angel. "He was just doing our official team greeting." Angel honked my boobs too.

"Hey! No! That is not our official team greeting."

"You sure?" asked Angel. He pointed to the rest of our team. All the guys had started honking the girls' boobs. Except Tanner. He was being very well behaved. But only because he'd probably already slept with all these girls. I still couldn't believe what Cole had said about Tanner being at Club Onyx with random girls all summer. *Asshole.*

"Huh," I said. "I guess it is our official team greeting." I reached out and grabbed Diablo's rock-hard pecs.

He smiled down at me. "So what's the plan?" asked Diablo. "Want me to distract the girls on the blue team with a little dancing?" He thrust his hips and his athletic shorts did absolutely nothing to hide his swinging bulge.

And of course I stared right at it. And gulped.

"Isn't it more important to distract the guys?" I asked.

"Good point. In that case, how about I tear those little shorts off of you and fuck you right there in the grass? After seeing that, all the guys on the blue team will be too horny to perform."

Angel stepped in front of him. "What he meant to say is that we're excited to be on your team and we're gonna give it 110%."

"Thanks," I said. I'd forgotten how sweet Angel was. And how devilish Diablo was. But I remembered Frankie telling me they were equally devilish in the sheets. I swallowed hard and my throat made a weird squeaking noise.

Angel smiled down at me. "We really do need a plan, though. Are we gonna slow play it or go all out? Or should we execute Operate Blue Balls for Blue? It's your call, Princess."

"I don't know what any of that means."

"Blue always lets Cole take the lead on every event. And he always kicks our asses. Earlier this summer me and Diablo went against him right from the start. But that didn't work. So last week we tried a different tactic and put scrubs against him at first and saved our energy for later. But that backfired horribly and we lost the first 14 events."

"And what's Operation Blue Balls for Blue?" I asked.

"Our last resort. If we can't beat Cole, we take him out of the competition."

My eyes got big. "You want to break his kneecaps?"

Diablo laughed. "If you want me to."

"But that's not what we're going to do," said Angel. "We were actually thinking that one of our girls could seduce him. And once they get him alone, they can just tease him and then leave him tied up in the woods with a horrible case of blue balls. That way even if he gets free, he'll be in too much pain to compete."

"Oh!" yelled Isadora. "I'll do it!"

Jealousy shot through me. I hated the idea of her sneaking off with Cole. And it would be a clear violation of Single Girl Rule #24: No blue balls allowed. Finish what you start.

I shook my head. Chastity had officially poisoned my brain. And today, she was the enemy!

"If anyone should do it, it should be me," I said.

I glanced over at Tanner glaring at me. Yeah, he was definitely jealous. I'd won Tanner over the first time by making him jealous. Could that really work again? And did I even want him and his perfect body and personality again? I tried to push the thought aside.

"But that won't be necessary," I continued. "Because I brought us a secret weapon: Ryder Storm. And you won't let us lose, will you, Ryder?"

"No way. Cole sucks."

"What was that?" I yelled. "I can't hear you!"

"Cole sucks!" he yelled back.

"What?!" I screamed at the top of my lungs.

"Cole sucks!" chanted my entire team. "Cole sucks! Cole sucks!"

By the time the chant stopped and we broke our huddle, I was feeling like I could take on the entire world. I hadn't felt so pumped up since before my final game of high school volleyball.

The blue team was staring at us. For just a second, Chastity and Cole looked a little intimidated.

That's right, bitches! You're going down. #ThisIsWar, baby.

Chapter 21

CODPIECES AND TURTLENECKS
Saturday

"Princesses, please join me to determine our first event," said Ocelot into his megaphone. He had gotten off the platform and was now standing in front of a giant prize wheel. Each brightly colored slice of the wheel had a different event written on it.

I tried to read them as I approached. There were a few standard events, like Tug of War, Dizzy Bat, and the Sack Race. But then there were some that I didn't recognize. *What the hell is Angry Swans? And Codpieces and Turtlenecks?* Surprisingly, none of the events sounded like things that would make me end up naked.

"Since the blue team are the reigning champions, red gets first spin. Princess Raven, please get us started." He stepped aside so everyone could see the full wheel.

I was worried I'd look like an idiot and not be able to spin the wheel properly. But after spending way too many afternoons of my childhood watching *The Price is Right,* I knew the proper technique. I stood on my tippy toes and grabbed as high up on the wheel as I could. And then I put all my force into spinning it downward.

I was relieved when it actually worked. The wheel spun and spun and spun. It almost landed on Codpieces and Turtlenecks, but instead it clicked over to the Egg Relay Race.

Okay, I can work with that. I'd been a beast at egg races back in elementary school. As far as I could remember, I'd never dropped the egg. And I wasn't about to break that streak now.

We had to field two girls and two guys, so I volunteered to be one of the girls. Isadora volunteered to be the other. I was a little worried that she'd severely injure her giant breasts by running in a bikini rather than a sports bra, but if she thought she could do it, then I guess I had to trust her.

There was no shortage of male volunteers, but ultimately I chose Tanner and Diablo. The running order was: Diablo, Me, Isadora, and Tanner as our anchor. My reasoning was that I wanted to get out to a quick start.

It didn't quite work out that way.

The second I saw the spoon in Diablo's hand, I knew I had made a mistake. His hands were so big that him holding the perfectly normal sized spoon looked like an average person holding one of those little plastic spoons that you'd get with an easy bake oven.

I must have given him a worried look, because he turned to me and winked. "Don't worry, Princess. I got this."

No. No, he didn't.

Especially because he was staring suggestively at my breasts instead of focusing. *Oh.* He was saying he was going to get *me*. Or maybe he was talking about the egg race. I had no idea.

Ocelot fired the starter gun. Diablo took off in a dead sprint, while the blue team's first guy took a much more measured approach. Unsurprisingly, Diablo's egg fell off his spoon before he had taken three steps. I cringed as the egg splattered on the ground. *What kind of monster decided to have a race with raw eggs? Why not like…water balloons? Or stress balls? Or literally anything else?*

"Dude, what the hell?" I yelled as Diablo came back to get another egg. "You can't go full speed!"

"I only have one speed. In both egg races and fucking."

Damn it, Diablo! "Please just slow down."

"I got this," he said. But he took my advice a little too seriously. Instead of sprinting for his second try, he walked at a pace that was slightly faster than an old dude with a cane. To his credit, though, he did keep the egg on his spoon. But come on! Why did he volunteer for this if he was so freaking terrible at it?

"This is a nightmare," I said to Tanner. "Do you have any spy tech we could use to turn the tide in our favor?"

"Nope. But I have something even better." He snapped his fingers and Nigel rushed over to his side.

I hadn't seen him before. But now I don't know how I'd missed him. He was dressed in a red cotton onesie that looked straight out of the early 1900s.

"Nigel, what are you wearing?" I asked.

"My workout outfit." He ran his hand down the fabric. "I've had it for decades but it's still good. They don't make things like they used to."

"Decades? Aren't you like…twenty something?"

"Me?" He looked confused for a moment. "Oh, yes. I'm a young lad. I meant it's decades old. I stole it from an old person. I'm a little thief." He wiggled his fingers.

"I'm sorry, what?"

He turned to Tanner, ignoring me. "You called for me, Master?"

"Did you bring your slingshot?" asked Tanner, not at all phased by Nigel admitting to stealing clothing from old men.

"Of course." He pulled one out of his back pocket.

What the hell? "Why do you have a slingshot?" I asked.

"Cougars."

I spun around and stared out into the woods. "Are cougars a big problem here?"

"Oh yes," said Nigel. "But really they're a problem for me everywhere. Older women love my boyish charm. Although technically they're not older…"

"Nigel!" yelled Tanner. "Let's stay focused, please. I need you to shoot the blue runner's egg off of his spoon."

Nigel grabbed a stone, aimed, and let it fly.

I could have sworn he missed by like three feet, but the egg still exploded as if it had been hit.

"What the hell?!" yelled the blue runner as he wiped raw egg from his face. "My egg just exploded!"

I started dry heaving at the sight of the egg on his face. But I was pretty pleased with the lead it earned us.

"How'd that happen?" I asked. "Nigel missed, but…"

Tanner and Nigel looked at each other.

"I don't think he missed," said Tanner.

"I never miss," agreed Nigel.

"You definitely missed." I'd even seen the grass move where the rock had landed.

"Then how did the egg explode?" asked Tanner.

"Magic?" I suggested.

Nigel's eyes got big. "I'm not a magical boy. I'm a normal boy. Right, Master?"

"Indeed. Nigel is a very normal boy."

Is he? Is he really? There was absolutely nothing normal about Nigel. And I still had my suspicions that Tanner was a vampire. Could vampires make eggs explode? I didn't remember seeing anything about that in the literature, but I'd have to double check.

Nigel turned and shot a rock at Chastity too. Right at her butt.

"Ow!" she shrieked and grabbed her ass. She turned and stared daggers at Nigel.

But Nigel had tucked the slingshot into his pocket.

"What did you just throw at me?" Chastity said.

"Who, moi?" Nigel pointed to himself. "Why would I throw something at you? I don't even know who you are."

Nigel was so good at sick burns.

Diablo *finally* made it back to the starting line. Isadora was all ready to go with her egg and spoon. Despite her lack of a sports bra, she was awesome at it. In fact, not only was she awesome at it, but her very bouncy display distracted the blue runner enough to make him drop his egg and have to go back to the start again. Cole and Chastity both yelled obscenities at him like they were dads at a six-year-old's soccer match.

We had a nice lead by the time it was my turn to run. I took off at a cautious but respectable pace. There was no need to hurry. Thanks to Nigel or Tanner somehow making that egg explode, we were a full runner ahead of them. I had plenty of time…

Where did she come from?!

Chastity sped past me.

Gah!

I hated her ridiculously long legs. It wasn't fair that they looked so good *and* were so fast. And why was she so good at balancing that egg on a spoon?

I picked up the pace, but there was no way I could match her speed. It was going to be up to Tanner to make up my lost time on the final leg against Cole.

But Tanner was busy jotting something down in a notebook.

"What are you doing?" I asked.

"Nothing," he said and quickly put his notebook back in his pocket.

"Tanner, focus. I need you to do whatever it takes to catch him," I panted as I made it back to the starting line.

Tanner snapped his fingers and Cole's egg rolled off his spoon.

"How'd you do that?" I asked.

"Magic," he said with a wink. And then he took off.

I didn't have time to be annoyed with him for messing with me. I was too busy watching the photo finish.

"Come on, Ryder!" I yelled as Tanner and Cole both leaned forward.

Everyone standing around the field looked to Ocelot in his ridiculous referee outfit.

"That one was too close to call. I'm gonna have to check the photo…" He glanced down at his phone. And zoomed in. "And the winner is…red team!"

"Yes!" I screamed and high-fived Tanner way harder than I should have. I turned to Cole. "Take that, sucker!"

Instead of coming back with a snarky comment, he just laughed. "Well played, guys. Well played." He shook hands with Tanner and patted him on the back. "That was one hell of a race. It's nice to finally have some real competition here." He flashed me his cocky smile and walked back over to his team.

Well that was rather sporting of him. It was really quite shocking. I expected him to be the sorest of losers. But instead he took it like a man. It almost made me feel bad about Nigel cheating with that slingshot. Or was it magic? *No. Magic doesn't exist.*

Ocelot called us back over to the giant wheel.

This time it was Chastity's turn to spin. Her boobs came dangerously close to popping out of her cut-off T-shirt, but somehow she managed to keep them covered as she spun. Round and round the wheel went until it landed on… *Salmon ladder?*

All the girls in the crowd cheered.

I turned to Tanner. "So what's happening here? Do we have to carry a bunch of salmon up a ladder? And more importantly…is it raw? Or cooked? Or alive?! And why are all the girls so excited about any of that?" Incorporating salmon into a race was a worse idea than using raw eggs, and that was really saying something.

"Just wait and see," said Isadora. "You're gonna love it."

Am I?

Ocelot led both teams on a short trek into the woods. Our final destinated appeared to be some sort of ropes course – there were nets and ropes and boards nailed into every tree in sight.

Wait a second. Ropes.

"Why are there so many ropes?" I asked Tanner. "Please tell me the salmon ladder isn't a BDSM thing. I'll freak out if raw salmon starts flying around and I don't have all my extremities free to dodge. And aren't the salmon back by the lake?" The further we got from the lake, the more worried I'd been getting that the salmon would be all sorts of rotten. The Society trying to get me naked at every possible turn was one thing, but their wanton disregard for food safety was despicable.

"There are no salmon," said Tanner.

"Then why is it called the salmon ladder?"

"I think it has something to do with the fact that it looks like a fish ladder."

I stared at him. "You're saying words, but they have no meaning." There were definitely salmon involved in this. I wasn't going to fall for his lies.

"You know…the thing that helps fish swim past a dam?"

I stared at him blankly.

"Just look," he said, pointing to where Ocelot was standing.

"For the salmon ladder," said Ocelot, "each team will field two women and three men. The team that climbs the highest total number of rungs wins the event. And if it's a tie, then whichever team finished faster wins."

Cole stepped up to the front and tore his shirt off.

My God. I knew he was going to look good shirtless, but *damn.* Those abs. And those pecs. And those tattoos… I couldn't decide which I wanted to touch most. But then a horrible thought occurred to me. Why was he stripping!? He should have been putting on a hazmat suit, not getting naked!

As it turned out, no salmon were involved. Instead Cole had to hang from a metal bar as if he was doing a pull-up. But instead of doing a pull-up, he had to somehow jump the bar up to a pair of rungs a foot above him. And then again, and again. Seven times.

It seemed like whoever designed this particular stunt engineered it so that it would make a man look as sexy as humanly possible. I was devastated when he got to the top and stopped.

But Tanner ripping his shirt off to go next softened the blow. In fact, he looked just as sexy. His muscle was leaner than Cole's and he didn't have any tattoos, but that didn't make him any less delicious. I actually preferred it. Because as much as I hated Tanner Rhodes, there was a piece of me that still really freaking loved him.

Tanner easily worked his way up to the top of the ladder. I gave him a big high five when he came back to the group.

"Ready to go next?" he asked.

I looked at him like he was crazy. "Hell no. No girl could do that."

Tanner raised an eyebrow and pointed to the salmon ladder. Chastity had stepped up to go next. It didn't even look like it took any effort for her to jump her way up to the top. And then she came over and handed me the metal pole.

"How?" I asked.

"It's easy," she said. "You just have to engage your core to create a moment of zero gravity. Then you can move the bar to the next rung."

Huh. "For real? It looks so hard."

"Na. You got this." She leaned in and whispered. "And if you play your cards right, maybe you can give the boys an accidental nip slip." Then she smacked me on the ass to send me on my way up to the ladder.

What?! No! I didn't want to give anyone an accidental nip slip.

I retied my top to be a little lower and tighter and then jumped up and hooked the bar on the first rung. Just like Chastity had said, it was nice and easy. And I hadn't even had a nip slip.

Ha! Easy peasy!

Now what came next? I looked up and tried to figure out how I was going to get the bar up to the next rung. I just had to engage my core to create a moment of zero gravity, right?

I tried to do that and… The bar moved about half an inch off the rung and then just fell back to exactly where it had been a second ago.

Minor setback. I adjusted my grip and got ready to try again with more force.

Instead of jumping the bar up to the second rungs, I somehow managed to toss the bar into the forest and rotated backwards, flailing my arms like a mad woman. I braced myself to flop against the ground, but instead a pair of muscular arms caught me as effortlessly as a Philadelphia firefighter catching a baby.

Tanner looked down at me with his brown eyes. God, he was so handsome. For a second we both just stared at each other. And my eyes may have darted to his lips.

I cleared my throat. "I almost had it!" I said.

"I know you did," he said. Even though it was a total lie, I still appreciated it. "But maybe next time don't throw the bar?"

"Good plan." I reluctantly hopped out of his arms and walked back to my team. I hoped I hadn't cost us our shot at winning our second event.

Luckily for me, the blue team's second girl was just as inept as I was. Well…not quite. But she still didn't get any rungs. And our second girl got four. So we were still within striking distance with two guys per team left.

I wasn't at all upset to watch the final two guys from the blue team, but Angel really stole the show. Every time he swung to jump up a rung, the outline of his massive cock was quite apparent. His brother Diablo was equally impressive in that area.

But the whole display was kind of ruined when he landed unevenly on the third rung and fell off the ladder. *Damn it, Diablo!*

That was two events in a row that he had totally sucked at. What was his deal?

I hoped that it was just a fluke, but over the next few events, I really started to see a pattern.

He dropped the baton during the 4x400 relay race. And then on the water balloon toss he kept popping the balloons. Granted…he was probably about twice as strong as anyone else there, so it made sense that he'd accidentally apply too much force and pop it. And it wasn't total sabotage, because Tanner and I did so well that we still won the event. But still. *Suspicious.*

Nigel folded his arms across his chest. "I told you that you should have let me do it, Mistress. I wouldn't have let you down."

I looked at his tiny little arms. There was no way he could have done it. His arms were skinnier than mine. "I'm sure there will be an event for you soon."

"But I'm very strong for my size. I'm much bigger in many areas than one might assume."

I stared at him. What exactly was he saying? I found myself glancing down to the front of his onesie. And…he was definitely filling it out. Really he was stretching out the material. *Why am I looking at the naughty bits of Nigel's workout outfit?!*

A slow smile spread across Nigel's face. And I not so subtly stepped a little farther away from him.

The next event was Codpieces and Turtlenecks, which turned out to be a fashion show for men. I couldn't quite wrap my head around how the scoring worked, but that didn't make the event any less entertaining to watch.

The first few guys came out in tight swim trunks. Let's pretend like they each earned an 8 for having great abs. Who knows? Maybe that really was how the scoring worked.

Then Cole strutted out. His walk was good enough that I wouldn't have been surprised if he got an invite to model at the next Miami Swim Week. But what I was really focused on was his MASSIVE erection tenting his swim trunks.

Oh my God.

He got to the end of the catwalk and popped his hip out *hard*. It would have looked super feminine and ridiculous, but with a boner like that, it was no wonder he was confident enough to make it work. He winked at me and tore off his trunks.

I expected him to just be fully nude, but instead he was wearing a little speedo with a huge metal codpiece.

"Oh, what a reveal!" gasped Nigel.

"We have a reveal too, right?" I asked.

Nigel stared at me. "That's like asking *are fax machines the best form of communication?*"

"So…we don't have a reveal? Damn it, Nigel! You said you had the perfect show planned."

"I'm confused. I just told you that I did have a reveal planned."

"No. You compared reveals to fax machines or something."

"Right. Fax machines are the best form of communication. Ergo we do have a reveal. Two, actually."

"And a codpiece?"

He made a sassy face.

Is that a yes? I hoped it was a yes. But honestly I was more focused on the fact that Cole's suit was a thong in the back. I had never seen such a tight, muscular ass. I kind of wanted to jump on stage and squeeze it. He struck one final pose before exiting the catwalk.

Tanner was next. But instead of swim trunks, he appeared to be wearing nothing but an ermine cape that covered his entire torso from his chin to mid-thigh. His walk could only be described as a sashay.

"Work it," growled Nigel. The violent eroticism of his tone made me deeply uncomfortable.

At the end of the catwalk, Tanner hit a power pose and tore off his cape to reveal…another cape?

"What the hell is happening?" I asked.

"Tanner's being very extra and you're just not getting it," said Nigel.

And then it somehow got even weirder. Because he then tore off that second cape. I kind of expected to see a third, but instead he had on a red mesh turtleneck and a codpiece. I was no codpiece connoisseur, but it was clear that Tanner's was much more tasteful than Cole's.

As far as I was concerned, he had earned a perfect 10 for bravery alone. Which meant that as long as our last model didn't totally blow it, we'd get the victory. I mentally patted myself on the back for finally making the call to sideline Diablo. I was tired of his sabotage.

"Please tell me that's Angel," I whispered to Nigel when I saw the tanned man step onto the catwalk in a ski mask and a red speedo. But I had a horrible feeling that it was Diablo.

"It was supposed to be," said Nigel.

Angel appeared at my side. "It's definitely not me," he said. "I'm right here."

Damn it! Had Diablo seriously forced his way on stage just so he could sabotage us? If his walk didn't go perfectly, I was going to lose my mind.

I could practically feel the ground shake as he stomped down the catwalk. It wasn't funny like all the other guys' walks had been. Instead it was super masculine. He was like a warrior marching into battle. And the way he stretched that speedo… It looked like he was smuggling a soda bottle down the catwalk.

At the end of the catwalk, he stopped, put both hands on his hips, and thrust. I thought for sure the violent motion would tear his speedo, but somehow the elastic hung on for dear life as his soda bottle bounced around.

For the second time today, I found myself thinking back to when I had run away from him and Angel. And what would have happened if I hadn't. I shifted in my chair and re-crossed my legs. I hadn't realized it was so hot out today.

It didn't matter what the judging criteria was. If the goal was to be funny - which I suspected it was - then Tanner's double cape with the mesh turtleneck definitely won the day. And if the guys were supposed to be sexy, then Diablo had won. No contest.

Or at least…it wouldn't have been a contest if Diablo hadn't tripped over his own feet and faceplanted on his was back down the catwalk.

Nigel cursed and jumped up onto the stage. He grabbed Diablo by the waistband of his speedo and angrily dragged him off.

Okay…so maybe Nigel was super strong. *Wait.* I suddenly remembered how he'd carried Chastity and me both up the stairs to my apartment. I stared at him dragging Diablo off the stage. How was Nigel so strong? It made zero sense.

I almost felt bad for Diablo. Was it possible that he wasn't sabotaging us and was just the clumsiest beef tower in the world? *No.* Something was up. He had forced his way onto that stage just to mess it up. But why?

There was only one explanation.

"I think Diablo killed Rosalie," I whispered to Tanner as we walked back to the event wheel. Ocelot had commended Tanner for being "wonderfully extra," but had ultimately awarded the victory to the blue team since none of them tripped and fell on their faces.

Tanner raised an eyebrow. "That's quite the accusation. Do you have evidence to back that up?"

"No. But how else would you explain why he's sucked so badly at every event? I think he's nervous because he knows that I'm Rosalie's sister and I'm onto him." The theory had made sense in my head, but hearing it out loud made me less sure.

"That feels like a bit of a stretch."

"Frankie told me that he and Angel have been members for at least five years."

"Again, not super incriminating."

I put my hand on my hip. "Okay then, Mr. Super Detective. Do you have any better leads?"

"No…"

"Then here's the plan. I'm going to show Diablo that picture of Rosalie and say that she's super into him. And that she's on her way to come watch the rest of the events."

Tanner stared at me. "And that will accomplish what, exactly?"

"It'll spook him. And then he'll freak out and call his accomplices."

"Oh, so now he has accomplices?" Tanner was clearly not getting my plan.

"Maybe."

"And how are we going to know when he calls his accomplices?"

"You're going to bug him."

"What makes you think I can do that?" asked Tanner.

I shrugged. "I don't know! You sell hair-changing tech to the CIA. I assume you have bugs too."

"Fair point. Okay, I'll bug him."

"Good. You set the bug. I'll go grab the picture." I knew the plan sounded crazy, but I was sure we were about to catch Rosalie's killer red-speedoed. There was literally no other explanation for Diablo's sabotage.

Chapter 22

THE SISTER-NAPPER
Saturday

"Is the bug set?" I asked, panting slightly from having just run back to the princess suite to grab my phone.

Tanner nodded.

"Okay, let's hope this works."

I walked over to the in-progress game of dodgeball and waited for Diablo to get eliminated. It didn't take long. He made a show of trying to catch a ball and missing, but I knew he did it on purpose. *Scumbag sister killer!*

"Hey," I said as he walked over to the sidelines. I tried to sound casual, but my voice squeaked awkwardly. I was so nervous that I was going to blow this.

"Hey, Princess," he replied. "Want to go behind that tree for a quickie?"

Angel ran over to grab a dodgeball that had just missed him. "What he means to say is that he's sorry for sucking so badly."

"Don't worry about it," I said. "It's just a game."

Angel nodded and ran back into the game.

"So is that a yes to the quickie behind the tree?" Diablo held his hand out for me.

"Not quite. Buuuuut, I did just get a text from my friend Oaklyn." I stared at him as I said Rosalie's society name. He didn't have much of a response. "She said she's gonna be here soon to watch the rest of the games. And between me and you...she's super into bad boys. Especially ones who are tall, dark, and handsome."

"I mean, who isn't?"

"Check her out." I pulled up the picture of Rosalie on my phone and showed it to him.

"Not bad," he said, nodding slightly in approval. He didn't seem the least bit shook. But I had expected that. After all...if he was some sort of deranged sister-napper, then of course he'd be a master at lying. But under the surface, I assumed he was totally freaking out. I had a feeling that within an hour he'd slip away to try to figure out how the hell Rosalie was coming back from the grave.

We ended up losing dodgeball, and the next event. And the event after that. But I didn't really care. I was completely engrossed in listening to the earbud that Tanner had given me. I heard every word Diablo said. But so far, none of it was about Rosalie.

Until...

"So Raven told me that one of her friends is coming to watch the games," said Diablo.

I looked across the field and saw he was standing next to his brother.

"Apparently this girl is super into bad boys," added Diablo.

"Nice. Is she hot?" asked Angel.

"Yeah man, she's a dime."

Damn right she is!

"Well that's great news for me," said Angel. "Once she sees how badly you suck at everything, it won't even be a contest."

"You can have her…I have other plans." Diablo slapped him on the back and walked away.

I turned to Tanner to see his take on what we had just heard.

"He doesn't sound very suspicious to me," said Tanner.

"Maybe he knows he's bugged and he's just playing us."

"I doubt it."

"Damn it! I thought for sure we had him."

Tanner pulled me into his big strong arms. "I'm sorry. But at least we've narrowed down the list of suspects. You're infinitely closer to finding her than you were just 24 hours ago."

I nuzzled into his chest. The smell of his sweat mixed with his sunscreen was so comforting. I wanted to just stay there the rest of the day. Tension melted off of me as he rubbed the back of my neck. And I realized that this was the first time in months that I'd felt this relaxed.

"In the meantime, we better focus on this competition. I still can't believe you agreed to take the princess suite."

I pulled back and looked up at him. "Why?"

"Cole really didn't tell you?"

"Tell me what?" *Oh God.* I should have known there was some horrible punishment for losing. "What happens to the princess at the end of this?"

"The winning princess gets an extra wish. And a token for their necklace."

Well that doesn't sound so bad. But I wasn't worried about what happened to the winner. "And what about the losing princess?"

Before he could answer, static crackled through my earbud. And then Diablo said, "Hey, girl."

I looked around the field to see who he was talking to. He wasn't competing, he wasn't by Angel...he wasn't anywhere to be seen.

"Hey," said a girl's voice.

"I think Raven is onto me."

"No surprise there. You're not exactly being subtle," replied the girl.

"Who is that?" I whispered frantically to Tanner. This was exactly what we had been waiting for!

Tanner shrugged and pulled out his phone. "Let's find out." He hit a few buttons and then turned the screen to show me a live feed of Diablo standing in a cabin with some blonde dressed all in blue.

She turned and I saw her face.

"Chastity?" I gasped.

Tanner looked a little shocked.

This wasn't possible. And yet... "Chastity helped Diablo kidnap Rosalie?" I couldn't believe what I was seeing.

"I'm so sorry," said Tanner. "But maybe it's not what it looks like..."

"What else could it possibly be?" I asked.

He pointed to the screen. "Let's listen."

"I've held up my end of the deal," said Diablo. "Now it's your turn."

"Oh is it now?" asked Chastity.

"Yeah. I've single handed made us lose like ten events."

Chastity nodded and seductively ran her finger across her lower lip. "You have…"

"Then I guess you better get on your knees, Princess." Diablo grabbed a pillow off the closest bed and threw it on the ground in front of him. "I've been waiting all day to feel those lips around my cock."

Chastity stepped forward and hooked her fingers into the elastic of Diablo's shorts. "Just my lips? Don't you want to feel my tongue? And my throat? And my tits?"

"Yes," groaned Diablo. His voice was tight with desire.

Chastity stepped back and flashed him a smile. "Well you're gonna have to wait a little longer. I only fuck winners."

"But you said you'd blow me if I threw the competition."

"I don't recall any such deal. Sorry, big boy." Chastity spun around and walked out, swaying her hips as she went.

"That's messed up," said Tanner.

"I know! I can't believe Chastity sabotaged us!" Although I was relieved she wasn't a murderer. Sabotage was pretty bad too though.

"I was more talking about how she just teased Diablo so hard. Poor guy is gonna have blue balls for days." Tanner shook his head in dismay. "I bet Cole put her up to that."

"You think so?"

"Definitely. Everyone knows that Cole is a total douche."

Based on my interactions with him thus far, that assessment checked out. "Then what do you say we go beat his ass?"

Tanner smiled and cracked his knuckles. "I've been waiting for you to ask me to do this." His eyes grew all stormy. Kind of like when I'd told him about the sex tape Joe had blackmailed me with. I loved when he looked angry, but…

"In Society Wars," I added. "Not literally."

"I knew what you meant," said Tanner.

Did he? Because it sure looked like he was ready to beat Cole's ass for real.

Chapter 23
RAMMING SPEED!
Saturday

We put our earbuds away and went back to rejoin our team. I had no idea what the score was, but I assumed we were losing.

"Where have you been?" asked Frankie. "We're getting our asses kicked!"

"How bad is it?" I asked.

"We're down 12 to 4."

My eyes got big. "12 to 4? Can we even come back from that?" I tried to do some quick math. There were 23 events. One point each. "Isn't 12 wins an insurmountable lead?"

"The final event is 5 points," said Tanner, "which means there are 27 points total. So we still have a chance, but we can only lose one more event from here on out. And no matter what, we have to win the finale."

"Or what?" I pulled him to the side out of earshot from the rest of our team. "I'm literally going to die if you don't tell me what happens to the losing princess."

"Cole's going to bang you."

What?! "But he said there were no strings attached when he offered me the princess suite!"

"Well, he lied."

"Damn it! He's such an asshole."

Tanner nodded. "Tell me about it."

"Well, what are you going to do about it? Are you going to sit back and let him win? Or are you going to save me?"

"This feels like a trap."

"What? Why?"

"Because a week ago I saved you from getting fucked by Cole. And then you told me that you never wanted to see my face again."

"You didn't save me. I drew the right card. And anyway, that was different."

He raised a questioning eyebrow.

"It was! I hadn't seen you for months. And then you just showed up and started messing with my life. It also didn't help that I was super-duper drunk at the time and extremely horny." *Shit!* Why did I tell him that I was horny? "I mean, I was horny at the time. I'm not horny anymore. Not because I masturbated. Fine, I *might* have taken a peek at Chastity's porn collection. But nothing happened." *Why am I still talking!?* Every word I said was making this so much worse.

Tanner laughed at me.

"It's not funny! I was so mad at you."

He reached out and ran his fingers through my hair. "Was?"

I slowly nodded. Yeah…*was.* It was hard to be mad at him when he was standing here smiling at me.

"So…you're saying that I shouldn't save you from Cole again?"

"What? No! You should absolutely save me. I'm so tired of him making me get naked at the worst times."

Tanner's face got serious at the mention of Cole getting me naked.

I couldn't help but smile. It really seemed like Tanner was into me. Was that why he had come back? So that we could give it another shot?

"Why are you smiling?" he asked.

"I'm just happy to have you on my team. Now are you going to save me from Cole?"

"And how do you expect me to do that?" he asked.

"I don't know! You keep pretending like you can do magic. How about you use some of that?"

"Okay."

Okay? He said it so confidently. Like he would actually use magic to make us win.

"Let's do this." He took my hand and led me back to the prize wheel.

Chastity was already there waiting. I was kind of mad at her. But also not. Because even though she'd seduced Diablo into throwing some events, she'd then recanted and told him that she'd only blow him if he won. And we were still losing. Which made me think that Diablo really did just suck at everything.

Or maybe Cole was just super amazing at everything...

"Princess Raven," said Ocelot. "It's your spin."

I grabbed the wheel and gave it a tug. *Please be an event that Tanner can make us win.*

It spun and spun until finally coming to rest on SACK RACE. *Oh hell yeah.* That was the perfect candidate for magic.

"So what kind of magic are you gonna use?" I asked Tanner on the way over to the field.

"The options are endless. I could fill one of the blue sacks with spiders. Or bricks. Or Nigel. Your choice."

"I like the Nigel idea."

"Me, too, Mistress Ash," said Nigel. "It would be my pleasure to hide in a sack. And tickle a sack." He held up his hand and demonstrated exactly how he'd tickle the opposition's balls.

"Eh," said Tanner. "That'll be too easy to trace back to us. Might lead to a disqualification. Let's just go with bricks."

I could picture it perfectly. Cole and Chastity would be out there with their smug, cheating faces. They'd be hopping along, about to cross the finish line. And boom! Suddenly there'd be a big brick in the bottom of their sack. They'd try to hop, but instead they'd just face-plant right into the grass as my team jumped to victory.

It was the perfect plan.

We stepped into our sacks and pulled them up around our waists.

"Ready?" I asked Tanner.

He nodded with a mischievous grin and turned to Cole and Chastity. "I hope you've enjoyed us letting you win…because from here on out, you're going down."

"I doubt it," replied Cole. "But good luck."

Ocelot fired the starting gun and the race was on. I hopped as fast as I could, but I quickly fell behind the three other superhumans. It didn't even make sense that they were all so good at sack racing. It was almost like they'd been practicing. Who in their right mind would practice hopping around like an idiot?

But it didn't really matter, because I had Tanner on my side. And he had magic. Or something like that. Seriously, his tech was top-notch.

"Uh," I said to Tanner as Chastity and Cole got way out ahead of us. "You better use that magic now."

"You sure?" he asked. "I thought it would be more exciting if I let them get out to a big lead first. The more they're winning by, the sweeter it will be when they eat bricks."

"Okay. I don't hate that idea. But you better not mess this up…"

The blue team rounded the cones on the far side of the field and started heading back to the finish.

Cole gave me a cocky wink as he passed. I just smiled, thinking about the horrible fate that was about to befall him.

Tanner and I hopped along leisurely while Cole and Chastity sped towards the finish.

"Tell me when," said Tanner.

"Wait for it…wait for it…" When our enemies were ten yards from the finish, I yelled, "Now!" *Eat bricks, suckers!*

Tanner snapped his fingers and… Cole and Chastity just kept hopping as if nothing had happened.

Tanner looked at his fingers in confusion. He snapped again, but still nothing happened. The blue team cheered wildly as their leaders crossed the finish line.

"What the hell, man?" I asked. "You were supposed to put bricks in their sacks!"

"I tried!" yelled Tanner. "I don't know what…" He stopped midsentence and went pale. It looked like he had seen a ghost behind me. "Shit," he muttered.

I turned around to see what he was looking at. Or in this case, *who*. It was a little man in a cropped purple vest and a matching fez. "Is that Nigel?"

"Give me a minute." Tanner jumped out of the sack and ran over to the guy. He was definitely dressed strangely enough to be Nigel. And was about the same size. But it didn't completely look like him…

I started to climb out of my sack but part of my sneaker caught on the fabric.

"Need help?" asked Angel. He didn't wait for an answer. He just picked me up while Diablo pulled the bag free from my sneaker.

"Thanks," I said. And then I ran over to where Tanner had been. I couldn't see him anymore, though. They must have gone behind a tree to talk.

I looked around when I got to the spot they'd been in. Sure enough, he and Nigel were standing behind a tree in a very heated discussion.

"Hey," I called.

They both looked over at me as I ran over.

"What's going on?" I asked. And then I realized that Nigel was still in his red cotton onesie. Which meant it hadn't been him in the purple vest and fez. "Who was that guy?"

"What guy?" asked Tanner.

"The one who you ran over to talk to."

"You mean Nigel?" he asked.

"No. I mean the guy in the purple vest. And the weird fez."

"Right. Nigel."

"Did you like my outfit?" asked Nigel.

"Yeah," said Tanner. "What'd you think? We thought it could be a good distraction for him to wear that during the next event."

I eyed him suspiciously. "Where'd it go?"

"Over there," said Tanner. He pointed behind a tree. And Nigel pointed behind a different tree.

"You're both lying. But I'm more concerned with why you didn't even try to win the sack race."

"I did try. But…" Tanner shook his head.

"Do you *want* Cole to fuck me? Because now if we lose one more event, I'm fucked. Literally."

Tanner ran his hands through his hair. The only time I'd seen him look this frustrated was when he'd run away from our make-out session at the Odegaard boutique. "I won't let that happen."

"With magic?"

"No. I don't need magic to kick Cole's ass."

Please let that be true. "Then what are we waiting for? Let's go win this thing!"

The next event was a tug of war. That was both good and bad. It was good because I was pretty sure our team was stronger. But it was bad because we were only stronger if Diablo was giving it his all. If he didn't pull his weight, we'd be screwed.

Ocelot and his striped-onesie-clad assistants watered down a patch of dirt to create the biggest, most disgusting mud pit I'd ever seen. I would have rather died than compete and possibly fall into that filth. But luckily, I didn't have to make that choice. This was a men-only event. And for some wonderful reason, the guys all decided to compete shirtless while us girls just got to sit on the sidelines and enjoy the show.

"Come on, red team!" I yelled.

Tanner looked over and smiled at me. He was at the very front of our line, and Cole was at the front of the other. The two men locked eyes and the tug of war began.

Neither team made much progress at first, but I wasn't complaining. With them pulling on the rope, all their muscles were fully flexed and shimmering with sweat.

Eventually Cole lost his footing. The second he slipped, Tanner pulled hard on the rope. It was just enough to tilt the scales in our favor. The entire blue team went face first into the mud pit, led by Cole.

"Wahoo!" I screamed, jumping up and down.

Tanner walked over and gave me a big high five.

"That was amazing! I knew you could take him!"

"Of course I can," said Tanner, as if he was insulted that I ever thought he couldn't.

"Don't celebrate yet," said Cole as he scooped a glob of mud off his face. "You're still losing 13 to 5." He walked by and slapped my ass, leaving a giant mud print.

"Hey!" I squealed. *Stupid cocky Cole.*

Tanner started to run after him, but I stopped him.

"Don't let him distract you," I said. "The best way to wipe that smug smile off his face is to just keep beating him."

And that was exactly what we did.

The next event was a game of giant chess: Tanner vs Cole. I got a little nervous when Cole took Tanner's queen, but two moves later Tanner called checkmate.

Holy shit that was fast.

Yes, Tanner's muscles were sexy. But seeing him dismantle Cole with his superior intellect was even more of a turn-on.

"Way to go, dumb-dumb!" I yelled to Cole as he stared in disbelief at the chessboard.

His usual confident smirk had returned when he looked up at me. "You're still losing 13 to 6."

Tanner shrugged. "We just wanted to make things interesting. We got this."

"Well, one more win for me, and…" Cole's eyes scanned my body. "Well, you know what happens next."

I gulped. Yes, I wanted to win more than anything. But maybe it wouldn't be so bad if I lost. After all…I had been telling Tanner the truth about how horny I had been ever since he left. God, what was I even thinking? My loins were out of control. *Focus!*

Chastity put her hand on her hip as Cole walked back to their team. "I told you you should have let me play. I would have whooped his ass."

She wasn't wrong. I'd once seen her beat our school champion in 60 seconds. And she hadn't even distracted him with her tits.

The next event was 2-on-2 basketball - one guy and one girl per team. It probably would have been smart for me to put Diablo or Angel in, since they were a good 6 inches taller than everyone else, but I still didn't fully trust Diablo. Tanner had good momentum going.

And I used to play basketball with my dad in our driveway all the time. That would probably be good enough for us to beat Cole and Chastity, right?

Tanner started off with the ball. He passed it to me and I tried to drive past Chastity, but she easily swatted the ball out of my hands.

Damn it! I hated how good she was at everything. Shouldn't her huge boobs get in her way?

I fared better the next time Tanner fed me the ball. Instead of trying to dribble around her, I just put the ball through her legs. Thanks to her ridiculous thigh gap, the maneuver worked. I nailed the layup and ran over to give Tanner a big high five.

Cole scored next, and then Tanner went in for a layup. As he jumped, Cole came up behind him and tried to block the shot. He missed the ball and hit Tanner right in the face. Tanner tumbled to the ground with a *thud.*

Ouchies. Tanner's elbow was suddenly missing a lot of skin. But he popped right up and immediately got in Cole's face. A few guys from each team had to jump in to keep them from throwing any punches. From there, Tanner took over the game.

Time after time, he drove straight at Cole. He wasn't at all afraid to put his shoulder into him. He even knocked Cole on his ass a few times.

At first I was loving it, but then I started to just feel kind of ignored. It quickly turned into Tanner versus Cole while Chastity and I stood around hoping in vain that someone would pass us the ball. At one point we just sat down.

"Oh yeah!" yelled Tanner when Ocelot blew the final whistle. We'd won. Or rather…Tanner had won. I walked over to celebrate with him, but he was too busy rubbing it in Cole's face.

When he finally turned to me, all he could say was, "Did you see that shot?"

"Which one?" He had taken so many that it was hard to tell which one he was talking about.

"The sky hook."

"Yeah, it was awesome," I lied. I had no idea what he was talking about. "Great win." I gave him a half-hearted high-five and walked back to the wheel to spin for the next event.

I couldn't help but feel a little disappointed that Tanner had ignored me so much. I hadn't been playing badly. Why hadn't he wanted my help?

Oh well. I decided to chalk it up as a bit of over-competitiveness. Guys were weird about basketball. The next event would be different.

My spin landed on Angry Swans. At first I thought it was going to be related to *Angry Birds*, but it turned out to just be a swan boat race.

There were a bunch of heats, but it was tied by the time we got to the final race: Tanner and me vs Cole and Chastity.

All the horrible spin classes finally paid off, because I was actually pretty decent at it. Despite that, we still fell behind a bit. Three quarters of the way through the course, they were a full turn ahead of us.

"We're never going to catch them," I said.

"What if we didn't have to?" asked Tanner.

"What do you mean?"

"How much do you know about 18ᵗʰ century naval warfare?"

"Uh…"

Tanner turned the rudder and started peddling like hell. "Ramming speed!" he yelled as we cut through the water directly towards Cole and Chastity's boat.

"What are you doing?!" I yelled. "Turn!" But it was too late.

Tanner masterfully guided us right into their broadside. Chastity shrieked as the head of their swan boat was taken clean off. And I shrieked too, because the force of the collision sent me flying into the lake. The decapitated swan's head bobbed in the water next to me before sinking below the surface.

"Take that!" yelled Tanner. He looked back and laughed as he peddled off towards the finish line…with me still stuck in the lake.

Stupid competitive asshole.

I started to tread water, but the lake was way colder than I'd expected. My muscles started to seize up and my teeth were chattering. I was about to freak out until I saw that Cole and Chastity had forfeited the race to come to save me.

Cole leaned over the side of their half-destroyed boat and stuck his hand out for me. "Grab on."

I reached up and Cole effortlessly pulled me into his boat. He rubbed his arm on my back to help warm me up as they peddled up back to shore. Rather than complaining to Ocelot about psycho-Tanner trying to kill him, he instead ran and got me a towel.

"Thanks," I said. Cole may have been the enemy, but right now he was acting more like my knight in shining armor.

"No problem. And make sure you hang on to that towel…you're going to need it after you lose." He winked and walked away.

Oh God. Why was I going to need a towel? I hoped it was because of more water rather than bodily fluids.

Chapter 24

#FREETHENIPPLE
Saturday

I didn't have a chance to fully dry off before Ocelot called Chastity and me back to the wheel.

"Ladies and gentlemen," began Ocelot into his megaphone. "After going down 13 to 4, the red team has won an impressive four events in a row. If they can get one more victory, then it'll all come down to the grand finale. Princess Chastity, would you please do the honors and spin for the next event?"

Chastity stepped up and tugged on the wheel. It spun and spun and spun. As it finally started to slow, I read the events that it might land on. Flag football, chicken fight, three-legged race, slip n' slide, sword fight… I wondered if that would be an actual fencing match, or if the guys would have to whip out their dongs and have a good old-fashioned locker-room sword fight. Knowing the Society, it easily could have been either. Alas, it was not to be. The wheel clicked past sword fight and landed on freedom race.

Freedom race? What the hell was a freedom race?

Based on how loudly all the guys on both teams were cheering, it seemed likely that the freedom race was going to be something wildly uncomfortable for me. Would I be handcuffed and have to try to get free before Cole claimed his prize? *Oh God.*

I started to walk back to my team to discuss our game plan, but one of Ocelot's helpers stopped me and handed me a big cardboard box. I opened it up to find a bunch of red bikinis inside.

Frankie skipped over to me with a big smile on her face, her braids bouncing with every step. "It's your lucky day," she said.

Was she being sarcastic? That was exactly the kind of thing you'd say to someone who was about to get bondage banged. "Why's that?" I asked.

"Because I'm a beast at tying knots."

Knots!? I'd kind of just been joking about the whole bondage thing. "Am I about to be tied up and spanked?"

Frankie laughed. "Maybe if we lose. But no, not for this event. Come on…we need to get some volunteers and then go get ready. We only have thirty minutes before the race begins."

Isadora and Giovanna were the first to volunteer. The rest of the girls on my team were less enthusiastic, but eventually we got three more takers.

Diablo raised his hand too.

"You want to wear one of these?" asked Frankie, holding up one of the red bikini tops.

Diablo laughed. "No. But I'd be happy to help tie them."

"Me too," offered Angel.

Frankie pursed her lips. "Nice try, perverts. But we don't need any help." She turned to me. "Let's go get ready."

We jogged off to the nearest cabin with the five other girls.

"So what exactly is the freedom race?" I asked.

"The best event," said Isadora. She and Giovanna had already gotten naked and were putting on the red bikinis.

"A race to see who can free all of us from our bikini tops the fastest," said Frankie. "It's kind of like #FreeTheNipple, only it has nothing to do with feminism and more to do with everyone seeing our boobs. Our job is to try to prevent that from happening by tying these bikinis as tight as humanly possible."

"Gah! I knew one of these events was going to end up with me naked."

Frankie laughed. "Not if I can help it. I feel like I've been preparing for this all my life." She gestured to her braids and all her hand-made bracelets. Lots of them involved leather straps and tons of little knots. "Here…put yours on and I'll tie you up." She tossed me one of the bikinis to change into while she went around helping the other girls.

Isadora and Giovanna respectfully declined her help. Instead of wearing the bikinis like normal people, they tied them in some weird style called the "upside down" bikini. Basically it turned their tops into slutty little tube tops that pushed their boobs together.

They claimed they did it to try to confuse the blue team, but I was pretty sure they just wanted their cleavage to look amazing.

I hid behind a bunk and changed into my bikini, holding the cups against my breasts while I waited for Frankie to come help. Eventually she came. I couldn't see exactly what she was doing, but the knots she was making certainly didn't feel normal.

She gave one final tug and then patted me on the back. "Don't worry," she said. "No one is getting through these knots."

I took a deep breath. "I hope you're right." And then something occurred to me. I was certain that Cole would be the one untying our knots. But who would do the dirty work for our team? Tanner wasn't my boyfriend anymore, but I didn't relish the idea of him ripping off a bunch of girls' bikinis. Especially Chastity's.

But as much as I hated that thought, he did seem extremely motivated to keep Cole from getting to see me naked. Which was confusing…because Tanner had made it very clear that we could never be together. *Right?* Gah! He was so confusing.

What really mattered, though, was if Tanner was any good with knots. Because I wasn't about to stand there and let Cole rip off my bikini top while Tanner floundered around like a schoolboy about to see his first pair of boobs.

"You any good with knots?" I asked Tanner once we were all changed and ready for the freedom race.

"I'm decent."

"Just decent?"

"Yeah," he said. "Nigel's the real expert."

I stared skeptically at the little man.

"I am. I spent decades on a sh…"

Tanner cleared his throat. "He spent a decade in boy scouts."

"That's definitely not what he was about to say." These two were being particularly sketchy today.

"Will you let me help, Mistress Ash?" asked Nigel.

There was no way I was going to leave my fate in his hands. "I'd rather Tanner do it."

"Good choice," said Tanner. "I may be okay with knots, but I'm *excellent* at untying bikinis."

I tried to ignore that comment. He'd probably been untying bikinis all summer while I mourned his disappearance. "Even when they're tied like this?" I turned to show him the crazy knots on my back.

"What the…?" he asked.

"Oh God. I'm so screwed." I wasn't sure exactly what Frankie had done back there with the knots, but surely the other team had done something similar. And Tanner looked like a deer in headlights.

"Maybe not," said Angel. "Diablo was serious when he offered to help you girls tie knots. When we were young, we got caught robbing a bank and the judge sent us to a wilderness camp. It was basically the Spanish version of boy scouts."

"You two were in boy scouts?" I asked. "I cannot picture you two in those ridiculous outfits."

"We made them look good," said Diablo. "Especially once we sewed ourselves some new pairs of shorts with extra room in the crotchal region."

Was he serious? He seemed serious. But I still didn't fully trust him. "How do I know you're not going to sabotage us?"

"I would never."

Oh, really? "I know that Chastity promised you a blowjob if you threw those challenges."

"Yeah," said Diablo. "But then she went back on it. So now I'm fully devoted to crushing her."

"Hmm…"

"Come on, you gotta believe I'll do whatever it takes to get her on her knees."

"Okay, fine. That checks out. But if you let me down, I'm going to kick you in the nuts so hard…"

"Deal." He stuck his massive hand out and shook on it with me. But seeing how big his hands were gave me pause. How could such big beefy hands untie such intricate little knots? It didn't seem like it was physically possible.

I was going to make a last-minute switch when Ocelot blew his whistle.

Shit!

Ocelot had set up a V-shaped platform. All the girls lined up on the platform, with Chastity and I at the center next to Ocelot. Diablo and Cole waited on the ends.

"On my signal," said Ocelot, "both men may begin untying bikinis. The first to get all seven opponents' tops completely off wins. Ladies, please put your hands on your hips. If you move your hands, your male teammate will have to freeze for 30 seconds before he can resume untying. Are we clear?"

We all nodded.

"Then let the freedom race begin!" Ocelot blew his whistle.

Diablo was as skillful as he'd promised. Within a few seconds, the first blue girl's top fell away from her chest. I hoped she would cover herself and give us a free 30 seconds, but she kept her hands at her side and let everyone see her breasts.

Cheers erupted from the crowd. So. Many. Cheers. There were at least a hundred people watching. A hundred! And if I lost, they'd all see me topless. Yes, I'd pranced around Club Onyx in my lingerie. But at least I'd been covered a little bit. If Cole undid my bikini, I'd be completely exposed. Would it be weird if my nipples got hard? Or would everyone be too distracted by some deformity that I wasn't even aware of?

I nervously glanced down the line to see how Cole was doing. Being the cocky bastard that he was, he kept one hand behind his back as he effortlessly undid Giovanna's top. A second later he freed Isadora's breasts as well.

Stupid upside-down bikinis! Had they even tried to tie difficult knots? Or did they just want to show everyone their perfect breasts?

Isadora answered that question by reaching up, jiggling her boobs, and then blowing a seductive kiss to the adoring crowd.

Ocelot blew his whistle. "Foul on red. Diablo, freeze for thirty seconds." A big LED timer behind Ocelot started counting down from 30 while Cole kept untying.

Fucking Isadora! If she was the reason that we lost this, I was going to tit-punch her so hard.

Cole kept one hand behind his back as he attacked the next bikini top, but after a few seconds, he gave that up and started going at it with both hands. Just as the penalty timer ran out he finally got the knot around her neck undone. The girl's face turned bright red as her top fell from her breasts. Cole undid the other knot and her top came off completely.

Oh my God. This was a mistake! I wanted to run, but that would surely result in us being disqualified. Which would then result in Cole getting to bang me. Probably in front of all these perverts.

Seeing Diablo work gave me some small hope though. He was quickly making up the lost time. And by the time Cole got my fourth teammate topless, Diablo had almost caught up.

A full two minutes passed before either of them got another bikini untied. Apparently both teams had arranged their girls from easiest to most difficult.

The crowd cheered again, and I knew that another top had fallen. Both teams had two girls left.

"Hey Cole," I said as he worked on Frankie's top.

He ignored me.

"Have you seen these lovely boobs that you're freeing? If you think Isadora's boobs looked good in that bikini, you should see them out of it." Saying that sentence made me feel so gross, but I had to do anything I could to distract him.

"I don't want to see Isadora's. All I care about is seeing yours." He turned and gave me his cockiest smile as the final knot on Frankie's top came free.

Shit!

"How'd you do that so fast?" demanded Frankie.

"I'm just that good." Cole didn't waste any time sliding over to start on my knots. His rough fingers brushing against my back sent shivers down my spine.

"You don't have to do this," I pleaded. "If you stop now, I'll let you do whatever you want to me."

"Tempting offer, but I'm already going to get to do that when I win."

Eh, worth a try.

"I have to admit, these knots were pretty good," said Cole. "But not that good." He yanked at the string on the middle of my back and all the tension went out of it.

Fuck my life. I looked down in horror, expecting my boobs to pop free. But by some miracle the fabric just barely stayed in place over my nipples. That wouldn't last long though. If Cole got through the knot on my neck, not even another miracle would keep my boobs hidden from the crowd.

Cole was silent in concentration for a few seconds. When he started talking again, I knew I was screwed.

"It was a valiant comeback," he said. "But alas, all good things must come to an end. With just a few more pulls…" He pulled once. Twice. And then he stopped. I could feel that most of the complexity of the final knot had been undone. "Just tell me when you're ready to lose," he said.

I looked over at Diablo, hoping that he had somehow caught up and was about to get Chastity naked. But nope…he still had two girls to go. And then something incredible happened.

The second-to-last blue girl's boobs were so big and there was so much tension on her bikini that when Diablo undid the middle string, one of the ends whipped forward and hit her in the face. She instinctually pulled her hand up to rub her cheek where it had hit her.

Ocelot blew his whistle. "Foul on blue! Cole, freeze for thirty seconds."

Ah! I was saved!

Cole let go of the final string and took a step back.

"You're lucky, Raven," said Cole. "But not lucky enough. The second that timer hits zero, your top is coming off."

"Not if Diablo finishes first," I replied.

"Not gonna happen."

"Come on, Diablo!" I yelled. "You can't let that timer run out!"

Diablo nodded and squinted at the top knot of the girl's bikini. A second later, the knot was free.

He had twenty-two seconds to get Chastity topless.

He approached her top with the same focus. But the clock was ticking down, and he wasn't making progress.

Twelve…eleven…ten…

"Hurry!" I yelled.

"I can't get it!" he yelled back.

Chastity looked kind of disappointed. I knew how badly she wanted to show off her perfect tits. But I also knew how badly she wanted to win.

Seven…six…five…

Come on! Come on! "Five seconds!"

Diablo growled in frustration and stopped working on the knots.

No! What was he doing?

"It's not looking good," said Cole. He took a step forward and rubbed his hands together, getting ready to pull my final string.

Three…two…

With one second left on the clock, Diablo reached around and grabbed the front of Chastity's bikini. With a roar, he tore her bikini in half. Chastity smiled as her ruined bikini top fell to the ground.

Oh my God! He did it!

I was about to celebrate when I felt Cole pull on my final string. The tension on the string went away and the fabric started to fall away from my chest. *Noooooo!* My hands shot up and *just barely* pressed my bikini top safely to my chest.

I let out a huge sigh. I'd saved myself! I wanted to turn around and slap Cole, but both my hands were otherwise occupied.

"Hey!" yelled Diablo.

I looked over to see what he was upset about. Was Chastity covering herself and not letting him see what he'd worked so hard for? It wouldn't have been against the rules since the race was over. But still…it would have been totally out of character.

That wasn't the issue though. Chastity was proudly standing with her hands on her hips, happy to show off her boobs to Diablo. Only she wasn't *really* showing them off, because her nipples were covered by bright blue pasties.

"Hey!" I yelled too, joining Diablo's calls of indignation. I turned to Ocelot. "She wore pasties! Isn't that cheating?"

"Technically it's not against the rules. And what do you want me to do about it? Disqualify them? Your team already won."

"But didn't Diablo cheat by tearing her top off?" asked Cole.

"I'll allow it," said Ocelot.

"Don't be a sore loser," I added. I held one hand across both my boobs so I could use the other to boop him on the nose. Nothing was more demeaning than a good booping.

He jumped back. "Did you just boop me?"

"Yup. Whatcha gonna do about it?"

He gave me a wicked grin. "You'll see."

Chapter 25

THE MOST INFLUENTIAL FASHION ICON OF THE 1940S
Saturday

The game for the grand finale of Society Wars was a childhood favorite of mine: capture the flag. Well, kind of. Instead of the teams playing in the front yard and back yard of some suburban home, the sides here were the girls' cabins and the guys' cabins. And instead of tagging people to get them out, we'd be using high-tech laser tag equipment.

But the most important change of all was that it wasn't a flag being captured. Instead, they were trying to capture me.

So it wasn't actually capture the flag at all. It was Capture the Princess.

Ocelot gave us each a list of rules and told us we had two hours to prepare our strategy. That seemed like overkill to me, until I realized that me not getting captured was the only thing keeping Cole from having his way with me. And based on my experience with him at the casino, I assumed he'd do it in front of the entire camp.

Just thinking about it made my palms all sweaty.

"Please tell me you're amazing at capture the flag," I said to Tanner.

"I've never played before."

Of course he hadn't. He'd grown up overseas or something. He'd never had a normal American childhood.

"But in war, as in business," said Tanner, "the most important thing is to know your enemy. In this case, that's Cole and Chastity. So what do we know about them?"

"They're dirty cheaters," suggested Diablo.

"Bingo," said Tanner. "Which means we should probably go somewhere a little more private before we start planning our strategy. Any one of these people could be a mole." He gestured to our dozens of teammates. Most of them were already doing some target practice with the laser guns. "Who do you trust?"

"Well I definitely trust Diablo." I smiled up at the giant man. "I'm forever in your debt for ripping off Chastity's bikini."

He patted my head with his Shaq-sized hand. "Any time, Princess."

I was pretty sure he was saying that he'd rip her bikini off any time rather than saving my life any time. But the way he said it was still comforting. I was glad to have him on my team now that he wasn't sabotaging everything.

"Trust anyone else?" asked Tanner.

"Frankie." She was, after all, my handmaid.

"You can trust my brother," said Diablo. "And my boy Nigel." At first I thought he was joking, but then he cupped his hands to his mouth and yelled, "Yo! Nigel! Get your ass over here!"

Nigel scurried over. "Greetings, Big Diablo," he said as the two did a ridiculous secret handshake that ended with Nigel gently cupping Diablo's ass cheeks while Diablo massaged his shoulders.

"What the hell is happening?" I whispered to Tanner. "Are they gay lovers?"

"Maybe?" he replied. He seemed just as confused as me. "I didn't know they'd ever talked…"

"What?" asked Diablo. "You don't like our handshake?"

"It was…interesting," I said.

Tanner held up his hand to get our attention. "We can circle back to that later. But for now, is there anyone else that you guys trust?"

We all shook our heads.

"I can vouch for Isadora and Giovanna," said Tanner.

I almost fell over in shock. "You can?" Since when did Tanner know the soapy shower lesbians?!

"Yeah. I recruited both of them to the Society. They're good girls."

"We need to have a serious talk about your definition of *good girls*. And do you really think they'll have a lot to offer in our war room?"

Tanner raised an eyebrow. "You'd be surprised."

"Indeed," agreed Nigel. "Never judge a bitch by her tits."

"Nigel!" yelled Tanner. "What did I say about using that phrase in polite company?"

Nigel shrugged.

I would have laughed if I hadn't been so nervous about losing the Society Wars. We had a battle to plan!

We rounded up the rest of our inner circle and headed to my princess suite. Tanner cleared a table and rolled out a map of the camp.

"So as I was telling Raven," began Tanner, "the key to winning this battle is to get inside the heads of our enemies. We've already established that Cole and Chastity are cheaters and probably have at least one spy in our camp, which is why we're having this meeting in Raven's princess suite. But what else do we know about them?"

"Cole is a big, dumb grade-A beefcake," said Nigel. I thought he growled a little bit at the end, but I couldn't be sure.

"Well he is big," agreed Tanner. "And he is fairly strong. But I don't think he's dumb."

"But you whooped his ass in chess," said Diablo.

"I did. But it wasn't because he was dumb. It was because he was overconfident."

I nodded. "Yeah…he's super cocky."

"So the question is: how can we use that against him?"

Uhhh… I had no idea.

It looked like Isadora was about to speak up, but Tanner spoke again before she could. "Before we answer that, it might be important to discuss his past strategies. Have any of you faced him during his undefeated streak this summer?"

"I've been here for all of them," said Diablo. "But he keeps changing his tactics. Sometimes he sits back and waits for us to attack, while other times he hits us hard within the first five minutes. A few times he's even split his entire force into two-man strike teams to hunt down our princess."

"Interesting…" said Tanner. "And what about the princess? Does he usually hide her in a specific spot?"

Diablo shrugged. "No idea. We've never found the blue princess, no matter who she is."

"You've never even spotted her?"

"Nope," said Diablo with a shake of his head.

"That's great news."

"It is?" I asked.

"It is," said Tanner. "Because it means that Cole has one hell of a hiding spot for her. If I had to guess, I'd say he probably hid his princess in the exact same spot every time."

Diablo gestured to the map. "But we've searched everywhere."

"Even in the cabins?"

"No. No one is allowed to hide in the…" Diablo stopped mid-sentence as a horrible realization came to him. "Shit, Cole is a cheater."

Tanner smiled. "Now you see why it's so important to know your enemies. I propose we task a third of our team with searching the cabins. All in favor?"

Everyone agreed.

"So we know how we're going to catch Chastity, but that's only half the battle. We'll still need to protect Raven from Cole."

Isadora cleared her throat. "I have a few ideas."

This should be good. I had a feeling she was about to suggest that she and Giovanna distract him with a threesome.

"We could honeypot him," she said.

I knew it! Wait…what does it mean to honeypot someone?

"But I doubt that would work," continued Isadora. "He seems to only have eyes for Raven."

"So what do you suggest instead?" asked Tanner.

"Well…Giovanna and I have also been part of all nine battles this summer. And no disrespect, but I don't think Diablo's assessment is correct. In every instance, Cole has sent out half a dozen scouts. And their recon has dictated the rest of his battle plans. I believe he has three basic maneuvers." She nodded to Giovanna.

Giovanna apparently knew what that meant, because she pulled a tube of lipstick out of her purse and drew a big red X on the map right in the center of our territory.

"Let's say Cole's scouts found us guarding our princess at that X," continued Isadora. "He'd respond with Maneuver Alpha - a full-on assault."

Giovanna drew a line of red Xs in Cole's territory. "If, on the other hand, his scouts saw *us* planning an offensive, he'd assume a defensive position and slaughter us as we entered his territory. Maneuver Beta."

Finally, Isadora took the lipstick and drew a giant question mark. "And if we tried to hide our princess to buy us time to search for their princess, then Cole would revert to Maneuver Charlie in which he splits his team into search parties. On the three occasions when this has happened, they've found our princess before we could find theirs."

I blinked my eyes. I had *not* been expecting such a nuanced assessment from Isadora and Giovanna. What had happened to the girls who loved taking group showers and flashing the entire camp?

"Which tactic would leave him most vulnerable?" asked Tanner.

Isadora took a moment to consider his question. "I think we've seen that all of those scenarios result in our destruction. So instead I propose we decorate the tree with false blossoms."

"Huh?" I asked.

Isadora and Giovanna looked at me like I was so dumb.

"Decorate the tree with false blossoms. You know…from Sun Tzu's *Art of War*."

What the hell is that?

Tanner nodded. "Oh, that's clever. You really think that will work?"

Isadora gave Tanner a wicked smile. "It's worked for us before. The details are classified, but let's just say that there's a terrorist sitting in jail somewhere still trying to figure out how he hadn't realized that the beggar on the side of the street was actually a female commando."

Giovanna laughed. "That poor guy. I'll never forget the look on his face when you tore off your wig and shoved your gun in his face."

What?! "You two were special forces?"

"Yeah," said Isadora as if it was totally normal.

Suddenly her in-depth assessment of Cole's battle plans made a lot more sense.

"So how do we do this false blossom thing?" I asked.

"Well…that depends." She turned to Nigel. "Could you sew up a second princess dress in the next hour?"

Nigel put his hand on his hip. "Was Adolf Hitler the most influential fashion icon of the 1940s?"

"Yes?" replied Isadora, sounding just as confused as I was.

"Damn right." Nigel snapped and walked away.

"Does anyone know what just happened?" I asked.

Diablo looked at us like we were all idiots. "He said he'd do it. How was that not clear?"

That wasn't exactly what I was asking. I was more curious about the fashion icon comment. But I guess Hitler had gotten a lot of people to dress a certain way…

Isadora turned back to the map. "Assuming Nigel can come through, we'll buy ourselves some time and take out a sizeable chunk of Cole's forces. But we'll still need to hide Raven somewhere."

Tanner spun the map around to get a better look at it. "That's it! Raven, how would you feel about a redo of our first date?"

"Are you suggesting that we fake an FBI raid?" I asked. "That would be pretty epic."

Tanner laughed. "No, after that."

"Distract them with the world's most delicious gyros?"

He shook his head. "Before that."

"You're gonna have to help me out here."

He pointed to the part of the map labeled *zip line course*. "While they're searching for you on the ground, you'll be perched in the trees. And if they do happen to look up and see you, just zip away."

"That'll give everyone a nice view," said Diablo. "Right up your skirt. I like it."

"What he means is that it's a great idea," said Angel. "I like it too."

So they both want to see up my skirt?

"But how is she going to get up there in her heels?" asked Frankie.

"Heels?" I asked.

"Well, technically boots." Frankie held up a pair of bright red, thigh-high boots covered in straps and...locks?

"What are the locks for?"

"To make sure you can't take them off."

"So you're telling me that not only do I have to evade 40 super athletes, but I have to do it in six-inch heels?"

"Yup! But hey, look on the bright side. It also makes you walk slower if the enemy catches you and makes you walk back to the feast area."

"Oh great. That'll make me feel so much better when I'm stuck in the mud."

"I got you," said Diablo. "I can carry you to the zip lines."

I didn't doubt that he could do that.

"Speaking of heels," said Frankie. "You should really start getting ready." She plugged in her curling iron.

"But you already did my hair and makeup."

"Yeah, and then you went and fell in the lake."

I shot a nasty look at Tanner. "Only because a certain somebody decided to go all kamikaze with our swan boat."

"It worked, didn't it?" asked Tanner.

I didn't bother answering him.

"Before you get ready, shouldn't we come up with a backup plan?" asked Isadora. "I'm not comfortable with our whole strategy hinging on the assumption that Chastity will be holed up in one of the cabins."

"Good point," agreed Tanner. Then his eyes lit up and he ran to the elevator. "I'll be right back. I just got the best idea."

Chapter 26

CAPTURE THE PRINCESS
Saturday

"You really think that'll work?" I asked when Tanner finished detailing his master plan. Frankie was almost done putting a few final touches on my makeup.

"Absolutely," replied Tanner. He sounded so sure. And who was I to question him? After all…he was the brilliant billionaire. If he couldn't come up with a plan to beat Cole, then who could? The fact that Isadora the supermodel commando had also helped with the plan made me feel even more confident about it.

But still. It would be up to me to execute the plan. If I slipped up, everything would be ruined. Especially my modesty. I quickly put the thought out of my mind. I couldn't dwell on that. It was too distressing…and distracting. I really wondered if Cole would actually bang me in front of the entire camp or if he was just all talk. Either way, I kind of loved that the threat of it was making Tanner so jealous.

Frankie turned my chair and put one final brush of highlighter on my nose. "All done!"

Tanner nodded in approval. "Wow."

Does he really mean that?

"Just wait until she puts on the dress," Frankie said. "In fact, you and the other guys all need to step into the elevator for a minute to give us some privacy."

Finally! Someone in the Society who understands privacy!

Tanner, Diablo, and Angel all left. I hadn't seen Nigel since he'd said that weird stuff about fashion-icon Adolf Hitler, but I assumed he was in the bathroom with Isadora and Giovanna. And even if he did happen to walk in and see me naked, it wouldn't be a huge deal since I was starting to think he had a thing for Diablo.

Frankie helped me into my dress…which was definitely not a dress. It was a ridiculously skimpy red monokini COVERED in crystals. It barely covered my boobs, and the back was just a thong. I kept telling myself it was less revealing than the lingerie I'd worn to Club Onyx, but I wasn't so sure.

"Since when is this considered a dress?" I asked.

Frankie answered by clipping a belt around my waist that had a long train of sheer fabric. "There. *Now* it's a dress."

"If you say so." I was at least happy that the weird skirt thing would help to cover my ass.

I slid on the torture-boots and then Frankie covered my arms in geometric bracelets. She finished the look by sliding a tiara into my very princess-esque braids.

"You look incredible," said Tanner.

I spun around. "Hey! Were you watching me get dressed that whole time?"

"Who, me? I would never do such a thing."

I put my hand on my hip and stared at him. I felt like I should cover my barely-hidden lady bits, but I also kind of loved the way he was looking at me. "Do I seriously have to wear this? I look ridiculous."

Tanner raised an eyebrow. "You look anything *but* ridiculous. I almost feel bad for Cole. He doesn't stand a chance against you in that dress."

"Why is everyone calling this a dress?"

Before anyone could answer, Isadora, Giovanna, and Nigel came out of the bathroom. I almost fell over when I saw Isadora. Partially because these boots made it nearly impossible to maintain my balance, but mainly from shock. Somehow, Giovanna had done Isadora's makeup to make her look almost exactly like me. And Nigel had sewn a passable replica of my princess "dress." It looked amazing on her.

"That's so not fair. You look a million times better than I do in this stupid thing," I said.

"I look just like you," said Isadora.

"Kind of. Only you actually look good. I just look awkward."

"You look stunning," said Nigel. "If you weren't my mistress, and my master's girlfriend, I would fuck you so hard."

Everyone in the room was silent. There was so much to unpack in that comment. Did Nigel really want to have sex with me? And did he really think I was still Tanner's girlfriend? I mean like…did Tanner tell him that? Or did Nigel just assume? I really needed answers here.

"Nigel!" yelled Tanner. "What has gotten into you today?" He shook his head. "We'll discuss this later. But for now, we need to focus. It's game time."

***

Our home base was a clearing in the center of a bunch of the girls' cabins. As the princess, I was required to start on a red platform, but after the games began, I would be permitted to run and hide.

My inner circle stood next to me. I tried to ignore how good Tanner looked in his battle gear. I'd seen him in sweatpants, suits, and tuxedos. But seeing him dressed for battle took his sexiness to a whole new level. The way his muscles bulged as he held his laser rifle… *Yum.*

"Are you sure you can't come with me?" I asked.

He thought about it for a second. "I want to. Believe me, I hate the idea of leaving you alone out there with Cole hunting you down. But if we really want to sell this illusion, then I have to stay with Isadora."

Was that really why? Or did he just think she looked better than me in the princess dress? I tried to shake the thought, but what Cole had said about Tanner having a different girl on his arm every night at Club Onyx had really gotten into my head.

"You have to trust me," he said.

Like I trusted you with my heart three months ago? I knew he was right, though. We had to try to sell the illusion that Isadora was me. "I do."

"Good. We got this." He gave me a high five and then started barking orders at the rest of our team. I almost tried to get his attention again, but I was distracted when Ocelot walked over and started securing the locks on my boots. He tugged on each lock to make sure it wouldn't come free. When he was all done, he said something into his radio and then asked, "Red team ready?"

"I think so," I said.

Tanner jogged over. "Troops are all set. Let's take this cocky asshole down. *Save Raven* on three." He put his hand out. The inner circle all put their hands in.

Tanner counted down, and on three, we all yelled, "Save Raven!"

I hope this plan works.

Ocelot's helper blew his whistle and the game began.

Phase 1 of our plan was simple - we were going to take out as much of the blue team as possible by decorating the tree with false blossoms. In this case, the tree was Isadora, and the false blossoms were her princess outfit.

Diablo swept me up in his massive arms and carried me away from the platform. I could have walked, but that would have left heel marks in the ground. And the only heel marks we wanted to leave were the ones being left by Isadora as she walked towards the ambush Tanner had set up with the bulk of our team. She made a halfhearted attempt to cover some of her tracks, but that was just to help sell the illusion. If we made it too easy to track her, Cole would smell the ambush coming from a mile away.

It would have been fun to watch Cole get totally demolished, but me staying that close to the camp would have been too dangerous.

"I can probably walk the rest of the way," I said when we were five minutes out of the camp.

"Nonsense," said Diablo. "You'd leave tracks. And anyway, carrying you is nothing. You weigh like ten pounds."

"Ten pounds?" I asked. "What do you think I am? A two-month-old baby?"

"But mainly I just love touching your ass." He shifted his hand down and gave my ass a squeeze.

"Hey!" I yelled.

"Shhh," hissed Angel. "I think I heard someone."

Diablo put me on the ground and then he and Angel bent a small tree down to cover us. I had no idea how they were strong enough to bend the tree. And I also had no idea how the tree didn't snap. But I didn't really care, because our hiding spot worked. A pair of blue scouts walked by us, none the wiser to our location.

"Shouldn't you shoot them?" I whispered. The scouts' had their backs turned to us. It would have been so easy for Diablo and Angel to pop out and take them down.

"No," replied Diablo. "Even if we take them out, they could still run back and tell Cole where they'd seen us. We'd be surrounded in minutes."

"But you're supposed to freeze when you get hit. And you definitely aren't supposed to communicate intel. That would be cheating!"

"Sure is."

Oh right. Cole's a dirty cheater.

Once the coast was clear, we continued towards the zipline course. We didn't encounter any more scouts on the way. I had been wondering how they'd hoist me up onto the zipline platform. But it turned out that there was no hoisting at all. Instead Diablo just gave me a good old-fashioned piggyback ride as he climbed up some boards nailed to the side of a tree. It was absolutely terrifying. If my hands slipped, I would have fallen right off his back and literally broken my ass.

Speaking of my ass, Angel probably had a pretty sweet view of it as Diablo climbed up the ladder. But at this point, I didn't really care anymore. I was pretty sure that just about everyone in the Society had already seen it. And that would be the least of my worries if we lost this game of Capture the Princess.

Diablo called Tanner and put him on speaker phone.

"How's it going?" asked Tanner.

"Great!" I said. "We made it to…"

Diablo put his hand over my mouth. "It might be bugged," he whispered. And then he said into the phone. "The package has been delivered."

"Excellent," replied Tanner. "The ambush went well. We lost about a third of our troops, but Cole lost more. As long as you guys can keep moving and avoid detection, we should be good to go."

"Did you take Cole out?" I asked.

"Nope. He wasn't part of the ambush."

"Damn," said Diablo. "We'll keep our eyes peeled for him. Over and out." Diablo hung up and turned to me. "Let's start moving."

We started zipping through the course. Diablo and Angel would look around each time we got to a platform, but my mind was elsewhere. I couldn't stop thinking about what Nigel had said. About me being Tanner's girlfriend. And then I couldn't stop thinking about what Cole had said about Tanner's scandalous ways. Luckily for me, my two guards had been part of the Society for years. And I knew they'd heard stories about Tanner's philandering ways. They'd told me as much at the Onyxies last year. What else had they heard or seen?

"So how well do you guys know Ryder?" I asked while we were stopped on a platform.

"Not that well," said Diablo.

"Yeah," agreed Angel. "We pretty much just know him as that weird dude who wears the flamboyant suits."

"And he was too scared to let us fuck you at the Onyxies," added Diablo. "But luckily for you, he's not here right now. So no one is gonna stop you from getting on your knees and gagging on our huge cocks."

"He doesn't mean that," said Angel. "What he meant to say is that you should probably slide out of that dress so that you're harder to spot. And to help you feel more comfortable being naked, we'll be happy to get naked as well. And then let's be honest…there's no way you'll be able to resist our massive cocks." He gave me a wicked smile.

"Hey!" I said. "I thought you were supposed to be the nice one!"

"I am nice. I'll even take a video that you can use to make Ryder jealous. Maybe then he'll realize that you're way hotter than all those girls he's been bringing to Club Onyx all summer."

The mention of Tanner with other girls made my blood boil. "Have you seen him with other girls?" I asked.

"Yeah. I just said he brought tons of girls to Club Onyx."

"I don't mean just walking around with them. I mean…"

"Fucking them?" suggested Diablo.

"Yes," I said. "Have you seen him fucking them?"

A branch cracking stopper our conversation. We all hit the deck and looked around for the threat. It must have just been a squirrel or something, though, because we didn't see any blue scouts. But I did notice something else…

"Where do they do maintenance on the swan boats?" I asked.

"Usually just right there," replied Diablo, pointing to the dock with all the swan boats. "Why?"

"Because the one missing the head isn't there."

Diablo pointed at each boat while he did a mental count. "You're right. Usually they have a dozen boats there. And I only count 11."

"Are you thinking what I'm thinking?" I asked.

"That depends," said Diablo. "What are you thinking?"

"On the map I remember seeing an arrow pointing to a cave on the other side of the lake. I bet that's where Cole has been hiding his princesses all summer!"

Diablo shook his head. "I can't believe we didn't think of that sooner. We have to call Ryder." He pulled out his phone and put it on speaker.

"Yeah?" answered Tanner.

"Have you found Chastity yet?" I asked.

"Negative. The cabins were empty." I could hear the annoyance in his voice.

I was going to tell him our theory, but then I remembered that he'd warned us about the phones being bugged. "Darn. Well, keep looking." I hit *end call* on Diablo's phone.

"So what's the plan?" asked Diablo.

"You guys have to go find her."

Diablo shook his head. "We were given strict orders to stay with you. You were about to take your dress off, remember?"

I ignored the second part of what he'd said. "What's the point of us hiding? You can stay with me as long as you want, but eventually they'll find us. Our only hope is for you to take a swan boat and catch Chastity first."

"Holy shit," said Diablo. "You're right. We need to catch Chastity before Ryder does."

"Huh?" I asked.

"That fucker," said Angel. "I can't believe we didn't see it sooner."

"I'm so confused."

Diablo looked so pissed. "Ryder made us guard you so that he could go find Chastity. Because he wants to be the one to fuck her."

"No. Ryder wouldn't do that." *Right?*

"Are you sure about that?"

"Yes," I said. But it came out all squeaky and weird. Because the truth was…I wasn't sure. Chastity was so beautiful. All the guys wanted her. So why wouldn't Tanner?

"Think about it," said Diablo. "Ryder spent all summer bringing other girls to Club Onyx. And now he sent you off into the forest with *us*. And he's already seen how handsy you get when you see our cocks."

"That little asshole!" Did Tanner really not care about me at all? I tried to stop the tears coming to my eyes, and it was actually pretty easy. Because I was done being hurt. Now I was just pissed. Of course he didn't care about me. He'd ghosted me for three fucking months. "You guys have to go find Chastity before Ryder does. Please."

They both stared at me.

"Come on," I said. I dropped to my knees. "I'm on my knees begging you."

"Oh really?" asked Diablo. He reached for the zipper of his pants.

"Ah!" I screamed and jumped back to my feet. "Not like that!"

"Us leaving you isn't worth the risk. Yes, we *might* get to bang Chastity if we catch her before Tanner does. But he could still beat us to her. Or Cole could catch you. Either way, we'd be left with blue balls. Staying here and seducing you though…that's a sure thing."

"What he means to say is that we'll be happy to go find Chastity," said Angel.

That wasn't at all what Diablo meant. But I was relieved that Angel could see reason. "Thank you!"

He smiled at me. "But only on one condition."

"Anything. Wait! No. Not anything. I'm not going to fuck you guys."

"If your plan works and we get Chastity, then you're off the hook. But if it doesn't work, then the next time we see you, no matter where we are or who you're with, you're going to give us a traditional society greeting."

"Which is…?"

"The second you see us, without saying a word, you get on your knees and suck our cocks until we cum all over your pretty face."

I gulped. The thought of that was absolutely horrifying. But also kind of hot... And it was better than the alternative of getting fucked by Cole in front of the entire camp. "Deal," I said. I stuck out my hand and we shook on it.

"See you around, Princess," said Diablo. He and Angel climbed down, ran off towards the swan boats, and then paddled into the lake.

I was all alone in the forest. And then a horrible realization washed over me. *Oh my God, what did I just agree to?!*

I tried to think back to the exact words. Had he said at Club Onyx? Or *anywhere?* What if I was just walking down the street and ran into them? Would I really have to blow them right there? Or what if they came to my work?! This was another incident just waiting to happen. God, Angel wasn't the nice one. He was a tricky little dildo!

If my plan didn't work and I lost this bet, I'd never be able to leave the house again. Which was fine. I quite liked my house. Especially with my giant closet that stupid Tanner had built for me. Although I was pretty sure he was gonna board it up and move all those magnificent clothes to some other girl's closet. *Jerk face.*

I was trying to think of ways to prevent him from taking back my closet when I heard a noise. *Shit! Someone is coming for me!* I grabbed some handlebars and zipped off the platform.

I was halfway across the zipline when I realized two things. First, I was not headed to another platform. I was angled towards the ground. And second, there was someone at the end of the zipline casually leaning against a tree. No, not someone. It was freaking Cole.

Chapter 27

200 POUNDS OF PURE MUSCLE
Saturday

Shit! Shit shit shit! I thought about letting go and falling to the forest floor. But I was like…20 feet up. In these heels, I was pretty sure my legs would shatter like toothpicks if I let go. I had no choice but to zip directly into Cole's outstretched arms.

I tried to scare him by coming in heels-first, but he just sidestepped and wrapped me up in his muscular arms.

"What's a pretty girl like you doing out in this forest all alone?" he asked as he put me down on the ground.

"Oh, you know…just enjoying nature." I tried to make a run for it, but Cole grabbed my wrist.

"Enjoying nature, huh? Is that so?"

"It is."

His eyes flared with amusement. "Do you mind if I join you?"

"I'd prefer if you didn't."

"Hmm…too bad. You're coming with me."

I smiled at him. "Make me."

He was more than happy to oblige. I squealed as he hoisted me over his shoulder. One of his hands was planted firmly on my ass.

"Hey! Hands to yourself, mister!"

"Sorry." He let go of my ass and I started to slide off of him.

I screamed and latched onto him. I really did not want to break my ankles.

"You should really make up your mind. Do you want my hands on you or not?"

"I want you to put me down."

"If I do that, will you be a good girl and come with me?"

"So that you can fuck me in front of the entire camp?"

He put me down on the ground but kept a firm grip on one of my wrists. "Of course. You've practically been begging for my cock ever since you got here."

"Excuse me?!"

He just laughed. Why did he find my misery so hilarious?

"How about we make a deal," I suggested. My mind was working overtime to figure out a way to get out of all this. But the only deal I could think about was the one I'd just made with Angel and Diablo. And if I didn't find a way to escape from Cole… *Oh God.*

"I'm listening."

I was about to offer him a blowjob, but then I remember that you always wanted to start negotiations with a lowball offer. "If you let me go, I'll consider forgiving you for tricking me into being the princess."

"Hmm…if I recall correctly, I saved you from having to room with all those sloppy girls."

I glared at him. "I trusted you, Cole. And you tricked me into gambling my body. For the second time!" And now Angel and Diablo got me to gamble my body away for a third time! What the hell was wrong with me?! I was pretty sure I had a gambling addiction. Did I need to go to my doctor for that. *Good God, no.* I could never see Dr. Lyons again. I was doctorless now. And I was going to die of a gambling addiction.

"I thought you were excited for the spit roast?" he asked, trying to distract me with food.

"Of course I'm excited for the spit roast. What girl wouldn't be? But I didn't need to be the princess in order to stuff my face full of delicious meat."

Cole blinked a few times and stared at me like I'd said something weird.

"Don't look so surprised. All the other girls in the society might be able to survive on lettuce and raw carrots, but not me."

"Fair enough," replied Cole.

"So do you accept my offer?"

Cole laughed. "What was it exactly?"

"You let me go, and I forgive you for being a jerk."

"Let me think about it… NO. I can't just let you go. My team has worked hard for this victory. And more importantly, I want that date with you."

Oh right, our other bet. "Fine. If you let me go, I'll still go on a date with you."

"And you'll also release me from my debt of nudity?"

Damn it! I had really been looking forward to being able to force him to get naked at the most embarrassing time. But I had no choice but to agree to his terms. I was at his mercy. "Yup. It'll be as if you won the bet."

"Tempting offer," said Cole. "But I still can't accept."

"What?! Why not?"

"Because..." He looked me up and down. "All I have to do is carry you a few miles to the feast grounds, and then you'll finally be mine. And thanks to our bet, I'll even get to take you out to dinner afterwards."

"Well aren't you the perfect gentleman."

"Only when I want to be." Cole's eyes bore into mine. His meaning was perfectly clear. What he was going to do to me was most ungentlemanly.

I shifted to try to cover myself, but it was impossible in this ridiculous dress. I'd dreamt of what it would have been like if I'd lost to Cole in poker. It was part nightmare, part fantasy. And now it was going to be my reality.

"You *really* want to bang me in front of the whole camp?" I asked.

His Adam's apple rose and fell. "There's nothing I want more."

"Why can't you just take me intimately in the woods?"

"That doesn't sound nearly as fun."

Damn it! I pushed my breasts together and conjured the sauciest of winks. "Then how about you tear this dress of off me and raw dog me against a tree?" *Oh my God, what did I just say?!* The words felt so dirty coming out of my mouth.

"As much as I would love to do that, it just wouldn't be fair to make my teammates miss out on the spit roast. Speaking of which..." Cole put his fingers into his mouth and whistled. Three blue scouts popped out from behind the trees.

"What do those losers have to do with the spit roast?" I asked. "If they're not bringing me delicious meat, then I'm not interested."

"Oh, they're bringing you meat…"

"Huh? I don't see any meat."

Cole laughed. "Wait a second. What do you think a spit roast is?"

He was being so dumb. Of course I knew what a spit roast was. "It's when you put a pig on a big stick and spin it over a fire. Everyone knows that." But then something clicked in my mind. I could have sworn that Chastity had told me about a different kind of spit roast once. What was it…?

Oh. Shit. My eyes got wide as I remembered Chastity's definition of a spit roast. It was something along the lines of a girl getting taken from both ends, as if she was the pig and the guys' dicks were the stick that she was roasting on. I thought back to my conversation yesterday where I'd told Cole how much I wanted a spit roast. I'd even said that I'd wanted to do it for my anniversary but my husband wouldn't let me. And if that wasn't bad enough, a few minutes ago I'd doubled down by saying how excited I was to stuff my face full of delicious meat. *Oh my God.*

"Wait, no!" I yelled. "I didn't mean I wanted *that* kind of spit roast!" *God, is that what Joe thought I wanted for our anniversary?*

"Sure you didn't," said Cole with a laugh. He definitely didn't believe me. And why would he with all the things I had said?

"I didn't!"

"Are you not happy with the selection I brought you? Is that it?"

I looked over at the three guys. They were perfectly handsome and well-built, but they were complete strangers. I wasn't just going to let them bang me in front of everyone! What kind of crazy slut did Cole think I was? And more importantly... "Why do you want to share me with one of them? I know guys like threesomes and all, but I always thought it was supposed to be two girls and a guy."

Cole shrugged. "It's not my place to judge what turns a woman on. Unless you're a furry. That's just weird."

"I know, right? And that's very progressive of you to not judge women's fantasies. But really...this is not my fantasy." *Right?* I'd be lying if I said I completely hated the idea of being pinned between Angel and Diablo...

"You don't have to be ashamed. And don't worry - I promise I'll still take you out on a date afterwards."

Weird. I was going to keep protesting, but then I realized there was a better approach to try to get out of this. "So you're not worried that I'll enjoy the other man more? Who knows...his cock might feel so good that I'll forget you're even there."

Cole just smiled. "It's pretty hard to forget about ten inches of cock inside of you."

I gulped and looked down at his crotch. There was no freaking way. Was he really that big? His codpiece had been huge during the fashion show, but I thought that was just for laughs.

Gah! Focus! I had to find a way out of this. Public sex was bad enough, but public sex with two men? I'd literally die of embarrassment. And possibly from internal bleeding if he was really as big as he said he was.

But how could I get out of this? I had already done a pretty good job of stalling to give Angel and Diablo time to catch Chastity, but it felt like my time was running out. Cole was intent on spit roasting me with one of his buddies. *Ah! That's it!* I had the perfect escape plan. Well, it wasn't perfect. In fact, it was extremely risky. But how much worse could this really get?

"Ten inches, huh?" I asked.

He just smiled at me with his stupid cocky grin.

"That's a shame. I was hoping for twelve. Good thing I have some options…" I turned to his friends and made a point of staring at their crotches. In Cole's shock, I was able to yank my wrist free of his grasp. I sauntered over to the three men. Or at least, that was my plan. My heels sinking in the mud made me look more like a drunk toddler than sexy slut. But whatever. The three guys were probably more focused on what I was about to do to them. Or let them do to me.

"I'm Raven," I said, sticking my hand out for one of the scouts.

"Garrett," he replied. When he went to shake my hand, I grabbed his crotch. His eyes got big.

"I'm a grabber," I said with a wink as I started rubbing him over his pants.

"Wow," muttered one of the other scouts.

Damn right. I hoped I looked sexy and confident, because inside I was dying of embarrassment. I had just introduced myself to a man by grabbing his penis.

Chastity would be so proud. Which, to be clear, was not a good thing.

I circled around Garrett, my hand still rubbing his pants.

"Hands on your hips," I ordered.

All three men slung their laser guns over their shoulders and put their hands on their hips. I couldn't believe it had been so easy. It was like they were little puppets on a string.

"Get in a circle."

"Huh?" asked Garrett. But the other two didn't hesitate. It ended up being more of a triangle than a circle, but whatever. The effect was the same.

In one swift motion, I let go of Garrett's rather un-impressive member, grabbed his laser gun, and shot both of his companions right in their sensors. The LEDs on their armor blinked and then went out. I turned to shoot Cole too, but he was too quick.

Cole beat me to the draw and shot Garrett's sensors before I could get the shot off. Which meant Garrett was out and his laser gun that I was holding immediately stopped working. Cole was safe.

Damn it!

"Nice try," he said. "But not good enough."

"I was so close."

"Not really. I saw it coming from a mile away. Enough screwing around though…it's time I got you back to camp so we can get this spit roast started." He scooped me up in his arms again and carried me through the woods. Even though he wasn't as big as Diablo, him carrying me felt just as effortless. More importantly, his grasp was just as firm. I had no chance of escaping, despite my wiggliness. And I got extra wiggly when I was nervous.

"So now that I took those losers out, who else is gonna get to bang me?" I asked.

"No idea," said Cole. "Maybe the whole team will line up and take turns with you."

"What?!" First it had been public sex, then a spit roast, and now it was going to be a gang bang?! "Is that even allowed?"

"Do you want it to be?"

"No!"

"You sure? It kind of seems like…"

I tuned him out as a weird feeling of déjà vu washed over me. I'd been here before. It all looked so familiar. The parting of the trees. The bushes. The rock that jutted out over the lake.

Then it hit me. I hadn't been here. But Rosalie had. This was the exact spot where the picture of her had been taken.

"Wait," I said. "Can we stop for a second?"

"No way."

"Cole, please…" My voice caught in my throat.

Shockingly, he actually stopped. He put me down and looked at me, his eyes filled with concern. "What's wrong?"

I didn't say anything. I just stared out at the lake. I couldn't believe that this was possibly one of the last places that Rosalie had ever been. I didn't know what I expected to find, but I couldn't look away. Maybe there was a clue around here…

Cole put his hands on my shoulders. "Really, what's wrong? If you seriously don't want to get spit roasted…"

"No," I said, cutting him off. "It's not that. It's my sister. Rosalie."

"Huh?" Cole looked around, I guess expecting her to pop out of a bush or something.

If only she would do that. "She went missing three years ago. She was in the Society, apparently. And just before she went missing someone took a picture of her in this exact location. That's why I'm here this weekend. To see if anyone knew her."

"I don't think I know of any Rosalies who have been in the Society," said Cole.

"That's her real name. Her Society name was Oaklyn Hope." I walked out to the edge of the rock overhang and looked out at the lake. *Where did you go, Rosalie? Who took you?*

Cole suddenly laughed. "You're messing with me, right? You're just trying to escape?"

"No," I said. "I'm dead serious." I looked around some more and noticed that there were eleven swan boats at the dock. Which meant Angel and Diablo had returned. "And anyway, you've already lost."

"Huh?"

"We found Chastity."

"Bullshit," scoffed Cole. "That's impossible."

"I admit, it was awfully clever of you to hide her in the cave. But I noticed that one of the swan boats was gone. And right before you caught me, I sent Angel and Diablo to go get her."

Cole gave me his cockiest smile. "Well that's a shame, because while Diablo and Angel are paddling around in the lake, Chastity is sipping strawberry daiquiris on the roof of the clubhouse."

"The roof? But the only way up there is to go *through* the clubhouse." I knew because we had considered it as a hiding spot for me. "So unless you're going to try to convince me that she scaled the wall in these crazy heels, then she cheated! Ha! You're gonna get disqualified."

"Do you remember how good Chastity was at the salmon ladder?" asked Cole.

"Yeah. She was a total freak."

"Well…earlier this summer they did a few renovations to the clubhouse. And I made sure to slip the builders some cash to get them to add a salmon ladder to one of the back walls."

"You clever bastard."

"Guilty as charged," said Cole with a stupid grin.

"You're not clever enough, though."

"Why do you say that?"

"Look below us," I said, pointing down into the lake below us.

Cole looked super confused. He shifted his weight and looked over the edge of the cliff. And I pushed him. He may have been over 200 pounds of pure muscle, but that weight just worked against him as he toppled over the cliff and into the lake.

I let out a sigh of relief when he bobbed back to the top. I'd been a little worried that he was going to hit his head and drown to death, but that seemed like a risk worth taking to avoid getting spit roasted.

Cole brushed some hair off his forehead and glared up at me.

"Sorry, sucker!" I called.

"What the fuck?!" he yelled back.

I held up the bug that Tanner had used to spy on Diablo earlier that day. "Ryder just heard everything you said. And as we speak, he's probably telling everyone on our team where Chastity is hiding. So by the time you swim to shore…this game will be long over. Who's the clever one now, bitch?!" I dropped the bug as if it were a mic, but it didn't really have the desired effect.

My victory celebration lasted all of three seconds - exactly the time it took for Cole to swim to the cliff face and start climbing. And I mean *really* climbing. I didn't even know how it was possible to scale a cliff so quickly.

Shit!

Chapter 28

THE SPIT ROAST
Saturday

I tried to kick off my thigh-high boots, but of course they wouldn't come off. Apparently the locks on them were not just for show.

Oh well. There was no time to mess with them. I just had to run as fast as I could and pray that Cole slipped and fell back into the lake.

My progress was extremely slow. My heels sunk into the mud if I put any pressure on them at all, so I had to basically speed-tiptoe through the forest. I must have looked like a total weirdo, but I didn't care. All that mattered was running away from Cole to give my team enough time to go get Chastity off the roof of the clubhouse.

About three minutes into my escape, I heard branches crunching behind me. A quick glance back told me everything I needed to know. Cole had made it up the cliff, and he was closing in on me. Fast.

I screamed and tried to run faster. It was no use, though. Any second, I'd be swallowed up in his soaking wet arms.

Damn it! When I'd seen him splash into the lake, I'd thought for sure I'd won. But now… I didn't even want to think about what was going to happen to me.

I looked over my shoulder once more. Cole's footsteps sounded like they were literally right behind me. Because they were. He reached out and…stopped dead in his tracks. The LEDs on his armor blinked out as Cole looked down in disbelief.

"Raven!" called Tanner as he jumped off a golf cart, his laser gun still pointed at Cole.

"Ryder! You saved me!" I ran over and threw my arms around him. He twirled me around, the scent of sweat and blueberries washing over me. For the first time since he'd left me on that boat three months ago, I was completely and unabashedly thrilled to see him.

"Of course I saved you. Did you really think I'd let you lose?"

"Not even for a second." Well…okay. Maybe for a second. Angel and Diablo had been very convincing about Tanner's intentions. But staring up at him now? I believed that he only had eyes for me. I was so happy that if he asked me right this second if I was stalking him in that sexy voice of his, I'd probably just say yes.

He put me down and brushed a loose strand of hair out of my face.

Please kiss me.

I thought he was about to, but then Cole cleared his throat.

Freaking Cole!

I looked over at him, trying to come up with the perfect snarky comment to sum up his epic failure. Not only had he lost, but he'd lost by telling me exactly where Chastity was hiding. What a dumb-dumb.

Before I could come up with a more eloquent phrase than, "You lose, dumb-dumb," Tanner cut in.

"Man," said Tanner, stepping towards his vanquished foe. "I have to admit, that was an epic showdown. Well played. And sorry that things got a little heated there in the swan boats. Sometimes I'm a bit too competitive."

Wait, why is Tanner suddenly being so nice to Cole? I kind of liked how much they fought over me.

Cole nodded and gave him a fist bump. "No worries. It was about time someone gave me some real competition."

"Well look at you two, suddenly being so mature," I said.

"Come on," said Tanner. "Let's get back to camp so we can celebrate." He scooped me up and carried me over to the cart. Then he turned back to Cole. "You need a ride?"

Cole shook his head. "Na. You won fair and square - you've earned some time with her. But don't let it go to your head. You may have won the battle, but you're going to lose the war."

"We shall see," replied Tanner. He hit the gas and sped off.

"We did it!" I yelled as the wind whipped through my hair. For the first time since I'd realized that Cole was trying to bang me in front of everyone, I felt like I could actually breathe.

"*You* did it," corrected Tanner. "One question though…why was Cole so wet?"

"He caught me sooner than I thought he would. So I had to improvise a bit to make sure we'd have enough time to track down Chastity."

"And…?"

"And I pushed Cole off the cliff into the lake."

Tanner burst out laughing. "Are you serious?"

"Yup."

"You know you could have killed him, right?"

"It seemed like a risk worth taking. He was gonna spit roast me with some rando!"

Tanner suddenly got serious. "So, about that…"

"What?"

"Um…well…"

I shoved his arm. "Spit it out." I didn't know what he was about to say, but I had a feeling I wasn't gonna like it.

"Don't be mad, but…" He paused.

"But what? If you don't tell me this instant, I'm going to push you out of this golf cart."

"Okay, okay. So Cole wasn't going to spit roast you with some rando."

"He wasn't?"

Tanner shook his head. "Nope. He was going to spit roast you with me." He pulled a blue bandana out of his pocket. "Did I forget to mention that I'm actually on the blue team?"

"What?!" *What the fuck is happening?*

"Last night Cole told me how excited you were to get spit roasted, so we came up with a plan to make sure we were the final two members of the blue team. I hope you're ready for a wild time." Tanner turned and undressed me with his eyes.

"You're joking."

"I'm not."

"But, but… You two hate each other!"

"We do. But I'm willing to put that aside for your pleasure."

Oh my God. I couldn't breathe. All things considered, I'd done a pretty good job of not freaking out all day about my potential punishment. I kept thinking that Tanner would save me. But now, he was going to be the one doing the punishing. *Wait a second!* I was finally going to get to have sex with Tanner! And Cole. In front of everyone.

It was hard to fully grasp the odd mix of emotions I was feeling. Excitement. Horniness. Sheer terror. Confusion.

Did this mean that Tanner wanted to be with me? Or was this some sort of weird anger bang to get me back for telling him I never wanted to see him again?

"What happened to you wanting to protect me? Just last week you totally freaked out when Cole almost banged me at the casino."

"I didn't want to miss out on all the fun."

"And DODO?"

"Banging you as part of Society Wars won't tip DODO off that we're together. Especially if you're banging Cole too."

We're together? I stared at him, trying to process everything he was saying.

"You look skeptical," said Tanner. "Isn't this what you want? What are you afraid of?"

"Um… Germs. AIDS. Public speaking. Centipedes. Being late."

"I feel like most of those don't apply to this situation."

"Sure they do."

Tanner nodded. "Well if it makes you feel any better, both me and Cole have been tested for AIDS. And centipedes don't really like it out here in the woods. I picture them more in basements."

None of that matters! I'm not freaking doing this! Right? Or am I going to do this? Because I really, really wanted to be with Tanner. Even though I knew I shouldn't. "What if I refuse?"

"Then we won't do it," replied Tanner like it was the most obvious thing in the world.

"Wait, what?"

"We don't do it. What kind of rapey perverts do you think we are?"

"The rapiest kind."

"The Society has a strict no rape policy. Didn't you read the contract? Rape is clearly prohibited in clause 49c."

"Oh right." I'd almost forgotten about that. I'd been kicked out of the Society before for violating that specific clause. Even though it had nothing to do with incident #2 and Dr. Lyons. Which, for the record, was the only time I'd ever tried to rape someone. And I hadn't even been successful at it. #RapingMenIsHard. I leaned back in the seat and took a deep breath. I almost even laughed thinking about my epic hashtag usage. Because of the word hard. And how un-hard Dr. Lyons had been when I'd groped him at the doctor's office.

Tanner pulled the golf cart to a stop and got out his phone.

"What's up?" I asked.

"Ah, found it." He handed me his phone. It was open to a princess suite contract on the Society app. He scrolled down and pointed to clause 4:

4) The losing princess shall be spit roasted at the victory banquet by two members of the winning team. The men participating in the spit roast shall be determined in the following way:

4a) Men who have a direct role in her capture get first dibs.

4b) If three or more men are involved in the capture, then the princess shall choose.

4c) If the princess is unable to choose, then the men shall have a rock-paper-scissors tournament. See clause 8d for specifics.

4d) If it is a solo capture, then the man with the most wins during the earlier events...

There were like 12 more subclauses that seemed irrelevant, so I just skipped to the next part.

5) Refusal to participate in the spit roast shall constitute gross misconduct, which results in immediate termination as specified by clause 49d of the Society's membership agreement.

5a) And in the case of refusal to participate, for her stay in the princess suite, including food and handmaid services, the princess shall be charged a total of $245,120.

I had to read it three times. If I didn't go through with it I had to pay that exorbitant fee for the room?! "Please tell me that $245,120 is payable in Monopoly money."

"Nope," said Tanner as he started driving again. "US dollars."

Shit! I had been saving money like a boss over the past three months, but not that much money. Not even close.

"I would offer to pay it for you, but I know you don't want me interfering with your love life."

"No! I didn't mean that. I take it all back. I want you to interfere with my love life." Obviously. I was considering letting him spit roast me. But if he just paid the fine I wouldn't have to.

"Nope." He shook his head. "I'm not falling for that trap."

"So you're really going to make me do this?"

"What are you so afraid of?"

"We already went over that."

Tanner laughed. "I meant specifically about the spit roast."

"It's like public speaking only a million times worse. Because I'll be naked. And having sex. With two men!"

"That's nothing to be ashamed of. And in a way…it's easier than public speaking. Giving a speech is hard work. Getting spit roasted is easy. Honestly, Cole and I have a lot more to be worried about than you. What if we can't get it up? Or cum early? Or accidentally make eye contact with each other?"

I laughed at the thought of it. "Well, that would definitely be embarrassing for you. But it's different since I'm a girl. You'll get high fives afterwards. I'll get slut shamed."

"The Society is a slut shaming free zone."

"I doubt that. But even if it is...I still don't want all those people seeing me naked. I have stretch marks on my ass."

Tanner slowed down and turned to look at me. His deep brown eyes drank in every inch of me. "Your ass is a work of art. And anyway, everyone here has already seen it thanks to that dress."

"This is *not* a dress!"

"As one of the most renowned fashion designers in the world, I have to respectfully disagree. Ah, we're almost here!"

It was fully dark now, but the feast area was impossible to miss. It was lit up like a Christmas tree with a gazillion white lights strung between the trees. A fire blazed in the center of it all, and I was pretty sure I saw a pig being spit roasted. To be clear - I'm talking about an actual pig on a stick spinning over a fire. Not a girl bent over between two dudes. And then a horrible thought occurred to me.

"Wait. Please tell me you aren't going to spit roast me over an open flame."

Tanner pretended to be offended. "Of course not! What kind of freak do you think I am?"

"The kind who wants to spit roast me with another dude!"

He laughed. "Guilty as charged. But luckily for you, I'm not a monster. If you really don't want to do it, then I'll pay the fine. Hell, I'll even find a way to let you stay in the Society."

"What's the catch?"

"The only catch is that you take a few minutes to make your final decision. This is a once-in-a-lifetime opportunity for you to experience something that most people can only fantasize about. Sex isn't something gross and evil that should only be done behind locked doors. It's beautiful, and it should be celebrated." He pulled the cart to a stop outside a tent near the feast area. The tent blocked my view, but I could still hear the ruckus of all the campers standing around the raging campfire. He hopped off the cart and put his hand on my shoulder. "I'll be back in five minutes. Think about it." He trailed his finger down my arm as he got out of the cart, just barely brushing my skin.

A shiver went down my back. I wanted him. I'd wanted him since the first day I'd set eyes on him. But not like this. *Right?*

Frankie popped her head out of the tent. "Hey girl," she said in her always-bubbly voice.

"Hey," I said absently. My mind was elsewhere.

She skipped over and grabbed my hand. "Come on. Let me touch up your hair and makeup. I want to make sure you look perfect before your big entrance."

Oh God. Big entrance? This can't be happening.

Frankie pulled me into the tent. It was primarily set up as a kitchen, with servers rushing in and out, but there was also a little vanity with those super bright lights. I sat down and Frankie started re-braiding my hair.

"I don't know if I should do it," I said.

"What?" asked Frankie. "You have to do it! You're going to have so much fun."

"You think so?"

"Yes. Just forget about all the people watching and enjoy yourself." She grabbed a medieval-looking goblet off a server's tray and shoved it in my hands. "Here, this will help."

I downed it in one gulp.

"Actually, I think you should definitely run away."

"What? Why?"

"Because as your handmaid, I'm second in line." Frankie looked so excited.

No! You don't get to have sex with Tanner. He's mine! And in that moment, I knew what I had to do. I wanted him. Despite the awkward circumstances. And I wasn't going to share him with someone else. Even if he was willing to share me. *God, I'd lost my mind.* "I'm going to need another drink."

Chapter 29
THE WHORE-PRINCESS
Saturday

Tanner was waiting for me outside the tent, just casually leaning against a tree. As if nothing wild was about to happen.

How can he be so calm at a time like this?!

He kicked off the tree and walked over, the hint of a smile playing on his face. He stopped a few inches away from me.

"So what's the verdict?" he asked. He reached out and ran his fingers through my hair.

"I'll do it," I said, my voice barely more than a whisper. Maybe if he didn't hear me, I wouldn't have to go through with it.

"What was that?" He cupped his hand to his ear and leaned in. "I couldn't hear you."

This is actually happening. I wouldn't share him with Frankie. I couldn't. "I said I'll do it." Sweat was pouring out of me by the gallon. This was shaping up to be more of a slip n' slide than a spit roast.

Tanner looked *so* happy. "Then let's go get this party started." He offered me his arm and led me towards where the music was blaring. Instead of entering from the front, we took a path around to the back, behind the main stage. There were curtains set up so that I couldn't see all the people. But I could still hear them.

Oh my God. Am I seriously going to do this? I started sweating even more and my stomach flipped over.

Tanner stopped behind the curtain and turned to face me. "Just to be clear - Cole and I are going to rip this dress off of you." His hand traced the fabric down from my shoulder to just above my breasts. He leaned in and whispered, his breath warm against my neck. "And then we're going to bend you over."

I was already drenched in sweat. But his words were starting to make me wet in a different place.

"And Cole is going to jam his cock down your throat while I claim your tight little pussy. In front of over a hundred people. That's what you want?"

Holy shit. His words sent a chill down my spine. Directly to my groin. I pressed my legs together. I'd never felt such a strange mix of excitement and nervousness.

I downed my third goblet of wine and nodded. "Yes."

He reached out and ran his thumb across my lower lip. "That's *really* what you want?"

I couldn't even speak. I was waiting for him to slip his thumb into my mouth, teasing me. I just nodded, because I was scared I was going to whimper.

Tanner pulled back and raised an eyebrow. Amusement danced across his face. "You, Miss Ashley Cooper, are officially a freak."

Am I? I guess I was. But he didn't have to rub it in. Besides, he was too.

"Oh," he said. "And I should probably mention one more thing before we go through this curtain."

"What?" *Is Dr. Lyons going to pop out and make it a foursome?* At this point, no filthy twist would surprise me.

"I wasn't actually on the blue team."

I looked at him in confusion. What was he talking about?

"Everything I said about working with Cole...that was all a lie. I'm still on your team. Our plan worked. We won!" He lifted his hand for a high five.

What the actual hell? "So I'm not about to be spit roasted?"

Tanner laughed. "No. Of course not."

"Are you fucking kidding me?! Why did you lie to me?! I was about to have a heart attack!"

"Because you're so cute when you get angry. And so very gullible. How could I resist?"

"So you're saying you just put me through twenty minutes of pure hell for no damn reason?"

Tanner didn't respond. He just kept laughing like he was the funniest person in the whole world.

You asshole! "I hate you." I slapped him right across his stupid face. And then I realized what this meant. I wasn't about to get spit roasted. We had won! I jumped into Tanner's arms and kissed him. Like...really kissed him. I dug my nails into his back and kissed him deeper than I'd ever kissed anyone in my entire life. Our other kisses had been hot, but this was pure fire. Apparently relief was an aphrodisiac, because all I wanted to do was rip his clothes off and mount him right there on the forest floor. Or maybe it was all the dirty talk getting to my head. Or his abs pressed against me. I'd been dying for him to kiss me again ever since he'd left.

"I fucking love you," I moaned in between kisses.

Shit. Not again! I'd already scared him off once by telling him that I loved him. Why the hell had I done it again?

I kissed him more, but the fire was gone. A second ago our tongues had been in perfect harmony. But now we were less harmonious than a chorus of 4th graders. God, those home videos still haunted my dreams. How did my parents put up with that nonsense?

Anyway…the kiss. I'd ruined it.

I pulled back and jumped out of his arms. I expected him to look angry. But instead he looked amused.

"You still love me?" he asked.

"I love you like a friend. You know how it is. It's just like the guys say. Love ya, buddy." I punched his arm. *Oh God.* Getting spit roasted would have been less awkward than this. And now my hand hurt. *Stupid huge biceps.*

"I've literally never heard a guy say that to another guy."

"Well it's not my fault that you only hang out with emotionally repressed homophobes. By the way, your prank was a total failure. I knew the whole time that you were messing with me."

Tanner laughed in my face. "Oh really?"

"Yeah. How gullible do you think I am?"

"Very."

Damn it! He was totally not buying my lie.

Ocelot poked his head through the curtain. "Ready, Princess?"

"For what?" I asked.

"To get spit roasted," replied Tanner.

"What?!" A split second after I said it I realized that he was just messing with me. Again. But the damage had already been done.

"Yup…not gullible at all," he said.

"I hate you."

He nodded. "We already established that."

Ocelot smiled at us. "I really hate to break this up, because you two are being absolutely adorable right now, but the victory ceremony can't start without you. And if we don't cut into this pig soon, we might have a revolt on our hands." He grabbed my arm and pulled me through the curtain.

"Ladies and gentlemen," boomed a voice through the speakers on stage. It was so loud that it almost knocked me over. "Put your hands together for today's victor…Princess Raven!"

All the campers cheered for me. I knew that there were a lot of people at the camp, but it seemed like so many more now that they were all crowded into one spot.

Thank God I'm not about to get banged in front of all of them. But then something even worse happened: Ocelot handed me a microphone.

What the hell am I supposed to do with this? I shoved it back into his hand. "I don't want that."

"Why not?"

"Because. I can't speak."

"You're speaking right now."

"I meant *public* speaking."

"It's not a big deal. Just announce your team's reward and then the DJ will take it from there." He shoved the mic back into my hand and escaped off stage before I could give it back to him.

I was going to chase him, but everyone was just staring at me.

Shhhhhhhhit.

I stood there frozen for what felt like an eternity. It was like I was a deer and the crowd was an 18-wheeler barreling towards me. Only this situation was worse, because at least the 18-wheeler would hit me and put me out of my misery. The crowd, on the other hand, seemed fully content to just torture me with their eyes.

Why couldn't I have gotten the public speaking gene like Rosalie had? She was so good in front of people. Talking to a crowd was like second nature to her. To me, it was pure torture. I was seriously considering dropping the mic and pretending it was a boss move and not a pansy move. But then the crowd started cheering.

"Wooo! Princess Raven!" yelled someone.

"Princess Raven!" yelled another. Soon everyone had taken up the chant.

At that point, I was pretty sure I blacked out.

What am I supposed to say? Oh right…rewards. For my team. Wait, what the hell does that mean? The only parallel I could think of was when my high school volleyball team had given out superlatives and varsity letters at the end-of-season banquet. Was that what I was supposed to do here?

I looked around for trophies. But there were none. Just tons of goblets. The DJ was dressed like a jester. And all the servers were wearing some weird cross between tuxedos and medieval livery. Oh, and there was a totally sweet throne that looked like it was straight out of *Game of Thrones.*

My nervous brain combined those two concepts - a sports banquet and medieval times - and I ran with it.

"My good people," I said into the microphone with a weird Scottish accent. "My good people, please. Settle down."

A hush went over the crowd. I had their full attention.

"For months we have struggled against the tyranny of the blue team and the whore-princess Chastity." *Whore-princess? Eek.* That sounded a lot harsher than I'd intended. And it didn't even make sense. They'd been battling Cole all summer. This was Chastity's first time as princess. "But today, thanks to the brave efforts of our valiant warriors, that all ended. Today we were victorious!"

"Yeah!"

"Go red team!"

I waited for the shouts to die down before I continued. "All of you played your part, but a few brave souls distinguished themselves above all else. Nigel, please step forward."

Everyone looked around. Eventually the crowd parted to let Nigel come up on stage. He looked so excited. "You're acknowledging moi?"

"Yes. Now please kneel."

"Oh." His eyes grew round with excitement. "For...sexual reasons?"

"What? No."

"But kneeling will put me right in line with..."

"Just kneel!" I whispered back, but the microphone caught it and amplified it a thousand times over.

Nigel knelt. And stared right at my crotch.

"Nigel," I began. "You did not face the enemy directly, but you faced an enemy far more ruthless than even the whore-princess herself." Why did I keep calling Chastity a whore? "You faced father time. And somehow, you emerged victorious. In little more than one turn of the clock, you crafted a dress truly fit for a princess. And with this dress, we sprung an ambush for the ages. For your fearless and masterful seamstressing, I reward you with…" I looked around. Where were the trophies? Other than my throne, the stage was pretty empty. "I reward you with the title of Seamstress of the Realm!"

Everyone was quiet.

Well that wasn't the reaction I'd been hoping for. Then it hit me. *Duh!* Of course they weren't cheering for him. I hadn't even let him stand up.

"You may rise, Sir Nigel, Seamstress of the Realm."

He stood and a few people cheered half-heartedly as he left the stage.

"Next I summon my most loyal handmaid, Frankie."

I gave an eloquent speech about her, but no one seemed to respond much to that either. *Man, tough crowd.*

Next was Isadora.

"Lady Isadora, please come forward," I said.

Isadora came forward and kissed my hand the way a subject would greet her king.

"Lady Isadora, for sacrificing your body in service of the kingdom…" I began. A few people snickered. *Oops.* I hadn't meant it like that. "Silence, perverts! I speak not of her deflowerment, but of her valiant bravery and her use of the classic gambit, tree with false bosoms. *Blossoms*. Blossoms! Her bosoms are not false."

I drummed on them to prove my point, but they didn't feel quite right. Now that I thought about it, they had looked way too perky when I'd seen them in the shower. They were definitely fake.

My face started to turn bright red. This was exactly why I hated public speaking.

Isadora saved me by flashing the crowd. The cheers she got made it clear that everyone preferred seeing her tits rather than my super awesome speeches, but I didn't really understand why. I mean, I was kind of slaying it. Especially for not having anything prepared.

The final superlative was the most important. "Ryder, please step forward."

He jumped up on stage from the front row. I'd been hoping he'd kiss my hand, and he delivered. His soft lips lingered on my hand for a beat longer than would have usually been appropriate. If he'd done that to a real princess, I dare say he would have risked being beheaded.

"Not only did Ryder outsmart Princess Chastity's dog, Cole, but he also bested him in one-on-one combat. If not for him, all would have been lost. For that, I name him Sir Ryder, Champion of the Emerald Oasis and Protector of the Realm. It would be my honor if you would join me by my side for the remainder of our celebration."

"It would be my honor, milady," replied Tanner. He kissed my hand again and stood next to me at the throne.

"How am I doing?" I whispered. "This feels so good!" I took his goblet of wine and downed the whole thing.

"Um…I think everyone is just waiting for you to start the spit roast."

My eyes got big. "*I* have to spit roast Chastity? How am I going to do that? I don't even have a dick!" The mic caught that last bit and magnified it through the speakers. Everyone went quiet.

Tanner laughed. "You just have to bring her to the stage. Angel and Diablo will do the rest."

Oh thank God. Wait, Angel and Diablo? Actually, that made perfect sense. They seemed to do everything together. And they'd already tried to double-team me once. I loved this for them. I brought the mic back to my mouth. "Bring out the whore-princess!" I cringed. I needed to stop with that.

The crowd finally gave me the response that I'd deserved this whole time. The spotlight shifted from me over to a cage in the corner. Chastity was chained up inside, and Angel and Diablo were standing on either side of it. But while most people had stayed in their outfits from the games, Diablo had changed back into his red speedo from the fashion show. Angel was dressed to match. They opened it up and dragged Chastity out onto the stage.

"Kneel before me, wench," I demanded. That sounded better than whore-princess in my head, but it was still pretty bad. Diablo gave her a gentle shove and she went to her knees. I turned to Diablo and Angel. "Please give me a moment alone with my prisoner."

They both stepped to the side. I handed the mic to Tanner and approached Chastity.

"Ah, Princess Chastity," I said, circling her. Then I crouched down to talk to her one-on-one.

"Ash!" she squealed. "You look so fucking hot in your princess dress. If my hands weren't cuffed, I'd honk your tits so hard right now." Then her face got super serious.

I already knew what she was going to say. "I'm so sorry about whore-princess thing. And the wench thing."

"Why? Those are such high compliments. #WenchesSlay. Besides, I'm the one that's so sorry."

"Huh?"

"I've totally broken Single Girl Rule 13: Always wing woman for the girl with the longest active dry spell. I promise I did everything I could to try to win so that you'd get all the dick."

Oooooooh. It all made sense now. I knew Chastity was competitive, but I'd kind of thought she was being a bitch by cheating. But in her mind, she'd just been trying to get me laid. In front of everyone. By two men. I took a deep breath.

"Did you at least give Cole a blowjob to convince him to spill the beans on where I was hiding?"

"No…"

Chastity frowned. "I hate that for you."

"I did push him off a cliff though."

Chastity laughed and tried to give me a high five, but her cuffs prevented her from moving.

"Do you want a royal pardon?" I asked. "I can probably get you out of this."

"Hmm…yeah, you are in charge. So I guess you could take my spot." She looked so disappointed.

"What? No! I meant just call the whole thing off."

"Are you crazy? Getting double-teamed by hot brothers is like…every girl's fantasy."

Is it? Is it really? I was pretty sure that she was thinking of the weird male fantasy of banging twin sisters. But if she was into it, then who was I to stop her?

"Alright then…" I stood up and walked back to my throne. Tanner handed me my mic as I sat down. I felt like such a boss in my throne. "Princess Chastity," I said. "For losing Society Wars, I sentence you to be spit roasted in front of the entire kingdom." I nodded to Angel and Diablo. They moved to either side of Chastity. The two men towered over her. "Gentlemen… Unsheathe your swords!"

Chapter 30

JUST FUCK ME ALREADY
Saturday

Angel and Diablo both hooked their fingers in their little speedos and pushed them down, freeing their huge erections. And when I say huge, I mean *huge.* Somehow they looked even bigger than I remembered from when they'd tried to double-team me in the shower on my very first society date. And when I'd booped them each on the tip at the Onyxies.

Up until now it had mostly been the male campers cheering. Now it was the girls' turn to cheer.

I expected the brothers to attack Chastity, but instead they stared at me. The desire was written all over their faces. And even though it wasn't for me, I found myself crossing my legs.

"Your orders, Princess?" asked Diablo.

Ummm… With Chastity still kneeling, both cocks were only a few inches from her face. The most reasonable command would have been for him to facefuck her. But I didn't want to leave Angel just standing there. Their heated stares made me wiggle in my seat. "Bring her to her feet."

Diablo and Angel each grabbed one of Chastity's slender arms and hauled her to her feet.

"Turn her to face the crowd."

They turned her.

I couldn't just sit here. I felt like I was about to combust. It had been months since I'd last had sex.

And I suddenly had too much pent-up energy. I got out of my throne and circled the trio, pausing in front of Chastity. "During the freedom race you wore pasties, while all of us other girls risked being topless. Why'd you do that?"

I leaned down. "Seriously…why'd you do that?" I whispered.

She laughed. "Because I didn't want to distract your suitors with my beautiful nips! I was trying to be the best wing woman."

Well that was the sweetest thing ever. Especially coming from Chastity. She *loved* showing off her tits.

"You're the best friend ever," I said.

"I know."

I stood back up. "Answer me, Whore-Princess!" I demanded, trying to put on a good show. "Why'd you wear pasties?"

"I'm a princess. It wouldn't be proper to show my tits to mere peasants."

I turned to address the crowd. "What do you all think of that? Was that cheating?"

"Yeah!" several men shouted.

"Rip her dress off!" screamed another.

"The crowd has spoken," I said. "Remove her dress."

Without hesitation, Angel and Diablo grabbed either side of Chastity's plunging neckline. The muscles in their arms tensed as they pulled. Her dress resisted for a moment, but the strength of the men proved to be too much. The fabric tore straight down the center, leaving Chastity completely nude except for her bracelets and her blue thigh-high boots.

"Ah!" she screamed, pretending to be embarrassed.

I was mortified for her. But she'd said she wanted this. She even just smiled and winked at the crowd. And maybe a little piece of me wished I was in her place. Seriously…why was I so wet right now? I tried to think about what I would want next if I was Chastity.

"Stroke them," I told her.

She tugged at her cuffs.

Oh, right.

"Uncuff her," I said.

Nigel ran over and undid her cuffs. She immediately started stroking both men, one in each hand. Within seconds, both of their erections were at full mast. *Fuck, this is so hot.*

"Get on all fours." My voice came out weird and squeaky.

Chastity dropped to her knees and put her hands on the stage, arching her back to stick her ass in the air.

Diablo crouched down behind her while Angel stood in front. Their huge erections were inches away from her.

All three looked to me as a hush went over the crowd. This was it. Their fate was in my hands. With one word, I could give them all the pleasure they craved. I swallowed hard. *And I can watch and pretend that it's me.*

I drew the moment out by slowly walking back to my throne. I was a little worried that if I stayed that close, I'd jump in. Tanner was sitting there with a disarming smile on his face. Could he tell how much this was turning me on?

God, I wished it was us on the stage. I wished he still wanted me. I wished I hadn't blown everything.

He locked eyes with me and raised an eyebrow as I approached.

"What?" I asked. *He can probably tell that I'm about to internally combust.* I could feel my cheeks heating. And I could have sworn his gaze heated too.

That sexy smile spread farther across his face. "I didn't say anything. By all means…please continue."

It sounded like an invitation for me to sit on his lap. *No. Reign it in, Ash!* Just because I was really into the scene playing out in front of us, it didn't mean he was. But geez, was he trying to make me so wet that it looked like I'd peed myself?

I sat in my throne and looked back at my subjects. They were still frozen just as I had left them. Chastity's innocence hung in the balance.

God, just fuck me already. I mean her. Obviously I meant her. I tried to shake away the thought.

As much as my oversexed brain wanted nothing more than to watch Chastity be impaled by over 24 inches of thick cock, as much as everyone here wanted to see it…it wasn't time yet. She may have been horny, but there were no condoms and no lube. If Diablo fucked her without warming the poor girl up, he'd probably tear her in half. I bit the inside of my lip, trying not to imagine that mix of pain and pleasure. I cleared my throat.

"Lick her pussy," I commanded. I could practically feel my own pussy throbbing.

"It would be my pleasure," said Diablo. In one swift motion, he hooked his arms around Chastity's legs and swung her up onto his shoulders, her pussy pressed against his face.

I squirmed in my chair as I watched.

At first Chastity squealed with surprise. But then she moaned in delight. "Oh fuck," she panted, squeezing her thighs around his neck to deepen his tongue.

Holy fuck. Why had no man ever done that to me?! I crossed my legs. I didn't think I'd ever been this horny in front of so many people before. Hell, I'd never been this horny, period.

"Permission to fuck her face?" asked Angel.

I looked at him skeptically. With Chastity sitting on Diablo's shoulders, her face was like 10 feet in the air. "Permission granted," I said, mainly because I was just curious to see how he planned to accomplish it.

While Diablo continued to feast on her pussy, Angel reached up and grabbed her arms. Then he pulled her backwards into an impressive back bend that put her mouth level with his cock. She grabbed his thighs to steady herself as he slapped his cock against her face.

Diablo must have done something fantastic with his tongue, because Chastity moaned loud enough for everyone present to hear her. Angel took that opportunity to ram his cock into her mouth. She didn't seem to mind one bit. In fact, it looked like she was actively trying to jam it farther down her throat.

Was it possible to come just by watching this? I uncrossed my legs and imagined it was me. I could practically feel each stroke of Diablo's tongue. I pressed my lips together and tried not to moan with need.

Tanner leaned over the side of my throne and put his hand on my thigh.

Fuck. Me. As soon as his skin touched mine, I did moan. God, had he heard that? I pretended to cough and told my lady bits to cool the hell down. "Enjoying the show?" I asked. But I already knew the answer thanks to the tent erecting in his pants. I wasn't the only one that was finding this incredibly arousing.

"Are you?" he replied. His words dripped with desire.

"It's…okay."

His hand traced up my thigh, brushing the thin fabric of my skirt to the side.

My inhale was practically a gasp. "You want to give them a command?" I asked. I wanted to know what he wanted. Because he didn't want me. Right? Or had I been reading everything wrong?

"Nope. I find it very interesting to see what makes you tick." His fingers explored even higher.

I moaned again. *Stop it!* "I'm just trying to be a benevolent princess." His fingers were so close to touching me where I desperately needed him. If I could just shift ever so slightly…

"Of course you are."

Chastity's sex scream brought my attention back to the trio. Her whole body shook with pleasure and three quarters of Angel's cock disappeared into her mouth. I could actually see it bulging in her throat. I swallowed hard.

I pressed my thighs together, but Tanner's hands pried them apart. There was no doubting his intentions now.

"What are you doing?" I hissed. "Everyone can see us!" But I didn't really care. Was he seriously going to touch me in front of all these people?

"You really think anyone is looking at us?" he asked.

"No, but still…"

"You're the princess. If you want me to stop, just give the command."

I didn't tell him to stop. In fact, I almost gave him the opposite command. With each passing second, his fingers danced ever closer to my aching pussy. But his progress was torturously slow.

"Fuck," I moaned. Of course, the mic picked it up.

Diablo and Angel both turned to me. "Is that a command?"

"Yes," I said, trying to cover for myself. My voice was all airy. *Oh God. Can everyone tell how turned on I am?* I swatted Tanner's hand away to try to regain my focus. "Put her on all fours. It's time we got this spit roast started."

The two giants pulled back and helped Chastity get on her hands and knees. She arched her back even more than she had before. It was clear she wanted it. And I couldn't blame her. Just *seeing* Diablo devour her like that had made me dripping wet. I snuck a glance at Tanner's crotch.

For just a second, I wished that Tanner hadn't been lying about conspiring with Cole. It could have been me up there with them.

"Shall we begin?" asked Diablo. He slapped his huge erection against Chastity's firm ass and Angel rubbed his tip against her lips.

I took a deep breath. This was it. At my command, Chastity was going to be ravaged by two huge men. Seriously…huge. Diablo's cock was nearly the size of her forearm. And in a second, it was going to be inside of her. In front of the entire camp. I was so horny I could barely even see straight.

I brought the mic to my mouth. "Let the spit roast begin!"

The crowd roared and the DJ turned the music up. Everyone in the crowd started dancing. Or more accurately, grinding on each other like no one was watching.

Chastity's eyes got big as Diablo guided his cock inside of her. "Oh God," she moaned, but her words were drowned out by Angel claiming her mouth.

Tanner shifted in his chair and put his hand back on my thigh. This time, I moved to meet his touch. His fingers dipped under the fabric of my dress and brushed against my pussy. I had to bite my lip to keep from moaning as his index finger grazed my clit.

"You may want to turn off that mic," growled Tanner. "Or not."

I fumbled with the power switch as one of his fingers slipped inside of me.

"Yes," I gasped.

Diablo and Angel were still on their first thrust, slowly stretching Chastity to accommodate their length and girth. Tanner matched that with his fingers. With each inch of cock that she received from both ends, I got a bit more of Tanner's fingers. And then they all pulled out.

"More," I demanded breathlessly.

Their second thrusts were much faster than their first, and so too was Tanner's. But it still wasn't fast enough. Not even close.

I couldn't wait any longer. I turned the mic back on and gave my command. "Faster."

All three men obeyed. Diablo grabbed Chastity's hips for extra leverage as he thrust faster and faster. Angel reaped the benefits. The faster Diablo went, the faster Chastity's lips moved over his cock. But best of all…the faster they went, the faster Tanner went.

"You're so fucking wet for me," Tanner whispered in my ear.

God, yes.

"You like watching this, baby? You wish this was us?"

Another moan rippled out of my throat.

"Anyone could look up here and see you fucking my hand, Ash."

I whimpered when his thumb circled my clit.

"Pretend that it's me bending you over, shoving my dick deep inside of you. Look at them and think of me."

I tried to focus back on what they were doing. Chastity must have been loving it just as much as I was, because just as I started matching Tanner's fingers with my hips, she started grinding against Diablo.

Now that the men had warmed her up, she was getting absolutely *railed*. And I could so easily picture it being me and Tanner instead. I thought I'd be jealous, but Tanner's fingers felt like heaven. It felt like he had hundreds of years of experience with those hands.

"Harder," I demanded without really thinking.

Diablo smacked Chastity's ass and thrust into her, burying himself all the way down to his balls. Saliva dripped from her mouth as she moaned onto Angel's cock. At the same time, Tanner buried his fingers inside of me, his thumb pressing against my clit a little harder. I threw my head back and moaned in pleasure. My breathing was ragged. I was close. And Tanner knew it.

He groaned like he was as turned on as I was, even though I wasn't even touching him. "I knew this was one of your fantasies, you dirty girl. I'm hard just picturing me being the one behind you. Claiming every inch of your tight pussy."

I moaned again.

His fingers moved faster and faster, hitting all the right places while my eyes feasted on the two men dominating Chastity.

"You have no idea how long I've been dying to touch you. To taste you."

God.

He circled my clit with his thumb. "When you said you've never orgasmed before…was that really true?"

I'd forgotten about that. But I was too turned on to be embarrassed. "Yes."

He groaned. "Well you're going to experience tonight. In exactly ten seconds."

Yes, please.

"Look back at me now," said Tanner. "Look at me when you come."

I turned my head away from the trio and back to Tanner. All I wanted to do was kiss him, but I didn't want to break whatever spell this was. I thought he didn't want me. But his fingers told a very different story. So did his dirty words.

"Now, baby." He pressed down on my clit again and my entire body shattered. Every muscle in my body clenched at the same time. My pussy pulsed around his fingers. I wanted to scream, but I had no control. My eyes rolled back and my hand shot out to grab his wrist and prevent his fingers from leaving.

"So fucking sexy," he whispered.

"Don't stop," I panted as he tried to pull back. "Never stop."

And he didn't. Within a minute, another orgasm washed over me. And then another. I was instantly addicted. How had I never experienced this feeling in my whole life? I needed a million more of them. From Tanner.

The only thing that stopped me from grinding on his fingers all night long was the DJ's voice on the speakers.

"Picture time!"

Everyone apparently knew what that meant, because everyone stopped dancing and all the campers in red charged towards the stage.

I pushed Tanner's hand away before anyone got close enough to see what he had been doing. *I hope.* My legs were still trembling from my orgasms. Diablo and Angel, on the other hand, gave zero fucks about people crowding around them. They just kept railing Chastity.

"What's happening?" I whispered to Tanner. My chest rose and fell with each breath. There was no way I was hiding the fact that he'd just been fucking me with his fingers.

"They're taking a group photo of the winning team. Smile." He pointed to the camera.

The flash was blinding, but I somehow managed to keep my eyes open for the picture. The photographer snapped a few more shots just to make sure she had a good one. And then as quick as she had come, she disappeared and everyone went back to the dance floor.

That left me in my throne, still in charge of Chastity's spit roast. And still wildly horny despite the multiple orgasms Tanner's fingers had somehow teased out of me.

"Should I have them switch positions?" I asked Tanner. I was way too into this.

"You can do whatever you want," he replied. "You're the princess."

"*Anything?*" I looked over at him.

"Anything."

"There's only one thing I want," I said, my eyes lowering to his lips.

"What's that?"

"Come with me and find out."

Chapter 31

MY ONE DESIRE
Saturday

I dragged Tanner off stage. This was it. He was finally going to be mine. All. Mine.

The second we were off stage and away from prying eyes, I jumped on Tanner and kissed him. Deeply. Passionately. I kissed him like I had before I'd messed everything up and told him I'd loved him the first time three months ago. God, I missed his lips. I'd missed everything about him.

I attacked his face as I squeezed my legs around his torso. For a few moments, everything melted away. All I cared about was the taste of his tongue on mine. The scruff of his face tickling my upper lip. His manhood pressing against me. He was huge. Maybe he was even bigger than Diablo and Angel. And I was about to find out for sure.

"Ash," he groaned into my mouth.

His groan drove me even crazier. I kissed him harder, my hands clawing at his strong back. I wanted to tear his clothes off and take him right there in the forest.

So I did. Because he'd told me I could do anything. And what I wanted to do was *him*.

I had never been one to have long nails, but they were long enough to rip into his cheap Emerald Oasis t-shirt. The fabric was no match for my horniness.

I threw the ruined shirt on the ground and jumped off of him. God, his torso was even better than I remembered.

"Did you spend the last three months working out nonstop?" I asked as I ran my fingers down his six pack. How had I been living without him this whole time? *Don't say I love you. Don't you dare say it.* If I could just keep my mouth under control, I could have him. *Maybe I'll just shove his dick in my mouth to prevent me from saying those three words that ruined everything.*

"I tend to work out more when I'm stressed."

"Are you stressed right now?"

"No…"

"Well that's a shame. Because I'm about to give you one hell of a workout." My fingers traced along his Adonis belt and stopped at the hem of his pants. I started undoing the button, but he put his hand on mine.

"Ash, we can't."

"Why not?"

"I've told you. I have a flaming genie penis."

I laughed and reached back for his pants. But he grabbed my hand. "I'm serious."

I glared at him. "Are you kidding me right now? I'm so horny I'm about to explode. Quit messing with me and fuck me."

"I can't do that. But I can take care of your needs in other ways." He licked his lips to show me exactly how he planned to take care of my needs.

Just the thought made my legs feel weak. As much as I wanted that, I wanted something else more. "No. I need your cock."

"Believe me, I want nothing more than to ravish your beautiful body right this instant. But I really can't." Tanner slid his hand between my thighs. "Like I said…there are other ways that I can please you." His hand slid higher.

"That's not the same," I said. But the moan that escaped my lips told a very different story.

His hand stopped. There was a cocky smile on his face. "So does that mean you don't want it?"

"No! Of course I want it. I want you." I'd take him any way I could get him. I'd been dreaming of this moment. Dying for it.

"There's only one condition."

"What's that?" I asked.

"You have to tell me exactly what you want. After all…you're the princess."

I didn't need another second to think about it. "I want your tongue." I'd already had his fingers. But I needed to know what it felt like for him to devour me like Chastity had been devoured. That would be enough. Anything he could offer me would be enough as long as I had him.

He stuck out his tongue.

"Not like that. Put that away, son."

He laughed. "Not like that, huh?"

"No, I want your tongue inside of me."

He leaned in and kissed me, his tongue probing my mouth. I kissed him back for a second and then pushed him off.

"Not like that either." *Although that was a really good kiss.* "I want you to lick my pussy." The words sounded weird on my lips. But I didn't care. I needed him more than I'd ever needed anything in my entire life.

"Well why didn't you say so?" He trailed kisses down my neck, across my collar bone, between my breasts. All while his fingers expertly undid the laces and buckles keeping my dress in place. The whole process was torturously slow.

God, hurry up! I pushed on his head to try to get him to go down faster, but his body was an unmovable mass of muscle, which just made me even wetter. He could move at whatever speed he wanted, and there wasn't a damned thing I could do about it. I was completely at his mercy.

The crisscrossed strings holding my top together were the first to go. My breasts sprung free from the tight material. Tanner took one my nipples into his mouth, slowly clamping down with his teeth.

"Oh God," I muttered.

He bit a little harder and twisted. It was like he had just cast a spell of horniness on me.

"Please," I gasped.

"I already made you come with my fingers," he whispered against my breast and kissed down my stomach. "And now I'm going to make you come with my tongue."

"You're driving me crazy, Tanner."

He laughed against my stomach and then pulled back. His eyes locked with mine. "Are you sure you don't want to go back to the stage? I'll kneel down right in front of your throne and eat you out in front of the whole camp."

Holy shit. "No. I just want you. Right here, right now."

His eyes were filled with desire. He looked like he was going to devour my body. Which was good, because that was exactly what I wanted.

But then he looked over my shoulder and his expression changed. I couldn't quite tell what it was. Surprise? Excitement? It was as if he'd had some sort of epiphany.

"I'm so sorry, Ash. But I have to go."

"What?"

"I just saw…" He shook his head. "No time to explain. I have to go." He planted a big kiss on my lips and ran off.

I squinted to try to see what he had seen, but it looked like the forest was empty.

What the hell had he seen?

I swallowed down the lump in my throat. I'd told him I wanted just him. That wasn't the same as saying that I loved him.

I could feel the tears biting at my eyes as I threw my arms over my exposed breasts. He'd left me. Again. And I still wanted him. I let the tears fall down my cheeks. Why did I still want him so desperately when he kept leaving me?

Chapter 32

OPEN ME AT MIDNIGHT
Saturday

Where the hell had Tanner gone? I didn't even under-stand how he'd disappeared so quickly.

And then I realized what was happening.

I breathed a huge sigh of relief. Tanner was mess-ing with me again. And I'd fallen for it. Just like I always did. *Gah! I really need to stop being so gullible.*

"Very funny," I called into the dark forest. "You got me again."

No reply.

"You can come back now."

Still no reply.

"Tanner, come on. I know you're messing with me."

Crickets.

"Tanner?" I called a little louder. "Well, I guess I better put these things away…" I took my hands off my breasts and jiggled them a little. Boobs would surely bring him out from his hiding place, right?

Wrong. He was nowhere in sight.

Shit. Had he seriously run away *again*? I stared into the empty forest and my heart dropped.

Whelp…this was officially the worst weekend of my life. I'd come here to try to find Rosalie. But instead I'd gotten completely sidetracked by Tanner and Cole. And almost been spit roasted. And then to put a cherry on top, I'd gotten too lovey-dovey with Tanner and scared him off. Again. Big, fat tears rolled down my cheeks. I wanted them to be because of anger or embarrassment. But I was crying because I was hurt. Tanner kept freaking hurting me over and over again.

All I wanted to do was leave this stupid camp and go back to being lonely and single. Because being lonely sure as hell beat the feeling of constantly having my heart torn to shreds.

I considered driving back to the city, but there were two problems with that. First, I was freaking exhausted. I'd been running around in the hot sun all day. But my physical exhaustion paled in comparison to my emotional exhaustion. Second, and perhaps more importantly, Tanner had driven me here. Which meant I had no car. I was freaking stuck at this stupid freaking camp. I wanted to scream, but I was worried it would draw the attention of wolves. Or bears. That would be just my luck. I could already see the headline. *Topless girl gets mauled by bear.* But the coroner would probably declare my cause of death to be extreme horniness.

I put my arms across my breasts. What the hell was I supposed to do now? Would Tanner try to give me a ride back to the city tomorrow? The only way I would agree to that was if I was allowed to repeatedly kick him in the nuts throughout the entire drive. And I doubt he'd agree to that.

Maybe I could hitch a ride with Frankie. Or Isadora. Or literally anyone without a penis. Except Nigel. It would be the weirdest drive of my life, but at least the weirdness would distract me from the deep depression I was soon going to spiral into.

Wait, how had Chastity gotten here? She'd probably driven with someone with a penis. *Gah.* I could figure out the ride situation tomorrow.

The more pressing issue was my exhaustion. And that was easily solved by hijacking a nearby golf cart and hightailing it to my princess suite. Luckily everyone was busy at the spit roast, so no one saw me driving back to my suite half naked.

All I wanted to do was collapse onto the cushy bed the minute I got back to my suite, but I wasn't a barbarian. My clothes were covered in mud and sweat and probably a bajillion bugs. Despite what Tanner said, I was pretty sure centipedes ran around in the forest, not just basements. A shiver went down my spine. Finding one of those devil bugs crawling up my leg would be a fitting end for the worst day ever.

I stripped off my dress, which didn't take long thanks to the fact that Tanner had been about two buckles away from getting me naked when he'd decided to run away like a little bitch.

Screw him.

I took a quick shower and then hopped into bed. I expected sleep to come immediately. But the second I closed my eyes, a fierce growl burbled up from my empty stomach.

Nope. Nope, nope, nope. My hunger could wait until breakfast. This day was officially over.

I shut my eyes and demanded my body to fall asleep. It didn't listen. All I could picture was that delicious spit roast. The pig. Not Chastity. Although what had happened to Chastity looked pretty delicious too.

Oh well. I would never get spit roasted, because I was done with men. The only way I was getting spit roasted would be by two dildos. How exactly would that work, though? Would I have to get the ones with the little suction cups? Maybe put them on opposites walls of a shower and then bend over between them? They'd have to be kinda floppy for me to maneuver between them. And what if I got stuck? With how today went, I'd probably get stuck and die if I tried that tonight. Not that I was seriously considering it or anything.

Yup…I'm definitely not going to be able to fall asleep.

I groaned and rolled out of bed. The minibar was unfortunately only stocked with alcohol - so much alcohol - and the room service menu said they stopped service at 9 pm. *What kind of shitty princess suite is this?* One for a 7-year-old princess with an early bedtime and a severe drinking problem?

It didn't really matter though. Random room service wasn't what I was craving. If I was being honest with myself, only one thing was going to satisfy my hunger tonight. I needed to taste that pig.

The only question left was…what could I wear back to the party? I'd die of hunger while trying to figure out how to put the princess "dress" back on. I could wear one of the plush bathrobes, but that felt like an invitation for Cole to sneak up and rip it off of me in the middle of the party. That left me with one option. I had to find something in the suitcase that stupid Tanner had packed for me.

I rummaged through the suitcase, throwing bikini after bikini onto the floor. To be fair, it wasn't all bikinis. He'd also been a gentleman and packed me a few skintight dresses, a push-up bra, and solid gold pasties.

I didn't know what I had been hoping to find. Of course that was what he had packed for me. Because he didn't know me at all. All I was to him was a pair of breasts attached to the most gullible brain in the world. I would bet my new gold pasties that he had run away so that he could go make fun of me with his bestie Matt. I was suddenly glad I'd set Matt on fire. Anyone who was friends with Tanner was an idiot. And idiots deserved to have their penises damaged. #PenisFacts. *I nailed that.*

I was about to give up my hunt for something to wear when something at the bottom of the suitcase caught my eye. It was fleecy and baby blue and had little cartoon pandas all over it. I reached in and pulled out the most beautiful set of comfy pajamas I'd ever seen.

They were absolutely perfect. Almost too perfect. I eyed them suspiciously. What was Tanner's angle here? Were they actually snap pants that would be easy for someone to tear off of me? Were they laced with some experimental tech that would turn them see-thru after ten minutes of wear? Or was Tanner just the sweetest guy in the world and included them because he knew I loved fuzzy jammies and pandas?

Definitely not that last one. Because Tanner was a dumb jerk.

I was debating how to test the pajamas for traps when the elevator dinged open.

"Pervert!" I screamed and dove into my bed. I held the covers over my head, hoping that whatever cannibal had come for me would just think the place was empty and go away.

I waited for them to say something. Or make a noise. Or anything. But everything was silent. Eerily silent. Like the silence you'd hear in a horror film just before the murderer pops out and stabs the dumb girl who walked into the basement by herself.

Was that what was about to happen to me? Or had I imagined the elevator opening?

I slowly lowered the covers to peep out. There was no one there. But there was a microwave-sized package sitting on the elevator floor. It was perfectly wrapped in shiny red paper and tied with a white bow. Somehow, seeing that was even creepier than seeing a murderous psycho. At least I knew what I was getting with the psycho. This could be anything. The top 3 most likely options were, in no particular order, a grainy VHS of me walking alone in the forest, a severed finger, or a bomb.

I kept both eyes on the package as I fumbled for my phone.

I wanted to call Chastity. But she was probably still busy getting railed by Angel and Diablo. So I had to resort to calling Madison. Which wasn't so bad, because she loved watching serial killer documentaries. She'd know what to do.

Three rings. No answer.

Come on. Come on! Why wasn't she picking up? This was a life-or-death situation!

It went to voicemail. I *almost* left her one, but I wasn't quite that desperate. If I did die tonight, I didn't want Madison to remember me as a monster who leaves voicemails. But that didn't mean I couldn't text her a bajillion times until she responded.

I navigated to the text screen. I was all ready to type out my last will and testament, but then I saw that I had an unread message from her.

Madison: On a date with Donovan. Wish me luck!

Who the hell was Donovan? And what kind of a cruel joke was the universe playing on me?

I wasn't even sure Madison liked dudes. And yet…she was out having the time of her life being ravaged by some gentleman suitor while I became the 7th victim of the Emerald Oasis Eviscerator. Was that a real serial killer? And had he killed 6 other people? Not to my knowledge. But it sure had a nice ring to it.

I took a picture of the package and attached it to a text.

Ash: I hope your date is amazing. And I can't wait to hear all about it. If I survive the night, that is. Which seems unlikely thanks to that package that just mysteriously arrived in my room. I'm pretty sure I'm about to get murdered, so I just wanted to say that I love you very much. Oh, and you and Chastity can share my awesome closet. <3

They weren't the most eloquent dying words, but they pretty much conveyed what I wanted to say. I decided to add one more line, just to make sure she'd never forget me.

Ash: P.S. I almost got spit roasted tonight.

I would have considered texting Liz instead. But I'd rather die than take advice from a furry. Hopefully the Emerald Oasis Eviscerator would kill her next. I tossed my phone onto the nightstand and tiptoed over to the package. Why was I tiptoeing? I wasn't really sure. But it felt like the right thing to do.

There was a little handwritten note on top of the package:

OPEN ME AT MIDNIGHT

The fact that it hadn't been written with random newspaper cutouts felt like a win. But also: *Hell to the no!* What kind of sick torture was this? If the Emerald Oasis Eviscerator thought I'd have the patience to wait two hours to open this, then he was insane. Then again, I already figured he was insane since he was a serial killer, so I guess that kind of tracked.

Yeah, I'm not waiting, asshole. I tore into the wrapping paper. At the same time, a horrible realization washed over me. If this package exploded, my final words will have been: "P.S. I almost got spit roasted tonight."

Fuck my life.

I braced for impact as the last bits of wrapping paper fell away from the package. But nothing happened. Inside was a normal brown box. It wasn't taped shut or anything, though, so the flaps sprung open to reveal…another package.

Actually, it was a heavy-duty safe. Like, one of those metal ones trimmed with blue neon lights that a rich dude would hide behind a Van Gogh in his home office. And there was a sticky note slapped on top:

Bad girl! I said to wait until midnight!
Now I'm going to have to punish you ;)

What the hell!? How did the murderer know that I'd open the first package early? And why was the tone of this second note so playful?

It was possible that the winky face meant that they were going to peel my skin off with a butter knife while forcing me to listen to Nickelback's greatest hits on a never-ending loop, but I was getting more of a sexy vibe. Which meant…

The package was from Tanner! Which made sense. He knew I liked to open things early when I was specifically told not to. Like when I opened his *just in case he disappeared* letter the second after I got it. Patience was not one of my virtues.

Was this why he had run away? If so, it better be freaking amazing. And the only gift amazing enough to make me forgive him was his penis. Although I hoped he hadn't chopped it off and put it in the safe. That would be disturbing. I'd rather the contents of the safe be somehow related to Tanner wanting to take me somewhere romantic for our first time.

Yup, that was the only thing I wanted in the safe.

Actually, that wasn't true. I would also be satisfied if Tanner had run off because he'd seen an adorable pregnant squirrel with the fluffiest tail and chubbiest cheeks in the whole world who loves being squeezed, and if said squirrel had been magically tamed to be my life-long snuggle companion.

Either one of those two things would be fine.

Although if it was the second one, I definitely needed to get some food. Because I was desperately hungry, and I didn't want to accidentally go into a hunger rage and eat Captain Nutsmuggler when he popped out of the safe at midnight. Not that I really thought that was going to happen. But a girl can dream. About receiving him. Not eating him.

I pushed the safe into my room and then slipped into my new panda pajamas. Usually I would have been mortified to be seen in public in such pajamas, but this was the Society. I'd just MCed a spit roast in front of these people. If anything, going back to the party in a conservative set of panda pajamas was just the sort of thing I needed to do to prove to everyone that I wasn't a huge slut. Maybe it would swing the pendulum a bit too far in the direction of total loser, but I was so hungry that I frankly did not care.

Anyway…the only society member's opinion I cared about was Tanner's. And if he packed those pajamas, then he must have thought they were totes adorbs.

I was super confident in my outfit choice right up until I pulled up to the party in my golf cart and realized that a hundred real humans were about to see me.

Whatever. That roasted pork was calling my name. The fat dripped off and crackled in the flames as the pig spun and spun. The enchanting aroma of bacon was completely irresistible. There was no way I was turning back now. I'd been dreaming of this moment for years.

I walked right up to the chef manning the fire pit and asked him to slice me off a piece of pork. And then I asked for seconds and thirds. And fourths. Fine! And fifths. Don't judge me. I was hungry AF, and I was still the princess of this damned party. As far as I was concerned, I was being a benevolent princess by leaving any pork for my loyal subjects…who were all completely ignoring me.

The spit roast had continued despite my absence. How in the world were they still going at it? Joe had never lasted more than 4 minutes and 23 seconds - don't ask why I knew that exact number - so it was shocking to see that Angel and Diablo were *still* railing Chastity with the same vigor as when I'd left.

My fanny flutters immediately returned. I couldn't help it. I'd finally experienced an orgasm. And now I needed one at least every ten minutes. Was this what tween boys felt when they first discovered they could jerk off? I ate more meat as I stared at the stage.

Yeah…Tanner better be planning to bang the hell out of me at midnight. His fingers had been amazing. I could barely even wait to see how his hard cock would feel deep inside of me. I smiled at the thought as I double-fisted my pork.

Someone finally noticed me and gave me a weird look.

Get over yourself, peasant. As if they'd never double-fisted their pork products before. #PorkLife.

I took another huge bite. It was delicious. Drool-worthy. The best meat I'd ever had. And yet…it wasn't going to be the best meat I put in my mouth tonight.

Chapter 33

VISIONS OF SUGARCOCKS
Saturday

Waiting for the safe to open at midnight was pure torture. It was like I was a kid on Christmas morning. Only it was neither Christmas nor morning, I was an adult, and my present was going to be a big, juicy dick.

So really it was nothing like Christmas morning. But the excitement was real.

I had hoped to fall asleep right after devouring the entire plate of pork - which, by the way, was even better than I had imagined - but sleep evaded me. Instead I just nestled snug in my bed, while visions of sugarcocks danced in my head. *Ew, not sugarcocks.* That reminded me too much of Joe and his sugarcakes. Which then reminded me of the video I had of him cheating on Sierra. I still hadn't decided exactly what to do with that. Sure, I could just show it to Sierra. The look on her face when she watched it would be priceless. And then the look on Joe's face when she dumped his cheating ass.

But I could also just hold onto the tape. Let Sierra marry him. And then show it to her a few years later and blow the whole thing up.

Hmmm…decisions, decisions.

There was no time to decide though, because MY ALARM JUST WENT OFF! *It's freaking midnight!*

Well, it was almost midnight. I'd set my alarm for 11:45 so that I'd have time to fix my hair and makeup before the safe opened. To have my makeup be anything less than impeccable would have been a horrible disservice to my extremely sexy panda pajamas.

I kept glancing over at the safe in the tub. Yes, the tub. I'd moved it there before bed in case it was a bomb. Or a squirrel. Either would be best contained by the bathtub. It was like they always said on the news: during a missile crisis or rodent uprising, the safest place to be was the bathtub. This was kind of the opposite scenario, but it still felt like sage advice.

As my phone ticked down to midnight, I hid behind the door and watched the safe.

Three, two, one…

Midnight was punctuated by a small *click*.

Well that was anticlimactic. I'd expected the safe to blow open and spew confetti all over the room. Maybe play some music. Or at least light up. But nope. All I got was a little *click*.

I crept over, still not *totally* convinced that it wasn't going to blow up, and gently opened the safe. Inside was a white leather box with ODEGAARD scrawled in blue letters. But it wasn't a shoebox like the ones Tanner had sent to my apartment. Instead, it was a thin rectangular clothing box.

I tore the lid off to see what kind of kinky lingerie he wanted me to wear for our first time. Shockingly, it wasn't lingerie at all. Instead, it just looked like a little pile of shiny black sequins. Like…so shiny. The shiniest. I didn't even understand how something so black could be so shiny. But it was.

I begrudgingly stripped off my panda pajamas and tried on the dress. As with every Odegaard design I'd tried on, it fit like a glove. Actually, it fit like a really short, sexy, strapless cocktail dress. And the matching gloves that came with it fit like gloves.

I looked in the mirror and checked out my ass. If I did say so myself, I looked classy AF.

The only thing I was missing was some shoes. But thanks to Tanner's ridiculous suitcase full of camp-inappropriate clothes, I had plenty of options. I was in the midst of trying on some sky-high black pumps when the doorbell buzzed.

"I'm coming!" I yelled, even though I doubted he could hear me at the bottom of the tower.

This is it. I smoothed my dress and took one last look in the mirror before boarding the elevator. *Don't tell him you love him. Don't tell him you love him.*

The doors slid open and Tanner…

Nope.

Not Tanner.

For some reason, Cole was standing there.

"What are you doing here?" I asked.

"Picking you up for our date," he said with his cockiest smile. "And let me just say…" His eyes scanned up and down my body. "You look absolutely stunning."

"Uh, no. I don't think so." Sorry bud, I have a date with Tanner.

"No? Then why did you do your makeup all sexy and put on the dress I got you?"

I looked down and pulled at the expensive fabric. "This? You didn't get me this."

"Yes I did."

"But it's an Odegaard."

"It is. That's what you always wear, right?"

"Wait, you really went out and bought this for me?" *What the hell is going on right now?*

"Yup."

I just stared at him.

"Shall we?" He held out his arm for me.

"Shall we what?"

"Go on our date. If we don't leave soon, we're gonna be late."

"I'm not going on a date with you."

"Yes you are." He said it with all the confidence in the world.

"And why would I do a thing like that?"

He raised an eyebrow and gestured to his torso. "Look at me. What girl wouldn't want to go on a date with me?"

"Hmmm…I don't know. Me?" I would never admit it, but he did look damn fine in his tuxedo. It was a shame he was such an asshole. And more importantly, he wasn't Tanner. Who would be here any minute now. Right? "If you really got me this dress, then what size is it?"

"Two."

I narrowed my eyes at him. "How'd you know that?"

"Because I bought it for you. And if you're asking how I knew your size in the first place…well, I've ruined enough dresses and had to buy replacements that I can guess a woman's size nine times out of ten."

"Ruined dresses? Replacements?"

He nodded. "If you're lucky maybe I'll ruin your dress later tonight."

"How?" I kind of regretted asking, but I was too curious. "Are you going to spill a drink on me or something?"

"You could say that."

I wasn't sure exactly what he meant by that, but the look in his eye confirmed that it was definitely a sexy spill rather than a clumsy one. I was more concerned by his earlier statement though. About him really buying it for me. Because that meant…

Shit.

Tanner had really run away. And then Cole had sent me the creepy elevator package, but I'd stupidly assumed that it was from Tanner. And now I was standing here, wearing the $3000 dress that Cole had bought for me.

"Ready to go?" he asked.

"You're really not listening, are you? I said I wasn't going."

"Yeah, but that's not really your choice. You owe me a date."

"From what?"

"Our bet."

I laughed. "Nice try, but you lost the bet. In fact, you're lucky I don't demand that you get naked right here."

"I'll be happy to get naked any time you want. But not because of the bet. The second you cheated, you automatically lost the bet."

"I didn't cheat." *Oh no.* How did he know about Nigel's slingshot?

"And now you're lying too. Pro tip: if you're gonna lie, you have to learn to look the person in the eye when you do it. Now can we please get going?"

"I'm. Not. Going." I hit the UP button on the elevator. I still hadn't fully processed the fact that Tanner had indeed left, but I had a feeling a breakdown was coming. And I was out of pork. Which meant I had no food to drown my sorrows in. So I was probably going to rip up my mattress like a wild, starving animal. *Oh no.* I already felt hungry again...

Cole stuck his hand in to stop the door from closing. "Are you mad about earlier? Is that it?"

"Uh, yeah. You could say that."

"Why?"

"Because you were going to spit roast me with some rando!"

"Those weren't randos. Those were my friends."

"That might make it worse. I'm not sure. Either way, you're a despicable pervert."

"Guilty as charged. But in my defense, I thought you were too."

"And what would give you that idea?"

"Well...you did strip down for a bunch of high schoolers at Club Onyx. And you made your little boy toy pleasure you on stage while you watched your best friend get spit roasted."

My face turned into a bright red tomato. *Kill me now.* I had been hoping that no one had seen that. If Cole saw it, that meant everyone probably had.

"Has anyone ever told you how cute you are when you get embarrassed?" he asked.

I punched his arm. *Ow.* Were his arms made out of bricks? "I hate you."

"You won't after our date. Come on, we're gonna have so much fun."

I wanted to say no. To tell him I was with Tanner. But the truth was, Tanner had left me. Again. And tonight I could either sit in my bed, eating twice my weight in pork and trying not to let my meat get wet from my tears and that was only if I was lucky enough to find more pork, or… I stared at Cole. I could go on a stupid date with stupid Cole to get my mind off of stupid Tanner. And honestly, the fact that Cole bought me this dress and went out of his way to surprise me made my heart skip a beat. Yes, he was cocky. But maybe I needed a date with a cocky guy tonight.

He put his hand out for me.

"If I go on this date with you," I said, "you have to promise me three things."

"Name your terms."

I held up a finger. "First, you have to promise not to spit roast me."

"I promise I won't spit roast you," he said with a smile. "Even if you beg for it."

God, why had I let Tanner finger me in front of a whole group of people? Now everyone knew I was a kinky bitch. "How gentlemanly of you."

"I try. What's next?"

I held up a second finger. "Second, you have to promise that I won't end up naked."

"What you do with your clothes is strictly up to you. But I promise that I won't remove your clothing without your permission."

I narrowed my eyes at him. That wasn't exactly what I asked him to promise. "So you won't trick me into flashing a group of high schoolers?"

"Hey, you did that on your own…"

"Promise you won't trick me into getting naked."

"Okay, fine. I promise."

"Good." I put up my third finger. "And third, promise that you will still honor our bet and get naked whenever I want. I'm agreeing to this date of my own volition, not because you won a bet. Which you didn't. You lost."

He nodded. "Even though you cheated, I did technically lose. So I promise to honor our bet."

"Alright then. You sir have yourself a date."

He scooped me up.

I squealed. *Oh my God, what is he doing?*

He laughed and carried me over to his golf cart. Then set me gently down onto the seat.

Oh. He was just being wonderfully gentlemanly. *Hmm.* Usually whenever he acted like a gentleman he immediately pulled one over on me. There was no way I was going to fall for his games again.

"I should warn you, though," I said as he drove. "If you ever break a promise to me, I'll kick you in the nuts so hard that you'll wish you were never born." Just because he was suddenly being a gentleman, it didn't mean I trusted him.

"Seems fair. But I also have a warning for you. Those promises only apply to this date. Because let me be very clear - on our next date, I am going to get you naked. And you may not be ready for it yet, but I saw you on stage. One day soon, you're going to *beg* me to spit roast you."

Chapter 34

TWISTED AND JERKED
Saturday

"Just move that aside," said Cole as he opened the door of his Ferrari for me.

Yes, he had a Ferrari. And no, I didn't have any idea how the liftman for the Society was able to afford a Ferrari. I figured they paid well, but not *that* well.

I reached down and pushed a duffel bag off the passenger seat. I hadn't realized it was open, though. Because as I moved it, a bunch of stuff spilled out - ropes, riding crops, spurs…

"If you don't mind me asking, why do you have a bag full of BDSM equipment?"

Cole laughed as he slid into the driver's seat. "That's my rodeo bag, pervert."

"Oh…" *Shit! Is he serious?* "Why do you have a rodeo bag?"

"You'll see." He winked at me and floored his Ferrari in reverse.

I gulped. This was definitely a mistake. What the hell had I been thinking getting into a car with Cole?! I'd officially lost my mind. "Where are we going? Some sort of weird midnight rodeo?"

"Nope."

"Then where? I feel like there aren't many options this late at night. Either you're going to take me to go get a Frosty at a Wendy's drive-thru, or you're going to take me to an abandoned shack and cut me up into little bits." *Oh no! Is that what the ropes are for?*

Cole hit the gas and we accelerated up a little hill. It almost felt like we were on a rollercoaster. Only instead of being at a theme park, we were in the middle of a deep dark forest. This thing must have had like a million horsepower. #Horsefacts.

"For the record," I said, "I'd rather go to Wendy's than be murdered."

"Well that's a shame, because you only made me promise that I wouldn't get you naked or spit roast you. You never said anything about murder."

"Seriously, where are we going?"

"It's a surprise." He turned the wheel and whipped us around a sharp bend in the road.

"What if I don't like surprises?"

"You'll like this one. Now sit back and relax. It'll be about 15 minutes before we get there."

His tone didn't leave any room for argument. I was just going to have to trust that he would follow my rules. Hopefully my threat to his testicles would be enough to keep him in line.

I leaned back in the plush racer seat and watched the trees zip by. Then my eyelids started to feel heavy…

"How does that sound?" asked Cole.

"Huh? What?" I mumbled, wiping some drool off my lip. *Shit. Did I fall asleep?* It had been a long day and I had every right to be super tired, but it still seemed embarrassing to fall asleep 5 minutes into our date. "That sounds great," I added, pretending like I'd been awake the whole time.

"You sure you heard me? For a second I thought you'd fallen asleep."

"Me? Ha, no," I scoffed. "What do you think I am, a little baby?"

"Alright then. Well, look alive. We're almost there." Cole turned off the main road and a second later a gate popped out of nowhere.

A guard stepped out of a gatehouse and put his hand up to stop us.

"Uh...is that guard holding a machine gun?" I asked.

"Technically it's an assault rifle. But yes, he's armed."

My eyes got big. "I don't know that we should be here..."

Cole laughed and blinked his high beams thrice in quick succession. The guard stepped aside and waved us through.

"Seriously, what is this place?" I asked as we drove up a windy path towards a *ridiculous* mansion. If the Emerald Oasis clubhouse was a castle, this was a freaking palace. "This looks like the kind of place where a bunch of mobsters would meet to bid on nuclear weapons and kidnapped virgins."

"That's only on Wednesdays."

Is he joking? I genuinely couldn't tell.

We came to a stop under the porte-cochère.

Cole reached over me and opened the glovebox. Inside were two masquerade masks. He put one on and handed me the other.

"So it's a masquerade party?" I asked.

"Yeah, I told you that."

Right. When I was sleeping like a baby. A valet opened our doors. Cole tossed him his keys and then slipped him a hefty wad of cash. I couldn't hear what Cole whispered to him, but I assumed he was telling him that he'd kill him if he dented his Ferrari.

Another armed guard stopped us at the front door. "Names?"

"Cole and Raven," said Cole.

The guard started flipping through a clipboard.

"You won't find our names on your list," added Cole.

"Then I suggest you turn your ass around. If you're lucky, I'll forget I ever saw you."

"Actually, I have a standing invitation from Kat."

The guard narrowed his eyes and adjusted his gun. "You really want me to call her?"

"Yes."

"Okay. But if it turns out that you shouldn't be here…"

"Yeah, yeah. You'll throw me out on my ass. Just call her."

"It's your funeral," muttered the guard. He turned away and said something into a mic clipped to his collar.

I wanted to ask who Kat was, but I was worried that any sudden movements would get me shot by Meathead McGee. That was the guard's name, I assumed. MM for short.

MM stared us down for a good five minutes until the door opened. A woman in a black leather catsuit and a cat-eared mask slid out.

Well…that's definitely Kat. She looked familiar, but with the mask covering half her face I couldn't quite place her. Had she been on one of the teams today? Or had I seen her at Club Onyx? I wasn't sure.

"Who…" she started. But then her face lit up. "Cole?! Is that you?"

"Good to see you too," he said.

She pulled him into a big hug. It lasted a bit too long for my liking. Not that I was feeling threatened by her or anything.

Okay, fine. I was feeling very threatened. Because not only were her breasts spilling out of her inappropriately unzipped catsuit, but I was pretty sure she also owned this palace. For a second I thought that she was Cole's sugar momma, but that wouldn't really make sense with how excited she was to see him. If he had been her house boy, he would have been locked up in this palace and forced to wear shiny gold hot pants while hand-feeding her grapes. Not that that was what Nigel did with Tanner.

Because Tanner was straight. And even though Nigel did some odd things, I certainly hadn't imagined him saying he wanted to fuck me. Nigel was as straight as an arrow. *I think.* It's possible it was more like…straight as a squash. So like slightly curved. And now I was thinking about penises. *Stupid orgasm and perverted brain!*

"Who's this?" she asked when their embrace finally ended.

"This," began Cole. He put his arm around my shoulders and pulled me into his side. "This is my girlfriend. Raven. Raven, this is Kat."

"Pleasure to…" *Wait…WHAT?!* Did he just say I was his girlfriend?!

"The pleasure is all mine," said Kat. "If you've been able to get Cole to settle down, then you must be truly special."

"Yup," was all I could think to say. I was still caught up on the whole girlfriend thing. Was that what he'd been discussing with me while I was asleep in his car? More importantly, if I had agreed to be his girlfriend, had I also agreed to a bunch of other crazy stuff? *Damn it!* Cole had an easy enough time tricking me into things when I was awake. I could only imagine what he'd tricked me into while I was asleep!

Kat led us inside. The foyer was about ten times the size of my entire apartment. And it contained exactly twelve more masked partygoers than my entire apartment. Because, you know…my apartment was currently empty. Unless Homeless Rutherford had snuck into my apartment tonight and thrown a masquerade ball.

The music got louder as Kat took us down a huge hallway lined with framed 8-foot-tall photos of cats. The first few were adorable, but then it just got kind of weird. No one needed that many pictures of cats.

The hallway opened up into a grand ballroom, complete with a DJ, a fully stocked bar, and tons of dancing guests.

"What will you be drinking tonight?" asked Kat as we approached the bar.

"Nothing for me," said Cole. "I'm driving."

"Nonsense," said Kat. She ran around behind the bar and then reappeared a second later with two identical room keys. Each was attached to a keychain with a little tag that said 236. She handed us each a key.

Cole pocketed his and I slipped mine into my clutch. Not that I'd be using it. I'd agreed to a date - not a sleepover.

"Well I guess that fixes that," said Cole. "I'll drink whatever Raven's drinking." He turned to me expectantly.

"Um…" I always hated ordering drinks. People were always so judgy about it. I mean, obviously I wanted something delicious and fruity. This party seemed fancy though, which meant there was likely an easy out. "Do you have a signature drink?"

"Sure do." Kat tapped the bar to get the bartender's attention. "Two Slippery Meows, please."

She got us our drinks and then returned to her hostess duties.

"What's up with that lady and cats?" I asked the second she was out of earshot.

Cole laughed. "Yeah, she's always had a thing for them."

Always? I took a long sip of my Slippery Meow. Other than flakes of 24-carat gold, I couldn't tell what was in it. But it wasn't half bad. Kind of bubbly but still smooth. "Is her name really Kat?"

"Katerina."

"And you guys go way back, huh?"

"We grew up down the street from each other."

"So she was your childhood sweetheart?"

Cole looked away. "Not quite."

"You've gotta give me more details than that. I mean, as your girlfriend I think I have the right to know."

He laughed. "If you must know, I had a huge crush on her when we were young. But that's done and dusted. She missed her chance."

"What happened? She didn't want to be spit roasted by you and your buddies? Shocker."

"Something like that."

"Wait, for real?" *What a pervert!* "I need the entire story immediately."

"Do you promise to never breathe a word of this to anyone?"

"Sure."

"Okay. So we grew up down the street from each other in a small town about 2 miles from here. As kids, we were inseparable. We rode our bikes to school together every morning. We spent our summer days playing outside and our summer nights hiding out in my treehouse. And when it got too cold, my mom would make us hot chocolate while we played with my Legos."

"Well that's adorable."

"Yeah. It was, until high school started."

"You got too cool for her?"

Cole downed the rest of his Slippery Meow in one big gulp. "Quite the opposite, actually. She joined the cheerleading squad. And instead of riding our bikes to school together, she started getting rides from the football players." He turned to the bartender. "Another one, please."

"So why didn't you join the football team?"

"I would have been killed. I weighed like a buck twenty back then. All elbows and knees."

"You're kidding."

"I wish I was."

"There's no way." I just couldn't picture it. It seemed impossible that such a hunk could have even been lanky and awkward. "I would have pegged you as the captain of the football team. Not some nerdy loser."

"Whoa, slow your roll there. I never said anything about being a nerdy loser."

"Weren't you though?"

"Yeah, I guess I kinda was."

"Please tell me you have a picture of that."

"Of course." He reached into his jacket pocket.

Oh my God, yes! I could not wait to see this photo.

But instead of pulling out a photo, all he pulled out was his middle finger.

I slapped his arm. "Hey!"

"Did you really expect me to be carrying around embarrassing childhood photos?"

Yes. Which I realized was ridiculous, so I said the first thing that popped into my head so he'd stop making fun of me. "When did you get hot?" *Smooth.*

"So you think I'm hot, huh?"

Shit! He'd caught me. "You're okay."

"Uh huh. Anyway, I got hot in prison. Getting picked up for knocking off that liquor store with Naked Bill turned out to be the best thing that ever happened to me."

I put my drink down on the bar and stared at him. "Naked Bill?"

"Yeah. My boy Bill. William, for long."

"I was more focused on the naked part." Actually I was more focused on the prison part. But I was curious about Naked Bill too.

"He had a tendency to strip when he got drunk. Anyway, let's dance." He downed his second drink and started pulling me towards the dance floor.

"No way. You can't just drop that bomb on me and then expect me to not have a million questions." I knew he was a bad boy, but that was a little too bad for my taste.

"Didn't you ever know anyone who liked to get naked while they were drunk?"

"Not that! I was talking about you going to prison."

"You actually believed that?" He laughed. "Yeah, that was a total lie. But I'm flattered that you think I'm that badass. Really I just got hot by joining a construction crew the summer before college."

I glared at him. "You know, you should really think twice before messing with me. I can make you get naked whenever I want, remember?"

"Go for it. In fact, that would be great. My tailor made these pants a little too tight in the crotchal region." He adjusted his junk.

Damn it! How was he so confident? If he had been threatening to make me take my dress off right now I would have been freaking out.

"Hmm…no, it's not time to get you naked yet. I'm going to save it for the worst possible time. It's gonna be epic." And I didn't want Kat to see him naked.

"If you say so. Now can we please dance? This is my jam."

"In a second. I never got the end of the story about you and Kat." I had to know exactly what I was up against.

"There isn't much left of the story. We went to different colleges. I didn't see her for a good 5 or 6 years. When we ran into each other again she was all over me, but I shut her down. Part of me still resented her for ditching me in high school."

Suddenly I saw Cole in a whole new light. All the muscles and tattoos and jokes were just his way of covering up his heartache. "I'm sorry she ditched you," I said.

"I'm over it. Wait a second…do you feel that?"

"Feel what?"

Cole gripped the counter while his body twisted and jerked. "The music…it's pulling me…" He held on tighter but the invisible force won out. He grabbed me and took me with him.

I wanted to ask so many more questions about his childhood, but I got the feeling that he'd already shared more than he was comfortable with. The least I could do to thank him was reward him with a dance.

I shuffled my feet and snapped my fingers, trying desperately not to look extremely awkward. I was pretty sure I failed.

"What the hell are you doing?" asked Cole.

"Dancing." *Gah! Dancing is the worst!* Whatever monster decided that dancing was a group activity should be shot. There was a reason that I only danced in the comfort of my own home when I was very, very alone. Or very, very drunk. I really needed another drink to do this…

"Unless your name is Uncle Frank, then that's not dancing. You have to feel the music." He grabbed my hands and helped me move to the beat. "See? That's not so hard."

When he held my hands it wasn't so hard at all. Actually, it reminded me a lot of dancing with Tanner at the Wineflix and Chill launch party. He'd made me feel comfortable too. Right before he ghosted my ass. *God, stop thinking about Tanner.*

We danced to that song. And then the next. And then he let go and started dancing all crazy. I went back to my classic shuffle/snap.

"Seriously?" asked Cole. "Back to that?"

"You don't have to rub it in. I know I'm a terrible dancer."

"You know what I think?"

"What?"

"I think you're afraid to make a fool of yourself. But the joke's on you. Because the only difference between a good dancer and a bad dancer is confidence. And you, Raven Black, are too hot to not be confident."

I was smiling so hard it hurt. Was I actually vibing this dude?

Chapter 35

WANNA SWITCH ROOMS?
Saturday

One dance at a time, Cole got me a little more comfortable with dancing. First he had me do the sprinkler. It was stupid, but it was easy. Then he started yelling out animal names for us to act out. The elephant was simple, but then he yelled, "Platypus!"

I stared at him in confusion. I hardly knew what a platypus looked like, much less how to imitate one.

Cole pressed his lips between his fingers to make a duckbill and then simultaneously rolled his eyes back into his head and stuck his tongue out.

I couldn't help but laugh. He looked totally ridiculous.

I still wasn't convinced that I could really let loose, though. Not until *Dancing Queen* started playing. Cole really embraced the song. For the next three minutes, he truly was the Dancing Queen. His dance was over the top and hilarious and extremely gay. But something about it gave me the confidence to join him.

"I'm the dancing queen!" we both shouted as we twirled around.

In that moment, something clicked. Cole was right. Dancing was all about confidence. And what did I have to not be confident about? No one was watching us. And if they had been, all they would have seen was a couple having the time of their lives.

We danced and danced and danced some more. I even tried a few of those horrible line dances. I still had no idea what it meant to cha cha real smooth, but whatever. Cole didn't care as long as I was shaking my ass on him. Which I was definitely doing. A lot.

So this is why people like dancing. I couldn't believe I'd been missing out on this my entire life.

I never wanted to stop. But eventually I got too thirsty to continue. I pulled Cole off the dancefloor to grab some water. I was planning on getting right back out there, but then I caught my reflection in the mirror. *Oh dear lord.* My black hair was plastered to my face with buckets of sweat and my face was super red from the exertion.

I excused myself and went directly to the ladies' room. I didn't have much makeup with me, but I was at least able to blot my face with a paper towel. Or two. Fine, I soaked twelve paper towels. But it was worth it, because by the time I was done, I no longer looked like a swamp monster.

"Need some lipstick?" offered the girl at the sink next to me.

Share lipstick? I'd literally rather get punched in the boob. "No thanks."

She shrugged and rifled through her purse. Then she pulled out a key just like mine, only it was labeled with an 008 rather than a 236. "Wanna switch rooms?"

"Uh…" I'd forgotten all about the rooms. Originally I wasn't even considering staying. But we were having so much fun dancing. It was super tempting to just dance the night away and then crash in a room here. Cole *had* promised to be a perfect gentleman.

"Is that a yes?" The girl was staring at me like I was a crazy person. Probably because I'd spaced out for 30 seconds thinking about tonight's rooming situation.

"Why do you want to switch?" I asked. It seemed awfully suspicious.

"I'm just tired of the same room night after night. Looking for a change of scenery."

Does she live here? Is she Kat's housegirl? If so, then I definitely didn't want to give her my key. I assumed Kat had given Cole and I one of the best rooms in the house. Meanwhile, her housegirl probably had some crappy room in the basement. "Thanks, but I think I have to pass. Have a great night." I grabbed my clutch and walked out. It was time to dance!

Or, more accurately, it was time to get super jealous. Because rather than waiting at the bar for me, Cole had migrated to one of the half-circle couches surrounding the dance floor. And he was joined by Kat and some other dude. Kat laughed way too loud at one of his jokes and gently pushed his arm.

I'm gonna cut a bitch.

I walked over and wedged myself between Cole and Kat.

"Hey, girl," she said. "Enjoying the party?"

I was until you came up and tried to steal my man. "This is seriously the best party ever. I never knew dancing could be so much fun."

"DJ Neon is amazing. Tom found him a few months ago, and now I can't imagine ever using someone else." Kat gestured to the guy next to her.

He leaned over and gave me a dimpled smile. "Hey, I'm Tom. Kat's husband."

Husband? "I'm Raven. It's so nice to meet you." Seriously. I had never been so happy to meet anyone. I suddenly felt silly for feeling so threatened by her. She wasn't trying to steal Cole…she was happily married.

The four of us chatted for a bit longer, but I was itching to get back to dancing. When *Get Low* came on, I demanded that Cole come dance with me. It was random, but in high school I'd always dreamed of grinding to that song. This was my chance. And it was everything I'd imagined and more. At first I wasn't sure I was doing a good job with my grinding, but the growing stiffness in Cole's pants put my mind at ease. I couldn't tell if he was ten inches like he'd claimed in the forest, but it felt pretty damn big.

The song ended far too soon. And then the DJ started playing the first slow song of the night.

Cole immediately spun me around. Our bodies pressed together and we locked eyes as he pulled me close.

"I know I promised to be a gentleman," he said. "But…"

I didn't wait for him to finish. I got on my tiptoes and pressed my lips to his. As he kissed me back with his pillowy lips, everything melted away. In that moment, me and him were the only two people in the world. I was weightless in his arms as we glided over the dance floor.

I had liked dancing earlier, but grinding didn't hold a candle to slow dancing with Cole.

My heart sank when the song ended, but it was like Cole didn't even notice. He just kept kissing me until I finally had to pull back to get a breath.

He ran his finger across my lip and stared at me like I was the most beautiful girl in the world.

"You know," I said. "If you always acted like this, I might not have made you make those promises earlier." I was actually kind of leaning toward letting him get me naked now. Maybe.

"Slow dancing makes you want to get spit roasted?"

"No!" I pushed him backwards. He stumbled and nearly knocked over two couples. "I meant the other promise."

"You no longer want to get me naked?"

"Not that either. God, way to ruin the moment. I was trying to be sexy."

He laughed. "You don't have to try to be sexy. I'm pretty sure it comes naturally to you."

Before I could respond, the DJ's voice blared through the speakers. "Who's ready for the final song?!"

Final song? But I want to keep dancing!

The rest of the dancing couples apparently didn't agree with me, because they cheered the DJ's words.

"Well, that's my cue. Game time," said Cole. He gave me a quick kiss and ran off the dance floor.

I chased after Cole. But by the time I got through the sea of dancing couples, he was nowhere to be found.

Where had he gone? And what had he meant about game time? And why did men keep running away from me?

I checked the bar first, and then I checked each of the couches. No sign of Cole.

The only place left to check was the bathroom. It was possible that he'd had a bathroom emergency and was too embarrassed to tell me. Right? *Or maybe he and Tom are spit roasting Kat.*

Nope, that wasn't it. Because Kat was walking towards me.

"Hey, Kat," I said. "Have you seen Cole?"

"Yeah, I just saw him go outside." She pointed to where she'd just come from and then hurried off.

I took off towards the door. Back through the cat-picture lined hallway and into the grand foyer.

Ah! There he is! Cole had just come in the front doors.

"Cole!" I called, but the damned foyer was so big that my voice never reached him. He must not have seen me either, because he turned and jogged up some stairs.

Where was he going? And more importantly…why was he carrying his rodeo bag?

Chapter 36

ROOM 236
Saturday

It didn't take me long to figure out what was happening.

Cole was headed to our room - room 236. And he'd been lying about his rodeo bag. I was pretty sure my original guess had been correct. It was a BDSM bag. Which meant he was definitely *not* going to be a gentleman tonight.

And that was totally fine with me.

I'd seen an entirely new side of him over the past couple hours. He wasn't just a cocky asshole. He was a former scrawny nerd with deep scars from Kat's bitchy claws. So he put on a cocky façade to prevent himself from getting hurt again. Tonight, though…the only one getting hurt was going to be me. In a sexy way, I hoped.

Oh God. I'd read some books about it and seen a few videos, but I'd never considered trying BDSM. I hoped he wouldn't be too extreme. I could handle a blindfold and some handcuffs, but I wasn't ready for him to alligator clamp my nipples to a car battery.

I started making a mental list of my hard limits as I climbed the stairs. No anal beads. No butt stuff at all, actually. Except light spanking. That would be fine. And handcuffs could be fun…

Focus! My hard limits brainstorm was quickly turning into a list of fantasies. You really can't blame me though. I mean…just a few hours ago Tanner had been the ultimate tease. And then grinding all up on Cole had got me hot and bothered all over again. I'd originally thought my panties were soaked from all my sweat, but now I wasn't so sure.

I got totally lost in Kat's mega mansion, but a nice couple finally pointed me in the right direction.

My palms were sweating as I fished the key out of my clutch and put it into the lock of room 236.

Here goes nothing.

A horrible thought occurred to me as I opened the door. I hadn't come up with a safe word! *Oh no!* That was like…BDSM 101. Always have a safe word. For some reason, the first thing that came to mind was, "Yes, Daddy!" I know it seems counterintuitive, but my reasoning was that such a gross phrase would immediately kill the mood for everyone involved. Which kind of made it the perfect safe word.

Room 236 was really more like *suite* 236. The door opened into a sitting room filled with sleek modern furniture. On one side was an open door to the bathroom, and on the other side was an archway into the main bedroom. Neon red light poured through the archway.

Neon red light? How very appropriate for a BDSM sex dungeon.

I straightened my dress and walked into the red room. In the center was a huge four-poster bed occupied by…

What the fuck?!

Tom was sprawled on the bed, completely nude except for a leopard print blanket strategically placed over his junk. "Hey baby," he growled. He crossed one leg over the other and stamped it against the mattress. "Ready for the time of your life?"

Oh God why?! What is happening?! In a total panic, I yelled out my safe word: "Yes, Daddy!" *Oh fuck my life.*

"Oooh, Cole didn't tell me you were such a freak. I like that."

I had never wanted to die more than I did in that moment.

I threw my hands out to block my view just as he tore the blanket away from his body. And then I ran like hell. Through the winding hallways. Down the stairs. Outside. Into the parking lot. That was probably far enough, but just to be sure I hid in the bushes for a few minutes.

What the actual fuck was that? There was so much to unpack about what just happened, including a number of horrible realizations about how bad of a person Cole really was. Because if Kat's husband was in my room, that meant Cole was…in Kat's room.

I had no idea what to do. But I knew who would. Chastity. I pulled out my phone and called her.

Please pick up. Please pick up.

My phone suddenly switched to video and Chastity's face popped up on my screen. Cum was dripping down her chin and I could see Angel thrusting in the background.

"Hey!" she said with a big smile.

"Jesus," I said. "You guys are *still* going at it?"

"Yeah. We took a little break, but then we decided to go back to my princess suite to keep the party going.

Wait, where are you? And where'd you get that bomb ass dress?"

"Long story short, I went on a date with Cole and it was a huge mistake and now I need your help."

"Whoa, slow down." She frowned and looked back at Angel. "No, not you. If anything I'd prefer if you sped up." She turned back to me. "You went on a date with Cole?"

"Technically I'm still on the date… I guess. Does it count if I'm sitting outside the party while he fifty-shades-of-greys the hostess?" I pushed some leaves to the side so I could stare out at the mansion.

"Like…bondage stuff?" Chastity sounded so excited.

"I think so. When he picked me up for the date he had this bag of ropes and stuff. He claimed it was his rodeo bag. But then I saw him carrying it into the party just before…" What I was about to say wasn't going to make any sense with no context. "Actually, I better start at the beginning." I rewound to when Cole had picked me up at midnight.

Chastity listened intently to the whole crazy story. And then she told me exactly what had happened on my date tonight:

"How did you not realize he took you to a key party?" she asked.

"A key party?"

"Yeah. I'll show you." She pushed Angel off of her and walked over to a group of guys playing poker.

Why was there a group of men playing poker in her room? What the hell had she gotten herself into? Did she suddenly have a gambling addiction like I did?

She grabbed the hat right off one of their heads and held it out. "Keys, please."

They all fished their car keys out of their pockets and tossed them in the hat. Then she closed her eyes, mixed them around, and fished one out.

"Who owns the Audi?"

One of the guys raised his hand.

"Wanna fuck me?"

I'd never seen someone get naked so fast. Chastity put the camera back on her face as he bent her over.

"So that's basically how it works. But usually it's done with couples to make sure that everyone gets to have some fun."

"Is that really a thing?"

"Apparently so. Because you just attended one! Or at least a variation of one. It fits, right?"

"I mean…I guess?"

"Well, what exactly did that girl say to you in the bathroom when she tried to switch rooms?"

"Uh…" I tried to think back. "She was tired of the same room night after night and was looking for a change of scenery. Something like that."

"Yeah, she definitely wasn't talking about her room. She was talking about her boyfriend. And speaking of needing a change of scenery…" She fished another set of keys out of the bowl. "Corvette!" she yelled over to the table. "It's your turn."

Another guy came over and got behind her as the Audi guy sulked off.

"That's more like it," she said, pushing back on the new guy. "Anyway, where were we?"

"That girl tried to swap keys with me."

"Exactly," said Chastity. "And while she was trying to switch with you, Cole must have switched with…what was his name again?"

"Tom."

"Right. He was switching with Tom. Which explains why Tom was in your room. And it also confirms that Cole ended up with Kat. Or at least *wanted* to end up with Kat."

"But why did he bother bringing me to the party if he just wanted to get with Kat?" But the second I said it, I knew the answer. "Oh my God…I was his ticket into the swinger party. He wouldn't have been allowed in if he was single."

"Yup," agreed Chastity. "That's what I was thinking."

"Man…Cole is even more of an asshole than I thought. I can't believe I kissed him." The thought of mixing saliva with him made me want to barf. The Society did STD tests on us, but it still felt pretty likely that Cole had AIDS. Or at least herpes. And now I had them too. And I couldn't even ask Dr. Lyons about it because I was a vomiting rapist who targeted hot doctors. I still didn't understand why I wasn't in prison right now. But this wasn't the time or place to start thinking about my incidents.

"So how are you going to get back at him?" asked Chastity.

"Hmm…" I got out of the bushes and walked over to where all the fancy cars were parked. "I could slash the tires on his stupid Ferrari," I joked. Kind of.

"And strand him at his lover's palace?" asked Chastity. "Speaking of being stranded…how are you going to get home?"

"Good question." I didn't exactly want to just let Cole drive me home whenever he finished with Kat. "I guess call an Uber?" I thought about the front gate security. "Chastity, what if I'm stuck here?"

"Why not call Tanner? Speaking of which, what happened to him?"

"Oh God no. He's worse than Cole." I plopped down on the hood of Cole's Ferrari, taking absolutely no care to not dent or scratch it, and caught Chastity up on Tanner's shenanigans in the forest.

"Wow, Tanner really is the worst," said Chastity. "I can't believe he blue-boobed you."

I laughed. "That's not a thing. I'm not in pain. I'm just insanely horny. And angry. Why do hot guys all have to be such assholes?"

"Most are. But not all of them. Don't forget about Dr. Lyons."

Why did she always mention Dr. Lyons when I was actively trying not to think about him? And why hadn't I given her a list of my incidents yet? She just wasn't getting it. "Just because he got you into the Society doesn't mean I should be with him."

"Why? According to our pro/con list, he's super handsome *and* sweet."

"He is. But something about him…"

"He's too nice?"

"No." There's no such thing as that, right?

"You sure?"

"Maybe…"

"Girls are attracted to bad boys," said Chastity. "It's just a biological fact."

"Gah. I just want a bad boy who isn't also a mean boy."

"Who says Dr. Lyons isn't a bad boy in the bedroom?"

I laughed. "I'm 100% sure he's not. Imagine if Cole was a doctor and I tried to seduce him like I did with Dr. Lyons? He would have fucked me so hard. Dr. Lyons, on the other hand, kicked me out and then showed up at my apartment to apologize."

"Yeah, what a little bitch," said Chastity.

"I didn't mean it like that. I just wish he was a little more…assertive. The perfect balance of sweet and confident." I almost added, "Like Tanner," but then I remembered that he was the worst. So instead I said, "Like the Sausage King."

"Oh, we're for sure going back to his restaurant this week," said Chastity. "But for now, we have something much more important to talk about."

"Which is?"

"I have the perfect…" She was interrupted by a giant cock hitting her in the face. And then one poked her from the other side. She laughed and swatted them away. "Boys! I'm talking to my bestie. Give me a minute." She looked back at me. "Anyway, as I was saying, I have the perfect… Ah!!!" Cum splashed onto her face from both sides. She looked so happy as the cum rained down on her. So. Much. Cum.

Usually I would have looked away. But tonight I was so horny that I just kept watching, wishing some guy who wasn't an asshole would want to drench my face like that.

But no… Tanner was scared of me. And Cole was more interested in his old high school crush.

The two dicks entered the frame again. She gave each a little lick and then shoved them aside with a laugh. "Naughty boys! I'm trying to talk to Raven."

"We just wanted her to see what she missed out on," said Diablo.

"You really did miss out," said Chastity. "Look at these things!" She turned the camera so I could see their huge cocks.

Angel and Diablo both smiled and made their cocks bounce a little.

"Next time maybe you'll get this view from your knees rather than through a camera," said Diablo.

Angel shoved him out of the frame. "What he means to say is that even though your plan worked today and you're off the hook on our deal…you're still welcome to give us a traditional society greeting any time you want."

"What's that?" asked Chastity.

"Basically a blowjob instead of a handshake," I said.

"Oh my God, I love that! And speaking of blow-jobs… I have the perfect plan to prank Cole. And it's going to be epic."

Chapter 37

THE GETAWAY
Saturday

"Nope…no way." I said. Chastity's idea for the prank was insane.

"Oh come on," protested Chastity. "It's perfect! Just imagine the look on his face…"

She had a point. If we did it right, it would be priceless. But executing it to perfection wouldn't be easy. "Even if I agreed to do this, how could we set it up in time?"

"Don't worry about that. I put things in motion twenty minutes ago."

"What?! But that was before you even told me about it."

"Yup. I knew you'd come around."

My heartrate doubled. *This is really happening. Shit!* "I don't know. Are you…" I stopped midsentence when something caught my eye. "Hold on. I think someone is climbing out a window." I squinted to get a better look. Some dude in a tux was climbing down three stories worth of ivy.

"Well that's amazing," replied Chastity. "Guess he didn't like his swap partner."

Another guy popped his head out of the window that the first guy had just climbed out of.

"Oh my God," I said. "Now there's a second guy."

"What? Yes! Tell me everything." Chastity sounded so excited.

"Okay…so the second guy is yelling something. And now he's climbing out the window too!"

"How far down is the first guy?"

"About halfway. But…oh wow. He just jumped. I'm pretty sure he just shattered both his legs. Wait, no. He did some sort of ninja roll and now he's back on his feet."

"Please tell me you're filming this."

"I would, but I'm talking to you. Now the guy is running towards me. The other guy is still struggling on the ivy. He totally sucks at climbing. But two security guards just came around the corner. The first guy has a decent lead though. Wait a second…" He passed under some floodlights, giving me my first look at his face. "Oh my God. Is that Cole?!"

"WHAT?!" shrieked Chastity. "Well, I guess that's good news. At least he didn't want to hang around after he got his revenge bang on Kat."

"Go, go, go!" yelled Cole. He was waving his arms frantically. The lights on his Ferrari blinked as he unlocked it from the edge of the parking lot.

"Gotta go," I said to Chastity. I jumped off the hood and climbed into the passenger seat. Cole arrived a second later and slid over the hood like a total boss. I leaned over the center console and threw his door open to hasten our getaway. I wasn't thrilled that he'd used me to get with Kat, but I didn't really want to be captured by those armed guards either.

Half the cars in the lot were parked in by other cars. But by some miracle, ours was right at the very edge. It was even facing the exit. Cole floored the gas and sped down the road towards the main gate.

The guard there stood in our way with his hands up. Cole didn't slow down. Or give any indication that he planned to go around him.

The guard raised his gun.

"Cole!" I screamed.

He still didn't slow down. I thought for sure the guard was going to open fire, but instead he dove out of the way at the very last second. The wooden bar behind him did nothing to stop us either - it just shattered into a million pieces as we sped through it.

"Wahoo!" yelled Cole. "We did it!" He raised his hand for a high five, but I left him hanging. I didn't know where that hand had been. But I had a pretty good guess. Which was why I definitely did not want to touch it.

"I hope you found what you were looking for," I said.

"I did. Wanna see?"

Ew. Had he filmed his sexcapades with Kat? "No thanks. Was that Kat's husband who was chasing you out the window?"

"Yeah. Tom apparently was not very pleased that I'd stolen from him."

Well that was a weird way to talk about banging someone's wife. Especially at a swinger party.

"Speaking of Tom…" said Cole. "What were you doing sitting out here? You were supposed to be distracting him!"

"Sorry," I said. "He's not really my type."

"Right. But you were still supposed to distract him. Didn't you remember the plan?"

"Ummm…"

"Damn it! You *were* asleep on the ride over, weren't you?"

"Maybe." *Oh my God.* Had I really agreed to distract Kat's husband in a wife swap so that Cole could get his revenge bang on? Even worse, it meant that he'd been planning that from the start. When he'd given me the dress. And asked me out. The dancing had seemed so genuine, though. And that kiss...

I shook my head. I was such an idiot. Or was Cole just a total asshole? Yeah...he definitely deserved the prank coming his way.

"So I guess we're not really boyfriend and girl-friend, huh?" I asked.

"That depends." He raised his eyebrow. "Do you want to be my girlfriend?"

"Excuse me? Did you seriously just ask me out five minutes after climbing out of your childhood crush's bedroom?"

"Technically not. Her husband chased me all around that damned mansion thanks to my partner abandoning me halfway through our mission."

"Oh yeah, all of that was totally my fault."

"Eh, I forgive you. If anything, the chase after-wards just made it that much more thrilling." He turned and gave me his cockiest smile.

Ugh, gross! Time to teach him a lesson. "You know," I said. "It's a real shame that I'm not really your girl-friend. Because if I was..." I rubbed my hand along his thigh. "Then we might have been able to have some fun on the car ride home."

His knuckles got white as he tightened his grip on the wheel. "Wouldn't that violate the promises I made?"

"Hmm…let's see. I don't need to get naked to give road head. And if I asked you to, I could make you whip your cock out right this second. So no, I don't think you'd be breaking your promises." I gave his thigh a squeeze and then pulled back. "But like I said, I'd only do that if I was really your girlfriend."

He shifted in his seat to try to hide the erection tenting his tuxedo pants.

"God, I'm so horny tonight," I said as I twirled a strand of my black hair. "First I had to watch that spit roast, and then I saw you escape from those armed guards like you were 007. What are you doing to me?"

He swallowed hard and stepped on the gas.

"Oh well." I pulled my phone out of my clutch and scrolled through my texts, pretending to ignore him. The longer he had to stew in his horniness, the better.

After a few minutes, I finally put my phone away. "You know what…screw it. I can't take it anymore." I pulled my hair into a messy bun. Just as I leaned over to unzip his pants, a siren blared behind us.

"Oh shit," he muttered, pushing me back to my seat.

I looked in the side mirror and saw the red and blue lights.

Oh shit is right.

I immediately started panicking as Cole slowed down and pulled to the side of the road. And then a thought occurred to me: If we were at a swinger party and Tom had willingly switched keys with Cole, then why had he chased him out of the house? The answer, of course, was that Cole hadn't just stolen Kat's body. He'd stolen something else.

I'd been wondering how the Society liftman was able to afford a Ferrari. Now I think I had my answer.

I just wished I had realized it before I'd become his accomplice in a heist.

"Cole," I said. "Did you take something from Kat's house?"

"Just be cool," he replied. "I'm sure this is just a routine traffic stop."

The officer tapped on the glass with his nightstick.

Oh God. Here we go.

Chapter 38

UNDER ARREST

Saturday

"Good evening, officer," said Cole, as if he wasn't about to be arrested and sent to prison forever. "Is there a problem?"

The officer shined a flashlight into our faces. "Do you know the speed limit on this road?"

"Forty-five, I think," said Cole.

"Then do you care to explain why you were going forty-nine?"

"I'm getting used to the acceleration on this baby," said Cole, patting the dashboard. "That's my bad. But I promise it won't happen again."

"You sure that's it? Or were you maybe distracted by your friend here?" The officer scanned the flashlight over my body.

I gulped. Not because I was nervous that I was actually in trouble. No...I knew that this was a Society cop that Chastity had sent to mess with Cole. Everything was going according to plan. But I'd forgotten how nervous cops made me, even if they weren't real. The siren had made my pulse skyrocket and I'd momentarily forgotten the plan. But as soon as the cop stepped up to the window, I remembered everything perfectly. And now I was more worried than ever...because of what Chastity wanted me to do to the cop. I took a deep breath, trying to settle my nerves.

"Tell you what," continued the fake officer. "I'm going to check your papers, and when I get back, I expect you to remember what actually happened. License and registration, please."

Cole grabbed the registration out of the glove box and then opened his wallet to grab his license. When he did, a little silver thumb drive fell onto his lap.

The officer fixed his flashlight on it. "What's that?" he asked.

"Just some photos." Cole pocketed it and handed over his documents.

The flashlight went out and the officer walked back to his car.

"What an asshole," said Cole. "I can't believe he seriously pulled me over for going four over the speed limit."

"Are you sure that's what this is really about?" I asked, doing my very best not to laugh. He seemed so pissed at this overzealous cop. And now I was going to turn the screws a little. "If there's anything that I need to keep quiet, you better tell me now."

"I'm pretty sure my insurance is up to date. It's possible the automatic payment didn't go through…"

"I'm not talking about that. I'm talking about what you stole from Kat." I said the last few words extra loud.

"Shhh," hissed Cole as the blinding flashlight returned to his window.

"Anything you want to tell me, Mr. Halifax?" asked the cop. His voice sounded significantly less friendly than it had earlier. He even put one hand on his pistol.

His acting was top notch. If I'd been in Cole's position, I literally would have shit my pants.

"Nope," replied Cole. Cole Halifax, apparently. Actually, I had no idea what his first name was. Cole was his Society name. Based on how much of an asshole he was, I had to assume that his real first name was Josh. Or maybe Chaz. Yeah, he was a total Chaz.

The cop shined the light in his eyes. "That's interesting. Because this car was reported as stolen a few months ago."

"What?!" asked Cole. "Stop messing with me." For the first time, his cocky voice sounded terrified.

The cop tightened his grip on his pistol. "Sir, please put your hands on your head and step out of the car."

Oh shit, that's my cue. I took a deep breath.

"Wait," I said.

The cop switched the flashlight to me.

"I'm sure there's a perfectly innocent explanation for all of this. If you'd just let us explain…" *Here goes nothing.* I hooked my finger into the top of my strapless dress and pulled down. The cold air bit at my exposed breasts.

Everyone was dead quiet for a second. I could hear my heartbeat pounding in my head. I had just flashed a complete stranger. Yes, the cop had been expecting it. But it was still incredible awkward.

The look on Cole's face, however, made it all worth it. There was a sheen of sweat above his brow and his eyes bulged out of his skull.

Then the flashlight went out and the cop walked away.

I immediately pulled my top back up. *Did that really just happen?* I mentally high-fived myself for having the lady balls to pull it off.

"Oh thank God," said Cole. He leaned back in his seat. His breathing was even heavier than mine. Which kind of made sense, given that I'd only had to flash some rando. He, on the other hand, had surely been thinking that he was going to go to prison for grand theft auto.

"I think what you meant to say is, 'Thank you for saving my ass, Raven.' "

Cole took a second to catch his breath. "I can't believe that actually worked."

"Why? Are you calling me ugly?"

"No. I just…holy shit. That was fucking intense."

"You have a lot of explaining to do. But for now, let's get the hell out of here."

Cole's hand shook as he turned the car back on, but he stopped before shifting into gear. "Shit, he never gave me my papers back." He looked over his shoulder nervously.

And then I heard the tap on my window.

I slowly unrolled it. I figured he was back to give us the papers. But I was wrong.

"Ma'am," said the cop. "I'm going to have to ask you to step out of the vehicle."

Huh? This wasn't part of the plan. He was supposed to pull us over, mess with Cole, and then leave after I flashed him. So why was he making me get out of the car?

I looked at him in confusion. My eyes landed on his badge. His real badge. Not some Society knockoff with their genie lamp logo in the center.

Oh. Shit.

My amusement immediately shifted to sheer and abject terror. I'd just flashed a real cop. And apparently, I had been riding in a for-realsies-stolen Ferrari.

"Step out of the car," he repeated. "Now." He stepped back and kept the flashlight trained on me as I opened the door and stepped out.

I squinted to try to see his face, but the light was blinding.

"Walk around to the back and put your hands on the trunk," he commanded.

I started walking, but my heel caught on something. I just barely caught myself on the side of the car.

"Have you been drinking?" asked the officer.

"Just a few Slippery Meows."

"Do you think this is some sort of joke?" He sounded so pissed.

"What? No. That was the name of the drink I had."

"So you have been drinking?"

"A little…" *Fantastic. Add drunk and disorderly to the charges.* I steadied myself and continued to the back of the car. The cold metal of the Ferrari stung my palms as I bent over and spread my legs like people do in movies. *Is this what he wanted?* It was a bit of a seductive pose. I definitely didn't want him to think I was trying to bride him with my body again. Once had been quite enough.

"Are you carrying any sharp objects?"

"No."

He stepped towards me and holstered his flashlight. "I'm going to pat you down. Unless you want to end up flat on the pavement, don't make any sudden movements."

He started at my ankles and slowly traced his rough hands up my legs. And up. And up some more. His fingers dipped just under the hem of my skirt.

I shifted a bit under his touch. *What is he doing?!* Showing him my tits hadn't been an invitation for him to feel me up.

But maybe he'd taken it that way.

He stopped just beneath my ass and then pulled back, continuing the pat-down over my clothes. He slid his hands along the curve of my hips and up to my breasts.

Is he supposed to grab them like this?

It felt a bit inappropriate. But I was more worried about what was going to happen next. Because he was inches away from my armpits, and they were extraordinarily soupy. If he touched them, there was a high probability that he'd either vomit all over me or arrest me for just being a disgusting sweat beast.

Luckily for both of us, he avoided my pits and arms all together. Which kind of made sense given that they were completely exposed in my strapless dress. Although my legs were exposed too, and he had certainly given them a thorough search. *Pervert.*

He pushed his radio call button. "Dispatch, this is Officer Foxtrot India 842. I've got a 10-99 at my location. Requesting backup. Over."

Backup?! My heartbeat increased even more. *And what's a 10-99?*

He grabbed my arms and pulled them behind my back. I chill went down my spine as he snapped the cold metal cuffs onto my wrists.

"Why are you cuffing me?" I asked. "What's going on?"

"You're a known associate of Mr. Halifax. I'm taking you in."

"In…to prison?" *No! This can't be happening.* I turned to him to try to plead my case. And for the first time, I got a good look at his face. Most of it was obscured by his big lumberjack beard, but I still recognized him.

"Dr. Lyons?" I gasped.

"That's Officer Ironside to you."

Oh right. I'd forgotten that Flint Ironside was his Society name. I laughed. Partially at the ridiculousness of his name, but mainly just because I was nervous to see him again. I hadn't seen him in months. Not since I ghosted him after we cheated on each other with each other. Incident #5 would always haunt me. And now I'd welcomed Dr. Lyons back into my life by showing him my tits. *I really should be arrested.*

But honestly…given how our relationship had gone thus far, that somehow felt appropriate.

"Is something funny?" he asked, staying perfectly in character.

I checked to make sure Cole wasn't watching and then lowered my voice to a barely audible whisper. "Seriously, this was awesome. Cole was totally freaking out. But can you take these handcuffs off me? They're a little tight."

"I will not take your handcuffs off. And your boyfriend should be freaking out. Because I'm about to bend you over his car and fuck you with my nightstick."

My eyes got big. What was he talking about?! This was *not* part of the prank!

Damn it, Chastity! I suddenly got a horrible feeling that she'd told Dr. Lyons about my desire for him to be a bad boy in the bedroom.

Or in this case…on the side of the road pressed up against Cole's Ferrari.

Chapter 39

PUNISH ME, OFFICER
Saturday

"I might be willing to let you and your boyfriend go with just a warning," said Officer Ironside. "But only if you can convince me that you two won't steal any more cars. And that you're sorry."

He knew this was all just a prank, right? "I'm so, so sorry, Officer."

"Tell me. Did you ever stop to think about how the original owner of this car felt?" He ran his hand over the trunk. "Imagine it was you."

"Okay…"

"One day, you go to the dealership. You aren't really expecting much, but then you stumble upon the perfect car. You take it for a test drive."

What the hell? Does he have a weird car fetish?

"You even start to fall in love with it. And then one day, you drive it to its favorite café to grab some garlicy deviled eggs. But then suddenly…poof. It disappears."

Oh, I get it. This was a metaphor for our relationship. *Wait…had he really been starting to fall in love with me?* I suddenly felt horrible about ghosting him. Because I knew exactly how that felt. Stupid Tanner. "That would really suck."

"Yes, it would. Now…you have a choice. I can either take you and your boyfriend in to the station and put you in jail. Or…" He pulled his nightstick from his belt. "Or I can punish you right here." He pushed the tip of his nightstick into my thigh and traced upwards. "So what will it be?"

I gulped. I'd thought he'd been bluffing about fucking me with his nightstick. But now I wasn't so sure.

"What's my punishment?" I asked.

"Whatever the fuck I say it is," he growled.

Holy shit. Dr. Lyons was too nice, but Officer Ironside was exactly the bad boy I'd been craving. Why hadn't he acted like this sooner? And why didn't he always wear a cop uniform? Because *damn.* He was wearing the hell out of it.

He dragged the nightstick higher up my thigh, not bothering to stop when he got to the hem of my dress. The cold metal stick brushed against my ass.

"So what will it be?" he asked.

On a normal night I would have resisted. But this wasn't a normal night. After everything I'd been through today, I'd never been so horny in my life. And honestly…what did I have to lose? Tanner and me clearly weren't going to happen. And Cole had proven he was a grade-A douchebag. At this point, Dr. Lyons felt like my best option. *Besides the Sausage King.* But the Sausage King wasn't here. And Dr. Lyons was. And his nightstick was dangerously close to my lady bits.

"Punish me, Officer."

"It would be my pleasure. But before we begin, I think a strip search is in order." He yanked my top down. With my hands cuffed behind my back, I could do nothing to block his view. His eyes lingered on my exposed breasts.

The way he was staring at me made my heart race. Like I was the most beautiful woman he'd ever seen.

He cupped my breasts in his hands, squeezing gently. His slow caress made my whole body feel alive.

"Eep!" I squealed as he pinched both my nipples and squeezed. Hard. And then he grabbed my arms and bent me over the trunk of the car.

The metal felt so cold on my breasts. But my attention was immediately pulled to the nightstick once again trailing up my legs. Slowly. Ever so slowly.

What is he going to do to me?

The nightstick dipped between my legs for just a moment, but then shifted and dragged it up over my ass. The fabric of my dress went with it, bunching around my cuffed hands and leaving my ass totally exposed.

I tried to look back at when he was doing, but he put his forearm into my back and pressed me onto the car.

"You don't move unless I tell you to move."

I didn't respond.

He spanked me. Not super hard. But not gently, either. "Do you understand?"

"Yes."

"Yes *sir*," he corrected and spanked me again.

"Yes sir," I said. But it came out as more of a moan. *Since when am I into spanking?*

"Good girl," he said, gently caressing the spot he just struck. And then I felt the cold metal of his nightstick again.

Is he gonna beat me with his nightstick!?

He traced the stick across my ass and hooked it under the band of my thong. One yank was all it took for him to snap the elastic. My ruined thong slid down my thighs and pooled around my heels.

I didn't know what a strip search was supposed to be like, but if they were always this sexy, then I really needed to look into doing some casual terrorism or something.

Officer Ironside tapped his nightstick against the inside of my thighs, forcing me to spread my legs further. I saved him some trouble and arched my back too.

I shivered as a gust of wind blew over my exposed bits. *Oh my God. What am I doing?!* The wind was a nice little reminder that I was outside. On the side of a road. A public road. Where anyone could drive by.

I stared to panic, but the nightstick was back on my thighs. Going up. And up. And up…

He's really going to fuck me with it. And I'd never wanted anything so bad in my entire life.

After hours of excruciating horniness, the cold metal nightstick brushing against my clit was *almost* enough to send me over the edge. He dragged it backwards and pushed slightly, forcing the tip of the stick into me.

"Oh God," I moaned. I arched my back more and thrust my hips backwards as much as my current position would allow. I'd never felt anything like this. It was so much thicker than Joe had been… Pain shot through me as it stretched my walls. But that pain was quickly replaced with pleasure.

My body had never felt so alive. The cold metal car on my breasts. The cuffs cutting into my wrists. The wind blowing on my naked skin. The thick nightstick plunging ever deeper…

He was going too slow though. I couldn't wait anymore. I needed all of it. Every. Last. Inch.

"Please," I whimpered. "I need more." I was so close.

He smacked my ass with one hand as he pushed the nightstick deeper with the other. And then he went faster. And faster. *God.* Every stroke brought me closer.

"What the fuck?!" yelled Cole.

Oh fuck. I'd forgotten that Cole had been sitting in the car this whole time. Hell, I'd forgotten about everything that wasn't in direct contact with my body.

"Freeze!" replied Officer Ironside.

I looked back as he pulled the nightstick out of me. He'd already drawn his taser on Cole with his other hand.

"What the fuck?" yelled Cole again.

"Sir, calm down. This is a standard strip search."

Cole balled his fists. "Bullshit. You were fucking her with your nightstick, you sick fuck." He turned to me. "Raven, did this asshole hurt you?"

"It's okay," I said. "I asked him to do it."

"You what?!"

"He said we could either go to jail now, or I could take the punishment." I bit my lip. "I chose the punishment."

Cole's eyes got big.

Officer Ironside stepped towards Cole. "I'm only going to ask you one more time. Get back in the car."

"Or what?" yelled Cole. "You'll shove your nightstick up my ass? Fuck you."

"You have three seconds."

"You think you're so tough, don't you? With your badge and your taser. Well how about you toss those aside and we can settle this like real men?"

"I don't need to fight you to prove I'm a real man. Just ask your girlfriend." He slapped my ass.

Cole lunged at him, but Officer Ironside expertly dodged to the side. He may not have been a real police officer, but he had been in the military.

I craned my neck to see more of what was happening, but my current position didn't give me much of a view. And I was starting to feel super awkward about having my bare ass just out there for all to see. It was an awfully awkward maneuver, but somehow I was able to stand up. I turned and leaned back against the car just in time to see Cole and Ironside squaring off.

"You don't want to fight me," said Ironside. His voice was laced with danger.

"Yeah, I do."

Ironside shook his head. "If you insist." He holstered his taser and put his fists up.

Cole charged him. The fight lasted all of three seconds. One second for Cole to close the distance between them. Another for Ironside to effortlessly dodge and put him in a headlock. And a third for Cole to lose consciousness.

Holy shit.

"Don't move," said Ironside as he hoisted Cole onto his shoulder. He carried him over and tossed him back into the driver seat.

Where does he think I'm gonna go?

He cuffed one of Cole's wrists to the steering wheel and grabbed the keys out of the ignition. And then he came back to me.

"Is he okay?" I asked.

"He'll be fine. Well…angry, but fine. Especially when he wakes up in a few minutes and sees what I'm doing to you." His eyes feasted on my naked body. "Come with me." He grabbed my arm and pulled me around to the front of the car. The taillights had provided some light when we were behind the car, but now the headlights lit us up completely.

I had the urge to hide my body, but my cuffed hands were useless.

"Does your boyfriend know how much of a slut you are?" he asked.

"Excuse me?"

"I could tell how much you liked that nightstick in your pussy." He pushed his hand between my thighs and stroked me.

I moaned under his touch.

"You're so fucking wet for me, Ash." He slipped a finger into me. "So how do you think I should punish you?"

There was only one answer. "Fuck me. Please fuck me."

"On the hood of your boyfriend's car?" He put a second finger in me. "You want me to fuck you like the whore that you are? You want me to make you scream my name while he watches?"

Oh my God. Every dirty word out of his mouth just turned me on even more. "Yes." That was the only thing in the world that I wanted.

He put a third finger in me. "If that's what you want, then it wouldn't be much of a punishment. Now would it?" He pulled his hand away and licked his fingers clean.

Is that sanitary? Actually, I didn't care if it was or not. Because it was fucking hot. Officer Ironside was a total stud.

"On your knees."

"But…" I said.

"Now," he growled.

I knelt on the ground. Luckily we'd pulled off onto a grassy shoulder so that I didn't have to kneel on the pavement.

He unzipped his pants and pulled his cock free. It was just like I remembered: 9 inches of rock-hard perfection. Only this time, it was way better. Because unlike at the museum, I could now see the man that it was attached too. He stared down at me like he owned me. And while I was handcuffed, he kind of did.

"Here's how this is going to go," he said. "If I say lick, you lick. If I say suck, you suck. And if I say choke, you fucking choke. And let me be very clear. You're *going* to choke." He ran his fingers through my hair. "Is that clear?"

"Yes."

He mollywhopped me with his erection. "Yes what?"

"Yes sir."

"Good girl." His harsh expression vanished, and for a split second, Officer Ironside was replaced by the sweet, somewhat awkward Dr. Lyons. "You're okay with this, right?" he whispered.

I nodded. He was being adorable.

"Of course you are, slut. Now lick."

Aaaand...Officer Ironside is back. I didn't mind, though. I was kind of digging Ironside. Actually, I was really digging Ironside. His filthy words had me soaking wet.

I flicked my tongue out against his tip. I expected his precum to be salty like it had been when I'd blown him at the museum, but it was surprisingly sweet. It was almost too sweet. *Almost.* I swirled my tongue around to get more of the sweet liquid and then leaned in and licked down his shaft.

"Suck."

I opened up and took him into my mouth. I slowly drew in a breath, just in case he was being super literal about the whole *suck* command.

He groaned as I worked my tongue around him.

"Are you sorry for what you've done?" he asked.

I nodded and said a muffled, "Yes sir." The motion pushed his cock towards the back of my throat.

"And do you promise to never do it again?"

I nodded again.

"I didn't quite get that," he said.

I nodded more and took him into my throat. My gag reflex kicked in. I had no choice but to pull back. Surprisingly, he pulled back too.

"I didn't tell you to choke yet. We'll get to that. But not until your boyfriend wakes up. I want him to see my cock bulging in your throat."

I nervously glanced at Cole. He was still slumped over in the front seat.

"I'll tell you what," said Ironside. "I believe that you're sorry. So I'm going to be generous with your punishment."

"Please say you're going to fuck me." God, I needed it. This entire day had been one giant tease. If he didn't fuck me, I was going to spontaneously combust.

"That depends," he said. "Your boyfriend is going to wake up any second. And when he does, you have one simple task: make him jealous as hell. If you can get him to honk the horn before I cum, then I'll bend you over that hood and fuck you harder than you've ever been fucked."

What the hell? Where did he come up with this kinky shit? "And if I can't get him to honk?"

"Then I'm going to cover you in so much cum that you'll look like the glazed donut I ate for breakfast. How does that sound?"

"Delicious," I said with a wink. *Especially if it tastes as sweet as his precum.* And then a thought occurred to me. When I'd jokingly made three wishes with Tanner, I'd wished for cum to taste like cookies. Was that why Dr. Lyons' cum was so sweet?

Of course not. Because Tanner wasn't a genie. He was just a jerk.

"Looks like your boyfriend is waking up," said Ironside. "Let's see how jealous you can make him." He put his hands behind his back and thrust his hips slightly towards my face.

Fuck Cole. This wasn't about making him jealous. I didn't care what he thought. This was about me and Dr. Lyons. And I was about to give Dr. Lyons the best damned blowjob he'd ever had. It would just be icing on the cake when Cole got pissed and honked the horn. Because then I'd get what I really craved.

I looked up at Officer Ironside as I leaned back in. But instead of getting right to sucking, I took my time exploring all 9-inches of his thick cock. The more I licked, the more he pushed his hips towards me.

Eventually he couldn't take it anymore.

"Suck," he demanded.

I slowly parted my lips, applying just the right amount of pressure as I took his shaft into my mouth. Slowly. Oh so slowly. I was only halfway down his length when his cock pressed against the back of my throat.

"I bet you wish your hands weren't cuffed so you could touch yourself."

I moaned. I desperately wanted that.

"Just imagine how good my cock is going to feel buried inside of you."

I wanted more. I wanted to jam him all the way down my throat and keep him there until I couldn't fucking breath. But I wasn't allowed to choke. *Yet.*

I pulled back and snuck a glance at Cole. Why hadn't he honked yet? After seeing him attack Dr. Lyons a few minutes ago, I thought for sure Cole would be freaking the fuck out. It wouldn't have surprised me if he tried to tear the steering wheel out of the car so that he could come try to fight him again.

Instead of freaking out, though, he was just calmly sitting there playing on his phone.

No, not playing. People didn't hold their phones perfectly vertically when they were playing. They held them like that when they were taking pictures. Or filming.

Oh fuck. No!

I'd starred in a sex tape before, and my dick of an ex-husband had blackmailed me with it to take everything from me in our divorce. I wasn't eager to repeat that. Especially not with Cole being the one in control of the footage.

"Are you really going to let him film us?" I asked.

"If he wants a record of me facefucking his girlfriend, that's his problem. Although it does seem like you're gonna have to try a little harder if you want to make him jealous."

Damn it!

I looked back at Cole. And he winked at me. He freaking winked at me! And then he had the audacity to give me a thumbs up.

Oh, it's on.

I fake-smiled at Cole and sucked Ironside again. With my head turned to face Cole, his cock bulged in my cheek. *Come on...honk the horn.* I turned back to Ironside and started blowing him faster and faster, my head bobbing up and down.

"You like sucking my cock while your boyfriend watches?" asked Ironside.

"Mhm," I moaned against his cock.

"I'm not sure he's gonna honk. Which is a shame, because I want nothing more than to destroy your tight little pussy."

I pulled back and locked eyes with him. "Then do it."

"Maybe. But first, it's time for you to choke." He grabbed the back of my head and yanked me onto his cock. It only went halfway down at first, but then he pushed my head down. The change in angle allowed his cock to fill my throat.

Holy shit. My gag reflex tried to push him out, but his hands were stronger. I couldn't breathe. But I didn't fucking care. I just wanted more. I leaned in further until my nose pressed into his flesh. All 9 inches of him were buried in my throat. And all I could think about was how this would feel in my pussy. I needed him to fuck me.

"Oh fuck," he groaned.

He let me go far too soon. I gasped for air, but only so that I'd be able to deepthroat him again.

"Have you ever sucked your boyfriend like this?"

"Never," I said. And I never would, because Cole was a stupid asshole. Who wouldn't freaking honk the horn!

After that, I pulled out all the stops. I sucked, I licked, I choked again. My eyes were watering and saliva was dripping down my chin, but I didn't care. I just wanted to be fucked.

I deepthroated him again, trying desperately to get Cole to honk the horn. But all it did was make Ironside groan again.

He grabbed the top of my head and pushed me off of him as he began stroking himself with his other hand.

"Don't cum yet," I started to say, but I only got half the words out before his whole body shook and his cum exploded into my mouth. It was just as sweet as his precum. Actually, it was sweeter. Cloyingly sweet. But it was still a million times more delicious than any cum I'd ever tasted.

I swallowed some down as he filled my mouth with more. And more. With my hands cuffed behind my back, I just had to sit there and take it. And I loved every fucking second of it. But God, I wished he'd done that inside me instead. Because I was seriously desperate for his cock.

A horn blared through the air.

Are you fucking kidding me?! Now he honks the horn? Now?!

I turned to glare at Cole as more cum splashed onto my cheeks. More and more and more. He hadn't been kidding about glazing me like a donut. By the time he was finished, lines of cum crisscrossed from my nose to my tits. And a little on my dress. Like a gentleman, he had completely avoided my eyes. Which was one of the many reasons why I was sure he was a better choice than Cole. Dr. Lyons could talk dirty *and* he still knew to never cum in a girl's eyes. It was the perfection combination.

If it had been Cole that had me on my knees, I was 100% sure he would have blasted me right in the eye. And then he'd have one of his friends pop out from nowhere to get my other eye.

Yeah, fuck him. And fuck him for not blowing that horn sooner. But he *did* honk the horn. Did that mean…?

"He honked the horn," I said. "That means you have to fuck me."

"Actually, that was them." Ironside hooked his thumb towards the street. A pair of taillights slowly faded into the dark night.

Oh my God. Some random people had just seen me get absolutely drenched in cum. And to make matters worse, Cole was still filming.

Officer Ironside hauled me to my feet and undid my cuffs. "I hope you've learned your lesson."

"I haven't." I dragged my finger across my cheek and then licked the cum off of it. "I probably need to be punished more."

He leaned in and whispered, "Believe me, I want to. But our first time isn't going to be on the side of the road in front of some other guy. You deserve so much more than that."

I looked up at him. He was so sweet. What guy cared about that sorta thing? Any other guy in the Society would have gladly taken me right on the hood of Cole's car without a second thought. But Dr. Lyons was different.

He pulled a key from his pocket and pressed it into my palm. It looked just like the key with the dice symbol that Cole had given me during my first visit to Club Onyx. But this one had a handcuff symbol etched into it.

"I'll be waiting for you." He stepped back and his eyes darkened. "Now go run back to your boyfriend, slut." He slapped my bare ass and made me jump a little.

I almost asked if he could take me with him in the cop car, but then I remembered Cole's video. If I didn't get back in that car and find a way to delete it, who knew what he'd do with it. Hell, who knew what he'd *already* done with it? For all I knew, he was livestreaming it on Instagram. *Shit!*

I pulled my dress down to cover my ass as I went back to the Ferrari.

This was going to be the most awkward car ride of my life.

Chapter 40

DELETE IT!
Saturday

"I knew you were a freak," said Cole as I slid into the passenger seat, "but *damn*. That was fucking hot."

Damn it! How had this prank failed so spectacularly? I would have lost my mind if I'd had to watch Cole with another woman. But he hadn't even flinched. In fact, judging by the impressive tent in his pants, he'd rather enjoyed it.

I was still searching for a witty comeback when Officer Ironside leaned through Cole's window.

"Good news, Mr. Halifax," he said. "I had a little chat with your girlfriend, and she convinced me that a *stiff* warning would suffice."

"Thank you, sir," said Cole. "Now can you please uncuff me from this steering wheel and give me my keys back?"

"Absolutely." Ironside reached through the window and undid his cuffs. Then he pulled Cole's keys, license, and registration out of his back pocket and tossed it on Cole's lap. "Stay safe out there." He started to walk away, but then stopped. "Oh, and you fight like a bitch."

Cole glared at him as he walked back to his police cruiser.

Maybe the prank hadn't been such a failure after all.

I burst out laughing.

"What's so funny?" asked Cole.

"Dude, I got you so good. You should have seen the look on your face when he said this car was stolen. Priceless."

"I'm confused."

"It was all a prank! Gotcha, bitch!"

"Oh damn," said. "That was pretty epic. But I'm still a little confused… If this was supposed to be a prank, then why did you put on a live sex show for me?"

"You can act all cool about it now, but I saw how pissed you were when you first saw him fucking me with that nightstick." I shifted in my chair. I was still unbelievably horny, and the thought of that nightstick did nothing to cool my loins. In fact, it had quite the opposite effect.

"Uh…yeah, because I thought he was some asshole cop taking advantage of you."

"But after he beat your ass you decided to just let him fuck my face?"

"He didn't beat my ass," said Cole. "He got lucky."

"Hmm…I dunno. It sure looked like he beat your ass. I have to ask, have you ever even been in a fight before?"

Cole gripped the steering wheel. "Did I do something to piss you off?"

"No, not at all. I love when the guy I'm crushing on uses me to crash a swinger party so he can revenge bang his childhood sweetheart."

"Whoa whoa whoa. Hold on." He looked at me like I was crazy. "You think *that's* what happened?"

"Of course that's what happened."

He shook his head. "Wow. I really wish you hadn't fallen asleep while I was telling you the plan."

"And what exactly was the plan?" I put *the plan* in air quotes.

"The plan was to get this." He held up the silver flash drive that had fallen out of his wallet earlier.

I knew he stole something! "What's on there?"

"I'm not 100% sure, but I'm hoping that there's a picture of Rosalie on here."

I blinked. *Did I hear him right?* "Why would Kat have a picture of Rosalie?"

"Because every week she takes a photo of the winning team at the spit roast. You said your sister had been at the camp a few years ago, so I figured Kat might still have the photo from that week."

Oooooh. So that was why Kat had looked familiar. I'd seen her a few hours ago at the spit roast. "Oh my God…"

"And yes, I had you pose as my girlfriend to get into Kat's swinger party. But that was the only way I could think to get in."

"Why didn't you just ask her? I thought you two went way back."

"Because this was way more fun. And there was this really awesome girl that I'd been wanting to take out on a date…"

"You seriously did all that just to get me some pictures of my sister? That's like…the sweetest thing anyone's ever done for me." And I'd returned the favor by…*oh my God*. What the actual fuck had I just done?

"Yes. And I'd do it again in a heartbeat. Although I'd prefer if you blew me at the end of the night instead of some random cop."

"Wow. I'm an awful person." I put my face in my palm and… *Ah! Yuck!* My palm stuck to all the cum. I pulled my hand away and wiped it on the seat.

"Hey!" yelled Cole. "What the hell?! Don't get that shit on my car."

I laughed. This whole situation was just so awkward. "I'm so, so sorry. If it makes you feel better, I hadn't planned for…" I gestured to the mess on me, "For this to happen. The plan was just for him to make you think you were getting arrested. And then I was going to act like a total boss and flash him. And then I was going to tell you that it was a prank and make fun of you for being such a scared little bitch. I had no idea Officer Ironside was gonna take it so far. If I had known what you were really up to, I never would have done it. I swear. I'll do whatever I can to make it up to." I bit my lip and glanced at his crotch, where his pants were still very visibly tented.

"Are you offering to blow me?"

"Maybe." *What am I doing?!* I had officially lost my mind.

He raised an eyebrow. "I don't want a pity blow-job."

"Oh," I said. It made sense that he was rejecting me. He must have thought I was disgusting. In the past 24 hours, he'd seen me get fingered by Tanner and then watched me blow Dr. Lyons on the side of the road. What man would want sloppy thirds?

"Don't sound so dejected. One day soon, Raven Black, I'm going to fuck the hell out of you. But not like this. For you, I have something…special planned."

"What does that mean?"

"Twice now I've been cheated out of fucking you in front of an audience. Let's just say I'm not going to miss my chance a third time."

I gulped.

"And anyway. You don't owe me any apologies for tonight. You already gave me some prize-winning footage." He grabbed his phone and pulled up his gallery. A gif popped up of Officer Ironside filling my mouth with cum. Somehow Cole had already found the time to convert it to black and white and added the caption: *Your girl loves when you speed. She loves it even more when you get pulled over for it.*

"What the hell is this?" I asked. It was so weird seeing myself like that. I looked like some sort of porn star.

"A gif of you taking a cumshot."

"I can see that. I was more concerned with why it exists."

"For the Onyxies, of course. Your little roadside blowjob fit the promiscuous girlfriend theme perfect." He stared down at his handiwork. "I'm not sure I have the caption just right yet, though. I was also considering: *Your girl is such a bad driver. You've always wondered how she never gets tickets.*"

"What the hell?"

"Yeah, you're right. The first caption was better."

"No! I wasn't talking about the caption. I was talking about the gif. Can you please delete it? I don't want everyone in the Society seeing me take a cumshot!"

"What? Why? It's so good. I really think we have a shot at winning this."

"Cole, please." My voice sounded desperate, but I was. Joe blackmailing me with my sex tape had been traumatic enough. I didn't need a repeat of that.

"But it's so hot."

"I don't care. I need you to delete it now please. And when you're done with that, can we please look at the photos you stole from Kat? I have to know if there's really a picture of Rosalie." The anticipation was literally killing me. This could be the clue I've been searching for all this time. The clue that would help me find my sister. Or at least help me find whoever killed... *No.* I didn't want to even consider the other possibility.

"Alright, fine..." He hit a few buttons and deleted my sex tape.

Thank God. I could suddenly breathe a little easier.

"And I'd love to look at the pictures," he said, "but we'll need a computer to get them off this flash drive. Did you bring your laptop to the Emerald Oasis?"

"No."

"Me neither. But my parents don't live far from here. They have one."

"What? You expect me to go meet your parents...like this?" I looked down at my cum-covered breasts.

"We'll be in and out. They'll never even know we were there. But if it makes you feel better…" He pulled off his tuxedo jacket and stripped off his shirt.

I didn't know why he was stripping, but I liked what I was seeing. His torso was covered in colorful tattoos. I wanted to know the history behind every last one of them.

He balled his shirt up and tossed it into my lap. "Use this."

I started putting it on.

Cole looked at me like I was completely insane. It was an expression I was used to seeing when he looked at me. "What are you doing?" he asked with a laugh. "I wanted you to clean up with it. Not wear it."

Oh, right. I wiped it over my chest and chin as Cole put the car into drive. I was relieved to finally be able to pull my dress back up over my breasts. But for some reason it didn't seem to want to stay up. *Damn it!* I'd been so happy to finally have a strapless dress that I didn't have to adjust every 5 seconds. I'd even danced for hours in it without once worrying about flashing the entire dance floor. Had Dr. Lyons torn the fabric when he yanked it down?

I kept playing with it as we drove through the forest.

A few minutes later we pulled up outside a cookie-cutter house on a picturesque suburban street. It felt like we'd been transported back to the 50s. If it hadn't been 4 o'clock in the morning, I was sure I would have seen at least one housewife gardening in a knee-length checkered dress.

"This is where you grew up?" I asked. "It's so…cute."

"You sound surprised."

"I just can't picture this house creating…this." I gestured to the tattoos snaking over his muscular body.

"Like I said. I wasn't always like this." He cut the ignition. "Now let's go see what's on that flash drive."

Chapter 41

TATE ABERNATHY HALIFAX
Saturday

"Are you sure we shouldn't knock?" I asked as I pulled at the top of my dress for at least the twentieth time.

Cole flipped through the keys on his keychain. "At this hour? No way. Like I said…we'll just be in and out. They'll never even know we were here." He unlocked the door and slowly opened it. I cringed when it creaked a little.

I knew this was his parents' house, but my heart was still pounding. The closest I'd ever come to sneaking into a house was when I used to help Rosalie sneak in through our bedroom window after a wild night with whichever guy she was dating that week. Me? I'd never even had a boyfriend to sneak out with.

I'd always wondered why Rosalie didn't just come home on time. But now I kind of understood. There was something thrilling about the adrenaline pumping through my veins. The thought of getting caught and having to meet Cole's parents was terrifying.

"Where's the computer?" I whispered.

He pointed down the hall. I tiptoed ahead as he eased the door shut.

Then everything happened all at once.

"Freeze, bitch!" yelled a deep voice.

I screamed bloody murder and threw my hands in the air.

My dress fell down.

The lights flicked on.

I stared down the barrel of a shotgun. And then I looked past it and locked eyes with Cole's father. Or at least, I would have. But he was staring right at my exposed breasts.

Fuck my life. I wanted to cover myself, but I really didn't want to get shot.

"Tate?" asked the woman who had hit the lights. "Is that you, honey?"

"Yes, it's me!" said Cole. Or Tate, apparently. "What the hell is Dad doing with a shotgun?"

"Language!" said his mom.

Cole looked down. "Sorry, Mom."

"What are you doing here?" she asked. "And who's this...?" She waved her finger at me and crinkled her nose. "This hussy?"

"She's not a hussy," replied Cole. Although my slutty little dress combined with my tits being out indicated otherwise. "Dad, will you please drop the gun?"

Cole's dad grimaced. And then he literally dropped the gun.

A shot rang out through the house and we all screamed.

Except for Cole's dad. He was too busy clutching his chest as he stumbled backwards.

"Brucey?" gasped Cole's mom just as Cole said, "Dad?"

Cole rushed over and put his arm around him, guiding him to comfort in an armchair.

"I," started his dad, but he was struggling to get the words out. "My chest. I can't breathe."

I just stood there watching the entire scene unfold, the top of my dress now clutched securely around myself. *Oh my God.* I was pretty sure I just gave Cole's dad a heart attack. By flashing him.

"Don't just stand there!" shrieked Cole's mom in my general direction. "Call an ambulance!"

"I don't have my cell phone!" I yelled back. I was totally panicking.

Cole tossed me his and I dialed 911.

"911, what's your emergency?"

"I think my…" *What is he?* I didn't want to call him my boyfriend's dad. "I think my dude's dad is having a heart attack." *Dude? Why would I refer to him as that?!*

"What's your current location?"

"2407 Windy Lane," I said. "Wait, no." *Shit!* That was my home address. Not Cole's. What was I doing? The pressure was totally getting to me. I didn't want to be responsible for killing Cole's dad. "Hold on." I turned to Cole. "They need your address." I tossed him the phone.

Cole calmly finished the phone call. And unlike me, he was able to give the right address.

The ambulance arrived a few minutes later. And then another came. *Two ambulances?* That seemed bad. Really bad.

Cole and I sat on the porch while the paramedics checked him out.

"I'm so, so sorry," I said. "I never meant to give your dad a heart attack."

"He's going to be okay," said Cole. But he didn't sound nearly as confident as he usually did. "And it wasn't your fault."

"I really think it was. You saw what happened…right?"

He nodded. "I did. My crazy dad pulled a gun on you. And for some inexplicable reason, you flashed him and gave him a heart attack. To be honest, it's not so bad of a way for him to go." He forced a laugh and looked away.

I put my arm around him and squeezed his shoulders. "You're allowed to be upset, you know."

He turned farther away and wiped a tear from his face. "Why should I be upset? Like I said, he's gonna be okay. I know he is."

"But he might not." *Why are the ambulances still here?* "I don't mean to be a downer. I just know all too well how much you'll regret it if you don't spend every last minute that you can with him. I'd give anything to have just one more minute with Rosalie."

He nodded and stood up. "Can you maybe come with me?" He put his hand out for me.

Of course. I slipped my hand into his and we walked over to the ambulance.

Please don't be dead yet. I wanted Cole to be able to say goodbye. Then at least he'd get the closure that I never got with Rosalie.

"What's going on?" asked Cole to the nearest paramedic.

"We still want to run a few more tests, but…"

"I'm fine!" called his dad from the ambulance. "Will you get these wires off of me? And why are you touching me *there?!*"

"We think it was a panic attack," added the paramedic. "Between thinking you were intruders, and uh…" He glanced at me and cleared his throat. "Other things. He got a little over-excited. We see this a lot in older folks. The excitement accelerates their heart, and they mistake it for a heart attack. And then they panic. And well…that's why it's called a panic attack."

"So he's fine?" asked Cole in disbelief.

"We're pretty sure. Yes."

"Oh thank God." Cole let out a huge sigh. "You didn't flash my dad to death!" He grabbed me and planted a big kiss right on my lips.

I laughed as he twirled me around.

His mom climbed out of the ambulance. "I guess you heard the good news," she said.

"That dad was just being a big drama queen?" asked Cole. "Yup, we heard."

Mrs. Halifax laughed with him. "I've always said your father is a big baby. You should see him when he gets the sniffles…"

"Hey!" called his dad from the ambulance. "I heard that!"

We all laughed and Cole's mom gave him a big hug.

"It's so good to see you, honey," she said. "But what were you doing sneaking in at 4 in the morning? And who is this?"

"This is Raven," he said. "Raven, meet my mom."

"I'm sorry I almost killed your husband," I said.

"It's okay," she said. "I'm pretty sure that was the most excitement he's had in years. Maybe a little *too* much excitement."

I looked away. I couldn't stand the awkwardness of this conversation.

She leaned in and whispered super loudly in Cole's ear. "She's really pretty. Is she your girlfriend?"

He laughed. "You're terrible at whispering, Mom. And we can chat later, but right now we really need to use your computer."

"We don't have it anymore," she said.

Cole cocked his head and looked at her like she was crazy. It was nice to see him give someone else that look for once. "What do you mean you don't have it anymore? I just bought it for you like two months ago."

"I don't know what to tell you."

"Did someone steal it? Is that why dad got a gun?"

"No, nothing like that. It just didn't work right."

"What do you mean it didn't work right?" asked Cole. He was getting more and more frustrated. "That thing cost like three grand."

Mrs. Halifax shrugged. "It worked great at first. But after a few weeks all these strange things started popping up every time we logged into the AOL."

The AOL? I held back a smile.

"You mean pop-ups?"

"Yes, pop-ups."

"You must have gotten some sort of virus." Cole and I briefly locked eyes. I was pretty sure we both knew exactly what had happened to that computer. *Porn.* Lots and lots of porn was the only thing I knew of that caused tons of pop-ups. Not that I knew firsthand or anything…

"That was what I told your father. So he took it to the Best Buy. They said it was a lost cause and told him to just throw it out, though."

I had to put my hand over my mouth to keep from laughing. I knew old people were bad with electronics, but Cole's parents had taken things to a whole new level.

Cole ran his hands over his face. "Are you serious? You know what, never mind. I don't need to use the computer I got you. We can use any computer."

"We don't have one. Our phones work just fine. Well, mine does. Your father's runs so slow."

He watched porn on his phone too? Cole's dad was as pervy as Cole was.

Cole turned to me. "Do you want me to drive back to the city? We can…"

"Nonsense," said Mrs. Halifax. "Only drunks and hoodlums are on the streets at this hour. You know, they say that driving tired is even more dangerous than driving drunk. And you both look exhausted. You're going to sleep on the couch, and Raven can take your room."

"But we really need to…"

"Tate Abernathy Halifax, you're staying the night. And that's final. Now give me your keys."

"It's okay, *Abernathy*," I said. I couldn't resist making fun of that ridiculous middle name. "We can spend the night. The photos will still be there in the morning." As much as I wanted to see the photos, I was freaking exhausted. And maybe a small part of me was scared to look at them. Right now I was so hopeful that the photos would give me the clue I'd been missing. The key to finding Rosalie. But I knew there was a high probability that it would just be another dead end. Or maybe there wouldn't even be a photo of her. The spit roast photos were only of the winning team. So there was a 50% chance that she wouldn't even be in it.

"If you're sure," he said.

"Great!" said Mrs. Halifax. "I'll go get everything ready." She ran off towards the house.

Cole and I looked at each other.

"My dad totally crashed the computer by looking at too much porn, right?" he asked.

"Oh for sure," I said. "And then tried to cover it up by throwing it out. Doesn't surprise me, really. I mean...like father, like son."

"I beg your pardon?" said Cole. "For your information, I've never crashed a computer."

"*Never?* You know I can ask your mom anything I want tomorrow morning, right?"

"Fine. I had a computer in high school that stopped working. But I swear it wasn't my fault. The thing was so old..."

"Your poor mom. Does she know how perverted you two are?"

"We're not perverted. We just have a nuanced appreciation for the artistic beauty of the female form."

I stared at him. "Mhm. Sure."

He laughed and pulled me into a hug. "Thanks for coming along on this crazy adventure with me tonight."

"Are you kidding? Thank *you* for figuring out a way to get that flash drive. It seriously means the world to me." I looked up at him and smiled. He may have been a filthy pervert, but he was also incredibly sweet.

A part of me didn't want tonight to end. Because in the morning, I'd either be one step closer to Rosalie, or still as far away from the truth as ever. And no matter what, I'd have to face the consequences of what happened tonight. Dr. Lyon's key was burning a hole in my clutch. Tanner was still a stupid runaway. And Cole…*Tate*. I let my head rest on his chest. I think I may have accidentally started falling for him. What the hell had I gotten myself into?

Chapter 42

LOOKING LIKE AN ABSOLUTE SNACK
Sunday

My entire body ached when I woke up. Literally every inch of me was sore.

Did yesterday really happen?

I rolled over and rubbed the sleepy out of my eyes. I hoped that when I opened them I would be back in my apartment. That the Emerald Oasis had just been the craziest sex dream ever. But nope. I was definitely *not* in my apartment. Because last time I checked, I hadn't redecorated with a bajillion posters of swimsuit models in seductive poses. Some of them had even forgotten to put on their swimsuits.

If I didn't know better, I would have thought for sure that I was in a frat house. But I did know better, so I knew that this was just Cole's childhood bedroom.

Makes sense.

"Cole?" I muttered.

He wasn't here. I couldn't believe that he hadn't snuck up here last night. I mean…I was lying naked in his bed. All he had to do was pick the lock and come snuggle me.

And yes, I know it was weird to be naked in his parents' house. But I wasn't about to sleep in my dress. And the clothes his mom had given me - a pair of sweatpants and an itchy t-shirt - were way too hot and uncomfortable.

Unfortunately, they were my only option unless I wanted to eat breakfast in the buff. Because as I looked around the room, I realized my dress was missing. Where the hell was it?

I threw on the itchy clothes and checked myself out in the mirror. I expected my red hair to be everywhere and for my face to look like a naked mole rat thanks to my invisible brows and lashes. But Tanner's bracelet fixed all that. My dark hair was a lot less susceptible to frizz than my natural hair. And it even made my brows and lashes dark.

Tanner may have been an awful person, but his bracelet invention was ridiculously awesome.

I followed the aroma of freshly cooked bacon all the way downstairs to the kitchen.

Cole and his dad were sitting at the kitchen counter while his mom added a stack of pancakes to an already ridiculous spread of food. Bacon, eggs, hash browns…all the best things. But the yummiest thing of all was Cole when he stood up to greet me. In his thin gray sweatpants and white T, he was looking like an absolute *snack*.

I tried to avoid checking out his package in front of his parents, but I couldn't help myself. Maybe he actually was as big as he claimed…

"Good afternoon," he said.

"Huh?"

He pointed to the clock. 2:30.

Geez. I couldn't believe I'd slept so long. Actually, I could. Yesterday had been the most exhausting day of my entire life.

"Grab a plate," said Mrs. Halifax.

"Please tell me you didn't wait for me to start cook-ing..." The thought was horrifying. Being late to breakfast was one thing, but making everyone wait until 2:30 in the afternoon? Mrs. Halifax would have been totally justified if she'd slapped me across the face with a pancake.

"We always eat a late brunch on Sundays," she said.

I couldn't tell if she was lying. But it was nice of her to not make me feel too guilty. In fact, I had a lot more to feel guilty about than just being late for breakfast. "I'm so so sorry for what happened last night," I said as I filled my plate with bacon and eggs, being sure not to make eye contact with Cole's dad.

"It's really fine," said Mrs. Halifax. "We're just so glad that Tate finally brought a girl home to meet us. I was starting to think he might be a gay."

I choked on my eggs. *A gay? Who talks like that?*

"Mom," said Cole. "Just because I don't bring girls home doesn't mean that I'm gay."

"Well I wasn't sure. You remember the Petersons, right? Their boy Trevor used to have all of those sexy lady posters in his room too. But then at Thanksgiving one year, well...let's just say the turkey wasn't the only thing getting stuffed at the Petersons." She shook her head. "Poor Mrs. Peterson still hasn't fully recovered from what she saw."

Cole's dad started laughing hysterically.

I officially loved his family.

I wolfed down a strip of bacon and then finally mustered the courage to face Cole's dad. "How are you feeling?"

"I feel great," he said. "Well, as good as you can feel after having a heart attack."

My eyes got big. "You really had a heart attack? I thought it was just a panic attack?"

"Panic attack? Ba! What kind of sissy do you think I am? It was a heart attack. The paramedics said it was one of the worst they've ever seen. But it's gonna take more than that to take me down." He puffed his chest out.

Cole looked at me and mouthed, "He's lying."

Ah, so Cole gets his perviness AND his cockiness from his dad. "Well I'm just glad you're okay," I said. "I promise we won't sneak in again."

"That's good, but don't be strangers either," said Mrs. Halifax as she finished the final batch of pancakes. "You two are welcome any time. I keep telling Tate to come visit more, but he's too busy for us now that he moved to the big city."

"I'll try to bring him back," I said.

"Thanks. Oh yeah, I almost forgot…" She popped up and disappeared into the other room for a second. When she returned, my black cocktail dress was draped over her arms. "Here's your dress, Raven. I hope you don't mind that I washed it. You really should be more careful with such an expensive dress. Whatever you spilled on it sure was hard to get out."

Oh my God. My face turned bright red. Did she know that she'd just washed cum out of my dress? Between Cole's teenage years and his dad's porn addiction, I was sure she'd had to deal with her fair share of cum stains. *She must think I'm such a slut.*

"Oh yeah," I said as casually as possible. "I think someone spilled cornstarch on me at the party."

Cole shot me a sideways glance.

Shit! Worst excuse ever. "Let me go put this with my things…" I took the dress and ran away to Cole's room as fast as possible.

I needed a minute before I could go back and face Mrs. Halifax after that, so I grabbed my phone and…

Twenty missed calls? That seemed bad. Especially since half of them were from Chastity. The other half were from Tanner. But I wasn't really interested in hearing whatever dumb excuse he had for leaving me last night.

I clicked on Chastity and called her back.

"Ash! Finally!" she said.

"What's going on? Are you okay?"

"Uh, yeah. I'm fine. But you're not gonna be if you don't get your ass to the office ASAP."

"The office? But it's Sunday."

"Apparently that doesn't matter to Mr. Frost. He may be hot, but he's such an ass. Speaking of hot guys… How did the prank go last night?" She sounded so excited.

"Well, Dr. Lyons facefucked me in front of Cole."

"Ahhh! I can't believe he had the balls to do it! Wait, you said facefucked? Not actual fucked?"

"Yeah. He said he'd only fuck me if Cole got jealous and honked the horn. But Cole is such a deranged pervert that he just filmed the whole thing."

"Oh em gee!" squealed Chastity. "You're totes gonna win an Onxyie. As long as he uses the right caption. How about… *You couldn't afford to lose your license.*

Luckily you have the best girlfriend in the world. Something like that. I dunno. I'll keep thinking. Send me the footage and I'm sure I'll get some better ideas."

"He deleted the footage."

"Damn," said Chastity. "Oh well. We can always film another. And next time, let me film it. I'll get the perfect angle to make his cock look *huge.*"

"There's not gonna be a next time!"

"You don't wanna blow him again?"

"No. I mean…yes. I don't know! I just meant I'm not gonna film it."

"But Single Girl Rule #7: Pics or it didn't happen."

Pics! "I can't believe I didn't tell you! Cole didn't take me to that swinger party to bang his high school crush. He took me there because Kat has been the photographer at the Emerald Oasis for years. He thought she might have pics of Rosalie from a spit roast. So he snuck in and stole her flash drive."

"And?"

"And I haven't looked at it yet! Cole took me back to his parents' house to use their computer, but his pervy dad had crashed it by looking at too much porn."

Chastity laughed. "Well get your ass back here. I can't wait to see those photos. And also, if you're not back by 5 pm, I'm pretty sure Mr. Frost is going to fire you. Or try to. I'm sure we can find a way to make him change his mind. Oh! And I can film it to replace the gif you lost. What angle do you think we should take with the caption? Should he be *your* boss? Or should he be your boyfriend's boss? I'm thinking… *Your boss fired you, but because he's a good guy, he still let you watch him fuck your girlfriend before security escorts you out.*"

"What? I'm so confused. It doesn't sound like the boss is a good guy at all if he fucks his employee's girlfriend. Especially after firing the poor guy. That's just adding insult to injury. And why was the guy's girlfriend even there for the firing? Did they both work at the same office in this scenario?"

"Who knows? But you can totally picture Mr. Frost doing that to someone, can't you?"

"I actually can, yeah."

"Perfect!" said Chastity. "That's what we'll go with. I'll go find a guy to stand in as your boyfriend for the gif. See you in a couple hours!"

"What?! No! I just said I could picture Mr. Frost doing that. Not that it was going to happen this afternoon."

"Then how else are you going to avoid getting fired? The email very clearly said that we *had* to be at the office by 5 pm."

"Let me see..." I put her on speakerphone and clicked through to my inbox. The first message was from Mr. Frost at 6:30 this morning. It was addressed to me and CCed to Chastity.

Good morning ladies,

Apologies for the short notice, but we need to talk. Meet me at the office at 5 PM.

-Xander Frost

Shit! This sounded serious. And I was almost certainly going to be late. Which was like...one of my greatest fears. Right up there with getting my liver punctured. "I'm on my way. If I'm not there on time, do whatever you can to stall for me." I ran downstairs and tore into the kitchen. My mind was going a million miles a minute thinking about what Mr. Frost could possibly want to talk to us about a 5 pm on a Sunday. Whatever it was, I was sure I wasn't going to like it.

"Everything okay?" asked Cole.

"We have to go."

"What?" asked Cole and his mom at the same time.

"A work thing just came up. Can you get me back to the city by 5?"

Cole glanced at the microwave clock. "It's gonna be close." He popped up and grabbed his keys.

***

We pulled up to my office with about 3 minutes to spare. The only reason we weren't super late was because Cole had sped like a madman...but only after making me promise that I wouldn't blow any cops to get him out of a speeding ticket.

"Thanks for the ride," I said. I gave Cole a quick kiss and jumped out of the car.

"Wait," he said. "You almost forgot this." He tossed me the flash drive. I snatched it out of the air and ran towards the building.

Chastity was waiting for me by the elevator.

"For someone who doesn't like to be late, you're really cutting this one close," she said, handing me a bag of work clothes as she jammed her thumb against the UP button.

After the elevator incident a few months ago, I'd promised myself that I'd never change in an elevator again. But desperate times called for desperate measures, so I broke my promise and stripped down on the way up to our offices.

I held my breath practically the entire time, just waiting for the doors to ding open at the most inopportune moment. Somehow, though, we made it up to our office without stopping at a single floor. Probably because no one else's boss sucked enough to make them come in on a Sunday. *Stupid Mr. Frost.*

Chastity tugged on my hair.

"Ow."

"Take your wig off. It feels like it's glued to your head or something."

I almost screamed. Glue and hair were not a good mix. But then I remembered it was just Tanner's fancy tech. I flid off the bracelet and my hair immediately turned back to red.

"What in the hell was that?" Chastity lifted a strand of my hair.

"Fancy CIA tech. There's no time to explain." We dashed off the elevator a second before the clock struck 5.

I let out a sigh. I expected Mr. Frost to be sitting right by the elevator counting down the time on his watch, but he wasn't.

"Uh, where is he?" I asked, looking around the office. The cubicles were all empty. And so were the offices.

"Of course he'd come late," said Chastity. "What a dick."

Our phones both buzzed. We pulled them out and looked at them.

One new email. From Mr. Frost.

Good evening ladies,

I'm running a little late, but I'll be there soon. Sorry for the inconvenience.

-Xander Frost

What a dick indeed.

"I can't believe him," said Chastity. "What do you think the odds are that he'd planned to be late the entire time?"

"Extremely high. He's the worst."

"Whatever," she said. "Honestly, the joke's on him. Because I need to hear so much more about this prank!" She jumped up and down with excitement. "How surprised were you when it turned out to be Dr. Lyons?"

"Pretty surprised. What exactly did you tell him to do to me?"

"All I told him was that you were looking for more of a bad boy."

Wow, really? "So he came up with all of that on his own?"

"Yup. Are you *sure* the video got deleted? I'd love to see him in action."

"Yes, I'm sure. I promise I'll give you all the details you want, but first…" I pulled out the flash drive that Cole had given me. I couldn't wait any longer, even if there was a chance that Mr. Frost would come interrupt at any moment.

"Right. The pictures!" She grabbed it from me and hurried over to her laptop. A zip folder popped up.

I took a deep breath and hit *extract all files*. And we waited. And waited. And waited.

Whatever camera Kat used must have had a bajillion megapixels, because we were only 10% done extracting over 100 GB worth of data.

It felt like the universe was purposefully torturing me.

And if having to wait wasn't torture enough, the universe went and made Tanner call me again. I glared at his name on my phone.

"Oh geez," I said. "Tanner's calling again."

"Aren't you going to answer it?"

"Why? So he can give me some lame excuse about why he left? No thanks."

"He's far too hot and far too rich for you to not at least hear him out." She swiped her finger across my phone to answer the call.

"What the hell?!" I mouthed angrily. What had happened to Chastity being #TeamDrLyons?

"Hello?" said Tanner.

"What do you want?" I asked.

"Oh thank God. I've been looking for you all day."

"Why? Clearly you don't like me. Why would you be looking for me?"

"I'm so sorry about running off last night, but when I tell you the reason, I think you'll understand."

"You have…" I looked at the screen to see how much time was left on the transfer. "Four minutes and thirty-two seconds to explain yourself." *Damn it.* I hadn't excepted for it to be so much time. It would have been much more effective for me to give him like…twelve seconds or something.

"Can we meet up? It would be better to show you."

"No thanks. Just tell me."

"Okay. You're going to want to sit down."

"Just tell me already." I didn't need to sit down to hear his lame excuse.

"I think I might have found a picture of your sister."

What? Another one?

"Ash?" he asked when I didn't respond. "Are you still there?"

"Yeah."

"That was why I ran off. I saw that photographer leaving the spit roast, and I realized that I'd seen her there every time I'd ever participated in Society Wars. So I ran after her and asked if she'd saved photos from past years. She drove a hard bargain, but eventually she gave in when I agreed to give her photography company exclusive rights to take all the Odegaard product shots for the next year. I was up all night drafting the paperwork."

My mouth dropped open. He'd run off to get me the photos too? And then I'd spent all night on a date with Cole? And blowing Dr. Lyons? What the hell had I done?

"I'm really sorry I left so abruptly," he added. "Usually I would have made Nigel do it, but I couldn't find the little bugger. When I texted him he replied with a voicemail where all I could hear was bubbles and him mumbling something about scheduled time off. Anyway, I didn't want to wait to get you those photos, so that was why I ran off so quickly."

Damn it, Tanner! Why couldn't he have told me where he was going? Or taken me with him? But no…he just had to run off. So then I went on a date with Cole. And blew Dr. Lyons. And now my stomach was twisted into knots. Tanner was the one who should be pissed at me, not the other way around. I put my face in my hands. *Fuck my life.* "Did you look at the photos yet?" I asked.

"No. I was waiting to look at them with you. But when I went to your suite this morning, you weren't there. And you weren't answering my calls. Where have you been all day?"

With Cole. I lifted my face out of my hands. I'd messed everything up. Cole was a freak and was able to forgive me for what I'd done with Dr. Lyons. But Tanner would have to forgive me for all of it. There had to be a way to explain all this. I liked Cole and Dr. Lyons, but I loved Tanner. No matter how much I tried to deny it, I did. That's why it had hurt so much when he left. I needed to fix this. "I got called into the office." It wasn't a total lie.

"On a Sunday?"

"Yup, courtesy of Mr. Frost."

"Man, that guy sounds like a real dick. When will you be done? I'll come pick you up and we can grab a late dinner. How about some Gochujang Palace?"

"That sounds amazing." *Shit!* Could I ever tell him that Cole got the photos too? Or about what happened last night? How could I ever explain that to him? *I thought you left, so I went out with that guy you hate. And then I let him watch me blow Dr. Lyons. And then I met his parents.*

My love life was a total mess.

Chastity waved toward the computer. The transfer had just finished.

"Hold on," I said. My love triangle - or was it a square? - would have to wait. It was time to finally see who Rosalie had been hanging out with at the Society.

I leaned over Chastity's shoulder as she clicked on the first thumbnail. A photo of last night's spit roast filled the screen. I was sitting in the throne, my face flushed courtesy of Tanner's fingers. The rest of the red team was all around us. But Chastity was only focused on one thing.

"Jesus lord have mercy," said Chastity, fanning herself. "I look fucking hot!"

"What did Chastity just say?" asked Tanner.

"Nothing," I said. "One sec." I put myself on mute so that Tanner wouldn't hear anything else. "See?" I said. "There's no reason to take sex tapes of me. You're for sure gonna win the Onyxies with that one."

"If it was a gif, definitely. But alas…this is just a still image. So it's not eligible. That's okay though. I'll just have to do it again and make sure I get a gif."

"Sure. Let's stay focused, though. We're trying to find a picture of Rosalie."

"Got it." Chastity saved the photo to her desktop and then went back to the list of files.

"It should be from early 2020," I said.

She sorted by date and then scrolled back and back and back.

"Here it is," she said. "Do you want to do the honors?"

I took the mouse and double-clicked the first photo from early 2020. *Here we go.*

A photo filled the screen of another spit roast. I looked away just as it came up. "Please tell me she's not the one getting spit roasted," I said.

Chastity laughed. "She's not. And she's not the winning princess either. I don't know if I see her at all…"

Damn it.

Chastity clicked to the next picture.

"Ash?" said Tanner.

I took myself off mute. "Sorry about that." I looked back at the screen. My eyes immediately gravitated to a couple in the back row. The girl had an awesome blonde braid and was smiling up at the guy like she was totally smitten. I was sure it was Rosalie. The only question was…who was the guy with his arm around her that looked equally as smitten?

The way he was turned made it hard to get a good look at him, so I clicked to the next photo. I rolled the mouse wheel to zoom in.

"Is that…?" I gasped. *No. It can't be.* My jaw dropped and the phone slid out of my hand. I didn't even hear it shatter on the ground.

"Yeah," said Chastity as she pointed to the guy next to Rosalie. "That's definitely Tanner."

That son of a bitch!

Ah! Tanner! What has he done?! And what is his secret? I promise all shall be revealed in *The Society Book 3*, coming soon...

In the meantime, you can see exactly what Tanner was thinking when he first caught Ash stalking him. And maybe learn his secret?!

To get your free copy of *The Society #Tanner*, go to:

www.ivysmoak.com/tstiw-pb

TikTok. Tag me - #ivysmoak - so I can join in on the fun.

And don't forget the most important Single Girl Rule of all – Rule #1: Boys are replaceable. Friends are forever. So make sure you come meet all your new besties in The Smoaksters Facebook Group! Where we dish about books and all the hot goss.

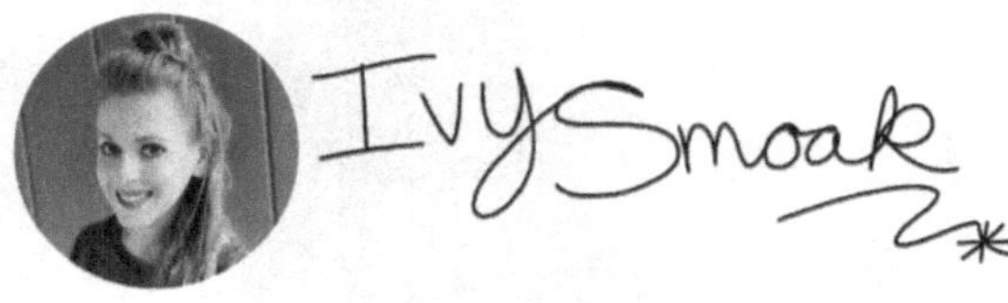

Ivy Smoak
Wilmington, DE
www.ivysmoak.com

About the Author

Ivy Smoak is the USA Today and Wall Street Journal bestselling author of *The Hunted Series*. Her books have sold over 4 million copies worldwide.

When she's not writing, you can find Ivy binge watching too many TV shows, taking long walks, playing outside, and generally refusing to act like an adult. She lives with her husband in Delaware.

TikTok: @IvySmoak
Facebook: IvySmoakAuthor
Instagram: @IvySmoakAuthor
Goodreads: IvySmoak

Recommend *The Society #ThisIsWar* for your next book club!

Book club questions available at:
www.ivysmoak.com/bookclub